Ryan returned fire, while J.B. frantically threw supplies into the chamber. Grabbing a sack of grens, the one-eyed warrior held one out to J.B. so the Armorer could see that the safety pin was firmly in place.

J.B. nodded, and they began to throw the deadly bombs wildly into the warehouse.

Shouting warnings, Sheffield and his sec men scrambled to reach the exit. Tossing the half-filled bag into the chamber, Ryan led the way into the gateway, then closed the door.

With pounding hearts, the two men waited for the swirling mists to engulf them, or for the chamber door to swing open again and for them to be brutally cut down by a hail of bullets from the hated blues....

**Other titles in the
Deathlands saga:**

JAMES AXLER

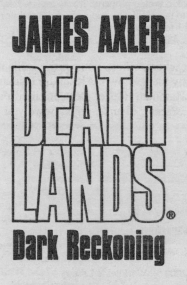

DEATH LANDS®

Dark Reckoning

THE BARONIES TRILOGY BOOK III

A GOLD EAGLE BOOK FROM

WORLDWIDE®

TORONTO • NEW YORK • LONDON
AMSTERDAM • PARIS • SYDNEY • HAMBURG
STOCKHOLM • ATHENS • TOKYO • MILAN
MADRID • WARSAW • BUDAPEST • AUCKLAND

To all my teachers, whose noteworthy skills helped forge
my meager own: Alexandre Dumas,
Dashiell Hammett, Lester Dent, Richard Falkirk and
Robert B. Parker. Thanks, guys. I owe you all a beer.

First edition January 2000

ISBN 0-373-62548-0

DARK RECKONING

...the dire time was finally here. We stood uncertain at the crossroads of total victory, and equally total defeat. A single moment's hesitation, the wrong word in a communiqué, a lone stray bullet could shatter all of our efforts and cast us once more at the feet of the beast.

But we chanced on fate, armed our guns and threw our resolve into the crucible of blood...

—Sir Winston Churchill,
Triumph and Tragedy, 1942

THE DEATHLANDS SAGA

This world is their legacy, a world born in the violent nuclear spasm of 2001 that was the bitter outcome of a struggle for global dominance.

There is no real escape from this shockscape where life always hangs in the balance, vulnerable to newly demonic nature, barbarism, lawlessness.

But they are the warrior survivalists, and they endure—in the way of the lion, the hawk and the tiger, true to nature's heart despite its ruination.

Ryan Cawdor: The privileged son of an East Coast baron. Acquainted with betrayal from a tender age, he is a master of the hard realities.

Krysty Wroth: Harmony ville's own Titian-haired beauty, a woman with the strength of tempered steel. Her premonitions and Gaia powers have been fostered by her Mother Sonja.

J. B. Dix, the Armorer: Weapons master and Ryan's close ally, he, too, honed his skills traversing the Deathlands with the legendary Trader.

Doctor Theophilus Tanner: Torn from his family and a gentler life in 1896, Doc has been thrown into a future he couldn't have imagined.

Dr. Mildred Wyeth: Her father was killed by the Ku Klux Klan, but her fate is not much lighter. Restored from predark cryogenic suspension, she brings twentieth-century healing skills to a nightmare.

Jak Lauren: A true child of the wastelands, reared on adversity, loss and danger, the albino teenager is a fierce fighter and loyal friend.

Dean Cawdor: Ryan's young son by Sharona accepts the only world he knows, and yet he is the seedling bearing the promise of tomorrow.

In a world where all was lost, they are humanity's last hope....

Chapter One

The howling alarms faded into blessed silence, and the ceiling lights of the redoubt flickered into life, as bright and strong as ever. Almost immediately, the seven bodies on the floor began to stir sluggishly.

As the burning waves of pain throughout his body slowly subsided, Ryan Cawdor opened his good eye and pulled a ragged breath into his aching lungs.

"F-fireblast," the man cursed weakly, his cramped muscles relaxing for the first time since he had entered the underground base. Never had the man encountered anything like this before. His skin had felt as if it were on fire, with flesh-eating ants digging inside his skull. A hot slug of lead in his gut would have been sweet relief compared to what he had just gone through for the past...how long? His mind was foggy about the passage of time, the endless searing pain blurring each hour into the next. Days, months? He had no idea. A rumble shook his belly, and a sour belch rose in his throat. Ryan was starving, so it had to have been quite awhile. Those blue-shirt sec men were going to pay for this, even if it took his last drop of blood. He'd chill every one of them!

Almost without thought, Ryan ran his hands over his clothing in an old ritual. The 9 mm SIG-Sauer pistol was still at his hip, the curved panga in its sheath. The ammo pouch was flat and empty, and he couldn't locate his Steyr SSG-70 sniper rifle anywhere nearby on the nearby floor. Had he dropped it outside? That would mean that the microwaves from the Kite satellite would have melted it into a puddle of useless steel by now.

Trying to rise, Ryan fumbled and slumped onto the cool floor beside a huge metal pump of some kind. The machine beat as steady as a human heart, performing some task involved in maintaining the nuclear reactors of the military redoubt.

The rad shielding around the subterranean base was the only thing that gave the companions some small amount of protection from the searing microwaves of the orbiting Kite, and going to the very lowest level of the redoubt had helped even more. But the sensation of being burned alive had only lessened, it never stopped, and eventually increased to where the one-eyed man felt as if he were being stabbed with a thousand needles, then red-hot knives. The agony robbed him of strength until there was nothing else to do but pass out, only to awaken hours later to the continuing bombardment.

Long minutes passed with only the sound of labored breathing breaking the silence of the basement. Gathering his strength once more, Ryan tried to force himself off the floor, and this time he succeeded. Struggling to his knees, the one-eyed man tried to focus on his friends, but was having some degree of difficulty doing so. Ryan realized he had to have taken more damage from the microwaves than he originally thought. Another score to settle with the blues.

Brushing back his wild crop of long black hair, Ryan noticed how shaky his hands were, the tanned skin red and irritated as if badly sunburned. He had spent a thousand days in the deserts of Deathlands, but never got burned like this. For a fleeting moment, he worried about cancer, then dismissed the problem. There was nothing he could do about it, so he turned his attention to other more solvable matters.

Catching his breath, the Deathlands warrior soon felt better. The odd trembling stopped, and he was able to focus his vision without trouble. The rest of the companions were scattered on the floor. Although their clothes were soaked with sweat, everybody seemed okay, each breathing without trouble and starting to move feebly. The low moans and curses were music to his ears. As the Trader always said, only the living bitched. The dead never complained about anything.

Sprawled in the center of the friends was a beautiful redhead, her clothes in disarray and laying frightfully still. Krysty Wroth usually healed faster than any of the others, including Ryan. But as the rest of the companions started to sit upright, she remained unconscious.

"Hey, M-Mildred," Ryan croaked, surprised to find his throat was sore. He had to have been screaming for a while. The thought didn't bother him. Anybody who didn't yell when being roasted alive wasn't tough; he was merely insane.

"Here…" the black woman whispered, then broke into a ragged cough. Her long beaded plaits dangling limply around her face, Dr. Mildred Wyeth clumsily fumbled to tug free a couple of buttons on her Army fatigues to wave fresh air into her stained clothing. She sighed in relief as her bra came into view, then again as she rubbed a hand over her chest, wiping off the sweat.

Aside from the sodden fatigues, the physician wore a gun belt with an empty holster at her hip. Nearby was her Czech-made ZKR target pistol.

"Sweet Jesus," Mildred panted, massaging her temples to ease the throbbing headache. "Feel like... I've been d-dipped...in acid. How...how long..."

Ryan could only shake his head in reply. His strength was returning fast, but he was a long way from normal yet. "Don't know how long," he said, trying hard not to stammer. "Days probably. Could be more, from the feeling in my gut."

Her own stomach rumbled in harmony. "Know what you mean. I could eat a Hummer right about now, tires and all."

"Hell, yeah," a wiry man agreed, holding his head in both hands as if afraid it was going to break into pieces. "H-haven't felt this bad since...poisoned back in New California." An Uzi submachine gun hung on a sling over the man's shoulder, an M-4000 scattergun partially hidden under a leg.

"How you doing, John?" the physician asked in concern.

By sheer effort of will, J. B. Dix yanked the shotgun from underneath his ass and managed a brief smile. "Not dead yet, Millie," he said, placing the weapon aside. Fumbling in the pocket of his battered leather jacket, he unearthed a pair of wire-rimmed glasses. Setting them carefully on his face, J.B. frowned.

"Black dust, they're warped," he cursed and started trying to straighten the bent frames.

"Go check on Krysty," Ryan ordered, standing

wearily. His boots felt strangely loose, as if he'd lost some weight. "She's not awake yet."

Nodding, Mildred crawled over to the supine redhead and placed two fingers on her exposed throat. Rasping for air, Krysty's chest rose and fell regularly, but her pulse was very weak. A trickle of dried blood marred a cheek from where Krysty had bitten a lip, and her nails were badly cracked from clawing at the floor. Worse, her animated hair lay limply on the cold concrete floor as if it were dead. Mildred knew the filaments were more sensitive to pain than norm hair, and especially sensitive to fire damage. The microwave bombardment had to have been a living hell for Krysty.

Thankfully, the redhead wasn't wearing her heavy bearskin coat. The feverish woman might have literally cooked to death wrapped inside the thick garment. However, a Smith & Wesson .38 revolver jutted from Krysty's gun belt, the hammer still cocked for firing. Gingerly removing the blaster, Mildred eased down the hammer and placed the weapon on the cool concrete. Thank God, the ammo hadn't ignited from the microwaves or else Krysty would have blown open her stomach, a bad way for anybody to catch the last train west.

Gently lifting an eyelid, Mildred waved a butane lighter back and forth. The pupils dilated in response, and Krysty muttered something too soft to hear.

"She's alive," Mildred reported. "She just took it a lot worse than us. Her hair, you know."

"Makes sense," Ryan replied, rubbing his cheek and finding a dense stubble. The one-eyed man now knew for certain that they had been unconscious for days. Whoever had been operating the Kite had been really serious about chilling all of them. A brief image flashed into his mind of a tall man standing next to Silas as the bullets slammed into the hated whitecoat, blowing away chunks of his screaming body. The stranger had been wearing a crisp blue uniform, not just a shirt, and he'd been carrying several holstered blasters. Logic said he had to be the sec chief for the Complex. At least their new enemy had a face, if not a name.

"Can you do anything for her?" Ryan asked, his mind returning to the problem at hand.

"I think so," Mildred replied, reaching for her med kit. She paused with a hand in midair. Damn, she had forgotten about tossing away the precious med kit in their desperate race to reach the redoubt. Every pound gone meant more speed, and the companions had barely gotten inside alive. Her med kit was miles away, probably reduced to ashes. She slumped in disappointment, too tired to feel angry at the loss, or hatred of the blue shirts, and forced herself to think about other things. There would be time for revenge later.

Krysty started to cough, and Mildred lifted the woman's neck to clear her throat. The redhead instantly breathed easier, and Mildred looked for something to use as a pillow. An old-fashioned frock coat was draped over the feeder pipe. Perfect.

Mildred appropriated the garment, folding it into a wad and sliding under the sleeping woman's neck.

"Anybody got a canteen?" Mildred asked hopefully, looking around.

Still working on his glasses, J.B. pushed the container closer with the heel of his boot. "Here you go."

Unscrewing the cap, Mildred poured a few warm

drops into the palm of her hand and wiped Krysty's face. It wasn't much, but that was all the physician could do at the moment. The water seemed to help, and Krysty's eyes fluttered open.

"Where…" she whispered, trying to rise. "Gaia… the redoubt…Tennessee…"

Mildred pushed her back down. "Lay still," she ordered. "Wait to get your strength. We're okay for the moment."

"Mebbe," Ryan growled, rummaging through his clothing for bullets. He found nothing, then checked the magazine of his pistol. Six rounds, that was it. Not good.

Muttering to himself, a pale teenager with hair the color of snow lifted himself off the floor with both arms as if doing a push-up, and blinked ruby red eyes.

"Not dead," Jak Lauren stated, sounding slightly shocked. The teenager was dressed in camou-colored fatigues. A big bore Colt Python was holstered at his hip.

"S-speak f-for yourself," a silver-haired man mumbled. One of his boots had come off, exposing a sock with a hole in the toe. The frilly white shirt and breeches shouted that the man could have come from another time, and the huge Civil War-era blaster holstered at his hip seemed to confirm it. He clenched an ebony cane in one fist, the silver lion's head loose enough to expose a few inches of the stainless-steel sword hidden inside the hollow sheath.

Grunting with the effort, Dr. Theophilus Tanner flipped onto his back, leaving the damp shadow of his body on the floor. He levered himself into a sitting position using the stick, then stared at the weapon for a moment as if unaware of what it was. Then, forcing open his grip, Doc dropped the weapon with a clatter. The imprint of the handle was clear on his palm as if it had been burned into the flesh.

"So we actually did make it down here," Doc rumbled in a stentorian bass. He glanced at the high curved ceiling and glass walls. "I was not sure if this had all been a dream, or a real event."

"Real enough. Just not sure how we got here," Ryan replied. "Everything after entering the front door is fuzzy."

Extracting a silk handkerchief with a blue swallow's-eye design from a pocket, Doc wiped his face, then used both hands to wring out the cloth. Water dribbled onto the floor. "I fully understand, my dear Ryan. Is everybody else undamaged?"

"I'm okay," Dean Cawdor said, leaning against the thumping water pipe, his body moving with each pulsation. A semiautomatic Browning Hi-Power pistol rested in a cracked leather holster on his right hip, and a huge Bowie knife jutted from a black nylon sheath on the other side, as if the enormous blade was balancing the weight of the adult-sized blaster.

Jerking a thumb, J.B. added, "Krysty is still out."

Doc frowned, then nodded. "Ah yes. Her hair, of course."

With the others awake and moving, Ryan took the opportunity to survey the underground reactor room. They were in the main access corridor that ran straight down the middle of the wide room. Stairs leading to the higher levels were at the far end, and some kind of processing water pump stood amid the companions. Long windows of unbreakable glass formed the walls on either side, letting them see the huge machinery beyond. But there were no doors to allow access. Perhaps this was a restricted zone, and the elevator intended for use by the nuke techs only.

A huge control booth filled the right side of the reactor room, with a pair of desiccated corpses in U.S. Army uniforms sitting at the complex panels. Ryan was impressed. For the bodies to be in that good condition after a hundred years, the booth had to be absolutely air tight. Damn good workmanship.

To the left was a still pool of clear water, with a maze of bubbling pipes and a steady glowing light at the bottom. Mildred had once explained that the glow was actually a powerful laser flashing a million times a second, but to the naked eye it seemed like a smooth shine. Ryan didn't care. Some levels of tech in the redoubts were far beyond his understanding. As long as the predark machinery maintained itself and continued pouring out electricity to run the redoubt, basically that was all he cared about.

Just then, something familiar caught his attention, and Ryan quickly went to reclaim his longblaster. The Steyr SSG-70 bolt-action rifle was undamaged, but the rotary clip in the breech was exhausted, and there were no more mags in his ammo pouch. Ryan shouldered the useless weapon. Even though they had no ammo right now, the companions sometimes found stores of weapons and ammo in the redoubts. Then he recalled where they were and bitterly cursed. The last time they had been here, the redoubt was completely clean, not a can of beans or a single live round remaining in the whole place. Plus, the mat-trans unit was turned off. Or had he imagined that? They would have to check the chamber first thing. That was top priority. Without some way out of here, they could be hit by the microwaves again, and the one-eyed warrior didn't think any of them could survive another bombardment like the last one.

"Hey, lover," Krysty said, limping across the room. Her flawless face was flushed from the effort of standing, but the woman was walking under her own power, the wild corona of her hair waving as if stirred by secret winds.

Ryan considered that a good sign. She had to be on the mend.

"Feeling better?" Ryan asked, reaching out to stroke her cheek. The filaments of her fiery hair coiled about his fingers, pulling the man closer.

Krysty took his callused hand in hers and gave a squeeze. "Still alive," she remarked, trying to conjure a laugh and only managing to weakly smile. "Which is a lot more than we can say about Silas, so I can't really complain."

For the nth time, Ryan realized how truly beautiful she was, his perfect match in every possible way, and a brief smile crossed his scarred face.

"I am most pleased to see you up and about, my dear Krysty," Doc said with a stately bow. "We were worried there for a moment."

"I'm fine, just starving," Krysty added softly, her stomach loudly rumbling. "Any of the MRE packs around?"

Ryan's own gut growled in harmony. "Not a crumb. We'll have to go hunting in the upper levels for anything edible still in storage. But checking the mat-trans unit is our top priority."

"Just in case we have to leave fast. Understood. But then food."

"Absolutely."

Doc cleared his throat. "Do you still require my coat, madam? If so, it is yours."

She shook out the frock coat and passed it over. "I'm not cold anymore," Krysty replied. "Thanks for the pillow."

"My pleasure. But you should thank the good doctor." He smiled. "I did nothing special."

"Aw, stuff it, you old coot," Mildred retorted.

"Hey, what's that?" Dean asked, pointing across the room.

Instantly, the adults spun with their weapons at the ready. There was something large and metallic hidden in the shadows underneath the stairs.

"Another door?" Jak asked, sliding a knife from his sleeve. "Never see before."

Checking his blaster, Ryan walked closer, with the rest of the companions close behind. Mildred flicked her butane lighter, and in the flickering flame they saw a large armored door set in the concrete wall. The frame was burnished steel, the massive portal veined with reinforcing flanges and bars.

"A second armory?" Dean asked hopefully.

Working the bolt on his Uzi, J.B. scowled. "Could be anything."

Ryan rapped on the metal with the barrel of his blaster. "That's solid vanadium," he stated. "Just like the main door upstairs."

"Nukeproof," Doc said suspiciously. "Could it be an escape route?"

"Never saw one in a redoubt before," Ryan replied. "But then, this redoubt has lots of armored doors sealing off sections. I think it might have been one of their secure sites."

"That would explain all the artwork upstairs,"

Krysty remarked. "Although why they thought paintings and statues were valuable I have no idea."

"Pretty," Jak commented succinctly. "But that all."

"It was a different time," Mildred said, sighing in remembrance. "A different world."

"Not make sense," Jak insisted.

Ryan snorted at the comment. "Lots of things about the redoubts make no sense. You know that."

"An enigma designed by a fool," Doc muttered.

Rubbing his jaw, Ryan nodded. "Something like that."

Going to the door, Krysty pressed her ear against the cool metal. "Can't hear anything," she reported. "J.B., think you can open this?"

"Why should we?" the Armorer asked, adjusting his glasses. The man seemed lopsided without his ever-present bag of explosives at his side. The collection of grens and plas-ex had been another loss in their desperate race for the redoubt.

"Could be another level, mebbe a storehouse full of weapons and food."

"Hmm. Hide all of the good stuff downstairs, eh? Does make sense," the Armorer replied, cracking his knuckles. "I'll give it a try."

"Hold," Ryan commanded. "Before we open any doors, I want a weapons check. I have nothing for the Steyr, and only six shots in the SIG-Sauer. Plus, my panga. How about the rest of you?"

"About the same. The scattergun is out," J.B. replied. "I have one clip for the Uzi with ten rounds. Nothing else."

"Three loads for the LeMat," Doc announced, patting the huge pistol on his belt. "And my sword."

"A full load of six," Krysty added, closing the cylinder of her S&W .38 revolver. "I found some loose rounds in a pocket. But no reloads."

"Nine rounds," Dean said, having already checked his blaster.

Scowling, Jak lowered his .357 Magnum Colt Python. "Two rounds," he reported. "And knives."

"One live bullet," Mildred added, closing the cylinder of her target pistol. "And a lot of spent casings for reloads."

"Fireblast, barely enough to go hunting," Ryan stated sourly. "And we sure as shit can't go after the blues with this little ammo. They'd blow us to hell with those damn rapidfires."

"Well, I can make black powder for Doc, and cordite for the rest of us," J.B. stated, "but it takes time. I'd need a month to cook plastique."

"You have the equipment to do that?" Mildred asked in surprise.

He grinned. "Sure. All I need is a file and a bucketful of quarters. Give me a few sunny days, and I can start producing guncotton and dynamite in under a week."

Mildred shook her head in disbelief. The man was amazing. Make dynamite from quarters? Sounded impossible, but if John said it could be done, that was enough for her.

Standing before the huge door, Ryan stared at it thoughtfully. Escape route, trap, or another level? A similar door was in the middle of the redoubt, separating the mat-trans section from the living quarters, something the companions had never encountered before in any redoubt. Hell, this could even be one of those deep storage lockers the Trader had told him about so many years ago, a special kind of vault designed to hold weapons and food in a sort of dry suspension for a thousand years. Of course, there could also be a dozen of those sec hunter droids inside to keep out intruders. The companions were too weak and low on ammo to risk tangling with those armored machines. Yet everything they needed could be behind that door—or sudden death. It was a big risk either way. Balancing the options, Ryan made a decision.

"J.B., check for booby traps," he ordered, taking a combat stance. "Doc and Dean, stand guard. Mildred, keep a watch on the stairs. Krysty, Jak and I will watch for anything unfriendly coming out. We retreat to the garage if we can't handle what's inside."

As the other companions moved into positions, J.B. ran his hands along the jamb and checked the hinges, then the big bolt holding the door closed. Next, he ran a small pocket compass along the surface of the metal. The magnetic needle didn't quiver once to indicate a hidden magnetic switch or mass proximity fuse.

"Looks clean," he said hesitantly, and spit on the locking bolt, wiggling it a few times to work the spittle inside the mechanism. His face clouded at the thought of the lost oil can, lock picks and probes, then he resumed working.

When satisfied, J.B. slid the bolt free and tugged on the handle. Nothing happened. "Heavy bastard. Give me a hand, will you?"

Grabbing the wheel, Ryan and Krysty helped the man force open the massive portal a few inches. Almost instantly, something large scuttled in view, three triangular eyes and long fangs reflected in the dim sliver of light.

"Close!" Jak ordered, as the thing shoved a clawed limb through the slim opening. The albino teen leveled his blaster and fired once, the discharge thunderously loud in the confines of the reactor room. A foot-long lance of flame reached through the door crack, the hollowpoint Magnum round smacking into the unseen creature and blowing off an eye stalk. The mutie gave out a high-pitched squeal, as greenish blood squirted onto the jamb. Stepping back, Krysty fired and missed, the slug ricocheting into the darkness. Ryan shot from the hip, and the claw blocking the door shattered, spraying green blood and gobbets of white flesh everywhere. Shrieking in pain, the creature scuttled into the darkness and the companions shoved the door shut with an echoing boom.

Dropping the Uzi, J.B. forcibly drove home the locking bolt, making sure it was solidly engaged. A split second later, something slammed into the door on the other side, then scratched the metal as if trying to dig through. Quickly, the companions retreated a few yards.

"Fucking crab," Ryan muttered.

"No way we're going in there again without light and lots more blasters," Krysty said, catching her breath. "Mebbe we better recce the top levels to see if Silas left anything useful behind."

"Doubtful," J.B. said, retrieving the Uzi. "But it's our best bet. At least the microwaves have stopped."

"Have they?" Jak asked pointedly.

Pensively, Dean looked up the stairs. "Could the Kite thing still be whatever, you know, beaming micros at us?"

"Perhaps they have simply lowered the intensity," Doc suggested. "But if we open a door in the upper levels, we start to fry again."

"Any way we can check?" Krysty asked.

"Maybe there is," Mildred said, rummaging in the pockets of her fatigues. "Ah, found it."

Carefully, she unrolled a tiny silver ball, the crumpled wrapper from the stick of gum from a MRE pack. Flattening the wad of metallic paper until it was relatively smooth, she then neatly folded it once. Doc already had his sword out, and she slid the folded piece of foil over the tip of the steel shaft.

Blaster in hand, Ryan understood what the two were doing. "Stay sharp," he said. "If the redoubt is no longer under attack, then we might get some company."

"Blue shirts," Dean said hatefully. The boy had his Browning in one hand, the Bowie knife in the other.

"Couldn't be anybody else," J.B. said, flipping a switch on the side of the Uzi with his thumb. The weapon felt uncommonly light.

"I want a three-on-three formation, with Doc in the lead," Ryan continued. "We go soft and silent, retreat if possible. If not, Jak, you got your throwing knives ready?"

The albino teenager holstered his Colt Python and flexed both hands. Black knives with leaf-shaped blades slid from inside his sleeves. "Throat," the teenager advised coldly, announcing his targets. "Can't breath, can't shout."

"Ready," Ryan said.

Extending the sword far out in front, Doc proceeded up the stairs at a slow pace. The steps were solid slabs of concrete, smoothed to a mirror sheen. The companions made no sounds as they slowly went higher and higher into the redoubt. There were no signs whatsoever of the base having taken any damage from the microwaves. The doors leading to the other levels weren't discolored or warped, no indications of scrap paper having caught on fire, the wall extinguishers hadn't burst. The leakage getting past the nuke armor of the base had to have just been enough to almost chill them, but that was all.

An hour later, the companions reached the topmost level of the base. Pausing at the stairwell door, Doc cocked the hammer of his LeMat, then eased the door open a crack and poked his sword through. The tiny scrap of metallic paper fluttered slightly in the breeze of the life-support system, nothing more. Withdrawing the sword, he widened the crack and glanced around the garage. Nobody was in sight.

"Clear," Doc whispered, flicking the piece of chewing-gum wrapper off the tip of his sword and sheathing the blade.

Ryan replaced the old man at the door, listening for the sounds of movement beyond. The silence was thick and heavy. Gesturing to the others to stay, and with Krysty and J.B. standing by the door ready to give cover fire, the one-eyed warrior slipped into the next room. Keeping low, Ryan darted from worktable to empty barrel, grease pit to stack of tires, never fully exposing himself until completing a full circle of the cavernous garage.

A hundred wags should have been parked here in storage—Hummers, APCs, trucks and even tanks, with drums of fuel and oil stacked in the storage bins behind wire gates. Workbenches lined the walls, the pegs above them empty of tools. Only the taped outlines of what should be there remained. Nothing was in sight, not a spare wrench or wiper blade.

"All clear," Ryan announced, standing in plain view and holstering his piece. "You can still see our bloody footprints on the floor. The tracks go straight to the stairwell door, nowhere else. None of them have been smudged. We're alone."

"Good," Krysty stated, tucking away her weapon and nudging Mildred. "What's with the chewing-gum wrapper?"

"Sort of an early-warning system," Mildred said, looking over the garage. "It wouldn't give us much advance notice of microwaves, but some is better than none."

"How does it work?" J.B. asked, easing off the bolt of the Uzi. The blaster had been under undue tension for days while they were unconscious. He only hoped the spring was okay and the rapidfire would still function properly.

Taking a seat on a pile of tires, Doc answered. "If there is a strong magnetic field, or the presence of microwaves, the foil will receive an identical charge across its entire surface and the two flaps will naturally repel each other, separating wide and fast. As long as they stay closed, we were not near any strong electromagnetic fields."

"Pretty good trick," Ryan grunted. "The whitecoats in your day knew about microwaves and sats, huh?"

Doc started to reply, then his features contorted in confusion. Conflicting emotions played across the time traveler's face, bordering on blind panic. The companions said nothing and turned their backs on the old man to continue exploring the garage. After what the whitecoats of Overproject Whisper had done to Doc, his friends understood if his mind wandered sometimes. He always came back, and he had never let them down in a fight. At least, not yet.

"Doesn't matter," Krysty said softly to Doc. "As long as it works."

Her voice seemed to calm the old man, and Doc faced the redhead, reason returning to his eyes. "Oh, most assuredly, dear lady," he said, displaying his oddly perfect white teeth. "The laws of magnetics are most adamantine. It works. Trust me."

"I always have."

Jak gestured with his blaster. "Check outside?"

Nodding, Ryan led the way along the zigzagging corridor to the front door. The passageway was wide enough to accommodate a semi-truck, and clusters of fluorescent lights hung from the high, curved ceiling.

"Dad, I always meant to ask, why does this zigzag?" Dean probed.

"Rads can only travel straight," Ryan said, slowing his pace. "They go right through stone or metal, but lead stops them. That's what these walls are lined with yards of lead. So one step out of the way and you're safe. All these extra sharp angles are just to be sure. One would do just as good a job."

Pursing his lips, the boy said nothing, filing the information away. Then, stooping to one knee, he inspected an object on the floor. "Hey, J.B., over here!"

The Armorer turned from the hip, the Uzi poised for action. "Trouble?" he demanded.

"Nope. Yours?" Dean asked, holding out a battered hat.

With a cry of delight, J.B. took the fedora and

straightened the brim into something presentable again. Easing it onto his head, he adjusted the angle and grinned. "Better," he stated. "A man just can't think straight with his brain exposed."

Reaching the end of the passage, the companions found the huge vanadium steel doors of the exit. The material was unmarked, but it had been designed to withstand the atomic fireball of a nuke blast. Their footprints led from the massive slab, the floor littered with spent brass, a few scattered leaves and dried splotches of green blood.

"Triple red," Ryan ordered, shifting the blaster to his left hand and using the right to tap an access code on the keypad on the wall.

The others spread out so as to not offer a group target. The companions had left something very hard to chill outside, and if the Kite hadn't done the job, the bastard might still be waiting for them to emerge.

Slowly, the portal rumbled aside. Instantly, a black hurricane roared into the tunnel, the companions staggering backward from the furious assault. The raging storm filled the corridor with streaming waves of some kind of dark material that stuck to their clothes and skin. Within seconds, it became impossible to see one another, much less what was outside the redoubt.

"Retreat to the garage!" Ryan shouted over the storm, an arm held in front of his mouth as protection as he strove to key in the code that would close the door.

Stumbling to the walls, they blindly followed the zigzagging passageway back into the redoubt. The fierce winds pounded them every step of the way, gusts knocking them against the walls and often to the dirty floor. Battered and bruised, the companions were forced to grab one another's clothing for support. As a group, they shuffled hastily away from the thundering onslaught of bitter tasting flakes.

Charging from the howling tunnel, the companions moved out of the way of the incoming cloud and took cover behind whatever was available, waiting for the outer door to close. The black cloud, resembling car exhaust, poured into the redoubt, covering everything from the grease pit to the rafters with a thick layer of soot. Ryan couldn't hear above the whistling wind, but as the exterior door finally closed, the storm abruptly died, whirlwinds of ash dancing across the thickly coated floor.

"By the Three Kennedys!" Doc shouted, then lowered his voice to a normal volume. "And what, pray tell, was that?"

Curiously, Mildred picked a flake off her encrusted shirt and watched it crumble in her palm. "This is all that remains of this part of Tennessee," she guessed, wiping her hand on her pants. "Should have realized this would be waiting for us outside. After so many days of being cooked by the Kite, the land has literally been burnt into ash."

Blue eyes staring from a blackened face, Dean blinked in wonder. "So the trees, the bushes, the grass..."

"Gone. All gone."

"Well, shit," Jak said, giving the word two syllables. The albino felt as if he had just escaped from the grave. The ash was inside his fatigues and already starting to work its way into his shorts and boots. He snorted to clear his nose and gagged on the aftertaste—fried dirt. Then he realized that's exactly what it was.

Stomping her cowboy boots, Krysty wildly shook her head, trying to assist her struggling hair to straighten out the tangles from the rough winds. Ash sprinkled to the floor, forming a small cloud around the dirty woman.

"Gaia! That was worse than any Deathlands sandstorm!" Krysty complained, beating at her clothes. "We're not going to get a single yard out of the redoubt without masks of some kind. We'd choke to death in minutes."

"Also need ropes to keep us together," Ryan added. Wiping his blaster clean, the man hawked and spit. Gray phlegm hit the floor. "We can make masks out of bed sheets. That's easy enough, but pointless. There's not going to be any animals out there to hunt for food. What the Kite didn't kill, this ash would soon suffocate to death."

"Make good cover nightcreep blues," Jak said. Then added, "If live get there."

Breaking into a ragged cough, Dean brushed the ash from his hair and tried to wipe off his face with a sleeve, but that only seemed to make it smear. Even worse, his blaster had caught the brunt of the wind when the main door opened. He couldn't risk firing the weapon until it had been thoroughly disassembled and cleaned. Tipping the blaster downward, powdery residue poured from the barrel. The situation was really bad. If anything attacked the group right now, they'd be dead meat, completely unable to defend themselves.

"Dark night, this sucks," J.B. muttered, beating his hat clean on the end of a worktable. "We got company in the tunnel, a hellstorm outside and the mattrans wasn't working."

"Looks like we're here for a while," Krysty agreed grimly.

Each of the companions was lost in thought for a moment as they watched the black ash swirling about to finally settle on the garage floor in a smooth ebony carpet.

"Enough," Ryan stated, putting as much force into the word as the tired man could muster. "If we can't leave, then I want a level-by-level search of the entire redoubt. There must be some food in here, tin cans, jars, MRE packs, self-heats. Bring what you find to the control room."

"Not the kitchen?" Dean asked, puzzled.

"Eat as we work," Ryan countered. "Silas was smart, but not a genius. If he turned off the mat-trans, then we can get it back on-line. Once we've had some food and a hot shower, then we can get busy."

"Gonna leave?" Jak asked, frowning.

Ryan started to stride across the filthy garage, leaving a contrail of churned ash in his wake. "Hell, no. We're going to finish the job of killing the blues," he said matter-of-factly. "Every one of the bastards."

Chapter Two

Thundering chaos ruled the land. Shriveled trees bowed under the violent maelstrom, and lakes of black mud sloshed onto caked shores. Whole bushes came out of the crunchy soil and flew away into the ash storm swirling around the Shiloh valley.

Shuffling through the hurricane, a slavering mutie flapped its loose lips over the long saber-toothed fangs that extended from its wide mouth. This was a good day, it thought. Food was near. A smell of blood hung in the air, which even the tempest couldn't hide. Something had died violently, and the mutie simply wanted whatever was left after the slayer had eaten its fill of the prey. Fresh meat was the best, but old meat was more tender.

As the mutie neared the top of a barren hill, the wind was so strong it had to dig into the soil with its clawed feet to keep from becoming airborne. Step by slow step, it relentlessly followed the odor of blood. Black ash streamed past the creature in an endless supply, and lightning crashed in the hidden sky above, but to its catlike eyes, the world was perfectly clear in a dozen shades of black and white.

Eventually cresting a hill, the mutie looked down a wrong-stone thing and made happy noises. Food lived in such places, juicy food. Correct-stone things reached high into the sky and only four-legs lived there. It couldn't catch those; too fast.

But wrong-stone things were flat and had many openings it could crawl through to find the food. Two-legs tasted good, and little two-legs couldn't even fight or run away. They merely made loud noises. Especially when eaten. It liked the death music they made, but the little food always became quiet after only a few bites. Big food lasted much longer, sometimes making death music for a day. Much fun.

The mere thought of fresh blood flowing down its throat made the mutie shuffle faster through the roiling clouds. Descending the sloped hillside, its scaled legs sank into the softened soil, going to its knees, sometimes going all the way to its hips. At one point, the world disappeared as it sank below the churning material. But soon its claws found hard soil, and the creature dug back into the storm where it was warm and safe.

Circling around a large boulder, something crunched under its foot, and the mutie dived upon the ground, hoping it was a fresh bone. But the broken thing was only the skull of a norm. A colony of worms writhed inside, the gray meat of the brain all gone. Annoyed, the mutie threw the skull away. It knew better than to try to eat the little worms. Even if chewed into pieces, they didn't die, and would eat their way out of a belly. That was a bad thing, because then nobody else could eat the body of the fresh dead, or else the little worms might also consume them. Thunder ruled the sky, rogs ruled under the dirt and the tiny worms ruled the dead.

The mutie paused as the word strangely resonated in its twisted mind. Born of distant human ancestry, the rad-blasted being felt questions about the odd life-forms start to form in the back of its lopsided head, but they faded before becoming fully formed. The shriveled lumps of its frontal lobes and anterior pons were utterly incapable of processing the simple data of a direct question.

Dropping to its hands and feet, the mutie start galloping toward the wrong-stone place. It could vaguely smell the two-legs and the fresh blood. There had to be much food to make such a strong smell, maybe more than fingers and toes combined. What a feast!

Then the monstrosity recoiled as another odor was detected by its single quivering nostril. Bad water, the stinky blood of metal-things-that-moved. Two-legs were always near bad water. It made you sick many suns if drunk. But they guarded bad water like kin. Maybe they worshiped it? Bad water, also meant boom sticks. When a boom stick spoke, the mutie would feel pain as its body jerked and blood began to flow from a tiny mouth that hadn't been there before. It couldn't understand how the noise could do this, but the boom sticks hurt very bad. They were to be avoided whenever possible.

Thankfully, the boom sticks were the only defense of the two-legs. The food couldn't see well in the dark, and barely heard anything. Grabbed from behind, the two-legs could only sing as it ate the meat and drank the warm blood. Two-legs were easy to kill.

The mutie smacked oversized lips, remembering when it had once gotten a small two-legs from the belly of its mother. The flesh was even more tender than a rotting corpse. Hopefully, there would be many of the wiggly two-legs, and it could take a couple back to the hive and trade them to the females for a chance to climb on top of them and thrust between their legs. That was the best of all things.

Clamoring down a short embankment, the mutie sloshed through a sluggish creek, the mud almost thick enough to walk on. Reaching the other side, it crawled up the bank and started slithering along the ground toward the wrong-stones. It could clearly see a huge gap in the stones, the opening filled with shiny-sharps and the thin humming vines that killed when touched.

Ducking behind the burned wreckage of a wag, the mutie burrowed into the ash and started to wriggle toward the waiting food. The smell of the blood nearly drove it mad, and it moaned in hunger, the guttural noise sounding almost exactly like the howling wind.

FOUR MUMMIES of cloth stood huddled before the wide gap in the stone block wall that surrounded the Tennessee ville. Oily rags were wrapped around their longblasters in an effort to keep out the windblown ash. The rags helped, but using the Kalashnikovs made them jam almost immediately. The ash got inside the breech mechanism through the barrel. Some sort of ribbed plastic covered the vented ends of the blasters, but after the first shot that meager protection disintegrated from the muzzle-blast. The sec men knew they could get off only one or two rounds before the fancy rapidfires would become totally useless. Sergeant Tucholka had suggested tying knives to the ends of the rifle barrels, but the guards refused. A knife on the end of a stick was what farmers carried as weapons, not sec men. Besides, if anybody got that close, they'd just use the knives properly—a quick thrust into the belly, a slice across the throat and loot the body before anybody else arrived.

Even masked by the storm, the base was a tiny oasis of green grass in the middle of a hellish vista. The wall encircling the ville held off the worst of the wind, but the ash peppered the buildings with brutal force, shoving sec men along the ground. The blues walking patrol tied themselves to posts driven into the ground to keep from tumbling away. With their faces wrapped in multiple layers of cloth for protection, the sec men could breath in the thick air, but no sounds or words would carry beyond a few feet, with visibility stopping at a few yards. If the orange clouds above flashed with lightning or rumbled with thunder, they had no idea. Even though they knew for a fact that the huge predark dish antenna rose above the ville, taller than a hundred men and wider than a twenty-minute run, they couldn't even see the concrete blockhouse it used as a support base for its massive steel girders and reinforcing struts. Ten men died walking off the cliff near the abandoned stone quarry before Major Sheffield, rather, Baron Sheffield, forbade any more patrols outside the wall. The ash storm utterly ruled the Shiloh ville.

Shifting weight from foot to foot, the sec men at the wall endured the raging storm, wishing they were stationed at the front gate. Those lucky bastards were safe inside a brick kiosk with windows and a stove. Probably had a dancing slave and were drinking beer, too. Then one of the guards jerked his head around, and took a half step forward.

"I just heard that weird noise again!" the private shouted, sliding his longblaster off a shoulder and clumsily working the bolt. Advancing to the end of the rope, he tried to see into the howling maelstrom. Ash and dust. Nothing else.

"Hey, me too!" added another.

"It's nothing," Tucholka muttered, hunched beside the burned wreck of a predark tank. Its thick armor was badly warped from the slave revolt, but the titanic wag still offered some degree of protection from the stinging debris. "Just the freaking wind! Told you that already!"

The second private stared at the hole in the wall. "You sure?"

"Shut up! I was trying to sleep!"

"You moron!" a corporal shouted in disdain. "That's how you got in trouble in the first place!"

Tucholka sneered at the man, then realized he couldn't be seen. "Stuff it, asshole!" the sergeant roared. "That's an order!"

The corporal yelled something that he couldn't hear and turned his back on the man. Saying nothing, the privates merely shifted position to keep a closer watch on the vulnerable gap in the ville defenses. Under the iron leadership of Silas Jamaisvous, the blues had captured hundreds of people from the surrounding communities, farms, hamlets and just people passing through Tennessee, forcing the slaves to dig huge stone blocks from the side of a nearby hill and build the great wall. The rock was only limestone, not granite, but it took power tools to carve granite and wags to move the massive loads. Nobody sane would give such things to slaves, no matter how well they were chained and watched.

The slaves had tried to get free anyway and had been dealt with harshly. Lacking any more workers, the wall remained unfinished with a single fifty-foot-wide gap in its expanse, a doorway perfect for cold-hearts and mercies, although muties were the real danger these days. The creatures seemed to be attracted to the dish for some reason. Maybe it was the soft hum of the transformers, or maybe they could see the microwaves beaming down from space to feed the ville electricity. Nobody knew for sure, and the muties weren't talking.

The hole was blocked as best as possible, stuffed solid with barbed wire and electrified with enough current to chill a horse. But armed men still had to stand vigil at the weak point of the perimeter. It was punishment duty, and they knew it. The sarge was guilty of sleeping on duty, the corporal stole shine from the kitchen and both privates had traded food to slaves for sex. Each of them had been caught in the act, whipped for disobeying orders, reduced in rank and assigned here as a last chance. One more mistake and they would be put in chains as the first of the new replacement slaves.

Wisely, each decided to eat a handblaster before going into chains. They knew what happened to slaves during the dark and lonely nights.

"Death before dishonor," the tall private muttered loudly, the words muffled through his heavy mask.

The loose ends of his wrappings lashing madly about, the corporal turned. "Huh? What was that?"

"Something my maw used to say every time she got ganged by the baron and his sons! Don't know 'xactly what it means, but she put a lot of stock in it as a curse!"

"Crap!" Tucholka yawned. "Rape is all sluts are good for! That, and cooking!"

The tall private bobbed his head. "My maw couldn't cook worth shit!"

"Which is why she got rode so much! See?"

"You're pretty smart, sir!" the second private said.

"Ain't a sergeant for nothing!"

Suddenly, a figure rose amid the barbed wire of the gap and grabbed the nearest sec man by the chest, the taloned fingers cutting deep into the cloth, ripping away a fistful of flesh through the encrusted rags. Blood gushed from the hideous wound, and the lifeless sergeant fell as the figure stuffed the still beating heart into its drooling mouth.

"Rad me! Muties!" the tall private screamed, firing his blaster.

Surging into action, the others cut loose with their Kalashnikovs, but the stuttering weapons got off only four or five rounds before jamming. The huge invader staggered from the impact of the 7.62 mm rounds, but didn't drop.

As they frantically struggled to clear the jams, the wind slowed for a second and the sec men got a clear glimpse of the mutie: giant fangs protruded from a grotesque face with one nostril and three bulging eyes. Twice the size of a norm, its whole body was covered with mottled skin, and long claws sprouted from the knuckles of stubby hands.

Swinging his blaster like a club, the short private charged the mutie. It blocked the attack easily and grabbed him by the face, its claws sinking into the wrapping and ripping off most of his skin. Shrilly screaming, the man stood transfixed, naked eyeballs staring from a visage of raw flesh and bare teeth.

As the mutie wasted moments consuming the dripping gobbet, the other guards slashed the ropes holding them in place. Even as the dying private collapsed, the creature charged the remaining sec men and they desperately dived out of the way. The mutie slammed hard into the tank, its claws raising sparks as they raked along the predark armor.

Struggling with his longblaster, the tall private got off another shot, and the mutie screamed as fingers exploded off its hand. Hooting in pain, it kicked out a clawed foot. Backing up, the corporal cursed as the wrappings were ripped away, exposing his bare chest with three thin lines across his flesh oozing droplets of blood. Death had missed by the thickness of a shirt.

"Ass sucker!" he shouted, and insanely charged, slamming the butt of his rifle into the thing's misshapen face. The wooden stock cracked from the force of the blow, fangs and yellow blood spraying into the storm.

The remaining private ducked low and slashed at its belly, but only scored a deep cut in the mutie's hip. The creature stabbed for his throat, and he raised the rifle to block. The weapon was knocked from his grip by the powerful blow, and the corporal stabbed the creature in the back of the neck from behind. Instantly, the being tried to turn, but was barely able to move with its spinal column damaged.

The corporal roared in anger and twisted the knife hard.

The mutie jerked wildly as if being hit with bullets from a dozen different directions. A chance blow from a flailing arm took the corporal across the face, and there was a crunch as his nose shattered. Blood began to spread across the cloth wound around his head.

"Son of a bitch!" he mumbled, and shoved the

knife in deeper, then jerked it loose to plunge it in again and again. "Dirty filthy mutie bastard!"

Shouting obscenities, the sec man slashed the creature across the belly, then upward. Writhing entrails slithered into view. As the dying creature fell to the ground, it weakly snapped at the nearest man, almost biting him in the groin.

Dropping their useless blasters, the guards savagely fell upon the thing, wildly hacking at the body until it was in several pieces. Then they stomped the remains under their combat boots, anger and fear fueling their rage. Minutes passed with only the sounds of their labored breathing and the snap of bones faintly discernible over the moaning storm.

THE PLEXIGLAS WINDOWS of the large brick building rattled from the force of the wind. The main door was bolted shut, and heavy blankets hung from the lentil, cutting the wind whenever somebody entered or departed. That helped, but it didn't completely stop the pervasive black grit from sweeping across the armory every time the door was used.

Sitting in the fireplace was an electric heater, the bright red coils steadily sending out waves of soothing warmth. Numerous gun racks dotted the wall. One held revolvers and boxes of ammo, another contained pump-action shotguns, while the rest were filled with AK-47 assault rifles, the metal shiny with fresh oil, the wooden stocks gleaming with polish. Stacks of loaded clips filled shelves, along with neat piles of ammo boxes. Crates of grenades were piled on the floor next to trunks of MRE packs. Originally, this building had been the armory for the Complex, but was now in the process of becoming the throne room

for the new baron of Shiloh ville. William Sheffield
always kept his weapons close, and his enemies dead,
as the old saying went.

An air conditioner was nestled in the wall, its front
masked with a heavy blanket and a lot of gray tape.
Something rattled nonstop inside the machine, the
noise fluctuating with every gust. On a small table,
off in a corner by itself, a shortwave radio was hard-
wired to a nuke battery from a military vehicle. The
speakers hissed with the usual background of static
from the isotopes in the atmosphere. A coffeemaker
bubbled softly on a sideboard, serving trays heavily
laden with loaves of canned bread, slices of canned
meat, and gray military cheese. A bottle of shine stood
near some glasses and a box of cigars.

A dozen sec men armed with AK-47s lounged before the fireplace, sipping coffee from ceramic mugs,
smoking cigs and cleaning their blasters.

Sitting prominently in the middle of the enormous
room was an ornate chair holding a big man who was
reading computer printouts. A willowy blonde stood
nearby, watching over his shoulder and making low
comments and suggestions.

The man was tall and heavily muscled, his neck
and hands corded with hard tendons. He was wearing
a crisp blue shirt and matching pants, the boots glossy
with polish. A huge .50-caliber Desert Eagle pistol
rested in a hip holster, with a sleek 9 mm Heckler &
Koch pistol riding in a shoulder rig. A white scarf
was tied about his thick neck, more to keep out the
draft than for any sartorial effect. His thick black hair
was cut short, and a pattern of tiny round scars
marked the left side of his face. It looked as if he had
taken a shotgun blast directly into the face and had

somehow survived. The truth was much more painful than that.

"Fucking weather," Baron Sheffield cursed, listening to the storm rage outside. Laying aside the report, he sipped at a mug of coffee, making a bitter face.

"Bah!" he said, throwing the cup onto the floor. "The blasted ash is into everything! The food, blasters...I'm surprised it isn't inside the fucking ammo!"

Thumbing live rounds into an empty clip, a sergeant asked, "How long can we expect the weather to be like this, my lord?"

"Another week, possibly more," Sheffield replied dourly, leaning forward in his chair. "Silas was an ass. Using the Kite to blast the whole countryside has only destroyed our food supply." The baron pulled a Tekna knife from his belt and imagined what he would have done to the old fool before allowing him to finally die. He was the fool for waiting so long before torturing the whitecoat. Silas would have told him everything! Eventually.

"Mebbe when the rains come..." a corporal started.

"The acid rain?" Sheffield stressed the word. "That'll only make things worse, not better, fool. How can farmers grow crops in ash with acid. Hell, there aren't any fields in this valley anyway."

"That problem is a long way in the future, sir," a corporal stated, smirking.

"Is that right?" Sheffield demanded coldly. "How comforting."

"Besides," a lieutenant quickly said to cover the blunder, "I thought there was plenty of food in the Quonset, sir." His voice was odd, scratchy and twisted. Two bullet scars marked either side of his throat, and there was a white patch in his dark hair where a slave's ax had struck, but failed to kill.

Sheffield scowled at the sec man. "We have six tons of MRE packs in the warehouse," he stated. "Our last gift from Dr. Jamaisvous. After that's gone, we'll be forced to get food from hunters and farmers as we used to do."

The corporal arched an eyebrow. "But sir, there are no more farms in the Shiloh valley!"

"Exactly. What the Kite didn't destroy, the ash has polluted. There won't be any new crops around here for years, mebbe decades."

"My lord," the blond woman said, "I have seen you use the Kite to break up acid rain storms and drive them away. Can't you do the same now with the ash?"

Thoughtfully, Sheffield stared at her. It was a smart suggestion. Collette never failed to surprise him. She was the only woman wearing the blue shirt of a sec man at the Shiloh Complex. Captured from a caravan passing through Tennessee, her youth and beauty had sent the girl directly to the gaudy house. She was attractive despite a large nose. The golden blond hair, emerald green eyes and her big breasts made men think of her only as a hot slut. Yet during the slave revolt, she had fought with the sec men against the other slaves. When the revolt was finished, she directed the grave diggers. That got her out of the chains, and because of her special talents, she soon became his bed warmer. Then over the long months, a lover, somebody he could talk to, and confide with. Collette was uneducated, but smart, and always gave good advice.

When Silas died and Sheffield took over the base,

he needed somebody he could trust to be the new sec chief, so he gave the job to Collette. A few of the blues grumbled over the matter. A former slave as their chief? It was an outrage! She fucked a couple, killed the rest and the men now obeyed her without question. That was when Sheffield discovered how good a fighter she was. Lean and strong, Major Collette was a chilling machine, an expert with blaster and knife. Plus, she sharpened her thumbnails daily, caring for them like a good blaster. Sheffield once saw her remove a man's eyes with those nails. The orbs popped right out, then she bit through the ganglia and spit the bloody orb back at the man's shocked face. Nobody fought with Collette after that incident.

The tattoo of a broken knife blade encircled by a ring of barbed wire was on the back of her left hand. The work was delicate, expertly done with lamp oil and a sharp pencil. The process was known to hurt like hell, yet Collette had done it to herself. As befitting her position, the woman was in good combat boots, loose denims and a blue shirt. A machete hung at her hip, while a small-caliber wheelgun was tucked into her belt and an Ingram M-10 machine pistol slung over a shoulder.

Under the frank appraisal of the baron's gaze, Collette smiled. Secrets were power in the Deathlands. Before Sheffield, she had been with Silas many times, but never as man and woman. She merely used her hands to satisfy the whitecoat. Some spit in her palm, and a few minutes later he was sound asleep. They all thought he was fucking her, more the fools they. But once he was out, she would steal food, look at the books and practice fighting techniques where nobody could watch. When the time came to act, she was more than ready. The private training got her out of the slave pens, and would someday make her the baron of a ville. Not even Sheffield knew she could read and write. When playing with his hair, or massaging his shoulders, the woman was also reading the reports he held. She knew more about the status of the ville than anybody, including the baron.

Collette had been very pleased when Sheffield chose her to be the new sec chief. It saved her the trouble of chilling the person chosen had it not been her. If everybody simply stayed out of her way and did as ordered, there would be a lot fewer corpses in the world.

"No, my dear, I do not dare to use the Kite," Sheffield said reluctantly, returning to the conversation. "It might make the weather worse, and if the winds get any stronger the dish will get damaged, even though it's already lashed down with every spare foot of chain we have. If it topples over, we're defenseless until it's repaired."

"Can the dish be moved?" she asked.

What an odd question. He gestured at the shaking windows. "Not at the present, no. The mil wags can still run in this muck, but the trucks and diesels stall the moment the air filter gets clogged."

"Machines need to breathe," She chuckled. "I've always found that so amusing."

"Have you, my dear?" the baron asked softly.

Collette smiled sweetly and nestled closer to the big man, making no verbal reply.

A sec man scraped his pipe clean with a small knife and loaded the bowl with a pinch of shagcut soaked in whiskey. "Storm ain't slowing or stopping for a while," he said, holding a flame to the bowl. "Plenty of time to decide what to do next."

"Perhaps," Collette countered rudely. Rising from her position, she turned to the baron. "Why don't you give me the access code for the Quonset hut and I'll have a full inventory on the supplies done."

"Nobody goes in there but me, or people I want in there," he stated, partially drawing the Tekna knife. "Ask again, Collette, and I'll slit your throat."

Rubbing her nose, the woman smiled. "I see that you have learned from the mistakes of Silas," she purred.

Sheffield grunted and sheathed the blade. Damn the bitch and her mind games. Always testing, always prying. Probably wanted to be baron herself someday. He'd have to watch out for that. "The whitecoat was an idiot. Burning the pollution from the land is a good plan. More crops means more people to rule. But to try and clean the land and air for the whole world? Who cares? Let them die, man and mutie."

"Just save the women," a sec man said with a chuckle, and the others joined the laughter.

On impulse, Sheffield grabbed his sec chief around the waist and pulled her close until warm breasts were pressed against his face.

"Sounds good," he mumbled, biting the fabric and the soft flesh underneath. "Might as well fuck. Not much else to do, but wait."

"Bedroom," Collette suggested, pressing harder against the man and spreading her legs a bit to guide his free hand between her thighs.

"They can watch," he growled, almost ripping open her shirt in his haste to expose her breasts. God, he loved those big milkers! They spilled free, and he ran rough palms over the large nipples. "Let them see how a real man does it."

"As you wish, my lord," she demurred, raking her nails through his hair.

Just then, a loud knock sounded at the door. Quickly, the sec men raised their blasters and assumed firing positions, as a corporal brandishing a handcannon walked across the room and threw the bolt. A blast of smoky air heralded a figure in bloody rags, the hash marks of a corporal barely visible through the layer of ash. He clutched a longblaster with a shattered stock and a badly bent barrel.

"Report," Sheffield snapped, shoving the woman away.

"My lord, we've been attacked," the corporal said without preamble, yanking the cloth from his face. "A mutie got in through the hole and aced two of us. My private and I finally stopped the thing, but we lost three men and a blaster chilling it."

"How did this happen?" Collette demanded, tucking the loose shirt into her pants without buttoning it closed. "Asleep on duty again, eh?"

"In this storm?" the corporal snapped. "It's the damn blasters! They jam after only a few shots. We had to take out the mutie with knives!"

"What about the Claymores?" Sheffield demanded, rising from his throne.

"None of them went off, sir. Ain't worth shit."

"Fuses are set wrong again," the baron muttered, worrying a fist. "Lieutenant Brandon, get on the intercom and assign more troops to the gap immediately. Then order the last two war wags to shove that dead tank into the gap. That'll cut the hole down from fifty feet to twenty. And have somebody reset the fuses!''

"Yes, sir!'' the officer replied. He strode across the room to a distant table and started to press buttons on a small control panel. A tired voice answered from the speaker, and he replied in a harsh tone.

Furious, a sergeant spit on the floor. "Shitfire!'' he growled. "What are we going to do about these fucking blasters? No matter what we do, no matter how much cloth we wrapped around them, they always jam!''

Glumly, a private added, "If the slaves ever find out, we'll have another revolt.''

"Got that right,'' another sec man agreed succinctly.

With a curse, Collette swung her squat Ingram around to point it at a musician chained to a chair near the fireplace. The slave continued to softly blow a happy song on her harmonica. She hadn't been told to stop and knew better than to disobey a command.

"Whoa there, sir! Ain't no need for that. Lorna is okay,'' a private said, stepping between the two women. "Totally faithful to the blues, she is. Good as a dog.''

"Idiot,'' Collette snarled, snapping the arming bolt. "Slaves are faithful only to the whip.''

The private turned to the baron. "Sir?'' he asked hopefully.

"Kill them both,'' Sheffield ordered calmly. "I won't have fools working for me as bodyguards.''

The sec man gasped and Collette fired from the hip, the chattering machine pistol hosing a stream of soft-lead rounds. The trooper tried to dodged out of the way and failed, his body spinning to topple onto the dirty floor. Unable to move, the girl simply continued to play the harmonica until the bullets came her way, slamming her backward against the chair. The tattered body slumped forward to dangle limply from the chains, the broken harmonica tumbling away to land in the fireplace next to the electric heater.

"Anybody ever speaks like that in front of a slave gets more of the same," Collette stated, slapping in a fresh clip. "We kill with blasters, but rule through fear. Understand?"

The men murmured agreement, trying to ignore the splashes of blood and gore adorning their uniforms.

"Wh-what about me, sir?" the wounded corporal asked hesitantly.

As if debating options, Sheffield waited a minute before answering. "You did good, Trooper. Go see the healer about that wound, then get some sleep. You deserve a rest. No patrols for a week. You're assigned to the bunker."

"Yes, sir!" He smiled and gave a crisp salute. The sec man hurried past the corpses and throne, heading down a long hallway for a distant section of the armory.

"That was generous," Collette commented, shouldering her blaster.

"Carrot and the stick," Sheffield replied. "Only a fool tries to rule by only one of those." Loosening the scarf around his neck, the baron sat in the throne chair and pulled the maps closer. "Lieutenant Brandon, take some men and drag the bodies outside. We'll save them for later in case we run low on food for the slaves."

"Right now?" the officer asked, glancing at the

billowing blanket covering the closed door. "But sir, the storm gets worse at night."

Sheffield lowered a map and said nothing, merely staring at the soldier.

Swallowing hard, the lieutenant gathered his weapon and joined the other sec men at the door. Covering their faces with masks of cloth, one by one the men slid under the blanket and out into the roaring tempest.

"Now we're alone." Collette smiled, removing her shirt completely.

"Later," the baron snapped, studying a map. "I have an idea that might solve our present problem nicely."

She leaned closer, letting him feel the warmth of her skin. "Tell me," the woman encouraged.

"We can't move the dish," he said, tracing a river on the paper with a finger, "but mebbe, just mebbe…"

"What?"

"Mebbe we can find another one."

Chapter Three

Separating into teams, the companions did a fast sweep of the subterranean base, going from level to level in quick procession. The base was larger than most, the half hour deadline stretched to the limit before the companions reconvened in the control room.

"Find anything?" Ryan asked as the others arrived. The man was standing in the control room, drinking from a canteen. On the floor, a pair of legs stuck out of the open access panel of the main console.

"We're alone," Mildred reported. "That's for sure."

"Good. Any food?"

Wearily, Krysty took a seat at a control board covered with twinkling lights. "Not a thing in the kitchen, or in the freezers," she said, a smudge of ash on her cheek. "There's all the water we could want, laundry facilities seem to work, a hundred soft beds. Just no food or weapons."

The big man frowned. "Nothing?"

"Not a grain of rice or a split bean. Zero."

"Damn."

Glancing across the room, Dean asked, "Any luck with the mat-trans unit?" The door to the chamber was closed as always, and a small sign on the door warned of no entry beyond that point for any personnel below B12 security levels.

"No bombs, it if that's what you mean," J.B. said, sliding out from the interior of a panel. The console seemed to be completely filled with endless wires. "Unfortunately, I have no idea why it won't work. Everything is in place and looks in good shape. But then, I have no idea how the mat-trans chamber works in the first place."

"Nobody does anymore," Doc rumbled, leaning against a wall. "Indeed, few did when it was brand-new. Now this is all lost technology. A virtual Atlantis underground."

"Damnedest thing," Mildred said, sounding puzzled, her face scrunched. "This control room is in pristine condition. Last time we were here, this place was busted to pieces from a major firefight, bullets holes everywhere and spent brass underfoot. Now it looks brand-new."

"You noticed that, eh? Us too," Ryan said, brushing a hand across the shiny top of the vid display. There wasn't even any dust, except for what they brought with them from the garage. "I think the old bastard repaired this redoubt for some reason. Mebbe by stealing parts from others."

Just then the door to the mat-trans unit opened and Krysty walked out. "The machine is still dead," she announced glumly.

"Broken?" Dean asked, digging in a pocket. "I found some tools in a drawer. Not much, just pliers and a few screwdrivers."

"Deactivated, more likely," J.B. said, accepting the tools and stuffing them into a pocket. "Silas wasn't fool enough to smash his only way out of here."

Ryan glared at the banks of comp screens, the

blinking cursors in each corner of the monitors waiting for commands to be given. "Fireblast, and only he would know the codes to turn it back on."

"Indeed, and it shall be most difficult to get them now, since you so permanently removed his head," Doc observed, twirling his stick.

"Wouldn't have told us the truth anyway," J.B. growled.

"Let me have a look," Doc suggested. Moving from console to console, the old man studied the comp screens intently. "This one seems to be the master," he declared at last. "All of these bases have similar setups, and this is usually the screen that lights up whenever we arrive."

"Got an idea?" J.B. asked, coming closer. "Let's hear it."

"I am going to try a hard reboot," Doc announced, opening the access panel to each console. Wiring and circuit boards were exposed in an endless array. "I shall just turn the whole system off, then back on."

"Won't that crash the system permanently?" Dean asked in real concern.

"It does not work now. Do you have an alternative suggestion?"

"Nope."

"Anyone else?" Doc asked, his hand resting on a keyboard.

The companions mulled over the plan, but couldn't suggest a viable alternative. The matter settled, Doc continued to open the access door to each console until he found the main power switch on the surge protector. The insulated box was in plain sight under the first console, nothing more than a simple toggle switch with a glowing indicator.

"This should kill the entire system," he said, placing a finger on the switch. "Ready?"

"Hit it," Mildred said. "The sooner we know, the better."

Doc flipped the glowing red switch and stepped back. The panel lights died instantly, and the control room grew silent as the comp hum died away. Only the ceiling lights remained bright, as those used a different circuit. Doc waited a few minutes for the capacitors to fully discharge, just in case the comps had crash protectors, then hit the master switch once more.

A dozens beeps heralded the return of the indicator lights, whole panels becoming illuminated. Every monitor brightened as the screens began to crawl with diagnostics as the system rebooted, then the comps did a systems check and began to scroll command codes.

"Work?" Jak asked, craning his neck to see over the others.

"Yes and no," Doc said hesitantly. "It looks like the unit is fully functional again, but we are still not going anywhere. It is asking for a password."

"Never did before," Dean stated.

J.B. shrugged. "It was a good try."

"We're not finished yet," Mildred said, biting a lip. She reached out for the keyboard, then withdrew her hand. "How long a code word is it asking for? Maybe it's the code for entering the redoubt."

"No, madam, this has six astrix in a row to fill," Doc mused. Then he narrowed his gaze and stared at Ryan.

"No," he muttered. "It couldn't be that easy."

Ryan blinked. "What?"

"There is only one way to find out." Doc typed in

a name and hit the Enter key. The comp hummed to itself for a few seconds, before coming alive, every screen in the room flashing DOS commands with a library of numbers scrolling by at unreadable speed. Then the monitors slowed their wild displays and resumed their usual appearance.

"Did it work?" Krysty asked.

Ryan grabbed a chair. "Let's see." Going into the mat-trans unit, he placed a chair inside and closed the door. Instantly, there was a telltale hum of power flowing to the machinery and they heard an unmistakable noise of the mat-trans unit working. Ryan waited a few moments before opening the door and there was no sign of the chair.

"Yee-haw!' Jak whooped, throwing his arms into the air. "We back on-line!"

Tilting back his fedora, J.B. whistled. "Used your name as the reboot command," he said. "Man, did Silas hate you, Doc."

"And I him in return. I plan to celebrate his demise every year, and drink a toast to the man who did the job." The old man took Ryan by the shoulders and looked hard at him. The frank emotion on the time traveler's face was embarrassing, but Ryan understood.

"There are three things that I must do in this world," Doc said slowly. "And now that Silas is dead, thanking you is the most important."

"Happy to do it," Ryan answered truthfully, slapping the man on the arm. "What's the third thing?"

Doc released his friend and turned away. "Going home to my dear Emily," he whispered almost too softly for any of them to hear.

Suddenly, a low whining noise could be heard

among the comp, closely followed by a familiar voice. "Greetings."

The companions spun. There was nobody in sight.

"Check the corridor," Ryan directed, drawing the SIG-Sauer.

"Oh, God," Mildred gasped, pointing at a comp monitor. "It's Silas!"

Astonished, the companions gathered around the glowing screen. It was unmistakably the dead white-coat, but not as they remembered him. This Silas was razor thin, with gaunt eyes and hollow cheekbones. A nervous tick jumped in his face, and his hands were those of a corpse. The picture stayed on the screen doing nothing, not moving or breathing.

"It's a recording," J.B. said in relief, releasing his grip on the Uzi. "Must have set it off with the reboot."

"Why isn't it talking, then?" Dean asked.

"Computers are brilliant, but stupid," Mildred said, walking to the keyboard and tapping a key. "We have to tell it we're here."

The still shot of the scientist flicked, then spoke again. "Greetings," Silas said in a harsh voice. "If you are hearing this, Major Sheffield, then I am dead and have finally given you the entry code to the redoubt. I held off for so long, Major, because I knew that once you had the code I was no longer needed. You can operate the Kite and dish now, and as the chief of my sec men you know the details of my plans." The picture smiled, as lovely a sight as the grave of a child.

"Sheffield," Ryan muttered, filing the name away.

"An advisory note. There is a pistol in the CO's office. Do not use it for the obvious reason. And do not use the door in the bottom level. The predark tunnels are full of savage muties, but light scares them away. Well, most of the time.''

"Thanks for the info," J.B. muttered.

"If it's true," Mildred warned.

The screen crackled for a moment. "The mutie outside the redoubt is for Ryan and the others. Hopefully, it will kill them as painfully as possible. If possible, I'll cage a puma in the art vault as a backup trap. Certainly there are lots of them to capture in the nearby woods. If there is time, I will also have the machines haul over more supplies and weapons from redoubt #5. The code for gaining access to the main armory is tattooed on my leg at the hip. Simply reverse the numbers, or else the sec hunter droids will attack.''

"Crafty old bastard didn't trust a soul," Krysty observed.

"Except this Sheffield," Ryan commented coldly. He was listening to the vid, but also paying close attention to the room behind the man. It looked like a tech lab, with lots of comps, and a stack of rainbow disks was visible in an open desk drawer. There was a window covered with iron bars and the silhouette of a man holding a longblaster. This was inside the Complex they had seen before, the old bastard's private rooms.

Pausing to mop sweat off his brow, Silas blew his nose and tucked the cloth away. "I hope that I was able to watch Tanner die screaming for mercy.'' He twitched. "Maybe the sight will even make my nightmares stop and I will erase this disk myself. Sleep, oh, God, what I would give for some sleep without dreams of Tanner and his bitch killing me over and over again.'' The man slumped and shook as if with fever.

"I wish you well completing the Great Plan. Once the atmosphere is clean again, normal rain will wash away the radiation, feed crops and the population will grow quickly. Soon there will be hundreds of thousands of healthy people to become citizens of the New America. Our America. An America of absolute law and order.''

"Baron Silas," Jak said, curling a lip.

The picture of Silas leaned toward the screen. "On a matter of security, Front Royal defied our authority and killed our representative, Major Overton. As soon as you have killed Dr. Tanner, assuming that I did not, then I strongly suggest you melt the ville into the ground. It would not be wise to let the word spread that anybody challenged our authority and lived.''

"Think the ville is still there?'' Krysty asked anxiously.

Trying to control the fury within, Ryan merely shrugged. There was no way of knowing if Front Royal still stood or was only a smoking hole in the ground. Hopefully, the unexpected death of Silas and the hunt for the companions screwed up the plans of the blues. There may still be a chance of saving his ancestral home. Load in another reason to ace the blues.

The vid of the old man paused for a few moments, as if to allow Sheffield to write down the idea, then continued. "Now a couple of suggestions. Never let the people know where you keep the computers that control the dish. Always make somebody else your public ruler of the baronies. Let any assassin go after him, and you can rule forever as the power behind the throne of New America.''

There was a long pause. ''I guess that is all. Good luck, William. Godspeed.''

The picture on the monitor flickered.

''Greetings,'' Silas said.

With a fast jab, Doc hit the Escape key and the vid disk stopped, frozen in the middle of a word.

''Arranged for his own successor,'' Mildred mused. ''But only told the man bits and pieces of how things work to keep him faithful. What a paranoid.''

''I liked hearing about the nightmares.'' J.B. grinned. ''Seems as if they were driving him insane from lack of sleep.''

''Good,'' Doc said grimly.

''Dad, if this Sheffield isn't here,'' Dean said slowly, ''then mebbe Silas never gave him the password.''

His father nodded. ''Makes sense, which means we're probably safe inside the redoubt.''

''Starving, but safe,'' Krysty retorted. ''Although it's something of a comfort to know a horde of blues isn't coming our way.''

''Good thing you killed him when you did,'' Doc rumbled, twisting the handle of his stick and drawing a few inches of steel into view only to slam it closed again. ''Or else he would have marched an army of blues in here and slaughtered us like sheep!''

Ryan had no response for the comment. You killed an enemy on sight. That was just common sense. He never could understand the sec men and barons who played games and gave chances to their prisoners. Raw stupidity. Chill and live, it was as simple as that.

"So, what now?" the big man stated, taking a seat. "Should we leave, or stay?"

"Kill blues," Jak stated angrily. "What mean, leave?"

"There's no food here," Ryan said, scratching his belly. "In a few days we'll start to sicken and couldn't fight fish in a barrel. But mebbe we can find food in another redoubt. Blasters, wags. Everything we need."

"We could also end on the other side of the continent," Krysty pointed out. "By the time we get back here, this Sheffield will finish that wall and be surrounded by hundreds of sec men. Never stop him then."

"I strongly recommend against a jump," Mildred said. "We need some time to get back on our feet. It always makes us sick, and after three days without food, it might kill some of us."

"Food," Jak said wistfully, his stomach rumbling.

Good. That was exactly the response Ryan had wanted. The message from Silas had taken some of the fuel from their engines, but now they were standing tall once more.

"Then we're agreed," Ryan said. "Okay, we search this whole place again, and I mean search from the periscope to the reactor, break open every closet, every desk and footlocker. See if there's anything to eat in this place, and I mean anything—used chewing gum, herbal soap, cigars, carpenters glue, anything at all. There has got to be some food here, and we're going to find it!"

His belly rumbling, Ryan headed for the elevator. "Come on," he said grimly. "Let's rip this bastard place apart!"

HANDS HELD behind his back, Sheffield paced the throne room in deep thought. "Ash storms, mutie attacks, I can't be bothered with this trivia!" he barked petulantly. "I'm so close to victory! I know how to operate the mat-trans unit, I know where the rest of the food and ammo are hidden. I just can't get to them!"

"Because he never gave you the entry code," Collette said. Sitting on the edge of a table, she had one boot on the floor, the other dangling in the air. "The code to the redoubt, that is. I assume it isn't the same code that opens the door to the Quonset hut?"

"Rads, no. The entry code is the last piece of information," he growled. "The whitecoat dangled it in front of me like a worm on a hook."

"Can't we blast a way in? Or dig?"

Standing still, Sheffield looked at the woman. It was time to tell her the truth. "They're nukeproof," he stated simply.

She gawked. "What?"

"The redoubts are nukeproof. Predark bunkers full of military stores and supplies."

"Shitfire," she whispered in shock. Then the sec chief stood. "We must gain entry."

The baron waved that away. "Impossible! The keypad has ten numbers and twenty-six letters. I worked the calculator program on the computer in the lab—he was teaching me for a while until I started to learn too much—and discovered that there are over a million combinations for the code."

Collette rubbed her nose, fingering the broken ridge of bone. "Millions, and it would take years to tap in every one," she mused, then tilted her head. "Do you still have the list?"

Dropping into his chair, Sheffield regarded the woman. "An interesting idea," he said, way ahead of her. "Send somebody to the redoubt and have him tap in codes off the list. Probably won't work, but it's only one man and worth the risk."

"A man we can trust," Collette corrected. "Once inside he becomes dangerous. Know anybody we can trust?"

"You, perhaps?" the baron asked softly.

Sensing danger, Collette switched tactics and laughed while undoing her blouse, then her bra. "I'm of much greater service here, my lord."

Amused, Sheffield watched as she fondled her breasts, the nipples hardening almost immediately.

"Two men," he corrected. "A slave to do the work, and an executioner in case he succeeds."

"Very wise, my lord," Collette whispered, undoing her gun belt and easing it onto the table. Her pants slid to the floor, and she was wearing nothing underneath.

"Just a gaudy slut at heart." He chuckled, unzipping his trousers. "I should bring some slave girl in and make you do her. I know you hate that. But you'd do it anyway for me. Wouldn't you, dear?"

Standing quietly in the corner, two young women waited for the commands to join the baron and his lover. One was pale and trembling, a virgin to sex of any kind. The other was swarthy and silently wept, knowing that any sound would mean a whipping.

"Yes, it is vile. Disgusting," the naked woman whispered hoarsely, gently fingering herself. "But ask and I'll do it. Anything you wish."

Drawing his handcannon, Sheffield placed it on a nearby table and motioned her closer. "Then come here, bitch," he growled deep in his throat, spreading both knees wide. "Crawl to me and beg for it!"

Dropping to the floor, the sec chief submissively approached her baron, licking her lips. Her long blond hair hid most of her face, but her eyes stared hungrily from amid the golden cascade, and she growled.

Sheffield watched as she knelt before the throne and took him fully into her mouth, lips and tongue striving to please him, spittle dribbling onto his pants as she mouthed his rock-hard cock. Soon he was breathing hard, his hips bucking, driving the flesh harder into her mouth.

"Oh no, not yet, woman," he said, pushing her away. Standing, he removed the rest of his clothing. "I have something else in mind for today."

"Do it," she begged from the floor, wiping her wet mouth with the back of a hand. "Don't ask, just do it!"

In blind lust, the baron lifted her off the floor by a breast, squeezing hard to make her whimper. Collette moaned in agony and raked her nails across his chest and along his throbbing manhood, tracing along the shaft until he cried out.

"Bitch!" he yelled, slapping her across the face.

"Please, no," Collette whimpered, knowing that was what he liked to hear.

Laughing, the baron grabbed her by the throat and squeezed until she thought he was really going to kill her. Panic struck, and she tried to escape, but it was hopeless now. He was much stronger and driven mad with lust.

Slapping her again, Sheffield simply shoved himself painfully deep inside her and started to thrust. Collette could only make inarticulate noises as he brutally assaulted her. And she knew there was worse coming. Much worse.

When Collette was baron someday, all of the men in her ville would be in chains and neutered, no, castrated, both cock and balls removed, sexless animals used only to draw water, pull plows and be used as target practice. Horrid filthy things, they should all die in screaming agony.

"Yes, more, please!" she begged, rolling her wide hips to engulf him completely.

"Stop trying to escape! You there, come hold her still!" Sheffield shouted at the slaves.

Instantly, the girls rushed forward to assist the baron. Each grabbed an arm and held Collette to the table.

Sheffield could barely speak, sex with Collette was so good it actually hurt sometimes. He grunted and squeezed her hips, pounding harder, sweat dripping onto her chest. The two hearts pounded in his chest, and he wondered if this was why they got along so well.

A soft explosion sounded from outside the armory, somewhere to the west.

"My lord?" one of the slaves asked, her eyes wide in terror.

"Just a land mine," he grunted, blurring the words. "Another mutie must have exploded."

"Soon," Collette agreed in a throaty whisper, thrusting hard, then shouting at the top of her lungs. "Oh, yes! Soon, my lord, soon!"

WISPS OF STEAM rising all around her, Mildred stood in the kitchen, using a wooden spoon to stir the contents of a huge stainless-steel pot on the main military stove. The grayish fluid bubbled steadily and gave off a pleasant aroma.

"How's it coming?" Dean asked hopefully. The boy dropped into a chair and tried not to drool at the prospect of eating.

"Pretty soon," the physician replied, sprinkling some salt into the brew. No matter how well stripped a larder may be, there always seemed to be salt left behind. Nobody ever thought of taking the big container. "This is purely survival food. It'll keep us alive, but I can't guarantee the flavor. However, it's all we have at the present."

Lugging a box full of empty whiskey bottles into the kitchen, Ryan set the crate on one of the score of tables that filled the room. It appeared that the base held a thousand soldiers and most of them could be fed at the same meal. "I'll be damn. That's beef of some kind," he said, sniffing. "Where did you find it?"

"Almost beef," Mildred said, taking a sip of the brew from the spoon. "It's boot."

Ryan frowned. "Army boot?"

"Good Lord no," Mildred said, adding another handful of tiny brown squares to the pot. The material sank into the brew without a trace, then started to bob to the surface. "Combat boots are mostly plastic and rubber. No nourishment there. I found some dress shoes in the closets. The polish helped keep the leather intact. I scraped off the plastic, that's what makes patent leather shoes so shiny, then cut them into strips, soaked the piece in salt water for a while to soften the material and leech out any lingering polish. Now it's in the pot."

"Boot," Jak said with a grimace. Near the sloshing

dishwasher, the teenager was using scissors to cut bedsheets into long strips. "Had worse."

"Have you indeed?" Doc asked askance, placing a fistful of lint-covered cough drops on an empty plate. It was the only edible thing he had found. "I am sincerely sorry to hear it, my friend."

"Not really," the teenager snorted. "Being nice."

Krysty entered the kitchen and put a cloth bag on the counter. "Got some roots here," she said, untying the bag. Inside was a scraggly collection of withered brown things as thin as spaghetti.

"Roots? Where the hell did you find those?"

She took a knife from a wall rack and started to dice the roots into little pieces. "Every officer in the base had some sort of plant on his desk. I pulled out the dead flowers and dug through the soil. Isn't much, but every little bit helps."

Carrying the stringy material to the pot, Krysty sprinkled them into the soup and took a whiff. "Fish?" she asked hopefully.

"Boot," Mildred said, adjusting the electric burner to a lower setting.

"Gaia, save us. Any rice or honey?" Krysty asked, randomly opening the cabinets. As long as rice was kept dry, it would last for centuries, and honey never went bad. Ever. It simply became a solid rock-hard mass, but once gently heated, the stuff softened to its usual form and was as delicious as ever.

"Not a frigging tea leaf," Mildred retorted grumpily. She placed a lid on the pot and moved to the sink for a glass of water. She opened the tap, and brown water gushed out to slowly clear into something drinkable. "The larder was vacuumed clean. There wasn't even an empty can in the garbage bin. Nothing but some salt and garlic cloves."

"Like garlic," Jak said with a smile. "Makes everything taste good."

"It also goes rancid over time and will kill you," the physician said. "Ptomaine poisoning. I threw it in the toilet."

Just then, J.B. entered the room, maneuvering around the sea of tables as he carried a stack of boxes. "Damn, that smells good," he beamed. "What's for dinner, Millie?"

Mildred glanced over a shoulder. "Don't ask."

His smiled faded. "That bad, eh?"

"Never mind the food. Did you find any weapons or grens?" Ryan asked. "There was nothing in the armory, or anyplace else I searched."

The Armorer glumly shook his head. "Not a loose round. Not even empty boxes or plastic wrapping on the floor. However, I found a Webley .44 revolver in the CO's office. Plus a nice box of ammo."

Joining him, Ryan scowled at the blaster. "That the one that Silas mentioned?"

"Yep."

"So what's wrong with it?"

J.B. lifted the handcannon and angled it into the light. "See? The barrel is blocked solid with iron. Pull that trigger and the back blast will remove your arm from the elbow down."

"Can you fix it, melt out the iron?"

"No way. I plan on placing it in plain sight near the front door in case anybody came visiting. Mebbe we can get them to shoot themselves."

Ryan lifted a cardboard ammunition box. "Worth a try. What about the ammo, rigged?"

"You better believe it. There's no cordite inside those cartridges. They're packed solid with plas-ex. Like loading your blaster with grens. Used that trick myself once or twice. It works great. But see here." He reached into a pocket and withdrew a grayish wad of something that resembled clay. "I took them apart, and now we have half a pound of plas-ex. About two grens' worth."

"All right," Dean said, beaming in pleasure. At least it was something.

The Armorer removed his fedora and placed it on the table. "Not really," he said, straightening the brim. "Don't have any timing pencils, detonators or any other way to set off the plas."

"Firecracker," Jak suggested. "Only made paper and twine."

"And gunpowder. We got none to spare. Doc's LeMat is the only blaster that uses black powder, and it's half of our remaining arsenal."

"Needs must, as the devil drives," Doc rumbled, drawing the massive weapon and putting it on the table. He made a gesture to slide it over.

J.B. waved him off. "Thanks, but I'm working on other stuff first. Keep that blaster loaded."

"I was thinking," Krysty said, pulling a chair away from the table and sitting down. "Even if we had wags and ammo, how are we going to destroy the Kite? We have nothing that can reach the sat in its orbit."

"Mebbe we could make it crash," Dean suggested.

"If we can reach the control systems, that's a good plan," Ryan agreed. The man spread a clean towel on the table and began to disassemble the Steyr. It was filthy with ash, and he wanted the rifle in good shape when they found ammo. "Comp systems are easy to smash. Only one Kite, and when the comps are gone, it's useless."

"Chilling the sat is easy," J.B. said to everyone's surprise. "Piece of cake. The problem is getting to the base undetected."

"While on my sojourn, I chanced to peer in the periscope," Doc said, taking a chair and pulling off his boots. The man wiggled his toes with obvious pleasure. "The storm seems to be lessening. When it stops, why not simply walk there?"

Sliding out the bolt and removing a spring, Ryan scowled. "And get chilled. There's no more trees outside, or bushes to hide behind. We'd be walking over open land in plain sight. Besides, we have less than a dozen live rounds and no usable explosives. They have motorcycles, mebbe another APC."

"Don't forget that chopper," Dean said.

"Yeah, we need a LAW rocket to take out that thing. Otherwise it'd be a death march."

"Front gate looked like it could stop a tank, so no use trying there," J.B. said, starting to clean his scattergun. "The stone wall has a gap, but the blues will station most of their guards there."

"Nightcreep," Jak suggested, stropping a knife on a whetstone. "Steal sec man blasters. Less them, better for us."

"Too risky. We can't steal weps from the blues until we go there, and we can't go till we got some more blasters."

"Catch-22," Mildred muttered. Then to their questioning looks she explained, "Predark talk for situations like this. You weren't allowed to leave the war unless you were insane, and if you wanted to go, then you were sane. Asking to leave meant you then had to stay, no matter what. Catch-22.''

Ryan slid the bolt home and dry fired the longblaster. The rifle clicked nice and solid. Find some ammo, and they were ready. ''Our best bet is to try the tunnel downstairs.''

Krysty considered the idea. ''Silas did mention the predark government had been digging them,'' she said. ''There could be tools in the storage lockers, explosives for the mining, medical supplies, lots of useful things down there.''

''Also a big ass mutie,'' Dean added. ''Sounds like the same problem to me. We need weapons to go into the tunnel to see if there are any weapons there to be found.''

''Muties aren't sec men,'' his father explained, starting to clean the SIG-Sauer. The one loaded clip he placed aside reverently. ''Okay, we've been through this place from top to bottom. What can we use to make some weapons?''

''Any brooms or mops in the closets?'' Krysty asked.

''Sure, lots. Army always liked things clean.''

''Good. We can use those as the handles. What can we burn?''

''I found some congealed oil in the grease traps of the garage,'' J.B. said, polishing his glasses with a cloth napkin. He placed them on his face and blinked his eyes into focus. ''The goo is useless for a wag, but we can soak rags in it and make torches. Remember, that mutie at the door didn't like the light.''

''Or getting shot,'' Dean added.

''Any chemicals we can cook into bombs?'' Mildred asked.

J.B. shook his head. "Nothing explosive. Some minor poisons, and I can make a ton of smoke bombs, but nothing deadly."

Tugging on an ear, Doc asked, "Was there any propane or oxygen remaining in the welding tanks I saw in the garage?"

"Only a few pounds of pressure, about ten seconds' worth."

"Not enough for a flamethrower." He sighed. "Ah, well."

"We have plenty of bottles," Ryan commented, nudging the case. "Just have to find something to put in them. Could we use the grease to make Molotov cocktails?"

The Armorer shook his head, then stopped and nodded. "Yeah, we can." He smiled. "I found some aftershave cologne in the barracks. That's mostly alcohol. I can cut the grease and make mebbe a dozen cocktails."

"Thicken them a bit with laundry soap," Mildred said, turning off the heat under the simmering pot. "That'll make it good and sticky."

"How about crossbows? Those are easy to make," Krysty said, starting to draw on the tablecloth with a pencil. "We can form the bow from steel bedsprings. This base has plenty of electricity. We can use the power tools to machine the shafts and carve the stocks from table legs."

"Fletching from feather pillows," Jak stated. "But still need arrowheads."

Rising from the table, Doc crossed the cafeteria and opened a drawer. "Plenty of knives here, although they are rather large. Could we perhaps cut them down to a more serviceable size?"

"Absolutely. There's a grinding wheel in the garage that'll do a fine job. This may just work."

"Hey! Remember the last time we were here and Doc almost got chilled?" Dean asked excitedly. "Where did we put the battle-ax and bayonets from the booby trap?"

"In the Art Room," Mildred answered. "I already checked. They're long gone."

"Shit." The boy's face slumped, then he beamed a smile and dashed away at a full run. "The Art Room? Yeah, be right back!"

"Homemade crossbows and bedsheet torches," Ryan growled, glancing at the doorway. "Mebbe we should risk a jump."

"Where?" Doc asked.

"Anywhere," Ryan answered, over his rumbling stomach. "Go to another redoubt, hopefully one Silas hasn't looted, grab some food or blasters, anything useful I find and jump back here using the LD button."

Hooking a boot under the table, J.B. leaned dangerously backward in his chair. "Last Destination button only works for thirty minutes. That's fifteen in, and the same out. Not much time."

"Traps," Jak added, brushing back his snowy hair. "Sec hunter droids, muties."

Ryan shrugged noncommittally. They could encounter any or all of those, it was a standard danger with any jump. Aside from not arriving at all. But they could also find a well-stocked armory with crates of MRE packs, LAW rockets, grens, even Stingers and IR antihelicopter rockets. They had hit the jackpot before, and he was sure they would do so again someday.

"Still got a few in the SIG-Sauer. That'll handle any problems," Ryan said confidently, patting the weapon.

"Mebbe," Krysty replied. "But the mutie outside took everything we had and came back for more. What's a 9 mm blaster going to do to another one of those?"

Thoughtfully, Ryan worked his jaw. "Yeah, I know. But what choice have we got?"

"Food first," Mildred directed, sampling the soup. It almost tasted like pork, which was a bad sign for a beef product, but she didn't think it would cause them any real harm.

"Found it!" Dean shouted, entering the kitchen. The boy was dragging an enormous plastic bag with faded pictures and writing on the outside.

"What that?" Jak asked, rising to help the boy haul it to the dining table.

"Silas mentioned hiding a cat in the Art Room as a trap for us. I figured it would have to eat, so I looked for food. Didn't see the cat, but found this bag in the closet."

Krysty squeezed the boy's shoulder. "Smart move. None of us caught that remark. You did good."

"Thanks," he said proudly.

"'Purina Cat Chow,'" J.B. read slowly, then turned the bag over. "Contents—rice, lamb, beef, wheat, veg oil, bunch of chems. This sounds okay."

"Better than okay." Mildred sighed in relief. "This solves our food problems for a while. More if we find any additional boots. Belts are good too. Less sweat to leech out."

Doc blanched. "Madam, please!"

"Sorry, but it's the truth."

Ryan gingerly took a nugget of the cat food and tried cracking it with his teeth. "Fireblast," he mumbled out of the side of his mouth. "Stuff is hard as rock and tastes strange."

"Bad?" Mildred asked in concern. She took some pellets from the bag and sniffed them carefully. It smelled like ordinary cat food. How could she tell if it was gone bad? The stuff always smelled awful.

"No, not bad, just strange," he said, swallowing with difficulty. "Hurt my teeth to chew. But I guess it's okay."

"Then it's dinnertime," Mildred said, taking a chair at the table.

Since the physician had cooked, the rest served. Ryan passed out bowls and spoons, while Krysty filled clean glasses with tepid water. Dean piled handfuls of the hard cat food on saucers, and Doc ladled out the thin gray soup, trying not to breath the fumes. Jak and J.B. kept watch with weapons in hand. They had been caught off guard once during a meal, but never again. Then the companions took their places and started to eat, none of them with very much enthusiasm.

Ryan ate steadily, ignoring the flavor and textures. Food was life. The one-eyed man would eat anything that didn't eat him first.

Krysty dipped one of the rock hard pellets into the soup, and then nibbled that. If anything, it tasted worse. "Sorry I lost my bearskin coat," the redhead said. "It was old and dusty, but it would have tasted better than this dreck."

"Amen to that," Doc said listlessly, taking another spoonful of the soup and forcing it down.

"Aw, shut up, you old coot," Mildred mumbled irritably, "and eat your boot."

Chapter Four

Night descended upon Shiloh Valley, or at least the clocks said it should be night. But there was no lessening or change in the terrible shroud of ash swirling around the ville like a black hurricane. A dozen sec men stood before the gap in the wall waiting for more muties to arrive. Fifty more men shuffled along between the brick buildings, patrolling for any other invaders. Three huddled in the kiosk in front of the main gate, the steel railing locked firmly in position. The slaves slept on the floor of the hut, since work was impossible. Nothing moved but the windblown ash; there were no sounds but the howling wind.

Then a single raindrop fell from the tortured sky and hit the ground with a sizzling hiss, like water hitting a hot stove. The ground sank out of sight where the droplet landed, a neat hole punched through the layer of dry ash.

A swaddled sec man walked closer to the spot and jerked back when he caught the delicate aroma of sulfur.

"Acid rain!" he shouted through his mask. "The rain has come early!"

But nobody could hear the warning. Struggling against the wind, the sec man reached the alarm bell and started wildly banging with all of his strength.

"Acid rain!" he screamed. "Rain!"

A few caught the muffled words and bolted for the nearest building as more drops descended from the mottled sky. Soon the sizzling noise rose to a deafening level, the ash compacting flat under the polluted deluge.

The guards at the wall cut themselves loose and headed for the bunker at the base of the dish. A private dropped his knife and had to untie the rope holding him secure. Stumbling after the others, he cried out as the rain hit his clothing and seared right through. Nuking hell, it was like touching a red-hot stove!

Going under the dish he was out of the rain, but he kept running. The wind could shift and he'd be dead in minutes. Somewhere far away, the alarm continued to ring as he crossed the encampment and finally made it to the bunker. Grabbing the handle, he tried to twist the latch but it remained firmly in place. Locked?

"Open the door!" the sec man yelled, pounding on the iron plates with a fist. "Open the fucking door!"

There was no response. Then a drop of rain hit him on the neck and he jumped from the pain, swatting at the point as if it were a bee sting. His fingers burned from the contact.

"Bastards!" he yelled, firing the Kalasnikov at the bunker. The rounds ricocheted off the armored door with no effect.

Dropping the blaster, he headed around the dish to try for the slave quarters. It was closer than the kiosk or the armory. Any building would do, but by now the rain was coming down in sheets, flattening the ash into something that resembled dirty concrete.

A sudden gust swept acid over the sec man, and he

shrieked as the cloth strips rotted away to expose his uniform, then the bare skin underneath. Frantically, he looked around for a canvas sheet, a tarpaulin, or anything he might use for protection. But whatever might have been available was now sealed under the hard covering of the solidified ash. The rain was pooling in gullies and trickling along to form streams that flowed toward the quarry.

The warning bell stopped ringing, and the trooper knew he was out of luck and time. Holding a hand to his forehead, he dashed into the rain, heading for the slave quarters. Stinging fire pelted him on the back, and pieces of his blue uniform flopped to his sides. He started to scream as the pain reached intolerable levels, but he kept going, combat boots splashing in the deadly water, the soles softening.

He crashed against the door to the slave quarters and grabbed the handle with both hands. Safety was only a foot away. He had made it. He would live! Yanking the door open, he saw a slave standing in his way. Grinning fiendishly, the woman struck the sec man with a bucket, the blow knocking him backward into the rain. He landed sprawling, the skin on his hands blistering instantly. As he shouted a curse, the water trickled into his mouth, swelling his tongue and burning the taste of sulfur down his throat. Recoiling, he tried to stand and fell face first into a puddle.

Sizzling agony washed his face, and he stood, realizing in horror that he was blind. Frantic, he ran for the dish once more and slammed into something large and hard. One of the support columns? He had no idea. The agony was overwhelming. He couldn't think. Run! He had to run!

The sound of an engine caught his attention and the

bleeding man stumbled in that direction, whispering for help, the flesh sagging off the bones of his exposed hand. There was a splash. He tried to dodge something and rammed into hot metal. A Hummer! Those were coated with plastic against the rain. He would be safe inside.

Grimacing in fear, the sec man inside the Hummer stayed motionless behind at wheel, his hand tight on the door handle to make sure it didn't open. The dying man beat on the glass with a bloody fist, the bones already showing. In a moment of compassion, the driver raised a pistol and pointed the blaster at the melting man, only to lower the weapon. The blast would shatter the window and let the rain inside. There was nothing he could do to help the poor son of a bitch.

"Sorry!" he shouted, fumbling for words. "Sorry."

Sagging out of sight, the man's cries got weaker as his skin flowed off, exposing muscles and beating organs. Soon only buttons, an ammo clip and some plastic pieces of combat boots would remain to mark the demise of the man.

Mercilessly, the rain continued pounding down upon the Shiloh Valley, destroying everything organic it touched.

RETURNING TO THE TOP FLOOR of the redoubt, the companions walked along the main corridor that led to the barracks. The last time they were there the hallway had been dark and lined with traps. Now it was well lit and spotlessly clean.

"Got to give old Silas that much," Ryan said grudgingly. "He was tidy."

"Anal retentive," Mildred commented.

Unsure of the meaning, Jak chose the dirtiest version he could think of and snorted a laugh. "Good one."

Going into the barracks, the companions found the four huge rooms were exactly the same as remembered—lined with bunks for hundreds of troops, small adjacent laundry rooms, and a line of lavs with rows of showers and stalls.

Choosing the most clean room, they checked once more for traps, then barricaded the door with a pile of bunks. Dean and Doc stood guard, while the others hit the showers and scrubbed themselves clean of days of sweat mixed with the bitter ash from outside. Then the others did the laundry while the albino youth and the boy showered in private stalls. The washing machines squealed unhappily, then sluggishly began to chug away. The bottles of bleach were bone dry, and adding water produced no results. But there were U.S. Army-issue plastic boxes full of individual packets of detergent and softener. In a few hours, the companions were scrubbed and wearing clean clothes.

Fed and clean for the first time in days, the companions chose the rooms reserved for officers, bolted the doors and fell soundly asleep. Nobody even dreamed.

Chapter Five

By the light of the silvery moon, the old man stared at the ruin of his ville, the melted stone towers, the burned huts, bits of cooked corpses sticking out of the flat acres of stone like insects caught in cool wax.

Reaching into a vest pocket, Baron John Henderson removed an antique silver snuff box, opened it and sniffed a pinch of the powder up each nostril. His body spasmed as the mixture of tobacco and jolt rushed to his brain, and suddenly he felt young and vibrant. As the drug took hold of his consciousness, colors changed hues, shimmering and melting into one another. The sensation of the experience made him feel giddy.

The baron of what remained of Casanova ville was wearing a predark business suit. He usually wore velvet slippers, but they had been replaced with stout leather boots. Tassels hung from an ornamental saber at his hip, but the fringe was stained and frayed. The big blaster in his shoulder holster was spotty, the gold filigree from the weapon forcibly pried off with a knife. Only the holster itself was in good condition, covered with fancy rainbow embroidery. The suit was clean, but not pressed, the buttons dim and scratched. Scabs from some disease dotted his unshaved face, his fingernails were caked with filth, his hair greasy and he smelled of urine. The reek was covered, somewhat, by the cloying perfume liberally applied to his old body.

But there was a fire in his eyes not fueled by the drugs, and his face radiated a strength of character that few men didn't fear.

Controlling his breathing, Baron Henderson knelt and placed a hand on the gray stone. It was hot, but not sizzling. Even after a week it was still hot. His grandson wouldn't allow the baron to visit the destroyed ville until he was sure it was safe. Safe. The very word tasted like shit in his mouth. What the hell was safe in Deathlands?

A well of fury rose within the baron, his grotesque face contorting in feral rage. Quickly, his grandson stepped forward and yanked his hand off the cooling lava.

"Dammit, I told you what it looked like," William Henderson said, inspecting the palm. It was red, but not burned in any way. "Just had to see for yourself, eh?"

The young Henderson was wearing camou-colored military fatigues, combat boots, with matching blasters on each hip. He was dressed like a soldier for combat, and only resembled his grandfather in the set of his shoulders and the madness in his face. The Hendersons had been breeding with their own bloodline for generations to try to purify the family of any weakness. Many were born without arms or legs, some unable to breath on their own. These were simply aced and burned, their very births denied. William had been the first whole Henderson in three decades, and while his body was perfect, even his grandfather feared the cold temper of the young Adonis.

Shaking off the youth's hand, the baron said nothing as he looked over the destruction of Casanova ville. Almost four hundred people had died in the attack, nearly half of his sec men and damn near every horse they owned. Plus, the wags and juice. The loss of slaves and blasters alone was heartbreaking.

"Fifteen minutes," the baron said aloud.

Crossing his arms, William nodded. "One of the guards was doing a slave in the bushes. He had just started when he heard the screaming and felt a wave of heat. Unfortunately, he didn't look up until he finished, and saw the castle slag to the ground like melting ice."

"You killed him, of course," the baron said, rising stiffly. Even the jolt couldn't remove all his pain these days. "The damn fool should have turned at once. Always time to hump a slut, but this could have been a chem fire, lightning strike, something controllable. There might have been something he could have done to save my ville!"

Narrowing his eyes to slits, William stared at the old reprobate, limbs quivering from the jolt, wine and semen staining his clothes as flies buzzed everywhere. Blood of his blood, the young man was still repulsed by the stinking whitehair.

"We strapped a knife to the slut and tied him down to a tree stump," William said. "Offered her freedom if she chilled him."

The baron stood taller, a faint smile playing on his chapped lips. "Original," he said with a chuckle. "Most amusing. The man died fast? No, wait. She took her time, savoring the kill. How long before he stopped begging for you to release him and switched to begging for you to chill him?"

"Two hours. The girl had style."

"Excellent. Bring her to my tent tonight."

"I can't. She's gone," his grandson replied. "I gave my word and set her free afterward."

Turning his back on the desolation of the congealing stoneworks, the baron shook his head sadly. "Honor and dignity, gods of the atom, what crap! I never should have let your idiot mother raise you."

"Really?" William said low and dangerous. "Yet it is only my word to my mother that keeps me here protecting you, you filthy disgusting old freak." He drew a blaster and pressed the barrel to the man's temple. "Black dust, I want to chill you more than I can say!"

The old baron grinned, displaying his assortment of stained and rotting teeth. "Then do it," he prodded. "Or shut the fuck up and get out of my way. You're as weak as your father was."

Snarling wordlessly, William cocked back the hammer and tightened his grip on the trigger, conflicting emotions storming across his handsome features. Then with a sigh, his broad shoulders slumped and he holstered the blaster. "I gave my word," William said softly, not really speaking to his grandfather. "And a soldier keeps his word, especially to himself."

"To himself most of all," the baron agreed, and the left pocket of his suit violently exploded, the heavy slug from the concealed blaster taking his grandson in the chest.

Stumbling backward, the young man hit a tree, a look of shock contorting his flawless face.

"Please," he wheezed, holding up a hand for protection while pressing a palm against the wet hole in his chest. Icy fire filled his limbs and a great wave of weakness stole his strength. It was quickly becoming impossible to breath. "Grandfather...!"

Drawing the .22 revolver from his smoking pocket, the baron aimed and shot the dying man again in the knees, the groin, then the gut, trying to make the pain as great as possible. Burbling blood filling his mouth, William fell to the ground, a fumbling hand clawing at his own weapon. The baron kicked the hand away and placed the hot barrel to the temple of his dying grandson.

"You didn't remember," he sang softly. "But I told you ten years ago that if you ever pointed a blaster at me again, you had damn well better use it, or I would use mine. Forgot, didn't you? That's a bad habit for a would-be baron."

William spit blood at the old man, hitting his cheek. The baron laughed and fired into the man's temple, exploding his head like a crushed egg.

"Forgetting a threat is almost as bad as forgiving an enemy. We rule by strength, not honor." The baron chortled through his nose, wiping the rivulet of snot on an encrusted sleeve. He repeated the phrase in a singsong voice, dancing a little step. "Forget, forgive, forget, forgive! Both of those won't let you live!"

Suddenly, sec men in liveried uniforms rushed from the bushes with a wide assortment of blasters in their hands. The officers held M-16s, the sergeants bolt-action longblasters and the privates all carried shotguns. There were no homemades. This was the baron's private guard, and they used only the very best his ville owned.

"Are you okay, my lord?" a burly sergeant asked, walking closer.

"Fine, fine," the baron said, holstering his weapon,

then quickly drawing the piece to reload. Spent shells were suicide in Deathlands. John Henderson knew he was slightly insane, but he refused to become stupid.

"My grandson and I had a discussion over whom should be the baron," the old man lied smoothly, sliding fresh shells into the revolver's cylinder. "I was asked to go into the bushes and retire myself. I told the boy no, and he accepted it with grace, dignity and honor."

Closing the blaster, Henderson tucked it inside his undamaged pocket. "You!" he snapped to a sec man. "Get me another suit!"

"Yes, my lord." The private saluted and dashed away.

The rest of the troops stood where they were, waiting for orders from their baron. He reeked like a used lav, and often chilled without reason, but aside from this one time, he had never lost a battle. The sec men had discussed the matter in detail days earlier, and rather than become coldhearts and attack farms, they would stay with the madman and see if he could get them another ville.

Henderson saw the decision in their face and approved. "By the way," he said, "did my grandson actually set loose the whore the guard was humping in the woods while my ville was being destroyed? He didn't really do that, did he?"

Averting their faces, the officers and privates mumbled assorted things under their breaths. Only a huge sec man spoke out loud and clear. "Why, yes, sir, he did. Never could figure out why, but it's not my place to question a superior."

"Sergeant, aren't you?" the baron asked, squinting up at the giant.

"Sergeant Thomas Smith, my lord."

"So tell me, Thomas, exactly how many other officers survived the attack? I only had twenty men with me when I went hunting that day."

Smith didn't correct the baron about being an officer. "Another five officers, my lord, and fifty more men were out fishing, or on patrol in the woods."

"Seventy troops, half dozen officers," Henderson muttered. "My grandson was my sec chief, and he turned traitor. I need a new commander of the troops. Okay, big boy, now you're it."

"Sir?" the sergeant asked, stunned.

The baron stared hard. "Don't make me think this is a mistake," he warned, resting a hand on his blaster. "Can't run a war by myself. Plus, I need an heir to carry on the Henderson name. My grandson committed suicide by challenging me. I'm offering the post to you, heir to the throne of...well, whatever ville we take over next. Yes or no."

"Yes," the sergeant said quickly, bending to a knee, "Father."

The baron chuckled softly. Even down on one knee, the bastard slab of beef was still taller than him. The freak had to be seven feet high! In a battle everybody would ignore the old man and concentrate on the giant. He was perfect cannon fodder. Yet there were more than muscles stuffed between his lumpy ears. He had answered without question or pause.

With an elaborate flourish, Baron Henderson reached out and touched the man on each shoulder with his warm blaster. "Then raise General Thomas Henderson, heir to the Iron Throne. What is your first command?"

"You," the general snapped, pointing at a private.

"Move my things to the dead man's tent, get me his wag and bring me his handcannon and belt holster."

"Sure thing, Sarge!" the man said, grinning.

Thomas backhanded the guard, sending him sprawling. "I'm your commander," he stated softly, almost too low for the others to hear. They had to lean in and strain to catch the words. "Obey me, or die. Your choice."

"Yes, sir," the cringing man mumbled from the dirt.

Raggedly the troops raised a cheer for the their new commander, the officers saluting the preening goliath.

Delighted, Baron Henderson smiled craftily at the young fool. That whispering trick was good; he'd have to use that himself. Without his grandson to direct a battle, he would have been forced to lead any charge himself. Now this huge idiot would do that for him.

"What are your orders, Father?" Thomas asked, looking very serious.

"We have gathered everything salvageable from the wreckage," Henderson said, taking another pinch of snuff with a shaking hand. He spilled most on his shirt but enough got up his nose to stop the trembling. "Now we go west, raid a few hamlets along the way for food, horses, anything else that we lack. Then, when we are ready, we strike at the enemy who did this to us, Nathan Cawdor of Front Royal!"

"Cawdor?" a lieutenant asked, puzzled. "But, ah, pardon me, my lord, but how you know he did it?"

"There were only three villes of any size in Virginia," he said, sneering, "BullRun, Casanova and Front Royal. Two have been destroyed. That leaves Cawdor and his brown shirts."

The troops murmured in agreement. They were more looking forward to raiding helpless farms than striking at the armed citadel of Front Royal. Muties or coldhearts, few whoever attacked the ville escaped alive. Maybe this melting thing was the reason why.

"And how, sir, we can stop a wep that fries stone?" a lieutenant dared to ask.

"Never question your baron!" Thomas snapped.

Then he turned to ask, "Do you wish to tell us your plan, Father?"

The private returned with a fresh suit, and the baron started to change. "Not at the moment," Henderson said, removing his jacket. His bare arms were as skinny as sticks, discolored with splotches and bruises. "But it cannot fail. Tomorrow, Front Royal falls and we shall rule the entire state from the Lantic to the Shens!"

Led by their new commander, the sec men wildly cheered, and Henderson tried not to laugh at them. They would all die in the attack on Front Royal. That was the key past the stone walls. But they would gain entrance, and soon afterward, the weapon that destroyed Casanova ville would be his to unleash upon the rest of Deathlands. Not to rule the groveling masses, but purely for the sake of retribution for being born into this horrid world. When he died, so would the rest of humankind. And the sooner the better.

Chapter Six

Dawn was just starting to break, when a blue shirt hesitantly opened the door of the armory and glanced outside. "Rain's over," he announced.

Baron Sheffield and the rest of the bodyguards exited the brick building, careful of stepping into any of the steaming yellow puddles. The landscape was like nothing any of them had ever seen. Everything was coated with a hardened layer of condensed ash. The ground was covered with gentle ripples, as if somebody had tossed a stone into a lake of lava, which instantly cooled back into rock.

"See who is still alive," Sheffield ordered, noting the piece of somebody partially buried in the weird stone carpeting. "Help anybody trapped, then get the slaves busy chipping this crap off the wags and the gate. Don't touch the gap in the wall. This can only help strengthen our defenses there."

"Sir!" The man saluted and dashed away.

"Nothing will grow in this valley again," Collette stated as a fact, hooking thumbs into her gun belt. "We have to move the base."

"But, sir, the dish..." a sec man began, pointing above them.

"Can be replaced," the baron snapped, studying the towering structure. "There's nothing special about it. We simply need a big dish antenna to communicate with the Kite. Moving the comps is easy. They hardly weigh a thing. Couple of hundred pounds.''

"Any ideas where, sir?" a lieutenant asked.

The baron started to speak when he noticed an old slave shuffling past the electric fence. "We'll discuss this inside," he muttered softly.

Returning to the throne room, the baron directed his staff around a table piled with maps, some plastic, a few hand drawn on deerskin, one or two made of yellow paper. Shifting the map of Tennessee to the bottom of the pile, he pulled another showing the East Coast of predark America. Corrections had been made to the coastline and land with a brown ink of some kind. "These are the other locations of big antennas," he stated, watching them lean in close to see. "Silas could have used any, but chose this one because it was the first dish he found." And it was near a redoubt, but that was none of their business.

Suddenly alert, Collette watched the baron's face, sensing he was withholding important information, and wondered what it was that she had just missed.

"Of all the possibilities," Sheffield said, stabbing the map with a finger, "these thirteen are our best bets."

"Ah, my lord?" a sergeant interrupted him.

"What?"

"Sir, I've been hunting over here in Georgia, and there's nothing there but desert and some cannie muties. Little green bastards got a taste for horse and damn near got me. Ain't no dish, though, sir."

"You dare to correct your baron?" Collette snapped, reaching for her blaster.

Magnanimously, Sheffield raised a hand, stopping

her. "Thank you, Sergeant. Fresh information is always useful. Any other corrections?"

The staff officers studied the maps and finally decided that one mistake was the only flaw.

"Good, that saves us a lot of time," Sheffield said, blacking out the site of Georgia Tech College. "Time we do not have to spare, or waste. I'll send two squads to recce the remaining six. As soon as they find one, they come back and I'll decide whether we go, or wait for a better location."

Conversation stopped as a slave girl entered the room with a silver tray of sandwiches. Sheffield flipped over the top map, and the blue shirts waited in silence until she had returned to the kitchen.

"Lieutenant Brandon?"

"Sir!"

"Take ten men with you. It'll be crowded in the wag, but you're sure to lose some along the way."

Coldhearted bastard. "Yes, my lord."

"Sergeant Campbell, do the same. Load the wags with all the fuel and ammo needed, then take what food can be stored inside. You can always raid villes for more."

"We're giving them the wags?" Collette admonished.

"Yes, *I* am assigning them wags," Sheffield corrected harshly. "My troops cut the time by half this way. It's a gamble, but one that *I* am willing to take."

"As you say," Collette demurred. The emphasis on certain of his words hadn't been missed by anybody in the room.

Rolling up the plastic map, Sheffield looked hard at the sec men. "You'll each receive a copy of the map just before you leave. Concentrate on your mission and don't worry about the other wag not coming back. I can monitor every word of conversation spoke inside them with the Kite," he lied. "Anybody goes rogue, and I'll melt the wag with the men inside."

"So we can ask you for help, sir?" Campbell asked.

Clever bastard. Sheffield frowned. "Doesn't work like that. I can hear you, but you can't hear me. Amplifiers, you know, system feedback." The baron had no idea what the words meant. These were simply things he had heard Silas say once while trying to fix a cassette player.

The men nodded in understanding, nudging the sergeant for asking a stupe question. Only Collette knew it was all a lie, but to the sec men, tech stuff was always accepted without question. She knew that most of the blues didn't know how an engine worked, or even their own blasters. Electronics was magic as far as they were concerned.

"Avoid the roads and use rivers whenever possible, and you'll make better speed," Collette said. "Also, less chance of hitting a roadblock and having to waste ammo on mercies or coldhearts."

"Riverbeds, you mean," Brandon said, smiling at her mistake. "Not in the actual water."

"No, she's correct. Use the rivers," Sheffield ordered. "The wags are amphibious."

Awkwardly, the men shifted their stances, trying to pretend they understood the words.

"The wags are waterproof. They can float," he added angrily. "Chill anybody who gets in the way. Put the fear of the blues into the bastards. Pave the way for our return."

"The first team will be designated Alpha. They'll

check the sites in northern Tennessee, eastern Kentucky and Pennsylvania.''

"Beta team will bypass Georgia, and recce the middle of North Carolina, south Virginia, then upstate.''

"Lot of ground to cover," Campbell stated, walking his fingers across the paper and trying to guess the distances involved.

"Yes, but there is a lot at stake," Sheffield said. Then he crossed his arms and smiled. Now was the time to give them the carrot. "The first team that finds what we need will be assigned as permanent guards for the new gaudy house. No wall patrols for the rest of their lives.''

The grim faces in the throne room brightened at the prospect, smiles abounding. It was a rich reward.

"When can we go, sir?" Brandon asked, hitching up his gun belt. "The sooner we leave, the sooner we come back with a new ville for you.''

Caught unprepared, Campbell shot the officer a hate-filled glance, but said nothing. Damn ass kisser.

The baron grunted. "Good man. You'll leave within the hour, and the slaves will start packing today. Once we have a goal, we leave immediately. This valley is dead.''

"About those two sites in Virginia," Collette started, rubbing her nose thoughtfully.

Spotted that, did she? Sheffield cleared his throat. "The first is near Green Cove ville, good walls and that's about all we know. The other is just east of Front Royal. I'm very glad that Silas didn't melt the place, because it may just become our new base.''

"Front Royal?" the lieutenant gasped. "But sir, they have wags, troops, an awful lot of our own

AK-47 blasters, grens, and Nathan Cawdor is known to be a chilling machine.''

"We can take them," Campbell growled. "They're just a bunch of farmers and whitehairs. Easy chilling.''

Scowling, Collette shook her head. "Front Royal is an armored citadel that no amount of troops can take. Only a fool or a madman would even try.''

"So what are we going to do if that's our best site?" the sergeant asked, worried. "Melt them a little with the Kite as a warning?''

"That would be a waste," Sheffield said, annoyed. "I can do much worse to Cawdor and his brown shirts. Much worse.''

"RISE AND SHINE, lover," Ryan said, walking naked from the steaming shower. He grabbed a towel from a pile and started to dry himself.

"I'll rise," Krysty grumbled from underneath the blankets, "but that's all. What time is it?''

"After noon," he replied, toweling his hair.

She cracked a smile. "Just getting up yourself, I see.''

"Second shower today for me," Ryan stated, tossing aside the damp towel and pulling on some clothes. "We spent most of the morning cleaning that damn ash out of the garage so we could work on the crossbows. Blasted shit gets up your nose and down your boots like its alive.''

"And you didn't wake me?" Krysty asked. "I looked that bad, eh?''

With a shrug, Ryan started to button a shirt. "You were hit the worst by the Kite and needed some extra sack time. That's all. Now go wash. Lunch is ready.''

Krysty sat upright on the bed, the blankets tumbling to her waist. "More soup?" she asked around a yawn, stretching her arms wide. "We should dip the arrowheads in it."

As always, Ryan felt himself responding to her beauty, but shoved those thoughts aside. There was too much work to do. "Too dangerous. It might rot the metal," he said, buckling on his gun belt. "Get moving."

Stumbling from the warm bed, the nude woman scratched herself as she padded across the barracks floor and into the shower. Minutes later, she emerged from the clouds of soapy steam scrubbed pink, her hair cascading down her back.

Ryan waited as she donned clothing, then they headed for the cafeteria. Lunch was the same as dinner. The companions forced down more of the hot gray soup and ate another generous helping of the cat food. It left a bad taste in their mouths that wouldn't go away even with brushing or gargling. But it eased the pain in their bellies and put strength back in their hands. Good enough.

Afterward, the companions spent the rest of the day finishing the crude weapons. Doc trimmed the dining-room knives to notched arrowheads, Dean lathed broom and mop handles into wooden shafts, Mildred used her delicate touch with a blade to split pillow feathers into fletching, Krysty used glue and thread to attach them, and Jak fixed the arrowheads into place with electrical tape salvaged from outlets and light switches. The arrows were ugly, but balanced. That was all they could ask for.

Ryan and J.B. did the heavy work. The big lathe cut table legs into stocks, and the long, flat metal strips from the beds became the cross-member pieces. The string for the weapons was the difficult part. Twine wouldn't take the tension. J.B. tried, and the hundred-year-old rope snapped every time. Mildred suggested hunting for a guitar, or a piano. The metallic strings of the musical instruments would be prefect for the crossbows, but none was available.

Ryan solved the problem by attacking the elevator with a hacksaw and removing the support cable. The main cable was a bundle of thin wires twisted together to form smaller cables, which were braided to make a thick one. It was incredibly strong, and as difficult as hell to get loose. The cable snapped free halfway through the operation and shot into the upper levels like a whip. The companions ran out of the shaft until the wildly lashing cable settled down and they could claim the smaller ones. The first tries were unsuccessful, then Doc suggested braiding a couple of the thin wires into a slim cable, like the guitar string that Mildred had suggested. It took the rest of the day, but seemed to work fine. When J.B. shot off some trial arrows, the bolts slammed completely through a wood desk and became embedded in the cinder-block wall behind.

"That'll do," Ryan said, hefting the crossbow. The weapon was slow to load and heavy to use, but the crossbow would silently chill from a distance, and that was all they wanted for it. They knew it was a gamble to check the tunnel before trying a mat-trans jump first. But the thought of going through the machine in their weakened condition was an even bigger risk. Even when well rested and fed, it took a lot out of them. The storm outside was still raging, so of their two choices, it was the least dangerous.

Mildred and Jak made some quivers from pieces of carpeting cut off the floor of the commander's office. Wire stitched them closed and their belts made effective straps.

"Two crossbows, ten arrows. That's all we got," J.B. announced, placing the weapons on a table. "Too much of the stuff cracked when we tried machining it into shape. There are lots more shafts and feathers, but no more arrowheads."

"Sharpen shafts," Jak suggested, drawing a knife. "Better than nothing." J.B. slid over a quiver, and the teenager got to work.

"Many hands make for light work," Doc said, drawing his own blade and starting to whittle on the next batch of shafts.

Rising from her chair, Krysty got a bowl from the cabinet, filled it with water and placed it between the men. "Be sure to char the points when you're done," she instructed, putting a butane lighter beside the bowl. "That'll make the wood harder, less likely to splinter when it hits."

Whittling away, the men nodded as shavings curled under the blades and fell quietly to the floor.

"This'll give us twenty-two arrows," Ryan said, drawing his blaster and checking the clip. "Anybody ever used one before?"

"Sure," Jak said, flicking a lighter into life. Holding the sharp tip of an arrow over the flame, he let the wood get black, then removed it quickly and doused it in the water. The difference between making it hard and setting it on fire was a matter of split seconds. A crossbow was how he had gotten his first blaster. It caught a mercie in the throat, and he finished him off with a rock. Jak got the dead man's blaster.

"How about you, Doc?" J.B. asked, sliding on an old pair of fingerless gloves. He had taken them off to do the lathing and machine work, but they were going into the unknown and he wanted to be ready for a fight. Anything could be beyond that door, any damn thing at all.

Pausing in his carving, Doc raised an eyebrow. "Swords and handguns were the chosen weapons of my day. Arrows were considered weapons of the red Indians of the plains."

"Mighty deadly in their hands," Ryan said, remembering a terrible day in the western plains when the companions almost hadn't survived. "Trader used to say that some triple-stupe bastard with a blaster would always get aced easy by a smart man armed with just a club."

"*The Art of War,* by Sun Tzu." Doc chuckled in amusement, putting another finished arrow aside. "Although a slightly garbled translation."

Ryan shrugged. "Just common sense."

"Well, I took an archery class in high school," Mildred said hesitantly. "But that was a long time ago."

"Good enough," Ryan said, sliding the heavy weapon across the table. "You two are the archers, then."

Lifting the slab of wood and steel, Mildred inspected the crude weapon. The stock was cut from a desk, the cross member attached with heavy bolts stolen from some piece of machinery. The trigger was a simple lever underneath that was to be pressed upward against the stock to release the catch. Grabbing the string, she pulled it backward until it locked on the catch with a solid click. Sliding an arrow between the notches, she shook the crossbow until the shaft fell out. Then Mildred did it all over again, until she could draw and load with a minimum of fuss. Nobody asked what she was doing.

"Should we have dinner, then hit the tunnel?" Dean asked hopefully.

"Tunnel first," his father decided. The soup was keeping them alive, but as their hunger lessened so did its flavor. "We don't know what's on the other side of that door. Could be a nice straight tunnel or a freaking maze. We need some way to make a map so we don't get lost, and there should be some way for us to mark the branches, just in case."

Krysty stood. "I saw some pencils and paper in the chief cook's office. Those should do." She crossed the room and disappeared into a small office.

"Any spray paint?" Mildred asked, slinging the crossbow over a shoulder. It was clumsy, but she could manage the weight.

Removing his hat, J.B. wiped off the sweatband with a cloth. "No paint," he said, replacing the hat. "I found a case of aerosol cans, but they were all dried out or had burst apart."

"Shit, worst redoubt we've ever been in," Mildred growled, as Doc handed her a full quiver. The physician slung it over her other shoulder, but the draw was awkward, so she shifted positions until satisfied.

"Blackboard in kitchen," Jak said, gesturing with his crossbow. "Chalk mebbe?"

"I checked, and it's gone," Krysty said, returning

with the writing materials. "And the markers are completely dried out."

"We'll use spent brass to mark our way," Ryan stated roughly, placing the empty Steyr on the table. "Everybody bring along a handful. Leave everything else behind. With luck, we'll be carrying things back here and don't want to be overloaded."

"Dad, who stays behind?" Dean asked out of the blue.

Frowning, Ryan realized the boy was right. The cellar door bolted from inside the redoubt. While they were in the tunnel, something might somehow creep into the base. They needed a rearguard.

"Want the job?" he asked.

"No prob," Dean stated resolutely.

"Good man," Ryan said, patting the boy on the shoulder. "Nobody else I'd rather have guarding my back than another Cawdor."

The young boy preened under the praise, then his usual serious expression returned. Dean was a seasoned fighter, and most barons were guarded by sec men with far less fighting experience.

"Here," J.B. said, passing him a couple of Molotovs. "We'll leave you these. Watch for splatter. These babies are messy. Grease and alcohol aren't exactly a prime mix."

"Check," Dean replied, rummaging in a pocket. He found a butane lighter and flicked it, adjusting the flame to its highest setting. In his opinion, these were the only wonders of the predark world worth having. Bullets got used and were gone, candles melted, light bulbs burned out, but the cig lighters survived the hundred years of radiation intact, and each was good for over a thousand times. Once, he had cooked a small rabbit over just the flame of a butane lighter. It made the meat taste odd, but he lived for another day.

Taking a torch, Ryan stuffed a plastic bag full of extra greasy rags into a pocket. "Ready?"

"Damn near," J.B. replied, standing. The carpetbag over his shoulder clicked from the Molotovs, and he opened the flap to stuff in some more cloth rags to keep down the noise.

"'Half a league, half a league onward,'" Doc rumbled in an odd singsong manner that indicated he was quoting somebody.

"Don't finish that," Mildred warned, cutting him off. Kipling was a good poet, but a damn poor military adviser.

Going to the bottom level of the redoubt, the companions gathered before the armored door and assumed combat positions. Going to the stairs, Dean readied a Molotov in case the others needed cover.

"No more than two torches at a time," Ryan warned, setting fire to his with a butane lighter. Oddly, the flame was weak and he realized the cig lighter was almost exhausted. Not good. "I'm on point. J.B. cover the rear."

"Gotcha," the Armorer said, igniting his own rag torch. Dense black smoke rose from the crackling flames, the smoke crawling along the ceiling like a living thing. Dean shifted position on the stairs to get out of its way.

"Remember the codes?" Ryan asked the boy.

Dean nodded. "When I ask who's there, only open the door if you give your real name. Albert, Alvin, anything like that means it's an ambush and don't open the door no matter what else you say. Any name like Roger, or Ralph, means run. I take the mat-trans and go."

"Immediately."

"Yes, Dad. Immediately."

The Deathlands warrior grimaced. There were more codes they had created over the years, but these were the only ones appropriate for this situation. Open the door, or not open the door. That's all there really was.

"Okay, open it," Ryan said, drawing his blaster and using a thumb to snick off the safety.

Doc threw the bolt, and the others lent a hand to heave the massive door aside. The cellar light illuminated a section of tunnel that stretched into the blackness. The floor was worn smooth, and arches made of the same black metal as the exterior of the redoubt supported the ceiling at regular spacings. Empty hoops along the wall showed where power cables should have been attached to lights.

"Damn fine workmanship," Mildred noted, studying the details of the braces. "Wonder what it was for?"

"Find out soon enough," Ryan said, extending his torch and entering the darkness.

The companions followed in close order. Pausing at the door, J.B. took a breath and walked through. Many years earlier he had been trapped for days underground with a rotting corpse. Tunnels and caves weren't his favorite places.

The torches crackled noisily, throwing dancing light along the rocky passageway for several yards. Then a shadow on the floor didn't dissolve under the light, but instead turned and charged with claws snapping.

"Mutie!" Ryan warned, lowering his torch.

Blinded by the light, the creature hissed loudly, but kept on coming. Shooting from the hip, Ryan blew off a leg, yellow blood squirting from the ghastly wound. The mutie howled in pain.

Mildred launched an arrow, the wooden shaft shattering into splinters on the rough shell. She cursed, and the crab was among them. Jak dodged a claw as Krysty fired, the bullet scoring a shallow line along the creature's shell. Ryan thrust a torch into its face, burning off an eye stalk. The mutie squealed, and Doc stabbed with his sword, skewering the thing in the open mouth. Squalling madly, the giant crab scuttled off into the darkness at remarkable speed, leaving a trail of blood behind.

"Tough little bastard," Mildred noted, notching a steel-tipped arrow.

"Can't let go," Jak stated, cradling his weapon. The teenager was leaning forward, as if already in pursuit.

Ryan snorted. "All that food? No way." Kneeling he critically studied the broken leg. The shell was abnormally thick. Arrows would never penetrate. They'd have to use the blasters. "Okay, one yard spread, double-time. Watch for spoor. Stay close and quiet. Our voices will carry for miles down here."

"Good," J.B. said, working the bolt on his Uzi. "Then so will anybody else's."

With Ryan in the lead, the companions took off after the mutie down the long subterranean passageway.

"Good luck," Dean said from the open doorway, blaster in hand. "Good hunting!" Slowly, the massive portal swung closed, the sweep of light narrowing to a slim vertical line, and then with a muffled clang it was gone. The bolts driving home sounded unnaturally loud.

Chapter Seven

Rolling over the barren landscape, the sputtering motorcycle braked to a halt in the front of the low hill. The swell was covered with the ash-colored concrete like everything else, and only its height made it visible above the sterile plain. Driving around the hill, the blue shirt stopped again as he found a small recess, a short alley that led to an imposing door made of black metal.

"This is it," the rider said, turning off the struggling machine and lowering the kickstand. Climbing off the bike, the sec man stepped out of the safety cage surrounding the vehicle and began to unlock the chains holding his passenger motionless against the gridwork of iron bars. Softly, the big engine began to tick as it started to cool.

Pulling the length of chain free from the man and bars, the blue shirt stepped away from the bike and drew a blaster.

"Okay, get busy," the sec man ordered, waving the weapon.

"Yes, master," the old slave said, rubbing his chaffed wrists and awkwardly climbing from inside the safety cage, heavy chains dangling between his scrawny ankles. Shuffling to the strange armored door, the whitehair couldn't help but gasp. The material was a black metal unlike anything he had ever seen. It was marred by fire, but still solid and strong. What blacksmith could have possibly made this colossal door?

"What are you waiting for?" the blue shirt demanded, squatting on the smooth rocky soil.

"Yes, master," the man repeated, rummaging around in his loincloth for the sheaf of papers the baron himself had pressed into his hands—along with a promise of freedom if he was successful. That he didn't believe, but this was better duty than mucking out the sewers or cutting stone in the quarry. Squinting at the print, he tapped in the first line of letters and numbers. Nothing happened.

"Keep going," the blue shirt snapped, lighting a cig and drawing the smoke deep into his lungs. "You only got this job 'cause you can read. Don't stop till I tell you to, or you'll taste the lash." He patted the knotted leather coil of the bullwhip hanging at his side. "Get me?"

"Of course, sir," the oldster whimpered, continuing to tap figures and letters into the little pad. Hopefully, he would soon find the key to the black door, the sec man would chill him then and his pain would end.

Then the realization hit him, success meant death! Redoubling his efforts, the old man started to type in the combinations faster and faster, praying and hoping the door would open soon.

THE TUNNEL STRETCHED for quite a way.

"Few droppings," Jak noted as they proceed. "No bats."

Keeping his torch high to avoid splatter from the grease, Ryan agreed. He had been in caves where the guano had been feet deep. Once he saw man drown in the stuff before they could throw a rope and drag the poor bastard to safety. But this tunnel was clean of bat shit, which meant there was no easy access to the outside. Then again, they were fifteen stories underground. Did bats fly that far to nest? He didn't know.

At an intersection, the companions paused to check the side tunnels. Both ended after only a few hundred yards. Whatever the military had been building down here was going to be extensive.

"Mebbe they were making a permanent vault for the art," Krysty asked softly.

"Makes sense," Mildred replied. "If you can say anything the government did in those days made sense."

"Don't like this," J.B. said, adjusting his glasses. "No equipment anywhere."

Ryan agreed. "Means that folks have been down here. Crabs got no use for hammers and dynamite."

After a while, the torches began to dim, so the companions took a rest and dropped the burning rags on the torches to the ground, then wrapped each handle with fresh strips and oil and lit them anew. When the job had been completed, they moved onward, leaving the smoldering rags behind to help mark the way home. The tunnel before them seemed to stretch forever.

An hour passed slowly, then Ryan gave a soft whistle and the companions froze, pulling their weapons ready. There was a shape in the shadows ahead of them twice as large as the crab.

He waited a few moments, listening for any noises, but only the crackling torches could be heard. Holding out his palm to the others, he closed it into a fist, then raised one finger. They nodded in understanding. Alone, Ryan proceeded carefully along the wall of the tunnel and found an ordinary concrete barricade blocking the end of the passageway. The yellow-and-black-striped slab barred further progress. Holding the torch at an angle, Ryan extended it over the waist-high barrier. In the reddish light, he saw a ledge beyond, a slope of raw unfinished rock leading into pitch darkness. It was an easy walk; no problem there. However, nothing could be seen above or below. The tunnel might have well stopped at the end of the world.

A movement from behind made him spin, and Krysty came from the shadows.

"Kill that torch," she whispered urgently. "They'll see you."

Dropping the torch behind the concrete barrier, Ryan stomped out the flames. Darkness filled the tunnel.

"Can you hear them?" she asked, only a vague form beside him. "Talking, laughing, a couple having sex, a child crying. It's a whole ville down there."

"Blues?" Ryan asked, straining to see. As his eyes slowly got accustomed to the lack of light, he began to make out shapes and forms below. A soft ethereal glow permeated the gloom.

On the bottom of the cavern, columns of rock rose in an irregular pattern like a wild forest of stone trees. Amid the vertical outcroppings were rows of huts and corrals full of something that moved. A low wall surrounded the underground ville.

Having seen enough, Ryan took her arm and they returned to the others.

"Kill that torch!" he whispered. "We found a ville."

Promptly, Doc dropped the torch and stamped out the flames.

Softly, Krysty added, "Can't tell whether it's norms or muties down there, but they have houses, a wall and some kind of animal penned for food."

"How see without torch?" Jak asked curiously. "Campfires?"

"There's a soft glow coming from the walls of the cavern," Ryan replied. He paused for a moment, listening for any sounds, then continued. "It's not much, just barely enough to see."

"Sounds worth a recce," J.B. said, hovering over the weakening light of the extinguished torch. "We can jack some of their cattle at the very least."

As the last few embers of the torch died, the darkness in the tunnel approached Stygian levels. "Krysty, you better stay here with the torches in case we need a guide home," Ryan decided. "And prepare some of the wooden arrows with oil and rags to use as an emergency flare."

"Consider it done," Krysty said, holstering her revolver. She had split her .38 ammo with Mildred so each woman had three rounds, but that was enough for this job. Besides, she was the logical choice. The redhead could hear better than any of the others, and often could sense things happening, or about to happen. There was no explanation for the ability, it was just something she could do. Same as her mother.

"Take," Jak said, passing her the crossbow and quiver. "Got knives. Just as silent."

The redhead slung the quiver and held the crossbow in both hands, testing its balance. "Thanks."

Then J.B. handed her a glass bottle. "Just in case," he said with meaning. The Armorer hated thinning his supply, but only suicides went into a hot spot without backup or an escape route.

"Arrows and knives only," Ryan stated, working the slide on his silenced 9 mm SIG-Sauer pistol. "We're doing a quiet recce. Only here to steal weps and food. No chilling unless necessary. Anybody get separated from the rest of us, or run into trouble, come straight back here. I'll take point with J.B. Mildred, cover the rear with the crossbow."

Taking positions, the companions exited the tunnel and waited until they could dimly see the subterranean ville below.

"Looks like a natural cavern," he said, doing a sweep with his binocs. "Hundreds of sides tunnels. Damn place is a warren of holes. Might be easy to get lost. Floor seems to be covered with lots of stalactites...stalagmites. Whichever. I never could remember which is which."

"Stalagmites might fall down," Doc rumbled softly, sword in hand, "but cannot because they grow up from the ground."

"That's good," Mildred complimented him.

"Thank you."

"Dark night, I see them," J.B. announced, adjusting the focus. "They sort of look like people, two arms, two legs, one head. About all I can tell at this distance. Doesn't seem to be any guards on patrol, or stationed lookouts."

"Even better," Ryan said. "Mebbe they don't have any enemies, aside from the crabs. Any weps?"

"Nothing that requires two hands to hold."

"Leaves plenty," Jak grunted. "Knives, handcannons, boomerangs, slings."

"We can handle those," Ryan stated, patting his pockets to make sure he knew exactly where everything was. "Okay, let's go."

"Ah, broiled crab for dinner," Mildred said, inhaling. "I can taste it already."

Going around the barricade, Ryan tested the slope, while keeping a hand on the concrete for support. The ground was rough and his boots didn't slip, no matter how hard he tried. The rock was as rough as sandpaper. Finally letting go of the barricade, he advanced a few steps, staring intently down the slope.

"Bottom is only a few yards away," he whispered, easing down the incline. "Single file, one yard spread."

J.B. was the first. The Armorer was a ghost in the darkness, but some pebbles came loose, bounding down ahead of the man. He froze motionless.

Ryan mentally cursed the noise and braced for an attack.

Across the expanse, some blobs of light started coming their way, but then sheared off to the right. Soon there came the sounds of a struggle, followed by a crunching noise and brief high-pitched squeal of pain. Something just been aced.

Moving more carefully, the rest of the companions reached the bottom and took cover behind some stalagmites and boulders. Moving from rock to rock, they zigzagged across the floor of the cavern, trying to stay behind cover. Most of the stalagmites rose a hundred feet tall, maybe more, the tops far beyond the weak illumination of the cavern walls, but a few were only inches high, mere toothpicks rising from the damp floor. They were very careful not to step on any and snap them off.

Examining the side of the cavern, Ryan saw the rock was covered with a silvery moss that gave off a weak shine. Suspiciously, the man held a rad counter near the fungi. Instantly, the device changed its soft musical hum to angry clicks as he got within a few inches.

"Wall moss is rad poisoned," he warned tensely. "Don't touch any."

The collection of boulders soon stopped, and there was only open space stretching from the rocky forest to the stone wall. The top twinkled like starshine, razor-sharp chunks of crystal lining the barrier like military barbed wire.

"What the nuking hell?" Ryan whispered in annoyance. "It's only a yard or so high. Can't be more than four feet max."

"Could be a trip line," J.B. suggested softly. "Or a marker for the archers."

Ryan admitted both were possible, only there wasn't a higher fence beyond the low one, just some huts. Studying the ville carefully, he suddenly understood that the huts weren't larger than the wall, but located on top of rocky mounds—no, piles of bricks. Deep underground, the locals lived underground again, but the doors were no more than a yard tall.

"Mutie runts," Jak observed under his breath. "Good. Easy picking."

"Bullshit, pygmies are fierce warriors," Mildred corrected, wiping a sweaty hand on her pants. She had to keep a good grip on the crossbow. The thing would have a worse recoil than a shotgun. "They have to be or else don't survive. In Africa, there were little natives deadly accurate with blowpipes and poisoned needles. They could chill a man on the run at a hundred feet. Small doesn't mean weak.''

In the center of the ville was a bubbling spring, the air rich in the smells of boiled meat and something else. A hoist of odd bits of metal and some wood hung over the spring, metal chains dangling out of sight in the water. The hot spring was their cooking pot.

"Not bad,'' J.B. muttered in spite of himself. "They're not mindless muties, like stickies.''

"Which makes them ten times more dangerous,'' Ryan said, then stopped talking. A low singing came from a large squat building with star-shaped windows.

"That looks like their temple,'' Doc ventured hesitantly. "Maybe we caught them on Sunday services.''

"Odd windows,'' Jak said. "Worship sky, mebbe.''

"It's probably been a long time since they last saw the stars,'' Mildred agreed. "If ever.''

Raising an open hand for silence, Ryan listened carefully. He could hear voices from most of the buildings to their right. Sounded like dozens of villagers, maybe more. But to their left they could hear only faint animal grunts.

"Head for the barnyard,'' Ryan ordered, creeping forward through the shadows. "There's too many locals to chance a raid. Runts or not, a hundred can easily kill five.''

Staying in the boulders, the companions started toward the left when a horrible smell began to infuse the atmosphere. The stink was easily identifiable as raw sewage, and soon they found themselves ankle deep in a gooey field dotted with tiny white sprouts, then grayish balls and finally huge mushrooms almost a foot high.

"Dinner," Jak said with a grin, stuffing mushrooms into his shirt. A few of the smaller sprouts went directly into his mouth. Two chews and he swallowed. The flavor was a bit salty, but tasted wonderful.

Mildred plucked a mushroom and inspected it closely. "These are okay to eat," she said, then greedily stuffed it whole into her mouth. Even raw it was wonderful.

"Mmm," J.B. mumbled around a mouthful, harvesting handfuls and stuffing them into his carpetbag with the Molotov cocktails.

Trying one himself, Ryan grunted his agreement and started yanking up the largest mushrooms. Ripping off the dirty stalks, he slid just the clean tops into his pants. After boot soup, damn near anything would taste great.

Filling the pockets of his frock coat, Doc smiled. "Hunger is the best sauce, my friend."

"Fucking A," Jak agreed wholeheartedly.

After taking as much as they could comfortably carry, the companions continued toward the farm. Mushrooms were good, but you couldn't live off them. Damn near no vitamins at all in the tasty fungus. Reaching a spot near the low wall, one by one the companions darted out of hiding and raced across the open field of stone. The jagged crystal bits sparkled dangerously on top of the wall, but they easily jumped over and resumed positions in the shadows at the base.

When they were all inside, Ryan led the way along the wall, the companions staying low where the darkness was thick. It occurred to Mildred that these might be shadows to them, but brightly lit areas to the runts. But before she could communicate the idea, Ryan called a halt as they reached a ring of small stalagmites rising close to one another. Inside the stony picket fence was a breathing sea of hairy bodies, naked pink tails whipping about as the sleeping horde squeaked and rubbed comfortably against their fat neighbors.

"We were right. This is a ranch," Ryan stated. "Just common rats. No signs of the big crabs."

"Mayhap the wall is for the crabs," Doc suggested. "To keep out the predators. I used to live on a farm, and there was no greater cursed thief than a fox stealing a chicken."

"Good, then rats lazy," Jak said eagerly, moving past both of the men. Going to the fence, the teenager darted out a hand and grabbed a rat, slitting its throat with a knife. The rodent barely squeaked before it died. Stuffing the body into a carpetbag slung over his shoulder, the teenager proceeded to catch and kill as many as he could before the fat sleepy rats got wise and moved away from his lethal hands.

"Sixteen," Jak said with pride, patting the bag. "Fresh meat tonight." With those words, the companions went motionless as something walked from the shadows. It was a runt.

Wearing a loincloth and soft boots covered with fringe, the mutie stood barely three feet tall. His skin was white to the point of being transparent, and blue veins were clearly discernible. His hands possessed elongated fingers, and both of his oversized eyes were a pale pink in color. Long black hair was tied with leather thongs on top of his head in two bushy tufts.

Pausing at the stalagmite fence, the runt sniffed the

air for a moment, a three-fingered hand drawing a crystal dagger from a rat-skin sheath. Then, moving even faster than Jak, it grabbed a bunch of rats by their tails and swung the bodies hard against the rock wall. The animals squeaked once as their heads smashed into pulp, and the mutie walked away humming.

"Just a cook," Ryan ventured once the runt was gone from sight.

"Those tufts must be feelers," Mildred muttered. "So they don't slam their heads on the sloping tunnels."

"We got food, and if they have stone knives, there's nothing else here to steal," Ryan stated bluntly. "Let's go."

As they headed along the wall, a runt staggered out of the darkness barely able to stay on his feet. Going to the wall, he lifted his loincloth and they heard a splashing sound. Sighing in relief, the mutie completed urinating and started back the way he had come, then turned abruptly and headed for the rat farm.

The companions tried to duck out of his way, but the runt was too fast and he gasped at the sight of the norms hidden in the wall shadows. Drawing a dagger, he inhaled for a scream and Ryan moved like a panther, crossing the few yards in a heartbeat. Violently, he slammed a fist into the mutie's face to the sound of shattering bones. The runt flailed its arms and dropped limply to the ground.

Moving past the corpse, the companions jumped over the wall and started across the open plain when an odd noise in the air above made them spin, braced for an attack. Unexpectedly, a net dropped from the sky, entangling their limbs and weapons.

"Two-legs!" another female runt called out loudly, advancing into view. "Live two-legs here!"

Shoving her weapon against the rope strands, Mildred fired the crossbow. The homemade arrow took the mutie in the throat, and the runt backed away, gasping for air as blood trickled down her chest.

A knife in each hand, Jak slashed wildly, the net parting at every touch of his blades. Soon the companions shrugged off the last few pieces of the restraints. Darting to the stalagmites, the companions paused to take stock of any wounds and see if there was any pursuit.

Nobody was running after them, but in the ville, a runt climbed on top of the temple and raised something small to its mouth. Ryan swung his blaster around in case the blowgun was pointed at them even though the range was impossible. But the runt aimed the thing toward the ceiling and blew so hard its cheeks puffed out. Nothing seemed to happen. Maybe it was also drunk and hadn't heard the warning of the others.

"Shit!" Mildred flinched, touching an ear. "Something just went straight through my head. That must be an ultrasonic whistle."

"Madam, that makes no sense," Doc replied, cocking the hammer of his LeMat handcannon. "The mutie talked to us normally. If we hear the same, why would one use an ultrasonic dog whistle?"

"Call dogs," Jak growled.

J.B. said nothing, but hastily hauled a Molotov from his bag, spilling mushrooms onto the ground.

"Ready the torches," Ryan said, flicking a butane

lighter. "The bright light should send these big-eyes powering away screaming."

The torches were prepared, but suddenly they noticed it was much easier to see one another. In horror, the companions realized the cavern was significantly brighter.

On the rooftop, the runt blew again, and the silvery moss on the walls flared with illumination until the huge cavern was as bright as daylight.

"Fireblast!" Ryan cursed, firing once at the runt. "Back to the redoubt!"

Clutching his stomach, the mutie tumbled off the roof just as dozens more boiled out of the temple and huts, screaming and waving weapons.

ROLLING ALONG the hard-packed ground, the LAV-25 was buffeted by the wild winds. The ash storm was over, and the acid rains thankfully gone, but now with nothing to stop or even slow them, the natural winds were ravaging the Tennessee valley. Dead leaves and loose dust peppered the wag until they were driving blind.

"See any road?" Brandon demanded.

"Can't see my own dick!" the driver shouted. "I'm waiting for us to hit a fucking cliff and die!"

"Ain't no cliffs in this direction," a corporal retorted, studying the compass in his shaking hands. "Stay in this direction, and we'll be fine!"

Cresting a hill, the armored wag started down the other side, when it began to build speed. The driver applied the brakes quickly, but there was no slowing of their progress.

"Shit!" he cried, stomping the brakes with all his might. "We're sliding free. No way to stop!"

Lunging across the interior of the wag, Brandon yanked on the mechanical brake and they felt the eight wheels lock tight. But the APC continued to slide down the smooth side of the steep hill, slowly starting to turn sideways.

"We're going to flip!" the lieutenant shouted, grabbing a ceiling stanchion. "Hold on, boys!"

The wind slammed small debris against the wag, as the vehicle continued to turn until it was traveling backward.

"Lock the rear door," a corporal shouted.

The nearest sec man barked a bitter laugh. "You lock the fucking door!" he shot back, clutching his safety harness with both hands. "I ain't leaving this seat!"

"Coward!"

"Asshole!"

The corporal drew a blaster, and the LAV hit something with a jarring crash. Every loose item the wag went airborne, shotgunning toward the rear. The sec men cried out as plastic crates slammed into legs and one man went limp, his skull crushed from the impact of a steel ammo box full of linked rounds for the 25 mm cannon.

"Release the brake!" the sergeant shouted, staring at the map on the floor in horror. "We got to get back control!"

"Why?" Brandon demanded.

"Lake!"

The lieutenant cursed and went for the release level when the wag slammed into something again, the impact making it spin like a mad top. The supplies went all over the vehicle, crates breaking open to spill MRE packs everywhere. A third impact straightened their course, and the driver fought the steering levers, trying to regain some control over the runaway war machine.

The duct tape covering an air vent burst free, and road dust poured into the craft like a river of smoke. In seconds the interior was filled, the men gagging and choking as they pulled shirts over their mouths in an effort to breathe. It was a trick they learned from the ash storm, but the dust was a finer grain, and it didn't work as well this time.

Then a sudden silence filled the APC and clean air streamed in through the vents.

"We're out of the storm!" a private shouted happily.

"And falling!" another cried, looking through the tiny slits of the vent. "Madonna save us! There's the lake!"

As the off-balance machine tumbled through the sky, the men flopped loosely in their seats, only the web harness holding them in place. Ammo boxes broke apart as the wag spun over and over, spilling live rounds into the mix of MRE packs, boots and vomit.

Then a deafening explosion slammed the craft from underneath, cracking teeth and splintering the Plexiglas covering the driver's ob slit. Bones audibly broke as the blues were violently heaved against the web straps. One sec man came free and slammed into to the armored ceiling, his head erupting into a pulpy mess of brains, bones and blood. The decapitated body fell, leaving an ear and some sticky pink matter clinging to the steel plating.

Dizzy from a blow to the temple, Brandon could barely focus on the fact they seemed to be rising and falling in a regular pattern. What the hell was this? Then the answer came like a fist from the dark.

"The lake!" he gasped weakly. "We landed in the bastard lake!"

"We're sinking!" a sec man cried, struggling with his harness. "I got to get out! I'm not going drown like a rat!"

"No, wait!" the officer shouted, raising a hand. "The LAV floats! We're okay!"

But the man struggled out of the web and stumbled toward the rear doors, walking unsteadily to the bobbing of the machine. "Horseshit!" he snarled. "Metal doesn't float."

"Sit down, Johnson!" the sergeant ordered in a booming voice. His commands were usually obeyed instantly, the fear of the bullwhip in powerful hands more than enough of a threat. But the scared man didn't even respond, as he clawed at the locking bolt for the rear doors.

"I said, sit down now!" the sergeant shouted, drawing his blaster and cocking the hammer. "We're afloat you triple-stupe fool. Open that and we sink!"

Another sec man reached out to grab Johnson, but the private fought free, ripping his shirt in the process. His face was white, his eyes wild with fear and he threw himself again at the aft doors, grabbing the locking bar with both hands.

The sergeant leveled his weapon and the blaster spoke. Johnson slammed against the double doors, a hole in his exposed spine, blood pumping onto the floor. Furious, the sergeant leveled the pistol to shoot again.

"Don't! Ricochets!" the lieutenant warned.

But the hammer was already falling. The large-caliber slug plowed through the dying man and slammed into the locking bar, knocking it loose. The left door swung wide as the misshapen slug bounced off the steel and zinged off the walls, floor and into the back of the driver's head. The dead man lurched forward, cracking the dashboard with his face, blood flowing over the controls.

The open door revealed the choppy waters of the lake and low hills rising in the distance. Fresh air rushed into the vehicle as Johnson toppled overboard and sank from view. Then a wave crested the door sill, washing over their boots and floating the airtight MRE food packs.

Struggling with the stubborn buckle of his safety harness, the sergeant dropped his blaster and tried to rip himself loose by sheer strength. Drawing a knife, a corporal neatly sliced through the woven nylon belts and rushed to the doors through the ankle-deep water. Another wave rolled inside, forcing the man back, and the craft began to list slightly downward.

Unsnapping the buckle on his web harness, a private stood and dived toward the rear. A sec man along the wall already had an arm extended. The first private grabbed the other's hand, and the sec man desperately reached for the handle of the armored door. Another wave washed inside, supplies caught in the current going out the open doors and floating away.

"Everybody cut yourselves loose and go to the front!" Brandon shouted, sawing desperately at the harness with a knife. "Got to balance the load and keep from tipping over!"

Fingers stretching to the limit, the private brushed fingertips against the waggling door, almost getting hold of the damp metal. Then another wave hit the wag, and the door sloshed closer for a split second.

In triumph, the sec man grabbed the handle and started to pull the massive door shut. It resisted going against the force of the waves, the water seriously slowing its progress.

"Pull, you bastards! Pull!" the private shouted through gritted teeth. Tendons rose from the sec man's arm, and the other planted a combat boot against the wall for greater leverage and grabbed the first man with his right hand.

"Come on you mutie sucking son of a bitch!" he roared, and the second man shouted in victory as the sluggish portal closed with a muffled bang.

The locking bar was shoved home, and the sec man slumped to the watery floor.

Finally free, Brandon went to the front of the wag and reached over the dead man to flip some switches. The motors struggled for a moment, then roared into life, a column of black smoke blowing skyward from the louvered exhaust port alongside the main turret. He slapped a big red button, and a steady pumping sounded from below. The water level in the machine dropped drastically until only a few small puddles dotted the rough floor.

"Sergeant, get in the turret and shout out directions!" the lieutenant ordered, dragging the dead man from the chair and sliding into his place.

Clambering up the short ladder, the sergeant threw open the top turret. Rough waves were on every side. To the west was a tall cliff and behind it a swirling wind storm, lightning flashing constantly in the clouds above.

"Head north!" the sec man shouted down below.

"You have the compass, jackass!"

He patted a pocket. Damn, so he did. "To your right! No wait, that's too much! Perfect! Now hold it steady! The shore is only a mile away!"

The eight big wheels spinning madly, frothing the water in their wake, the LAV headed for the nearby land.

Things below the surface of the lake were already fighting over the body of the sec man, tentacles lashing wildly as multiple muties engaged in mortal combat over the flesh. The scattered MRE packs floated away unnoticed, the waterproof wrapping reflecting the dim sunlight like golden flakes on a silvery pool.

As the LAV-25 sloshed onward, the officer sure hoped the other wag had escaped the storm without so many deaths. They were the last hope for the project, and he had already decided that if there was no dish at any of the three locations, well, they would just keep the wag and take off on their own. A man could make himself a baron with a fighting craft like this!

Then he threw a look at the radio speaker in the ceiling.

"Well, we survived," Brandon said quickly. "All hail Baron Sheffield!"

The men noted what the officer was looking at and even the ones with broken bones cheered as heartily as they could. The baron wasn't with them, but Sheffield was still very much in control of his troops.

"Sir, Johnson is aced," a private reported from the rear of the vehicle.

The lieutenant glanced over a shoulder. "You're the guy who closed the door, right?"

"Ah, yes, sir."

"Then you're the new driver. Take his shirt and blaster. When we hit the shore, strip the dead of boots and ammo, anything else we might need. When we reach the shore, toss them out."

"We need to bandage the men, and should check the APC for damage, too," the sec man suggested, yanking off the corpse's gun belt and blaster. He could cut the hash marks off the dead man's shirt later. The blaster was a lot more important.

"More to the right!" the sergeant shouted down. "That's it, sir. Hold your course!"

"We'll do both on land," Brandon said gruffly. "But let the local animals attack the body as a diversion. Get me?"

"Yes, sir. Better them than us."

"Words to live by," the officer muttered under his breath, glancing at the silent radio speaker.

Chapter Eight

Charging through the stone columns, the companions headed for the slope that led to the redoubt. Weighted nets fell from the sky, landing everywhere. The muties were throwing blind, hoping for a catch, but the stalagmites blocked the nets and many simply wrapped harmlessly around the columns.

Reaching the base of the slope, J.B. turned and fired two rounds at the screaming mob. A runt fell sprawling, a dozen others behind him tripping over the corpse. But the rest arced around the pile of wiggling forms, many twirling slingshots at their sides.

A rock smashed on a column, the missile exploding apart from the impact. Doc recoiled, a bloody cut on his cheek.

"Bounders!" he shouted, and fired the LeMat.

The thundering blast of the Civil War weapon echoed wildly in the confines of the cavern. The runt with the sling flipped backward, a hole drilled completely through his chest. Slowing their advance, the other muties angrily shook their weapons and shouted. Then a dart of fire shot by overhead and impaled a runt. The others backed away quickly.

Glancing upslope, Ryan saw Krysty standing at the mouth of the tunnel struggling to reload the crossbow. Then he narrowed his eye and raised the SIG-Sauer, firing at the runts that were crawling spiderlike along the sheer wall of the cavern yards above the tunnel opening. He hit one, dislodging the mutie, and it fell silently to its death on the rocky floor. Another was only wounded and began to retreat, but the rest spread out and started to converge on the woman from every direction.

Loaded crossbow in hand, Krysty stuck her head out for a second and saw the runts coming her way. She shot at one, the arrow entering its neck all the way to the feathers. The little humanoid still crawled on for another yard before going limp and plummeting away.

"Molotovs!" Ryan shouted, drawing his panga, the long blade shining in the light of the silver moss.

"Way ahead of you!" J.B. shouted, and threw a lit bomb at the runts among the stalagmites. The bottle arched high and crashed in the middle of the muties, coating them with the deadly mix of the alcohol and wag grease.

Their bodies covered with flames, hair sizzling like fuses, the runts dashed insanely about, setting others on fire, until the unharmed muties turned their weapons on their burning comrades, mercifully cutting them down and ending their screams.

Her .38 Smith & Wesson spewing flame, Krysty blew the head off a runt. Then a rain of stones hit the barricade, one going past her head so closely that for a split second the woman saw her own distorted reflection in the lump of crystal. She fired again and another fell off the rock face. But more were crawling behind, fresh troops arriving every minute.

"Now what?" Mildred demanded, launching an arrow into the chanting throng. It missed one, merely nicking his throat, but it slammed directly into the chest of the runt behind him. The mutie beside the wounded male snatched away his dagger and started forward.

Rocks from the slings were slamming into the slope and boulders as steady as machine-gun bullets. Ryan fired twice more, runts grabbing their ruined faces as they dropped, but more took their places, the chanting starting to rise in tempo as the muties prepared for a rush.

Then a squad of female runts in stiff leather armor, carrying bone-tipped spears and round shields studded with crystal shards, burst through the mob.

"By the Three Kennedys!" Doc roared, waving the smoke away from the muzzle of his huge blaster. "Sec men!"

Ducking out of the way, Mildred dodged a barrage of rocks. "Those shields are going to be trouble," Mildred grunted, notching in a fresh arrow. Four of the steel-tipped ones remained. She had to make each one count.

"Not," Jak stated, and, stepping out from behind a boulder, the teenager leveled his blaster and fired. The steel-jacketed .357 Magnum round plowed through a shield, knocking a runt off her feet, the slug plowing into the female behind her, and sending several more to the floor in disarray.

As Jak dived for cover, J.B. stood and lobbed another Molotov, with devasting results.

Crossbow in hand, Krysty waited for a runt to stick his head around the mouth of the tunnel. She thrust the crackling torch into his face with enough force to dislodge the crawler. His hair on fire, the mutie hit the slope and rolled downhill to smack into a stalagmite with a sickening crunch.

Mildred put a steel-tipped arrow into a warrior, then, as she loaded a wooden shaft for a regular mutie, she cried out, dropping the crossbow and grabbing her head.

"It's that whistle again!" Mildred shouted, her face contorted in pain.

"They're going to cut the lights," Ryan said in comprehension. The little bastards were smart. The companions were trapped, and the runts knew it. They would never make it up the exposed slope alive. It was too easy to pick them off. Only two shots remained in the SIG-Sauer, and Doc and J.B. had about the same. He needed a diversion, or someplace to fall back and take the fighting hand-to-hand where their size and strength would work against the little warriors.

A fiery dart streaked across the cavern from the tunnel overhead, the burning arrow heading toward the caves on the left wall. Ryan glanced at Krysty, and she looked to the right instead. He nodded, and she smiled. Then he pointed to either side of the barricade, and Krysty hastily withdrew into the passageway. Five more runts crawled around the edge and dropped into the tunnel, just as they all heard the shattering of glass. A fireball blossomed to fill the tunnel, the muties dying where they stood, flapping their arms as the Molotov consumed them whole.

Shouting a battle cry, the armored warriors started forward and J.B. shot four with the Uzi. Three dropped, and one staggered away, wounded in the thigh. The rest quickly retreated behind stalagmites and threw spears.

"That's it," the Armorer said, pushing the blaster

behind his back to get it out of the way. "I'm down to four Molotovs and my knife."

"More than enough. Give me one, Jak another," Ryan ordered, grabbing a bottle. "When the place goes dark, we make a firewall directly between us and them."

A lone spear arched high into the air to come down just behind the companions. The runt warriors were testing the range.

"Won't hold long," Jak stated, sheathing a knife to take the bottle. The Colt Python had only one round, and he was saving that for their mass attack, the best chance to get more than one runt with the single round. And the closer, the better.

"It'll do the job," Ryan stated, watching Mildred flinch as the silent whistle was blown once more. "On my command we head to the right. Got it? The right!"

Another spear came their way as the moss began to dim, then the whole cavern abruptly went dark.

"Now!" Ryan shouted, and the two Molotov went flying.

The whiskey bottles crashed yards apart, the splattering fire forming pools that spread. The runts retreated a few yards, shouting in fury. Then Ryan lit the rag on the third bomb and sent it flying toward their left with all his strength.

The muties seemed to have been waiting for this, because they charged in that direction, heading for the cave Krysty's arrow had gone into.

"Now," Ryan said softly, running toward the right.

They nearly reached the side cave when a runt spied them and yelled a warning. Ryan shot him down, and with his last 9 mm cartridge got a female warrior in the armpit. She stood transfixed for a second, then toppled over as if boneless.

Reaching inside the cave, the companions lit the torches and threw them on the floor at the opening. Now anybody entering would be in plain sight, while the companions would stay in darkness. Spears flew through the flames, hitting the walls and throwing off sprays of sparks.

Retreating for additional distance into the cave, Ryan bitterly cursed when he saw they were trapped. The cave was merely a hole in the cavern wall that opened onto a granite bridge that stretched over a black abyss and ended on a sheer rock face. Nothing but endless space was visible below.

Doc spit out a word that had never graced his lips during his own era, then he said it again more forcibly.

"Yep, this is going to be bad," Ryan said, holstering his useless blaster. "There's still a lot of them, and we have nowhere to go."

"We could always jump," Mildred said, glancing into the gloomy pit. There wasn't even a moaning wind to emphasis the depth of the yawning crevice. Just total silence.

"Always knew I'd get aced someday," J.B. said stoically, tilting back his fedora. "Only hoped it was in bed making love with Millie one last time." It was the first time J.B. had ever mentioned their sexual relationship in front of his companions.

The physician turned at the pronouncement and grabbed the man by the jacket lapels, pulling him close. The lovers kissed hard, then broke apart fast as another spear came out of the tunnel, sliding along the rough ground.

Notching the final arrow, Mildred placed the loaded crossbow on the bridge for anybody to grab, and she drew her Czech-made .38 ZKR target pistol. She was going to make those three rounds last for as long as possible.

Just then a screaming warrior dived over the torches and rolled along the ground undamaged. She warbled a cry, and more jumped through the flames successfully. Going to one knee, Doc leveled his blaster, holding the cannon with both hands.

"Wait," Ryan advised.

Inside the passage, the armored runts gathered into a group, seemingly having to gather their courage before attacking. But soon they were frothing at the mouth and bellowing a challenge. The muties swarmed toward the norms.

"Now," Ryan said calmly.

Doc took in a breath, held it and fired. The muzzle-blast illuminated the darkness to daylight. The leader spun, arms outstretched, throwing blood across the others. The runts howled and covered their faces, dropping weapons and stumbling in the gloom. A couple bumped into each other, then walked straight off the bridge and plummeted out of sight.

Doc fired again, the second blast scoring two kills. Then J.B. threw the last Molotov, the liquid fire splashing over a group of warriors carrying a basket. Screaming in agony, the creatures dropped the basket and started to beat at their burning bodies with empty hands. Holding the crossbow, Jak waited for an undamaged target, when harsh blue light came from the basket, along with a sputtering and hissing noise.

"Retreat!" Ryan shouted, walking dangerously backward until he was flat against the rockwall. The muties had a bomb or dynamite in there, maybe left-overs from the predark mining. "Cover your ears!"

The companions slapped palms over their ears as protection from the concussion just as the wicker basket erupted in a tremendous explosion. The entire cavern seemed to shake as stalactites rained from the ceiling, then the granite bridge cracked, large pieces dropping off. The companions clawed at the sheer wall for any purchase, when the rock shattered, the painted plaster falling away in pieces to expose a hidden tunnel. Without hesitation, Ryan and the others swarmed into the new opening just as the shuddering granite bridge broke completely apart and fell into the inky blackness.

Chapter Nine

The dining hall of the fortress at Front Royal was brightly lit by a hundred thick candles and two roaring fireplaces. Servants carried in platters of food, serving the dirty sec men and grimy civilians hastily gobbling down the food on their plates.

At the head of the table sat Baron Nathan Cawdor. His clothes were patched, but clean, and blasters rode at each hip. A monstrously huge .50-caliber Desert Eagle pistol rested in a position of honor in a shoulder holster. The weapon had been pried from the cold gray hand of Overton, would-be baron of Front Royal, as he lay sprawled in the mud.

Nathan watched his troops consume the repast like muties at a fresh corpse. Thankfully, the hunters had done well, better than anyone had hoped for, and the ville had venison and bear meat by the ton in the smokehouses slowly being cured for the coming winter months.

The repairs to Front Royal were almost complete. Nathan had taken a great risk using sec men and civilians together on the task of rebuilding the keep and the barbican at the front gate, but the gamble had paid off. There had been no attacks by muties or coldhearts while his troops were busy with the construction and too tired to fight. Give the men a few days, and the ville would be able to properly defend itself again. That's all, just a few more days.

"Anybody need a beer?" Nathan asked the assemblage, hoisting a tankard of bathtub ale. It was slightly green, but eminently drinkable.

"Down here, my lord!" a stone mason called out, waving a hand wrapped in rags in lieu of a glove.

Nathan rose from his chair with the tankard in a fist, and the sec men and civilians roared their disapproval. Even the servants looked askance.

"My lord!" the stone mason gasped, rising to block the man. "This isn't allowed! A baron serving the troops?"

Nathan stared hard at the man. "I'm the baron," he said succinctly, "and shall do as I please. When my workers are exhausted, I do what is needed."

"Which is why we would die for you, my lord," a sergeant said bluntly. "Any man of us, and happy to do so! But we'll never let you do such a thing as this!"

The others murmured in agreement. "The day you serve us food," the stone mason added, almost sounding angry, "is the day we revolt!"

Nathan slammed the tankard on the table, rattling dishes for yards. The Cawdor temper was as famous as it was deadly. "Those are hanging words, Corporal," Nathan said gruffly.

The man remained adamant and shrugged. "Then hang me, Baron. But I'll be rad-blasted before my baron brings me a drink!"

"And what about the lady?" a woman asked, entering the hall carrying a wooden tray of beer mugs. Lady Tabitha Cawdor wore her long hair free, the tresses almost reaching to her trim waist. She was in a loose gown of royal brown, heavy pants peeking out from below the pleated skirt. Boots and belt were without polish, and an M-16 longblaster was slung over a shoulder. Her hands were heavily scarred, as was one cheek. She moved stiffly, but with her head held high as befitting the wife of the local baron.

Clumsily, she moved to the table and placed down the tray with some difficulty. The men dared not speak. They knew the tortures she had gone through and considered her more than a lady.

"My lady," the officers said, bowing. "We are honored by your presence here."

"Thirsty, too, I hope," she replied, laughing and wiping her forehead. "Drink your fill. This is a day of celebration. The barbican is complete. The chief just rammed it with a wag at top speed, and the gate held. The repairs are finished."

The whole room roared its approval, and a servant took the tray, passing out the beer to eager hands.

"To the baron!" a farmer shouted. The workers thundered the name "Cawdor" over and over.

"And to the good health of our new heir!" a cook added from the back of the hall. "Five pounds going to two hundred, young Alexander Cawdor!"

The assemblage lifted their mugs high and drank in silence.

"Praise be," the sec man said with a grin, new life showing in his lined face. "May he follow his good father, and not his triple-damned mutie loving uncle, Harvey."

The workers and soldiers paused, glancing nervously at the baron. Nathan said nothing, then slowly stood and spit on the floor.

"To hell with Harvey!" he bellowed, brandishing a mug, and the hall erupted with cheers.

Reclaiming his chair, Nathan drank from the mug and placed it aside. "How are you feeling, my love?" he asked softly. The nearby workers pretended they could hear nothing.

Weakly, Tabitha smiled. "I'll live, and our son grows stronger every minute. I had to find him a second wet nurse to feed that outrageous Cawdor appetite. But that wasn't a problem since so many children had been...lost in the war."

Nathan placed his hand on top of hers and gently gave a squeeze. "We're lucky our son lived, which is why I assigned the two of you twenty guards. The ville means nothing if you aren't safe."

Hands under the table, Tabitha pursed her pale lips. "Do you really think such extravagant precautions are necessary? Sullivan has been burned, Overton is dead. Who would dare to attack the heir of Front Royal now?"

"Too many," Nathan growled, leaning back in his chair. The more prosperous the ville became, the more coldhearts attacked, and mercies raided the outer hamlets. The M-16 from their own armory, and the AK-47 blasters taken from the blues were handling the problem easily, but the ammo was getting low quickly, and they had no way of reloading the 7.62 mm rounds. A gunsmith tried using black powder instead of cordite, and the weapon nearly exploded into pieces. Doc Tanner had told them the secret of turning black powder into gunpowder, but that mix of chems was even more powerful. Something purely for cannons, once the blacksmiths finished making them. If ever, he added sullenly.

"Any word from Ryan or the others?"

"None," she answered. "Is that bad?"

"Neither bad nor good. My uncle could survive skydark itself." He poured more beer in the mug. Death wasn't a topic for such a day. The corpses were buried. It was time for the living to forget. "And how does the weather look?" he asked, changing the subject.

"Clear," she replied, a smile almost returning to her tired face. "No sign of a storm. Sorry."

"Shitfire," the baron cursed, and reached into his jacket for a predark steel tube. He fondled it for a second, then opened the container and handed a fat cigar to the nearest man. "Pass this down to Dundee. I bet him there would be acid rain by the end of this week, but he said no. As always, he was correct."

"You wanted rain, my lord?" the man asked, shocked.

Tolerantly, Nathan smiled. "You're new here, yes? Thought so. Front Royal needs the acid rain to make sulfur for our black powder. It's why we have gutters and sewers. Every deadly drop becomes powder in our blasters."

"Damn me for a mutie." The farmer chuckled and passed the cigar to the next sec man down.

The predark stogie made it to the old man with only a dozen sniffs taken of the aged tobacco. Dundee tucked it away in a shirt pocket. His joints never failed. There had been twinges of a coming storm, but then they faded unnaturally fast, as if the rain had abruptly gone elsewhere. Damnedest thing.

Just then a line of servants arrived with baskets of fresh bread and brimming tureens of stew, the chunks of meat and vegetables swimming in gravy thicker than winter mud. It was food for workers, not dainty tidbits for barons.

"More soup?" a maid asked, gesturing with a ladle.

"Rads, no," a burly sec man replied, wiping his mouth. "Two bowls of your stew is all any man can hold."

"Some men have bigger appetites than others," the redhead whispered provocatively.

The sergeant laughed and winked at her. She tousled his hair playfully, then walked away to serve the stew to other workers.

Suddenly, there was a commotion at the far end of the hall, and the servants danced out of the way of a hurrying sec man. His clothes were dappled with mud from hard riding, most of the loops in his belt and bandoleer empty of rounds. There was a half-healed wound on his neck, a dirty rag serving as a bandage.

Nathan lowered his mug as the man approached.

"Baron Nathan, bad news," he announced in a single breath.

"Report."

"Scouts have reported they spotted Baron Henderson alive in the woods!"

The dining hall grew quiet as Nathan frowned. "Impossible. His ville was melted! Who reported such a thing?"

"Me," Clem said, striding forward. The sec chief was as lean and brown as a starving bear, and considered twice as dangerous. The mountain man was dressed completely in fur, including his boots. A wide leather belt circled his waist, carrying a pouch and a hatchet, his chosen weapon for in-fighting. A bolt-action Enfield longblaster rested on a wide shoulder, and a bandoleer of ammo was slung across his chest.

Without removing his hat or blaster, Clem took a chair and grabbed a mug, only to find it empty. "Shit!" he cursed.

Tabitha pushed a tankard to Nathan, who relayed the beer closer. "Then I must accept the report as true," the baron stated. "So the old devil is still alive, eh? His grandson and so-called healer, also?"

Ignoring the mug, Clem lifted the tankard, draining it in a series of steady swallows, a little of the green beer dribbling down his chin. Placing the empty container aside, he belched mightily. "Dark night, I needed that. T'ain't shine, but it'll keep your heart pumping."

"Glad to hear it," Nathan said, motioning a servant to fetch another tankard. "Give me details."

Pulling out a plug of tobacco, Clem bite off a chaw. "Yeah, Baron Henderson and his weird offspring are both alive," he said while chewing. "They got about fifty sec men. No wags, no slaves, no sign of that crazy healer. Must have perished in the attack of whatever the hell it is that's been melting these villes."

"At least it has stopped," Tabitha said, nibbling on a small piece of bread.

Removing his coonskin cap, Clem scratched his beard. "At least for the moment. Baron, just in case our ville starts melting, do we have supplies hidden outside?"

"In Overton's cave," Nathan replied, drawing his blaster and checking the load. Satisfied, he holstered the piece. "It's a good spot, and I saw no reason not to use it."

"Agreed. Then I guess we're ready for trouble."

"Chief, what if Henderson attacks?" a lieutenant asked bluntly.

Nathan answered instead. "With only fifty men? I wish he would!"

Clem wasn't so sure about that. Henderson was a crafty bastard, but he said nothing. It had been a long day, and something told him it promised to be an even longer night.

WALKING THE WESTERN parapet of Front Royal, a sec man in a brown shirt paused to squint at a disturbance in the trees, while carving a tiny ship out of a piece of scrap wood. There seemed to be a group of men coming toward the ville with wags and horses. It might be traders or immigrants, but at that range he couldn't tell. Better safe than dead, as the old saying went.

Sheathing his knife, the sec man pocketed the partially carved ship and slid the M-16 blaster off his shoulder. With weapon in hand, the man strode toward the warning bell, then staggered as a terrible pain took him in the side. Glancing down, he saw the feathered end of an arrow jutting from just above his belt. As he opened his mouth to shout, blood flowed over his lips, and he gagged for air, a wave of weakness washing over him. Instinctively, the guard knew he was dying. A cold clammy feeling filled his belly from the volume of blood flowing out of the wound. His guts had to be slashed to ribbons.

The sec man rallied his strength and tried to walk. He had to warn the ville that invaders were coming! His vision was blurry, the brass bell shifting between a mile away and directly in front of him. He reached out to slap the clapper dangling underneath and touched only air. But it was so close! Or was it? Black dust, he couldn't tell how far away it was, his vision was so bad.

Now two ghostly bells slid up and down before the dying man, and cold sweat trickled down his body. Forcing himself forward, the guard lunged for the bell and fell flat on his face, the granite feeling oddly warm and comforting against his cheek.

"Can't...die..." he said aloud, forcing himself to crawl on hands and knees. He couldn't see the bell any longer. The world was tinged with red as if the daylight were fading. He had only moments to live. He knew that, but he'd die as he lived, protecting the ville and his baron. Raw fury fueled his strength, adrenaline pumping through his slowing heart. In ragged stages, the sec man stood and tried to draw his blaster, but the weapon clattered to the parapet, making no noise as it hit the stonework and bounced into the courtyard below. How could it not make noise? Black dust, he was already dead. The guard felt sick and lightheaded at the same time. A fog masked his sight, and he could sense his heart beating slower, and slower, inside his cold chest.

Grimly, the walking corpse lurched toward the edge of the wall when another arrow slammed into his chest, piercing his heart. Total silence engulfed the sec man, and he died never knowing if he reached the edge of the parapet or not.

THE COBBLESTONE STREETS of Front Royal were quiet. The market was closed, the children at home having dinner, the bars serving their first rounds, the gaudy house just opening its door for business. An old man was washing his hands in a horse trough, a sec man walking patrol whistled a tuneless song and a blacksmith banked the fires of her forge as a preparation for going home.

The blacksmith closed the doors of her shop and turned toward the tavern, already thinking of beer and bread when the body fell from the sky and slammed against the cobblestones with a sickening crunch, blood spewing from the mouth of the dead man from the impact. A cat screeched at the sight and dashed away.

"Shitfire!" a farmer shouted, dropping a sack of turnips and backing away in shock.

But the blacksmith glanced skyward, then rushed forward. Gingerly, she turned the dead man over and saw a familiar face. It was "Admiral" Peters, the sec man who couldn't swim, but loved boats. The Admiral had arrows through the kidney and the heart, and his blaster was gone.

"Coldhearts!" the blacksmith bellowed at the top of her powerful lungs. "The ville is under attack! Sound the alarm! Coldhearts!"

People began to race for cover, a bell was beaten and soon the drawbridge was lumbering upward, a team of six strong men struggling to close the vulnerable door.

"FIRE!" Baron Henderson commanded.

The line of sec men launched another whistling flight of arrows at Front Royal. In the distance, another guard fell off the parapet of the ville, tumbling into the moat where he disappeared with a watery splash.

Picking his nose, Henderson smiled in delight. The

baron had chosen this location with extreme care. It was a low ground swell with the setting sun behind their backs, making it difficult for the others to see them. And a few steps backward put them out of line-of-sight, making blasters useless. There were trees on either side to hide his men, and even a creek to water the horses. Henderson had no idea why Baron Cawdor would leave a spot like this open for invaders. Maybe he wasn't as smart as Henderson had heard.

A picket line of sec men were spread out in a wide arc before him, the archers sending waves of arrows over the high stone wall of the ville. He wanted as many sec men dead as possible before the alarm was sounded, but then he wanted the alarm sounded as loudly as possible.

Behind the hill was his can opener, a machine he had found in a predark book for children. Henderson couldn't read, but there were pictures and the device was simple to build. His troops had used it to smash several small villes along the way, and it was unstoppable. Front Royal would be his within the hour. They wouldn't dare to use their melting machine on their own ville.

"Why the fuck haven't they sounded the alarm yet?" Henderson complained, wiping a hand clean on his pants. Then the old man caught the faint clanging of a bell.

"Took them long enough!" he snorted angrily. "I'll fix that laziness with a touch of the whip once I'm in charge!"

A galloping horse stopped near the old man, and the rider jumped off to salute. "My lord, the forward area is secure."

"Any casualties?" Henderson asked with little concern.

The rider smirked. "Not on our side."

"Good, go join the snipers in the trees near the front gate. When the brown shirts start running out, cut them down inside that fancy barbican of theirs. I want it blocked with their dead so none can escape."

"As you command, my lord." The man saluted and hopped on his horses to ride around the castle to the other side.

"Stop shooting," the baron commanded. "Join the rest of the snipers in the trees. They know we're here by now."

Squads of men were running along the parapets, some big man in furs seeming to be directing things. There was no sign of Cawdor or his hot little wife. Henderson had special plans for that juicy blonde. Oh yes, very special plans.

The archers broke ranks and ran for the cover of the trees. Laughing, Henderson strolled over the hill to look at the can opener. A team of twenty horses struggled to haul a heavy wooden wag through the tangles of wild grass, raising clouds of gnats.

"Don't go to the crest," he commanded. "They can shoot at us from there. Park it just below the top, where we can shoot them, but they can't hit us."

"Yes, Father," Thomas rumbled, sliding off his horse and passing the reins to a sec man. "But what if they smell a trap?"

The old man grinned. "It's already too late."

The wooden machine was huge, a flat platform on wheels, a tall set of braced stanchions, with a cross arm longer than the base, and a lot of rope. It had taken them less than a day to build.

"It's called a catapult," Henderson said, as the sec man pegged the wheels in place to prevent the contraption moving. "It launches a fifty-pound rock three hundred yards. Good accuracy, too, if the wind isn't too strong."

The wind was still that morning, with no sign of a storm.

"We're going to use rocks again?" Thomas asked, puzzled. "I don't think rocks will harm those thick walls like the log palisades of those hamlets."

"You are correct. Rocks would do nothing here," the baron replied. "We're going to use dynamite bombs."

Near the catapult, more sec men were lugging tiny wooden barrels, no more than a demijohn in size, from the rear of a covered wag.

"Each of those small barrels is filled with nails or broken glass, and has a half-stick of dynamite inside," Henderson explained, pausing to take a pinch of snuff. His box was almost empty. There had better be jolt in that fortress, or else he'd skin the survivors alive until some was found. "Once we get the timing right, they'll explode in the air, showering the ville with shrapnel like a shotgun blast. There won't be a man, woman or dog alive inside those walls within a few hours. My grandson... I tried it on a gang of muties once just to see and blew them into pieces."

At the ville, sec men lined the parapets or stood in every window, the vented barrels of the M-16s sticking out like porcupine quills. They were waiting for a siege ladder to appear, or a mass attack. What fools.

"They're in position," Henderson said eagerly, wiping spittle off his chin. "Launch the first bomb!"

The fuse was lit, and the rope holding down the

cross arm cut. The arm traveled a brief arc and slammed violently against the stopping bar. The whole catapult shook, but the barrel in the scoop flew over the hill toward Front Royal. It fireballed only yards short of the wall, the windows shattering, men disappearing, the water in the moat seeming to boil under the barrage of nails and glass.

The browns rallied within seconds, the return fire chewing the ground along the top of the hill as they strived to reach the machine behind the mound of dirt.

"One inch longer fuse." Henderson laughed, openly rubbing between his legs. "I want to see blood on this shot!"

The next barrel sailed over the wall and detonated above the city. Roofs collapsed, and screams of pain sounded from the dying and wounded.

Suddenly, the defenders in the windows started shooting at the trees on either side of the hill. Their sporadic fire became a steady stream of rounds, ripping the foliage of the forest apart. More than once the blind firing was rewarded by a yell of pain, or the scream of a dying horse. The Casanova troops dashed from the thick greenery to take refuge behind the hill.

"Why would they do that?" Henderson whispered softly. "It makes no sense. No sense at all! Unless…"

Without further comment, Henderson quickly climbed onto a horse and galloped for the horizon. The rest of his troops were shocked at the behavior. The fight had only begun. What was happening here? A few of the wiser sec men saw the frightened face of their leader, grabbed horses and madly rode after the man. One corporal refused to release the reins of his mount, and a lieutenant shot him dead to get the stallion.

"Father?" Thomas cried out, watching the old man disappear into the distance. What could he be up to, some sort of trick to fool the browns? It had to be. They were winning the fight, soon Front Royal would be theirs!

Then in the woods, a man screamed in hideous pain. A blaster chattered. Another scream. A third begged for mercy, his words cut off abruptly. Then the monsters came out of the bushes on either side of the invaders.

The huge, massively muscled beasts only vaguely resembled the primitive dogs they had been bred from. Clearly a lot of mastiff was in the mixed blood, perhaps Doberman, maybe some mutie also, for the titanic animals stood chest high at the foaming muzzle. Pointed fangs filled their long mouths, their black coats as shiny as a wet road.

Silently, they moved among the yelling men, biting a groin and casting away the flesh, only to dart forward and attack another victim. They never stayed to savage the body or eat what they removed. It was uncanny, nightmarish.

Plowing through the troops, the black beasts bypassed the terrified horses and charged for the catapult crew. Thomas couldn't believe it. How smart were these things? The first dodged a stream of bullets from a rapidfire and leaped upon a sec man, tearing out his throat, blood gushing from the grotesque wound. Shaking its head to toss away the bloody gobbet, the dog charged again and took another man in the groin. He dropped, screaming in a high-pitched voice, and fired at the beast, but missed. The dog savagely closed its powerful jaws on his exposed throat. There was a snap, and the noise stopped.

Now the remaining sec men started to fire at one another as the deadly canines darted from man to man, removing a hand, ripping out a throat, or a belly. One dog paused to swallow and was cut to pieces by cross fire from the blasters. None of the others made that lethal mistake.

A beast sprinted toward Thomas, and he fired a blaster point-blank in its face. The slug plowed a bloody furrow along its head, and the creature closed jaws on the hand holding the weapon. The sec chief shrieked and fired again, the blast going through the dog, and he recoiled with only stump at the ragged end of his arm.

"Henderson, you lying bastard!" he roared, trying to draw his second blaster with his left hand. The big man got it free of the holster but dropped it to the ground. The dogs took this as their cue, and several converged on the weakening man. He caught one by the neck and shook it with a jerk, the neck snapping like a twig. Then another dog got him between the legs, as a third attached to his throat. Thomas went down, his hand clawing for the knife in a sheath on the wrong side of his body. His screams didn't last long, and soon there was only the sound of ripping flesh on the far side of the hill.

"HOW MANY MEN did we lose?" Nathan demanded, wrapping a strip of cloth around his bloody arm. The wound was minor, but it would take a healer to remove the sliver of glass.

"Six, far as we know," Clem replied, sliding a fresh round into his Enfield. "What was that thing called again?"

"Catapult," Nathan repeated, cradling the arm. "I

planned this defense against mercies with a piece of predark artillery, a Howitzer or a mortar, but it worked well enough against the catapult.''

''More than well enough, my lord.'' Clem grimaced, looking out the window at the dogs tearing the bodies apart. They would continue to do so until recalled. There was no way anybody could have survived this slaughter. Nathan had released every dog the ville had, including the half-trained pups and bitches.

''So much for Baron Henderson,'' Clem said, allowing himself a small smile of contentment. ''We're never going to hear from that rad-blasted son of a mutie again.''

''MUTIE DOGS,'' Henderson spit, urging the horse to greater speed. ''Never saw that coming. Bloody, clever Cawdor. But not clever enough for me!''

''My lord!'' a lieutenant shouted, riding close. ''Where do we go from here?''

''To the south! We'll need an army to take Front Royal!'' Henderson shouted, a string of drool dripping from his mouth. ''So I'm going to steal one!''

Chapter Ten

As the LAV-25 rolled along, the ragged woods thinned to flat grasslands and the ruins of predark buildings rose on the horizon. Standing in the open turret, Sergeant Campbell could see the pieces of the paved street beneath the strips of grass, potholes and sewer grates dotting the expanse. The crumbling buildings stood like the rotten teeth of a decomposing corpse—windows and doors, gone, nothing existing above the second level. Curiously, the sergeant of Beta team noted that the destruction seemed to be mostly caused by fires and looting. He had seen ruins where the buildings were sheered off at exactly the same height from a nuke blast knifing across the land. Skydark had to have been one bitch of a show for the few survivors.

In a weedy fountain, a bronze statue was covered with a layer of green moss and speckled with bird droppings. Wooden posts marked a long-gone fence, and a steel post stood where some sort of sign had to have been. Campbell grew nervous when he noticed how quiet the ruins were—no birds sang, and nothing moved in the weeds or grass.

As the LAV rumbled into an open area, he called for a halt. "Scotty, check our location," the sergeant ordered, jacking the bolt on the 25 mm electric cannon. The hairs on his nape were stiff, but there was nothing dangerous in sight. Maybe he was just tired. More coffee. Yeah, that's all he needed.

The rear doors of the APC swung open, and Scotty stepped out of the wag, his blaster sweeping the ground for targets. The rest of the sec men remained inside the wag, keeping a grip on their Kalashnikovs.

After a few minutes, the private tucked away his blaster and clumsily checked the huge sextant Collette had given them. The antique was solid brass and weighed several pounds. Carefully, he balanced sun overhead through the billowing clouds, shot the horizon with the half-mirror, then did a few calculations.

"This is the place, Sarge," he announced, lowering the sextant. "Trans University. Any sign of a ville, or dish from up there?"

"Not yet," the sergeant growled, cupping his hands around his face to try to see better. "No wait. There's something to our north. Big, white. Could be a dish."

"But no ville?"

"Nothing."

"Shit."

"Motherfucker!" a sec man cursed, grabbing Scotty by the shirt and trying to haul him inside the vehicle. "Bear!"

The private pulled loose and turned to see. A hairy giant was padding their way. The huge grizzly stood ten feet tall, its fangs and long claws bared for a fight.

Laughing in contempt, Scotty slid the AK-47 from his shoulder, aimed and fired a short burst into the animal's belly. The bear stopped as if hitting a wall, then screamed a challenge and rose to its hind legs, which made it appear even larger. Scotty put another burst into its throat, and the animal staggered, slumping slowly the ground and going still.

"Good shot," Campbell called from behind the cannon, as he eased his grip on the trigger. "About time we had some fresh meat."

"Thanks," Scotty said, walking over to the beast and putting one more round into its ear. The head jerked from the impact, and the beast exhaled into death.

"Son of a bitch," a corporal gasped, then chuckled. "The bastard was faking."

"Seen them do that before," Scotty said, kicking the body a few times just to make sure. "Bears be smart. Smarter than dogs."

"Griz," a sec man said, scowling. "Nasty tough."

Climbing from the turret, Campbell jumped to the ground. "I like bear," he stated. "Better skin it quick, though, or the bugs will start chewing the hide."

"Take the meat, sure," Scotty said, drawing a knife. "But why are we going to tan it?"

"Present for Collette," Campbell said. "She likes fur and knows how to say thanks to a real man."

The sec men laughed at the image of their sec chief spread-eagled on a bed begging for it. They had all been there and wanted to go again. The bitch was a roller coaster with a tongue.

"So how are we going to tan it?" the corporal asked, unsure.

Scotty rolled his eyes. Ville boys! Didn't know nothing about nothing. "Scrape off the fat with a knife, then we all piss on it and rub in some salt. That'll do until we can get it home."

"What do you mean, piss on it?" he demanded.

Suddenly, a winged creature darted in from the woods, landed on the bear and plunged a barbed beak into the corpse, ripping out a bloody chunk of flesh.

The sec men stepped back and drew their blasters. The mutie looked just like a screamwing, only it was much bigger, twice, three times the size!

Scotty fired at the screamwing, stitching a line of holes across the bear and the mutie. The slugs slapped the thing around but didn't penetrate its leathery hide.

Looking directly at the sec man, the screamwing launched itself off the bear and crossed the twenty yards separating the two in only a second. Scotty cried out as the mutie buried its beak into his chest, struggling to remove whatever internal organ it had hooked with its beak.

"Chill it!" Campbell shouted, and opened fired with his Kalashnikov. The rest of the troops did the same, and Scotty was torn to pieces under the fusillade of bullets, his arms flailing wildly.

The human corpse dropped, and the screamwing struggled out from under the dead man, a ropy piece of intestine dangling from its wicked beak. It stared at the humans as it consumed the tidbit in a few swallows.

A private broke ranks and ran for the ruins, but the rest stood firm, their blasters blowing a hellstorm of lead at the gory killer. The 7.62 mm rounds impacted all around the beast, a hole was punched through a wing, a bloody score along one side of its body. Barely scratched, the mutie narrowed its hate-filled eyes to slits and lifted into the air, angling its taloned feet at the gunners.

Dropping his Kalashnikov, Campbell drew his handcannon, aimed and fired. The .45-caliber round from the Colt pistol slammed into the creature like the hand of God, completely removing its head and neck. Blood pumping from the ghastly wound, wings still flapping, the headless mutie flashed forward to crash into the side of the armored LAV. Cursing, Campbell fired again and again at the creature until it stopped flopping on the ground.

"Fucking muties!" he cursed, dropping the half-spent clip and slapping in a fresh one. "Getting meaner every damn day. Hey, Adams, check Scotty."

Grabbing a predark med kit, the man rushed to the still form and rolled over the body. "Aced, Sarge," the healer announced glumly, looking at the exposed lungs and heart. "Nothing I can do to help."

Campbell holstered his piece. "Shit, and he was the only one who knew how to operate the sextant. It's yours now, Adams. Learn how to work that thing fast."

"Me?" he gulped. "Yes, Sarge."

"Mac, get his blaster and boots," the sergeant ordered, retrieving his longblaster. "Corporal, you skin the bear. No sense wasting all that fresh meat. Randy, man the 25 mm and shoot anything that ain't us. The rest of you apes stay with me. We're going to do a fast recce of the area to see if there are any more of those things around."

"Didn't know a mutie could, like, you know, mutate," a private said hesitantly, staring at the mutilated body of the screamwing. A breeze ruffled its wings, and the man froze for a moment.

"Well, now you do," Campbell growled, heading for the nearest building.

In a tight group, the sec men entered the old structure through a gaping hole in the wall. Most of the ceiling was still intact, but the entire floor was covered with dried leaves. Endless shelves of books covered the walls, protruding into the room as if the walls weren't enough to hold all of the volumes.

A private ran his hand along a shelf, the books exploding into dusty smoke. Dried and useless. Anything useful had been looted long ago.

Exiting the library, they briefly checked a dirty dining room overgrown with thickets, then a small building with its second floor acting as a roof. The floor was bare ground, and a row of wooden crosses lined the walls, dusty skeletons still attached to the thick beams by rope and nails. The torso of each was intact, but the leg bones were smashed in almost exactly the same place. Tiny pieces of white cloth marked with a faded red cross still clung the skeletons, and one skull had a scalpel buried in its left eye socket. Another had a stethoscope knotted around is neck.

"Whitecoats," a sec man growled, and spit at the skeletons.

Campbell snorted. "Locals probably busted their legs to make them chill faster."

"Where's the fun in that?" a private asked angrily.

"Civilians," the sergeant agreed. "Dumber than ville boys."

A sec man appeared in a doorway ahead of them, his face sweaty.

"Hey, Sarge," he said, licking dry lips. "Sorry that I ran, but that mutie was—"

The concussion of the handcannon boomed across the inside of the ruins, making dust rain from the ceiling. The sec man slammed into the wall and slid to the ground, a bloody hole in his arm.

"Strip the coward naked," Campbell ordered, holstering his piece, "and leave him alive."

"No, please," the man begged as the others advanced and began to rip off his uniform. He tried to stop them, but the blood loss was already stealing the strength from his body. Soon, he was nude in a pool of his own blood. "Sarge, don't leave me like this! Please!"

A corporal backhanded the cringing man across the face. "We can't hear the dead, Arnie," he said, sneering, and kicked the other man directly on the wound.

The pain flared beyond tolerance, and the sec man fainted dead away. Stopping at the doorway on the way out, Campbell waited until the others were outside, then surreptitiously tossed his unconscious brother a sharp knife. Rules be damned. It was the least he could do for family.

By the time Beta team had completed a security sweep of the ruins, Adams was finished with the bear, thick steaks piled in a tin bucket normally used for drawing water from creeks. The scraped skin was attached to the outside stanchions of the LAV with short pieces of rope, the hide dripping with piss and shiny with salt crystals.

"Good job," Campbell complimented him, inspecting the hide. "That'll cure fine. Okay, rest period is over. Everybody back in the wag. We still got to find that dish."

Gratefully, the sec men climbed into the safety of the APC and closed the door, sliding the locking bar with a loud clank. The driver started the diesel engines, and the armored vehicle rolled away from the ruins. Laying abandoned in the middle of the road was a reddish lump. The skinned carcass of the bear glistening in the sunlight, long black lines of insects already marching over the meat, carrying it away piece by piece. As the LAV disappeared into the thickets, a muffled cry rose from inside the ruin of the hospital, then a body hit the ground. Almost instantly, the insects began to angle toward the new bounty of fresh food.

Less than an hour later, the LAV-25 plowed through a line of thorny thickets, and the driver whooped in delight. Campbell smiled and slapped the sec man on the shoulder.

There on the ground directly ahead of them was a near duplicate of the blockhouse back at the Shiloh ville, and rising majestically above it was a framework of girders and struts supporting an enormous dish. The structure looked solid.

"Hot damn!" a sec man cried, peering out a blasterport. "We're going to be the pussy patrol for rest of our lives!"

"Not yet," Campbell said, scratching his head. "We got to make sure it's intact. But it looks mighty good, boys. Mighty fucking good! Adams on the 25 mm, Mac stay in the LAV. You two come with me."

Grabbing their blasters from a wall rack, the men kicked open the rear doors, fingers on triggers. Nothing stirred in the grass. Cautiously, they stepped from the wag and circled to the blockhouse. Campbell tried the metal door, but it was rusted shut.

"Need explosives to open that," he stated, stepping back and looking at the dish towering above them. "Rest seems okay, though."

The framework was badly coated with rust, but still stood ten times the height of a man into the cloudy sky. The dish itself spread above them like a slice of white ice.

"Perfect!" a sec man said, sighing.

Experimentally, the sergeant reached out and slapped the main support girder. The steel vibrated from the soft blow, making the entire structure tremble slightly. With his heart in his throat, Campbell waited, but the quaking didn't stop, it only got worse. Soon pieces of rust started to sprinkle to the ground as the framework began to wobble.

"Oh shit, get back!" he shouted, sprinting for the LAV. The others were right behind him.

The driver of the wag stared in horror as cracks appeared along the struts, spreading like some horrible disease, the gaps widening as the metal yawned apart, braces shattered into dust.

Frantically, he started the engine and threw the APC into reverse, slamming on the gas pedal. The vehicle spun all eight tires in the damp grass, then they reached dirt and the wag lurched backward, racing away from the falling dish.

Campbell grunted a curse and headed for the nearby trees. Those would offer some protection, if only they got there soon enough! Then the air driven before the falling dish slapped the men off their feet and threw them at the woods like broken toys.

The sec men inside the LAV cried out as the wag slammed into a tree, coming to a abrupt halt. Struggling with the stalled engines, the driver could only watch as the weakening supports broke completely apart and the huge dish fell from the sky, its shadow falling over the APC like a shroud. A man screamed, another covered his head with his arms, and the dish thunderously slammed into the ground only inches from the vehicle, a strut scraping the wag's armored prow.

The predark material crumbled into a compact pile

of debris, spewing a cloud of dust and pulverized plastic. More pieces fell, a few bounced off the wag with loud bangs, and the crushing noise continued for minutes. Chunks of the dish fell to the ground only to break apart again and start the whole process over, but on a smaller scale. Only the cracking and shattering of the plastic, and the groan of the twisting metal could be heard. Nothing was visible within the roiling dust cloud.

Fifteen minutes passed before the noise of the destruction reached a level low enough for the men to shout at one another, and finally the weak breeze blew away enough of the dust to make seeing possible again.

Rising from a bush, Campbell glared at the mountain of plastic debris piled high before the LAV. He wanted to be furious, but the driver had done the correct thing. If he had stayed, the LAV might have been buried under that crap forever. He walked closer to the destruction, surveying the unlimited wreckage. There was nothing left of the predark dish except for twisted scraps of plastic and lumps of rusted metal.

Turning, the sergeant looked for his men and saw their still forms sprawled on the ground. One was at the base of a tree, his blood and guts spread along the track like jam. The other lay pinned in place with a long shaft of white plastic shoved through his body. Fuck! Four men down, and this only their first stop.

"Okay, you assholes, start digging!" he shouted. "We got a long ways to go if we want to reach the next dish by sundown!"

Grumbling unhappily, the weary sec men started to climb out of the turret of the wag and began the odious task of clearing a path through the debris.

STEPPING OUT OF THE WAY of the crumbling plaster, Ryan and the others looked across the chasm along the shattered remains of the granite bridge. The explosion had sealed the cave on the other side completely.

"No way we're jumping that," J.B. stated.

Keeping a hand on the wall for support, Mildred peered into the depths below. "Not even a splash or a crash," she said softly, tilting her head to listen. "How deep is that hole?"

"Doesn't matter," Ryan stated, flicking a butane lighter and studying the cave around them. Only it wasn't a cave, but another tunnel identical to the one leading from the redoubt—the same smooth floor, arched walls, concrete braces supporting the ceiling, bare metal hoops for wiring not installed.

Going to the edge, Jak lifted the loaded crossbow from the floor and made sure the wooden arrow was firmly in place. This was their last weapon.

"Maybe the bridge was also part of this tunnel," Doc suggested, sheathing his sword and locking the blade with a twist. "But a subterranean earthquake collapsed the area, and only the reinforced floor of the tunnel remained."

Lifting a piece of plaster from the floor, J.B. inspected it closely. It was plain white on one side and painted to resemble rock on the other. Triple strange. "But why would anybody hide this tunnel?"

"Escape route?" Jak suggested. "Or no want runts find."

Taking the torch from his belt, Ryan lit the oily rags and started forward. "Only one way to find out."

There was no silvery moss on the tunnel walls, the darkness seeming to swallow the crackling light of the two torches. The drilled shaft echoed their steps as the companions walked along.

Reaching an intersection, Ryan held out his torch to try to see down the side passages. The right ended in a rockfall, slabs of granite sealing the tunnel completely. But the left side went on for a distance. Faint noise could be heard in the tunnel, voices, and some sort of dragging, moist sound. Frowning, Ryan covered his mouth and jerked a hand toward the main tunnel. Once they reached it, he walked away from the side tunnel a few yards before speaking.

"That sounded like the runts," he said.

"Good news, bad news," Mildred muttered, turning the knife in her hand nervously.

J.B. tilted back his fedora. "What the hell is the good news?"

"If they got here, then there's a way back to the main cavern," she explained. "We're not cut off."

"Do here," Jak said, offering the crossbow to the woman. Mildred took the weapon and the teenager gestured, a knife sliding into each hand. "Never know what hit."

"Not here. There's no cover," Ryan countered. "We need someplace to ambush the muties. Can't go back to the bridge. The other side branch is blocked." He turned and heading farther along the tunnel. "We keep going. Any ammo left?"

"Not a single round," J.B. stated grimly, patting his clothing.

"Everybody got a knife?"

"I daresay yes, my dear Ryan," Doc rumbled, sliding his sword free once more.

The tunnel continued for hundreds of yards, with the noise from the runts becoming fainter until it was lost completely. But the companions kept going. Just because they couldn't hear the runts, didn't mean the little muties weren't still after them.

Suddenly, Ryan raised a hand for a halt. A faint blue star shone straight ahead of them. They waited a few minutes but the light didn't move, or alter in any way. Ryan waved a hand forward, and as the companions cautiously advanced, the star became a beam of bluish light piercing the darkness. The companions kept to the side of the tunnel to offer as small a target for snipers as possible.

"That's not daylight," Ryan said, squinting against the smoky flames of the torch.

"More like a halogen light," J.B. stated incredulously.

Mildred shifted her grip on the crossbow. "Down here?"

He shrugged. "That's what it looks like."

"Could be," Ryan muttered, dropping the torch and grinding out the flames. "We crawl from here. Mebbe this is the way to the surface."

"Ash storm okay by me," Jak said stoutly. "Least could run if need."

Extinguishing the second torch, the companions went on the floor and crept toward the strange illumination until the light filled the tunnel brightly. Knowing they were in plain sight, they waited for an attack, or any response, but only silence greeted their presence.

Slowly, Ryan stood and walked into the light until he could see the front end of some sort of machine. It was a truck with a broken grille. Its left headlight was smashed, but the right blazed. Large rocks were strewed across the floor, slabs of stone stacked behind the wag as if it had been caught in an avalanche.

His palm tight on the handle of his knife, Ryan edged past the chunks of limestone. Glancing into the cab, he saw two corpses dressed in blue uniforms slumped against the dashboard. Their heads were split open, slivers of windshield protruding from their slack faces.

Sheathing the blade, Ryan whistled twice, and the rest of the companions rushed forward to join him at the wreck.

"Dark night," J.B. whispered, taking in the scene. "How did this get all the way down here?"

"Quake?" Jak asked, running a hand over the machine as if unsure it was actually there. The metal was cold under his touch. "Been here while."

"Can't have been here for very long. The headlight is still working," Mildred offered. "No, that's wrong. The nuke battery would power the bulb until it burned out. Might have been here for weeks, months."

Reaching in through the broken window, Ryan pulled a sandwich off the top of the dashboard. He squeezed the bread, and it crunched slightly. "Only been a couple of weeks," he said, sniffing the food. Smelled like peanut butter. Definitely predark supplies. He took a bite, chewed and swallowed. "Days," he corrected, breaking the sandwich into pieces and passing the morsels around. Everybody wolfed his or her portion and started to loot the vehicle.

Pulling open the door to the truck, Ryan grabbed the body of the blue shirt as it fell out sideways. The corpse had a blaster in its belt, and an AK-47 rested on the floor. Ryan tossed the handcannon and gun belt to J.B. and appropriated the Kalashnikov. Briefly, the one-eyed man checked the weapon, dropping the clip to make sure it contained ammo.

"Fireblast," he cursed, holding the magazine in the light. "The clip is bent. No way this'll feed properly."

"Mine's okay," J.B. said, jacking the slide. "Got a full load of .45 rounds."

At the other door, Doc struggled with the handle. Impatiently, he used the silver head of his swordstick to break the window and grab a second longblaster from the hands of the other sec man. He tossed the weapon to Jak and yanked a shoulder bag free of the corpse's stiff arms.

"Fucking A," Jak said, sounding pleased. "Let runts come now!"

Yanking open the canvas bag, Doc grinned in delight. "And here is even better news," he said, lifting a handful of loaded clips into view. "Spare ammo by the pound, and lots of grens!"

"Yo," Ryan called, holding out an open hand.

Doc tossed the man a clip, and Ryan slapped it into the breech of the rapidfire, working the bolt to eject a live round, then dropping the clip to insert the bullet again.

"This one works," he said, satisfied. "Give me two more. There are a lot of runts."

"For a while," Doc agreed ominously, walking around the wag. He gave Ryan two more and passed several to Jak. Judiciously, the old man then handed an explosive charge to everybody. The last six he kept in the bag and slung it over a shoulder.

"What kind are they?" Mildred asked, studying the

military sphere. The ball was colored green with a black stripe. She didn't know that code.

Holding the gren in the headlight, J.B. checked the colorations. "Steel shrapnel," he announced. "High explosive, antipersonnel."

"Shit!" If they used them in the tight confines of the tunnel, the ricochets could tear them into pieces.

Dragging the body from behind the wheel, Ryan checked the floor and the glovebox. Nothing useful there, except for a metal ring of keys, which he pocketed. Those might come in handy later. Pushing the seat forward, the one-eyed warrior checked the storage compartment behind the seat. He found some gnawed chicken bones, empty brass, a length of rope, a crowbar, a bullwhip, a thermos, some heavy towing chain, a coil of fuse too coated with blood to ever be useful, a blanket and some loose envelopes of shiny plastic.

"MRE packs," Ryan said, tossing them out behind as he dug for more. The packs were loose, scattered amid the tools and junk as if completely unimportant. Sheffield had to be rolling in predark supplies. Ryan cut his hands unearthing the Mylar envelopes, but he didn't care. There was enough food for days.

The companions grabbed the packs off the floor and filled their pockets. Everybody wanted to dig into the food here and now, but this was neither the time nor the place. Jamming an envelope into her carpetbag, Mildred noticed a tiny speck of light on her shoe. It wasn't same shade of blue as the halogen headlights, and she held out a hand to catch the dot on her palm, tracking it back to the pile of rocks. Another buried truck? She hesitantly placed an eye to the opening and gasped.

"Sweet Jesus," she whispered in astonishment.

Just then, a noise came from down the tunnel, and Ryan hurriedly killed the headlight. Darkness swallowed them whole. Instantly, the noise stopped.

"Runts here," Jak whispered.

Tugging his hat on tight, J.B. drew his Colt .45 pistol and snicked off the safety. "Any idea how many?"

"All," the teenager answered grimly.

"Let them come," Doc rumbled, pulling the pin from a gren and dropping it into a pocket. Sticky tape held the spoon in place, and he broke a thumbnail digging the end free and unwrapping the charge so it was ready for use. With a good enough bounce, he could get the charge past the runts and it would blow behind them, the shrapnel tearing them to pieces. For a brief instant, Doc was back in his own time standing before his students explaining this to them as they recoiled in horror, then reality returned and the scholar prepared for bloody warfare.

"Hold the grens," the Armorer said suddenly, holstering his piece. "I may have something better. Give me a second."

Moving fast, J.B. went to the cab and found the thermos. Unscrewing the top to make sure it was empty, he used a knife to break the vacuum seal and freed the glass container inside. Gingerly lifting out the tube, he carried it to the front of the wag and tried to lift the crumpled hood. It was stuck, so Doc and Jak helped get it loose. Knowing what the man was doing, Ryan moved behind the steering wheel and put his hand on the ignition switch. Locking the hood into place, J.B. gave Jak the tube and fumbled with the engine until finding the flexible hose that led to the carburetor. He sliced it off with a knife, took the hose and stuffed the end into the glass container.

"Go!" he ordered.

Making sure the wag was in neutral, Ryan cranked the engine, the headlight dimming as the starter struggled to turn the dead engine. The fuel pump wheezed loudly, telling of a break in the diaphragm, but gas squirted out the end of the hose and dribbled into the tube.

"Full!" J.B. said after a minute.

Ryan released the ignition switch and the lights came to life with full force.

Mildred handed J.B. rags she had cut from a sec man's shirt. The Armorer stuffed a piece of cloth into the glass tube and tilted it for a few seconds to moisten the fuse. Then he tied the wet rag around the neck of the bottle and screwed the plastic cap back on tight.

"Not much, but it'll catch them unawares," he said, handing it to Mildred.

Placing the crossbow aside, she nodded, pulled a butane lighter from her pocket and tested the flame to make sure it was at the maximum setting.

Swinging open the door to the cab, Ryan assumed a firing stance behind the barrier. "Range," he demanded, resting the Kalashnikov on the dashboard, the barrel sticking through the smashed windshield.

"Close," Jak said, a hand resting on the tunnel floor. "Can feel coming."

Moving with a purpose, the rest of the companions shifted some of the loose rocks into a crude wall on either side of the chassis, and crouched behind the cover, checking the found weapons again to make sure they would function.

The scuffling sounds grew louder and when the voices became clear, Ryan pulled the switch, bathing the runts in the bright clear light.

They screamed and covered their faces, many dropping their weapons and backing away. However, towering amid the runts was a monstrous creature of some kind, abnormally large. Its slick skin shone with moisture, and a writhing nest of tentacles reached out from below its miniature snarling face. The eyes were mere slits, the mouth filled with needle-sharp teeth.

Now he knew what had been inside the temple of the runt ville. The runts had brought along their god to finish them off.

"Fire!" Ryan shouted, triggering the longblaster in a chattering spray. The word echoed down the tunnel, and the runts shouted in rage, shaking their spears as the big mutie moved forward with a grinding noise, the tentacles grabbing hold of the support columns and pulling its massive body along across the floor.

"Go for the face!" J.B. shouted, firing the blaster steadily, the big bore .45 booming in the underground tunnel.

The two Kalashnikovs stuttered in strident fury, the twin streams of 7.62 mm rounds stitching the god across its lumpy body. Greenish blood pumped from the puckered holes and the beast roared, extending a forked tongue toward the companions.

The ropy muscle hit the grille and wrapped firmly around the exposed metalwork. As the wag started squealing into movement, Doc lunged and the tongue dropped to the ground, sliced in two, green ichor smeared along the man's slim sword. A greenish froth filled its mouth, and the mutie howled in rage. Spurred on by the awful pain, the lumbering creature dragged itself toward the norms even faster.

Out of ammo, Ryan and Jak dropped their exhausted clips and slapped in spares, while Mildred put an arrow into the mutie's left eye, the shaft disappearing into the gelatinous hide with no appreciable effect.

J.B. snapped off two fast rounds from the Colt, the thunderous discharges illuminating the passageway as bright as day. The .45 slugs scored deep grooves across the beast's head, removing a chunk of slimy flesh the size of a dinner plate. The creature rumbled in pain and redoubled its forward speed.

Rushing toward the mutie, Mildred lit the fuse of the Molotov and threw the bomb.

"Too high, madam!" Doc admonished, a deadly gren balanced in his grip. He debated throwing it now, then realized her target and braced himself for the results.

Tumbling through the air, the glass container smashed to pieces on the ceiling directly above the mutie, pouring its contents of liquid fire upon the beast. Coated with flames, the creature rose upward, bellowing a wordless scream. In blind rage, it threw itself to the right, slamming into the tunnel walls as it tried to shake off the fierce orange thing eating its flesh. The passageway shuddered, loose debris raining to the tunnel floor as the mutie tried again and again to pound out the flames. The runts rushed forward to help, only to have their god crush them under its burning body. A retched stink filled the air. Green blood welled from its mouth, pouring onto the floor and then, incredibly, catching fire as the flames dripped onto the life fluid.

Retreating quickly, the companions stopped firing and watched as the subterranean god began to fry inside and out. The light and heat grew into a hellish bonfire, and still the thing struggled to reach its tormentors. Soon a devil's skull with bulging eyes stared at the tiny humans, its stump of a tongue stabbing outward but failing to hit the mark.

Taking careful aim, Ryan triggered the Kalashnikov, the bullet smashing apart the cooking skull, the great wad of brain tissue expanding through the cracks until the gooey pieces dribbled to the floor. The runts went deathly still as the howling monster violently shuddered, then lurched forward one last time before dropping lifeless to the ground. Fed by the blood of the dead god, the fire raged out of control for minutes, then quickly died.

As the flames expired, the companions braced for the expected attack. But it didn't come, and they heard the runts chanting something musical.

"Trick," Jak said, working the bolt on the AK-47 to clear a jam.

"No, I think they mean it," Ryan said, lowering his blaster. "We aced their god."

Mildred barked a humorless laugh. "So now we're the gods?"

"Care to test that theory?" J.B. asked, keeping a steady two-handed grip on the Colt.

Stepping out of the cab, the one-eyed warrior approached the crackling corpse and saw the runts scamper away from him, bowing their heads respectfully.

"Speak talk?" Ryan demanded, standing brazen in the beam of the headlight.

"We speak," a runt muttered. He was dressed in armor like the female warriors, with a spear and leather shield. There was an elaborate weave of bones in his graying hair. "Machine god no kill, we worship!"

"I chief!" another male stormed. "You no talk machine god!"

"Machine god?" Jak asked.

"Machine-gun god is more like it," Doc muttered.

As the challenger strode forward, Ryan calmly shot the chief dead and the rested covered their faces in fear.

"No kill! No kill!" the grayhair begged from the ground.

"You chief," Ryan stated, and, taking the shield of the aced runt, handed it to the old runt.

Astonished, the mutie accepted the shield with reverence, then stood tall before the others. "Bow before new chief!" he screamed, spraying spittle from his loose-lipped mouth.

The others obeyed, moaning the song once more. Facing the much larger norm, the chief went to one knee and lowered his misshapen head. "What machine god want us do?"

"Return to your homes," Ryan said, resting the stock of the Kalashnikov on his hip. "We follow."

"Yes, god!"

"And bring best rats. Many mushrooms."

"Bring all?" the chief asked fearfully.

Trying not to choke on the stink of the burning slug, Ryan knew food had to be very scarce down here. "One rat for each finger and toe," he said. "Then I give great gift."

"Gift?" the runt asked fearfully.

Magnanimously, Ryan waved a hand at the dead creature. "Eat fill of old god. Make strong!"

The chief runt could only gawk at the incredible offer. He tried to speak several times and finally got out, "Hail, machine god!"

On cue, the rest repeated the words. But one young male mumbled something under his breath. Turning, the chief charged at the heretic and smashed the leather shield on the youth's head again and again until he dropped senseless to the tunnel floor.

"No challenge gods!" the grayhair shrieked. "Obey-obey-obey!"

The remaining runts doubled the level of their cheering, while several began to loot the body of their fallen leader.

"What now?" J.B. asked, sidling closer. Acting casual, he tucked the Colt into the holster, but he kept his hand on the butt of the blaster.

"We take the food and get back inside the redoubt," Ryan said. "After that, we eat and lay some plans. Mebbe the runts here can help us get through the wall around the ville."

"Better than that," Mildred said, gesturing with her head. "See the rock wall over there? Remember the huge explosion we heard when we first approached the Shiloh base? That was their stone quarry exploding during an avalanche."

Jak looked at the bodies laying near the crushed wag. "Overseers?" he asked.

She nodded. "Yep. Just on the other side of those rocks is their base."

"Dark night," J.B. exhaled. "We got a back door."

With a stern expression, Ryan started toward the wall, then paused. "We only get one chance at this," he said solemnly. "We dig our way out, and the blues will find the hole pretty damn fast. Got to do this at night, and with more weps.''

"Which means we have to chance a jump," Doc said, wrapping the tape around the handle of a gren, and carefully sliding the pin back into position. He eased the charge into the canvas bag and took his swordstick by the top. At this range the grens were useless, but his Spanish steel would make short work of the primitive troglodytes.

"A jump," Ryan repeated. Shouldering the long-blaster, he started to walk through the worshiping mob of little muties. "Do we have another choice?"

HITCHING UP THEIR PANTS, two sec men walked from the lav of the Shiloh ville situated near the stone quarry when one of them stopped in his tracks.

"Hey, what the fuck was that?" the private asked, looking around. "Sounded like a blaster on full-auto."

The sergeant bit off the end a cigar and inserted the tobacco fully into his mouth to moisten the leaves. Setting the end on his back teeth, he struck a match and lit the end of the cigar until it glowed cherry red. "Couldn't be," he stated. "Ain't nobody got rapid-fires but us."

"Mebbe so," the private replied hesitantly, tightening his belt. "But I think we better report it anyway."

"Sure," the sergeant said, puffing, completely unconcerned. "You do that. Collette loves wild reports of ghostly blasterfire. Give you a big kiss."

Following the man back to the barracks, the private paled at the very thought of angering their volatile chief and debated the wisdom of such an action.

Chapter Eleven

The tall grass almost reached the ob slit of Alpha team's LAV-25 as it traveled through the waving expanse of wild wheat stalks. Braking to a halt in the middle of a rolling field, the driver set the brakes but didn't kill the engine, the big Detroit power plant chugging over steadily.

The vented muzzles of AK-47 longblasters jutted from every blasterport. One of the back doors was swung open, and Private Michaels stepped to the ground, blaster in hand. Some birds pecked at apples in a tree, and somewhere nearby a stream babbled over stones. A loon called for its mate, and a swarm of bees buzzed around the rusted hollow of a mailbox jutting from the ground.

"Keep me covered, boys," Michaels said, holstering his piece and opening the heavy wooden case hanging at his side. Extracting the sextant, he shot the sun and started the simple calculations.

"Well?" Lieutenant Brandon asked impatiently. Soft wind ruffling his hair, Brandon stood in the open hatch of the turret, an arm draped across the 25 mm cannon.

"We're in Kentucky," the healer reported, his pencil busy. Then he looked up. "Yep, this is where the dish and some pissant ville are supposed ta be."

No structures were visible for as far as they could

see, only gently rolling hills of low grass, some mountains to the north and a young forest to the west.

The lieutenant scowled. "You sure?"

Michaels carefully double-checked the compass, and then the sextant once more. "Yes sir, this is the area. Map shows a big city dish right here where we're standing."

"Seti," the lieutenant corrected him automatically. "Not city."

"Sure. What does that mean, anyway?" the man asked.

Brandon had no idea, but would never admit a weakness in front of his troops. "Shut up," he snapped. "That's baron stuff."

The man accepted the rebuff and packed the sextant into its cushioned box. He knew the predark instrument was much more valuable than him, and took extraspecial care of it. If it got broken by his hand, the healer died.

"Okay, get out and stretch your legs," Brandon commanded, rising from his chair. "Hit the latrine and let's get some coffee on. We got two hundred more miles till the next dish."

"Hopefully," a private said, nursing the broken arm in a sling.

As the sec men climbed from the wag and started to gather wood for the campfire, Brandon heard an odd thunder in the distance. Glancing at the sky, the sec man saw purple clouds, laced with fiery orange and crackling with sheet lightning. Nothing unusual there. Yet the noise got steadily louder, and the blues moved toward the APC, grabbing their rifles and checking clips.

"Davies, take the 25 mm," Brandon ordered. "Tell us if you see anything!"

The man popped into the LAV and started up the short ladder to the turret when men on horseback galloped into view from the valley below. The riders were half hidden by their mounts, but the sec men could still see the males were stark naked and heavily covered with scars in decorative patterns. Their long golden hair was streaming wildly, and the newcomers had wide Oriental eyes and dark skin. Bandoliers of ammo crossed their broad chests and blasters rode at every hip, yet they carried long spears in their hands.

"Fucking coldhearts," the lieutenant said, calmly drawing his handcannon. "Ace them and take the blasters."

The sec men cut loose with their Kalashnikovs, the rounds hitting man and beast with little effect. A blue cursed and rummaged for a box of grens, when the top turret of the LAV-25 rotated to point the 25 mm cannon at the horsemen. The electric Gatling whined for a moment, building speed, then cut loose with a roaring staff rod of destruction. Riders and horses exploded into grisly bits as the high-explosive shells tore through their flesh. The first line of the riders vanished in the brief salvo.

With amazing precision, the other barbs reared their horses, walking them about on hind legs, then started to gallop away from the armored war wag.

"Again," the lieutenant ordered, laughing and holstering his piece.

The Gatling roared, and half a dozen more of the riders were blown to pieces under its furious assault before the rest made it to the safety of the ridge and disappeared.

"Won't be seeing them again." Brandon laughed, rubbing his hands. "Now, how about that coffee?"

Suddenly, a row of riders rose from behind the hill, their long spears soaring into the air before cresting their arc and descending toward the sec men with fearful accuracy.

The blues scattered, but it was too late. One caught a spear in the shoulder, the lance going completely through and burying itself to the hilt in the soft soil. Another was caught through the boot, a third in the hand, his longblaster smashed to pieces.

Trying to step out of the way of the falling missiles, Michaels was hit in the mouth, the barbed lance going straight down his throat and out his ass, impaling the man like a pig on a spit. Still horribly alive, the blue lashed his arms about feebly, unable to scream with the wooden shaft completely filling his torn and bleeding gullet. A steady stream of red trickled out, forming a puddle around his boots.

Cursing vehemently, the lieutenant fired from the hip, blowing Michaels's head off and the grisly corpse stopped moving.

"Chill those motherfucks!" Brandon yelled, and the LAV-25 rolled to the crest of the hill. The silent riders were galloping madly along the valley plain below, way beyond the range of the ineffective Kalashnikovs.

A soft electric whine heralded the roar of the 25 mm cannon, coming to deadly life again, spraying annihilation onto the distant coldhearts. The ground behind the horsemen churned with explosions as the armor-piercing rounds hit the soil and detonated. The noise and spray urged the barbs on, but the Gatling swept over the riders, killing the men and animals indiscriminately. Only a single rider made it to the trees and disappeared from sight. The sec man at the

Gatling drilled a couple of short bursts into the greenery, then stopped wasting ammo.

Standing on the hilltop, Brandon fired a few rounds
from his blaster at the escaping killer, then slapped in
a fresh clip. Turning, he saw the carnage of his
squad—three badly wounded, one dead. As Brandon
watched, the sec man with the lance through his
shoulder snapped off the shaft and gritted his teeth as
he pulled himself loose. Blood gushed from the
wound, and he stuffed in a dirty piece of cloth. The
other men pinned by the lances did the same, painfully freeing themselves by sheer determination. Only
Michaels stayed in the same position, the remains of
his head lolling to one side as his arms swung loosely
from the gentle wind blowing over his upright corpse.

"Who were they?" Brandon demanded, breathing
heavily. "Who the rad-blasted fuck were those
guys!"

A sec man dropped the empty clip from his AK-47
and slammed in a fresh magazine. "Barbs," he replied angrily. "I heard tell of them as a kid. Outlanders that ride the Kentucky plains, chilling everybody."

"Cannies?" a private asked, a friend bandaging the
wound in his shoulder.

The corporal scratched under his cloth cap. "Nope.
They just ace you. Don't take blasters or food. Don't
rape the women. Just kill folks, is all."

Brandon stayed on the hilltop, watching the valley
below for any signs of more barbs. "Why didn't they
use those blasters?" he demanded, puzzled. "Give
them a better chance at least. They lost more men than
they chilled."

"Those are just trophies from aced foes," the private explained slowly, as if in disbelief. "They never use the blasters. Just those spears. Or so I heard."

"Guess it's true," another man stated, wrapping his bloody hand.

From the turret, Davies swung the cannon aside. "You mean they save blasters like we do ears and dicks?"

"Yep."

"Outlanders," the sergeant stated gruffly. Grabbing a lance, he yanked it loose from the soil. The weapon was over eight feet long, the barbed spearhead made of steel that shone like winter ice in the sunlight.

"Fresh steel," he muttered. "These crazies can make new steel and use spears?"

"Lances," Brandon corrected, finally turning away from the forest. "That's no spear."

The sergeant inspected the weapon curiously. "What's the difference, sir?"

Brandon took it from him and pointed. "A spear has a head. This wep is sharp from the grip to the tip. A lot more deadly."

"Yeah, I saw that."

After stripping the healer of his blaster, gun belt and boots, the sec men boarded the LAV-25 and drove away in silence. As the wag dwindled into the distance, a lone man rose from the tall grass near the still-warm corpse. He was breathing hard, and his muscular chest was coated with a sheen of sweat. With knife in hand, the outlander stared hatefully at the escaping iron box. But the barb wasn't overly concerned, because he knew the ways of the fat norms. Confident in their own safety, they would stop at night and make a campfire to cook food. They would sleep in woven cloth, with only one or two inside the box with its chilling machine. The men inside would be the first to die, then all the rest.

Scooping up a handful of earth, he stuffed his mouth full and swallowed the rich dirt. Life renewed filled his body, and on foot the scarred warrior began to chase after the machine people. In his mind, he was already wearing their blasters.

RICH SMELLS of roasting meat permeated the kitchen of the Tennessee redoubt, four of the sixteen ovens radiating waves of heat. Wearing an apron, Krysty laid a platter full of fried mushrooms on the counter and Dean carried it to the table, snatching a couple with his bare fingers. Doc gave everybody a serving, and the companions dug in without talk.

"No more for me," Ryan said, pushing away the plate of tiny bones. He wiped his mouth with an Army napkin and released a tremendous belch.

"In Arab countries that is a mark of appreciation," J.B. said, then chuckled, slicing a small steak off a nondescript roast. He knew it was rat, but fresh meat was healthier than the predark foods, even if the MRE packs did taste better.

"Damn straight. Best rat I ever had."

"I raided the MRE packs," Krysty said from the kitchen. "Some salt and pepper, a little mint, and rat cooks just fine."

"Mint?" Mildred asked, her fork paused before her face.

The redhead laughed. "Toothpaste."

"Mushrooms best," Dean mumbled, his mouth stuffed full as he shoveled in more roasted meat. He didn't care what it was, as long as there was plenty. The more he ate, the hungrier he seemed to be.

Wisely, Doc used a spoon to ladle the growing boy another heaping portion of the mushrooms. "Don't forget to take some vitamins from the MRE packs after dinner," the man said. "Apparently, the blues had no idea what the tablets were."

"Fools," Jak said, chewing on a leg bone.

Ryan added, "Dead fools."

"Millie, what did you do with the boot soup?" J.B. asked, ripping open a plastic pack and taking a bite of the cherry-nut cake inside. A hundred years old and it was still moist. Predark whitecoats probably thought the mat-trans was their greatest invention. His vote went for vacuum-sealed food packs.

"I sealed the rest in a couple of pots and put them the main refrigerator," Mildred said, pouring hot water from a tea kettle into a cracked mug. It had some sort of an anchor logo with a Latin phrase that was too faded to read. "We have fresh meat now, and the MRE packs for later, but it never hurts to have spare rations tucked away. When we needed it, the soup kept us alive."

"Barely," Jak said in earnest honesty. He added a sprinkle of powdered milk into his coffee, then some sugar. The teenager took a sip and felt the soothing warmth spread through him like a healing potion.

"Damn," he exhaled in satisfaction.

Going to a sink in the kitchen, Ryan washed and went to the weapons table. They had food now, and a way into the home base of the blues. Blasters were now their top priority.

Before they left the tunnel, J.B. had drained the oil from the wag, and once they were back in the redoubt, he filtered it carefully through some washed sheets until satisfied it was pure enough to lubricate the weapons.

"Two crossbows," he said aloud, taking inventory. "Eight arrows with no heads. Twelve AP grenades, two pounds of plas-ex with no detonators. Two gallons of fuel, but no bottles to make Molotovs, a roll of fuse we can't get clean enough to work, a Colt .45 with ten rounds and two Kalashnikovs, each with two 30-round clips, and six loose rounds."

"Better than before," Doc commented, picking his teeth with a sharp bone. "But hardly a cornucopia of ironmongery."

Rising from the dining table, J.B. carried a coffee cup to the weapons on display. "About twenty rounds were damaged and not salvageable," he said, taking a sip. "But I saved the powder, mixed it with some ash from the garage and got three loads for Doc's LeMat. The rest I keep."

"Where did you get the lead?" Dean asked, mopping his plate with a piece of canned bread.

"I had spare lead and wadding," Doc rumbled in reply, patting the handcannon at his belt. "Just no powder or primers. John Barrymore, you are a wonder."

"Do what I can," the Armorer said, finishing his cup of coffee. "Just don't fire that monster too close to me in case I made the mixture too strong."

Slung over his shoulder was the canvas bag that had held the grens they had found. It now served the Armorer as his replacement munition bag. Mildred had appropriated the other bag found in the wag. It was lighter, some sort of polyester mix that was waterproof. She had washed it a dozen times to get the bloodstains out, but some still remained as faint impressions of the original owners. Mildred was already busy rebuilding her stash of med supplies: boiled cloth on sandwich bags for large wounds, some tampons found in a footlocker for small-caliber bullet wounds, a couple of kitchen knives she had ground to razor sharpness on a grinding wheel in the garage, a plastic bottle of boiled water. The physician even used a hacksaw to cut some copper pipe from under a sink to make trach tubes and to drain pus from infected wounds. A pair of pliers and a small set of tweezers completed the kit. It was a start. No matter how well trained any doctor or surgeon was, he or she couldn't do much without the tools of the trade. Bare hands could kill a lot faster than hers could cure. Sad, but true.

"Rats are done cooking," Krysty announced, coming out from behind the counter. "Just have to let them cool for a while, then we can stuff them in the fridge."

"We have enough food for a week," Mildred said, topping off her mug. "Which leaves us with the problem of blasters."

Ryan lifted an AK-47 and ran his hands along the wooden grip. "We have the element of surprise with that tunnel into the quarry," he said, working the bolt and listening to the smooth sound of well-oiled parts. "And we can steal more clips from the blues as we ace them."

"Truth, indeed, my dear friend," Doc intoned. "Yet we need much more plastique to destroy the Kite."

"A hell of a lot more than we have at present," J.B. said. "That's for damn sure."

"No time make more plas," Jak stated calmly, testing the draw on one of his many leaf-bladed throwing knives. "So we jump."

"I just got a belly of food," Ryan said, crossing his arms. "Sure like to keep that for a while before puking my guts out after a bad jump."

Krysty took a seat at the table. "How long should we wait?" she asked, glancing at the physician.

"Hour should do," Mildred answered hesitantly, unwrapping a stick of chewing gum. "Two would be better, though."

"Then we make a jump in two hours," Ryan stated, already disassembling a Kalashnikov for one more thorough cleaning.

As THE LAV-25 drove through the collection of ramshackle huts, the locals watched the armored wag fearfully.

Standing in the turret, Campbell kept his hand on the 25 mm cannon in case of trouble. The wag also came with a 7.62 mm electric machine gun, but Baron Sheffield had removed the blaster to cover the hole in the wall at the Shiloh ville. Reluctantly, the sergeant agreed. Their longblasters and the grens should be enough firepower for any amount of opposition encountered. Especially with a pesthole like this.

The ville was no more than a small creek feeding a muddy puddle, surrounded by huts made from refuse and roofed with mud. There wasn't even a fence of cut logs to keep out the muties, and anybody could make one of those. The locals were either triple-stupe and lazy, or else had a shit load more blasters than they were displaying. Only a handful of badly repaired bolt-action longblasters were visible, and none of the men carried extra rounds in their belts. Those were probably just showpieces used to frighten cold-hearts. The sec man had encountered that trick before many times. A big man with a bushy beard had a handcannon tucked into his belt, and there were a lot of cartridges in the loops. But if there was any powder between the lead and the shell there was no way of knowing until the hammer fell.

Everybody else was carrying axes and shovels, including the women. Campbell snorted in disgust. Farmer weapons. Useless against the LAV, and they knew it. This was all a bluff.

Then he jerked back as he realized metal struts stuck out from the roof of the main hut, and that the walls sloped gently downward...it was the dish, flipped over facedown. Now he could spot the smashed remnants of the support girders used among the others huts, and the crumpling ruins of the blockhouse that had once contained the controls and electric motors to angle the dish at the sats in space. Gone, it was all gone, used by stinking farmers to make huts! A blind rage filled the sec man, although he kept his face calm. The dirt-eating mutie lovers were going to pay for that.

"Stop right there, outies," the bearded man ordered, holding up a hand. "Make a move and we'll cut you down."

"Now, we don't want any trouble here, whitehair," Campbell said with a smile.

"Trouble is what you'll get!" the man shot back, resting a hand on his blaster. "We got you covered good and tight. What you doing in Settee ville?"

Seti ville, the damn fools. "Just here to fuck your women," Campbell said, drawing his Colt and shooting the man in the throat.

Instantly, the rest of the blues cut loose with their Kalashnikovs through the blasterports. The farmers threw the axes and died. The people with rifles cast them aside and pulled crossbows into action. Snarling in rage, Campbell flicked on the cannon, and the people disintegrated under the barrage of shells, their bodies blown to pieces.

Kicking open the back doors, the blues charged onto the street and started to chill every male they saw, young and old. Many tried to flee for the woods, but they never reached the trees alive.

Firing his Kalashnikov at the scurrying figures, Campbell laughed in delight. His troops were tired from being bounced around in the APC for days and needed some exercise. This mud pit would do fine for some R&R until they left for Virginia to hunt for the next dish.

Separating from the howling mob, a scraggly white-hair dashed into her rickety hut and came back with a huge handcannon. She cocked the hammer and pulled the trigger, but the big bore blaster only made a soft bang and sprayed out some pretty sparks. A laughing blue shirt shot her in the hip and stomach. As the whitehair fell, she fired again, the weapon booming in discharge. A round slammed into the turret just below Campbell, missing him by an inch.

Snarling, the sergeant flicked the cannon into operation for a moment, the old woman and her hut vanishing in thunder and flame.

The slaughter was over within minutes. The blues herded the surviving women into the middle of the ville, making them stand in the muddy hole. Ruthlessly, they weeded out the ugly, the old and the pregnant, the lifeless bodies splashing into the dirty water.

"Please, not my daughter," a woman begged, hugging the whimpering girl. "She ain't never been with no man!"

Brutally slapping her hard across the face, Davies grinned as he pulled the mother out of the mud by the collar of her tattered dress. "Good! I like them fresh," he said, leering. "Going to do you both, so you better show her how it's done right, or I'll hurt her real bad!"

Striding from the LAV, Campbell started for another girl in a tattered white dress, when an older woman darted from the crowd and grabbed him by the leg.

"Take me. I ain't much with looks," she pleaded, "but I can do things no young'un can. Dirty things you never thought of. Make a gaudy slut gag."

Campbell hauled the woman to her feet and ripped open her dress, her bare breasts spilling into view. The woman made no sound as he squeezed her soft flesh until tears filled her eyes.

"Yeah, you'll do," he said, pinching a nipple. "Okay, boys, take what you want and ace the rest. This slut is mine."

As the sergeant pushed the woman toward the wag, the other blue shirts forced the remaining females into the ruin of the dish. Laughing and jeering, the men forced the women to strip each other naked and tie themselves to the tables and beds with their own clothing. Soon, only the sounds of muffled sobs and the slap of wet flesh could be heard in the isolated ville.

TWO HOURS LATER, the companions gathered in the control room of the redoubt near the door to the mattrans chamber.

"Made straws for teams, draw," Jak said, holding out a fist. A collection of plastic broom bristles jutted from his pale hand.

Scowling, Ryan shook his head. "Too risky. We go in balanced teams. Two each, point and anchor. J.B. with me. Krysty with Dean, Jak with Mildred."

"Who goes first?" Dean asked.

"Ryan or me always take point," J.B. said, polishing his glasses. "Same goes for here."

"And what about me?" Doc asked.

"Jumps hit you too hard," Krysty stated, brushing back her waving hair. "We can't take the chance of you passing out for hours. The LD button only works for thirty minutes. We'd lose you forever."

"Besides, one of us should be fully awake here just in case of trouble," Ryan added gruffly. "I want that damn cannon of yours ready to cover my ass in case we come back with a sec droid chasing us."

Doc said nothing for a few minutes, then relaxed his tense stance. "Then, you may consider me, Paris," the man pledged. "None shall breech these gates of Troy."

Arming themselves from the meager supply of weapons, Ryan and J.B. each took a Kalashnikov, one extra clip and two grens. Except for their knives, the men left behind their other weapons. There was no sense carrying deadweight when they would need every ounce free to haul back supplies.

"Krysty, take the Colt. You and Doc stand guard here behind the comp console," Ryan directed, slinging the Russian rapidfire over a shoulder. "Shoot anybody with us that's carrying a blaster. Jak, Dean and

Mildred, take grens and stand guard in the hallway. Kill anything that gets past Krysty and Doc.''

''May Gaia protect you,'' Krysty said.

Nodding his thanks, Ryan turned toward the chamber door. After he and J.B. stepped inside, the one-eyed man closed the door and waited. As always, the mechanism paused for a few moments, as if waiting for a destination code to kick in. Then the machine began to activate a random jump.

Slowly, a swirling mist began to cloud the chamber, twinkling lights like tiny stars shooting through the metal disks of the floor. Then the thickening mists masked the men, and it seemed as if they dropped through the solid floor into infinity.

Wild visions filled their minds, and Ryan grimly knew it was the start of a jumpmare. Sometimes the illusions were pleasant, fantasies of blue skies, green pastures and sex. But more often they were horrid visions of doom and pain. This time it was an endless kaleidoscope of disjointed scenes: Ryan standing above the body of his brother Harvey, a black horse galloping into the horizon silhouetted by a swollen red sun, Krysty glancing over her shoulder and smiling just as a bullet plowed through her skull, removing most of her features. Ryan's hands were covered with blood, burning blood whose fumes rose to fill the skies as sirens howled and jetfighters soared away launching salvo after salvo of missiles that streaked off into space, the contrails twisting and darkening into loaves of fresh bread. The smell filled his mind, his stomach lurched with pain, and then the merciful veil of unconsciousness claimed him.

GASPING FOR BREATH, Ryan shook uncontrollably, bitter bile rising into his mouth. He forced it back down, only to have it rise once more in rebellion. Nearby, J.B. was sprawled on the cold plastic, twitching and shaking.

Precious minutes ticked away before the men were able to force themselves erect and take stock of their surroundings. The walls of the chamber were solid yellow, almost a gold in color, with tiny flakes of bluish material.

"New...redoubt," J.B. croaked, wiping the sweat off his face. "Never been here before."

With fumbling fingers, Ryan hit his wrist chron, and the second hand began to sweep. "Come on," he muttered, using the AK-47 as a crutch to help get to his boots. "Only got...twenty minutes remaining."

Weakly, the men opened the door and stumbled into a control room that was a near duplicate of the one they had just departed. The control room was clean, the comps humming softly, the screens scrolling with coded commands. Outside the control room, the corridor was streaked with fire stains, doors buckled in and the jambs partially melted.

"Clean," J.B. reported, checking the rad counter on his lapel.

Shifting the grip on his longblaster, Ryan grunted, saving his breath. Advancing to the next level, the stairs began to get cleaner and soon they smelled green growing plants.

"Hydroponic garden?" J.B. asked, his hands easy on the Kalashnikov submachine gun. The weapon had an eight-pound trigger as a safety precaution against firing if dropped or jostled. The Armorer had adjusted that, and now the blaster worked on a hair trigger.

Two pounds of pressure, and it would spit subsonic lead at 600 rounds per minute.

Tense, Ryan tested the air again, but there was no trace of the hypnotic perfume of that deadly flower from Georgia. Lots of plants were mutated, some of them even better than in predark days. But not that thing he and Krysty had found inside that deadly sports arena.

Bypassing all other levels, the men headed straight for the armory. Most of the redoubts were exactly the same, and the companions could find their way through the redoubts with their eyes closed, a feat that had saved their lives several times. Only a scant few were oddballs, with unique designs or layouts. Thankfully, this wasn't one of them.

Passing a skeleton on the stairs, they entered the garage and stopped. There were no tools on the walls, no wags in the parking spaces, even the fuel drums were missing. Those were often empty, but almost always still in the redoubt.

Worse, the entire roof of the redoubt was gone, windblown trash and leaves filling the garage. A warm breeze blew over the men as they glanced at the unfamiliar stars overhead. None of the known constellations were in view.

"Resembles the Southern Cross," Ryan said irritably, looking upward.

J.B. shrugged. "Could be. But why would the American government set a redoubt in Australia?"

"Why would they put one in Japan or Russia? Or seal that tunnel closed with plaster? Who the fuck knows? The old whitecoats were crazy."

"Mighty odd," the Armorer agreed.

Somewhere in the back of his mind, Ryan felt as

if an important piece of the puzzle of the redoubts had just fallen into place, but he couldn't understand its subtle meaning. This was something he would have to think hard about later.

A beeping sounded from his wrist chron. "Ten more minutes," he announced. "Five to reach the mat-trans unit, gives us five. Double-time to the armory!"

The men sprinted across the garage, only to find the corridor that led to the armory was also carpeted with leaves, the door sagging on broken hinges, fronting an empty room. The hundreds of shelves were vacant, and not a single ammo clip or loose round was anywhere in sight.

Going to a pile of junk, J.B. lifted the top off a crate marked Claymore Mines. Inside there were only empty slots in the mass of foam cushions.

"Nothing," J.B. stated, and sailed the lid across the room to crash into a distant wall.

"This redoubt has been looted long ago," Ryan agreed, glancing around one last time before heading for the stairs. "Let's go."

Returning to the mat-trans unit, Ryan's watch began to beep a warning as he hit the LD button. The electronic mists rose from the floor, engulfing them once more.

"Are we late?" J.B. asked, worried. "Did we miss the thirty-minute mark?"

"Find out soon," Ryan growled, clutching his longblaster and bracing for the coming onslaught of jump sickness.

Chapter Twelve

Splashing through the wetlands, the LAV-25 of Alpha team rolled over snakes and logs with equal ease. Gators bawed at the vehicle's approach, but backed away from its bad smell and retreated to their secret underwater lairs. Humming insects bobbed about the machine, searching for flesh to feed upon, but found only impenetrable steel and sizzling hot exhaust, the reek killing them in midair. Snug inside, the sec men relaxed in the cool breeze of the air conditioner and ate a meal from MRE packs.

The armored wag dipped as its front wheels found a deep hole, then leveled as the back wheels spun in the mud and forced the APC onto hard ground. Thick Spanish moss hung in curtains off the sickly trees, black birds with two heads flying slowly through the humid air. Everywhere the rusted bodies of predark cars dotted the wetlands. Hoods had been removed, displaying mossy engine blocks to the inclement weather, or exposing gaping holes where the engines had once been. Some of the wags were completely submerged under the water, only their roofs showing, or thin antennas sticking up like metallic reeds.

Smoking a cig and eating a sandwich, Lieutenant Brandon wasn't surprised by the condition of the vehicles. Auto junkyards could be looted for lots of things—tires to resole boots, windshields removed to be windows in a house, seat cloth to make clothing. Radiators made good stills to cook shine, old-fashioned batteries had lead plates inside to melt into new bullets. Sometimes there were even tool kits in the trunks, or better, suitcases full of clean clothes and sometimes even blasters. The fuel tanks were always empty. There were magnets in the radio speakers a smart person could use to make compass needles, the needles coming from manual carburetors, not those fancy injector things. Those were useless. Floor mats sown together made rain gear that could keep you alive in an acid rain storm, and paper maps in the little dashboard box could be used when you went to the lav. The plastic ones were only good for patching a small hole in a roof, but the papers ones were very good. Oil pans were good cooking pots, hubcaps could be used as plates. Safety harnesses could be made into belts, and you could use the mirrors to reflect candlelight, making one as bright as two. And for reasons lost in time, a lot of cars carried bags of sand or rock salt for no reason anybody had ever figured out.

Rolling over the wrecks, smashing bodies and cracking windshields, the LAV-25 plowed relentlessly through a hanging wall of creepers, passing a tiny island in the shallow water. A few trees covered with moss partially hid a ramshackle hut of tin and plywood. Rusty license plates shingled the roof, strips of fibrous material from the dashboard firewalls peeking out from underneath, and shiny hubcaps dotted the walls, but there was no way of knowing whether those were for protection or merely decoration.

A hairy man clothed in rags and mirrored sunglasses stood by the hut, a homemade blaster made from exhaust pipes tightly clenched in both hands. As the wag neared, he cocked back both hammers until the rocker-arm springs clicked into position, ready to drive the nails forward and set off the twin charges. Loaded with window glass squares and lug nuts, the man braced himself against the numbing recoil of the big bore weapon.

Having no interest in wasting ammo or time, the driver rolled past the hermit, Brandon calmly eating his sandwich as he tracked the man with the 25 mm cannon merely for fun, but with no intention of firing.

THE HERMIT WATCHED the wag until it was a tiny mote in the distance, then as it disappeared into the vines and moss.

"Damn fools," he mouthed over toothless gums. "Think that toy's gonna save them? Haw!" The laugh startled some birds, and they took to the sky on ebony wings. Faraway, a stinger called for its mate, and something large splashed into the water.

"Idiots," the man snuffled, and went inside the tin hut to start to cook dinner. The nets had caught a lot of catfish this day, and he planned to fry the whole batch. He'd make stew from what he couldn't eat at one sitting, and the rest he'd poison and feed to the gators. About time to make some new clothes.

As he was rattling the pots and pans, an odd sound made the man turn, and he gasped in shock.

"Who the hell are you?" he demanded, reaching for his makeshift weapon. The lance took him full in the chest, going completely through and burying itself halfway through the back wall.

Stealthily, the lone barb entered the hut and started to eat the raw catfish quickly. There was no dry earth in the wetlands, and he needed food badly. The men in blue shirts were near. Soon he would have them and the feasting would truly begin.

AS THE SWIRLING electronic mists faded, Ryan and J.B. rolled limply on the floor. Opening the door, the other companions rushed into the chamber and checked them for damage.

"No wounds," Mildred stated, running her hands expertly over their forms. "No broken bones, either. Just jump sickness. Help me get them into the room across the hall."

"Not control room?" Jak asked, surprised.

"They might be asleep for hours," the physician said. "A double jump can hit hard. Only be in the way in the control room if there's any trouble."

The teenager grunted in agreement.

"Unfortunately, I see no new blasters," Doc noted, taking Ryan by the shoulders, while Jak got his feet. Krysty and Mildred did the same for J.B. The unconscious men mumbled while they were hauled out of the chamber, but the words were too low to understand.

Laying them on the carpeted floor in the office across the hall, Mildred slid sofa cushions under their heads to make the men comfortable. "Sleep is the best thing for them now," she said. "I have a big pot of black coffee warming in the kitchen for when they wake up."

Tenderly, Krysty brushed a hand along the scar that ran down Ryan's face. "I'm just glad they came back alive," she stated softly.

"Me too," Dean said.

"Both tough," Jak praised. "Hard chill."

Standing, Doc rumbled, "Hard is not the same as impossible, my young friend."

"Guess it's our turn now," Krysty said, taking the AK-47 from Ryan and checking the clip. Not a shot had been fired. Good. She took the spare clip from his pocket, along with the two grens. Dean took the other blaster from J.B. and the grens.

Slinging the blaster over a shoulder, Krysty undid her gun belt and gave the Colt .45 to Jak. "Stay sharp," she warned.

"Razor," the teenager said grimly, buckling the blaster around his waist. Jak checked the draw and settled the gun belt a little lower on his hips.

Closing the door to the office, the companions went back into the control room, Jak and Doc taking positions behind the console, with Mildred staying in the corridor, a primed gren in each hand.

"Ready?" Dean asked, swinging open the door to the mat-trans chamber.

Briefly, Krysty checked her wrist chron, making sure it was working. "Ready," the redhead answered.

Entering the chamber, they closed the door, sat and waited. Moments later the primary circuits flared with power, and the mists swirled into existence around their heads and boots until a silent hurricane of twinkling stars engulfed them, the lights flashing faster and more brightly with every heartbeat....

OUTSIDE, THE SUN WAS starting to set, colored streamers of clouds filling the sky like a tortured rainbow. Softly, the wind moaned over the bare landscape of Shiloh valley, the hard ground vacant of even leaves or dust. What the compacted ash hadn't trapped, the acid rain had dissolved or washed away.

Tapping steadily on the keypad next to the big black door, the old slave gasped in astonishment as the massive portal set into the strange hillock suddenly rumbled open, showing a long corridor. The walls were smooth, the high ceiling lined with glowing light tubes unlike anything he had ever seen. The floor was dirty with a thin layer of ash, and laying prominently in sight was a handcannon. A shiny new blaster just lay there waiting to be taken.

Furtively, the whitehair cast a glance over his shoulder to the snoring sec man wrapped in a blanket and leaning against the Hummer. The low campfire cast a reddish glow over the man and wag, making them appear to be painted in blood.

As the slave took a hesitant step toward the blaster, he inadvertently touched the keypad, and the mammoth door began to close. Hastily, he jumped out of the way, and it sealed with a resounding boom. Instantly, the sec man was standing, his blaster out, eyes blinking away the sleep.

"What the fuck was that?" he demanded, the muzzle of the weapon swinging back and forth.

"Just thunder, sir," the slave said, looking at the darkening sky. "Nothing important, sir. Just thunder."

Suspicious, the sec man studied the growing twilight, then sat again, wrapping the blanket around his shoulders.

"Toss some more wood on the fire," the blue shirt ordered around a yawn.

"Yes, sir. At once, sir," the whitehair replied, all the while mentally repeating the sequence that opened the portal to the bunker over and over. Freedom was close. Soon, very soon.

LAYING ON THE FLOOR of the mat-trans chamber, Krysty and Dean violently heaved for several minutes, their stomachs rebelling at the instantaneous transportation. As the sickness slowly faded from their bodies, the woman and boy struggled to their feet and glanced around the mat-trans chamber. Lights glowed in the patterned metal disks set in the floor and ceiling. The armaglass walls were a pale blue streaked with soft gray.

"I think I know this place," Krysty said, feeling confused. For some unknown reason she was trying to hear the sound of a distant siren. But there was only silence.

"Not familiar to me," Dean countered, going to the chamber door, which opened easily. The woman and boy were triple-alert, their weapons up and ready.

The next room was rectangular, roughly five yards by three, and quite empty except for some wall shelves and a plastic table with a copper bowl. There was residue inside that resembled dried blood. Acting on impulse, Krysty tapped the bowl with a fingernail, and it rang with the clarity of a bell. Spent brass was scattered about on the floor in a variety of calibers. Then it all came rushing back to her.

"Gaia, protect us," Krysty whispered. "This is the first redoubt! The big one in Alaska! The first redoubt we ever jumped to, that is."

Cradling the AK-47, Dean brightened. "The place with the big armory where Doc first got his LeMat and J.B. his Uzi?"

"Yes." The woman sighed, her shoulders slumping. "That's the redoubt I mean."

"Hot pipe! Let's get going!" Dean cried, stumbling for the hallway door. "Dad told me this place has the biggest armory of any redoubt! We can make a couple of trips with the LD button and get all the ammo and food we need! Clothes, missiles, grens. We could load a wag and drive into the chamber!"

"Don't bother running," Krysty said, slumping against the cool wall. "This base is useless to us."

Already partially out the door, Dean turned with a stern expression. "What do you mean?" he demanded anxiously. "It's got everything we need!"

"And more," Krysty agreed sadly. "It's also the biggest redoubt we ever encountered. Miles and miles wide. I remember it taking us an hour to walk to the main intersection of corridors, and then it was even farther to the armory."

Dean glanced at his chron. Seventeen minutes to go. "Aw, shit." He frowned, then started for the door again. "We can at least take a fast recce. Mebbe something got dropped."

Her red hair coiling nervously, Krysty rose and followed the boy into the control room. Panels of consoles blinked in silent rhythms as the great machine conferred with other comps, testing circuits. There was some spent brass on the floor, and an empty cigar box on a console, the plastic smeared with brown stains that vaguely resembled old blood.

Resting the Kalashnikov on a shoulder, Krysty tried to recall if anybody had been wounded on their last jump here. Finn had been shot, somebody else also. Was it Henn, or Okie? They had also gotten a new member of the crew, Lori Quint. She had been with Doc for quite a while before... Krysty shook her head to dispel the dark thoughts. Too many dead. It was difficult to keep track.

"Nothing," Dean announced, returning from the

hallway. "Might as well leave." Petulantly, he kicked over a chair and stomped back to the mat-trans chamber.

"Mebbe in the next redoubt," Krysty said hopefully. "We find a lot of bases with a few supplies remaining. Only need one of those."

"We'll find blasters," the boy agreed confidently. "Just a matter of how soon."

Climbing inside the chamber, they hit the LD button and let the swirling mists and twinkling lights cast them into nothingness, and beyond.

As THE NOISE of the chamber faded, the door to the hallway swung open and a stooped graybeard in furs walked into the control room. The old Russian scanned the room, certain that strangers had invaded the redoubt.

"Could have sworn I heard voices," he muttered, glancing around. Then he placed a hand on the control console and felt the heat rising off the comps.

"Yes, visitors," he hissed. "I will have to do something about that."

Then he began to randomly press buttons and flip switches, smiling as lines of data began to scroll up the banks of comp screens and a distant hum increased in volume.

"They won't come back!" The man laughed. "Gone forever."

FALLING THROUGH infinity, Krysty and Dean hurtled through the electronic void when they felt a jarring lurch and knew that something was terribly wrong. A dimly seen floor materialized beneath them, and both were seized by bitter cold. Somehow, the air felt slow and it was difficult to breath. As the mists vanished, their clothes became instantly soaked and each realized they were underwater.

Skeletons of rotting bodies drifted past the choking pair, the rusted remains of blasters laying on the slimy armaglass floor. Dimly seen through the cloudy water, the chamber door was marked with discolorations and deep scores. The other prisoners had died trying to get free before drowning.

Frantically, Krysty reached out for the LD button, but Dean was already there. As the button was depressed, the mists began to build once more, and they fought to keep from trying to draw in a breath of air. Hearts pounding, each thought their aching lungs were about to burst when they dropped once more into the artificial abyss of nothingness, but this time unsure of where they were going, or if they would get there alive...

THE SHALLOW WATERS of the Pennsylvania wetlands gradually became dry land, and Alpha team's LAV increased speed as it moved effortlessly across the fields of stubby grass.

"Sir!" the gunner in the turret called. "Something big on the horizon!"

"A ville?" Brandon asked, dry shaving with a plastic razor from one of their packs.

"I think it's a dish, sir!"

Dropping the blue stick, the officer rushed to an ob slit. "Half speed," Brandon ordered. "We want to recce the area first."

The wag slowed to a crawl, and the sec men crowded the ob slits and blasterports to catch a glimpse. Sure enough, rising above the morass of trees was a dish, just like the one at their base, only much bigger. Almost double the size.

"Jackpot," the corporal announced grinning around a cig, and slapped a private on the shoulder.

"We still have to check out the ville," the lieutenant countered. "But so far, so good."

Rolling closer, every weapon at the ready, the sec men could see that the predark dish was intact and in near-perfect condition. The concrete bunker at its base was almost identical to the one at their own ville. The framework of supporting girders seemed intact. A heavy infestation of thorny vines covered the dish and frame, but the slaves could clear those away in a couple of hours.

"We found it," the driver shouted. "Hot damn, we found one!"

"Shut up," Brandon ordered, staring out an ob slit, a hand resting on his holstered blaster. "How stupe are you?"

"What do you mean, sir?"

He pointed with a thumb. "See that? The animals aren't checking this wag out very closely. It's strange, but not frightening."

"Wags been here before," the corporal puffed. "Stay hot, boys. We could have company."

In response, the gunner in the turret slapped the breech of the electric cannon, making sure the ammo belt was firmly in place. "We're ready," Davies said confidently.

"Everybody out," the lieutenant ordered brusquely. "I want a perimeter sweep of fifty yards in every direction. Chill anything you find. We're not going to make the same mistake twice!"

Grabbing their blasters, the blues exited the vehicle

and spread out in a loose circle, plowing through the bushes and tall weeds, their blasters steadily chattering at anything they found. Soon, dead animals and birds were strewed across the ground, pumping their blood onto the dry soil.

While the troops were busy, the corporal walked to the blockhouse and risked shaking one of the support columns. The steel girders didn't move.

"Strong as chains!" the sec man called out happily. "We got a winner, sir. This dish is perfect shape."

"Any holes or cracks?" the lieutenant asked, walking closer.

"Smooth as a whore's tongue."

"Good," Brandon replied, and pulled the map from his pocket to check their location. "Now there's supposed to be a big ville nearby, just to the west. We find that, and we can go home."

Just then, a sec man cried out and disappeared from sight. The others recoiled, and another man screamed as he slid into the dirt, the grass closing over his head without leaving a trace. His cries seemed to echo from underground for a few moments, and then there was only silence.

"Muties!" a corporal shouted, firing his AK-47 in short bursts at the greenery underfoot.

A gray tentacle snaked up from the ground and grabbed a second blue shirt around the chest, the thorny tip sinking into his flesh like a fish hook. Quickly, the sec man next to him fired at the ropy limb. The slugs blew a hole through the tentacle, exposing only strange undulating fibers inside, no meat or bones. Convulsing, the gray limb dragged its captive headfirst into the soil, leaving his blaster behind.

"It's underground! Shoot the grass!" Brandon ordered, running for the APC. What the fuck was this thing, a plant or an animal? Both could be killed with blasters, but only if they could see it. And dirt was about the best bullet stopper there was. Some villes were merely surrounded by a wall of cloth bags filled with dirt. Arrows, bullets, nothing could get through that. A few feet underground, and the thing might as well be armor plated for all the good the Kalashnikovs would do.

The lieutenant fired his handcannon wildly at the soil as the others hopped about for their lives, the AK-47s spraying lead at the grass. When he was close enough, Brandon threw himself at the open doors and landed inside the wag. With a kick, he closed the door and threw the lock.

A third tentacle shot straight up into view, and the corporal hacked at it with his Bowie knife. The blade became embedded halfway through and the limb was withdrawn, taking the knife. Wordlessly, the corporal retreated and a sec man charged forward, shoving his blaster barrel into the ground while firing.

"No!" the corporal shouted, hastily raising an arm for protection.

The Kalashnikov chattered briefly, then seemed to expand, the breech stretching and breaking apart, as the jammed weapon exploded. A flash from the blast masked the man, then he was back, staring in horror at the tattered stumps of his arms, blood pumping from the open ends with every heartbeat. His mutilated face contorted in a wordless scream. The sec man staggered, and his pants and shirt turned red from the thousands of deep cuts in his flesh. Blood was everywhere and he fell to the ground face first, transfixed from the shock and the pain.

As if this were a signal, the field erupted with writhing tentacles: one snatched a bird hopping on the soil; another crushed a rabbit hidden in a bush. The men yelled in fear and fired their weapons in every direction. The weird limbs shook with the passage of the bullet through them, then headed directly for the source of the noise.

A blue shirt near the framework of the dish was hooked and dropped his blaster to grab the metal struts with both hands. His screams increased as another tentacle caught him in the thigh, and his flesh started to rip away in pieces as the mutie tried to claim the struggling food.

"No, you nuke-sucking bastard!" he screamed, then, as his weakening hands slipped off the struts, the man pulled the ring on a gren and released the arming lever. "Fuck you! Take you with me, motherfuck!"

The lashing tentacles hauled the sec man from sight, the loose soil filling the hole after he was gone. Then a muffled blast shook the field, and all of the tentacles shot stiffly into the air as a section of the ground heaved skyward.

"Hurt you, did we?" a private snarled, hauling a gren from his pocket. "Then try this!"

Following his lead, several of the blues tossed explosive charges, then ducked. Thunder shook the field, and when the roiling smoke cleared two more sec men were in pieces, others badly wounded. The tentacles grabbed the chunks of warm meat and took them away.

"Stop that, you idiots!" the corporal commanded. "Davies, use the freaking cannon and chill this mutie freak!"

The 25 mm cannon cut loose, blows chunks of greenery sky-high, fireballs blossoming under the furious assault. Instantly, dozens of the tentacles lashed at the wag, slapping the hull with ringing force as they tried to gain entrance.

Now with a visible target, the blues concentrated their firepower on the LAV, cutting a limb in two. As the tip fell away, yellowish fluid squirted from the stump. Suddenly, a quake shook the field and the back end of the LAV dipped into the soil. The lieutenant and the gunner screamed from within the APC as the vehicle dropped another yard lower. The big diesel engines started with a roar, the double rows of studded tires spinning in the loose soil, trying to find purchase.

The remaining sec men rushed toward the sinking LAV, firing their blasters at the sticky soil, a few tossing grens. Cutting himself off in the middle of a warning, the corporal backed away from the scene as quietly as possible, waiting for the slaughter.

Exhaust spewing, engines roaring, wheels spinning, the LAV bucked like a living thing as it tilted awkwardly, first this way, then that way. Out of control, the cannonfire swept through the defenders, blowing the sec men to pieces. The corporal used the gory diversion to race away from the area and desperately climb up the support column of the dish until he was high in the sky.

Tentacles, vines, limbs, whatever the hell they were, rose from the land by the dozens, grabbing everything, every bloody boot and severed hand. In moments the blues were gone, and the limbs crawled over the hull of the struggling APC, jabbing into the air vents and blasterports, wrapping around the studded tires, the door handles, stanchions, seizing anything that offered a solid grip. Holding his breath, the corporal watched as the men inside the vehicle fought for their lives, firing through the blasterports and shoving out grens. The electric cannon never stopped firing, the 25 mm shells tearing up the landscape as the machine was inexorably drawn lower and lower into the churning soil. The headlights flared on, and somebody tried to open the back doors, the latch rattling loudly. Soon the grass reached the ob slits, rose over the stanchions, and then the hood, until only the turret itself was visible.

As soil covered the exhaust ports, the noise of the engines abruptly ceased. Then the top hatch was flung open and the lieutenant crawled into view. A tentacle caught him by the wrist, and Brandon fired a blaster, blowing off his own hand. Another ropy limb wrapped itself around his calf, sinking the barb deep into his leg. Openly weeping, the sec man fired his blaster twice more at the thorny vines that held him prisoner, then reversed the weapon and fired. The bullet removed a chunk of his skull, but the dying man was still breathing, his single remaining eye staring wide in horror as the LAV was hauled below the field and out of sight.

Somewhere below the rippling waves of green grass, there came a short ripping noise of the electric cannon using its battery power to strike at the enemy one last time. Then a deep and terrible silence engulfed the wooded area.

Dripping sweat, the corporal stayed where he was, trying to control his breathing. Minutes passed, then an hour, before he decided to risk moving. Climbing down the girders, he eased a boot to the ground and waited, ready to instantly climb back into the maze of struts at the slightest sign of disturbance. When nothing occurred, the sec man realized the mutie had to be busy with its food and this was his chance to escape.

Gently lowering the other boot, he then took off at a run, grabbing a blaster from the ground as he passed by, angling for the imagined safety of the forest. The roots there should be too thick for the weird mutie to travel through. Rock would be better, but he was a long distance from any real mountains. The forest would do. He'd travel out of there by jumping from tree branch to tree branch if necessary, until he was far away from this chilling zone.

Reaching the edge of the field, he leaped over a log and landed with a thump, then froze motionless. Shitfire, he'd made noise! Slow minutes passed while the blue shirt waited for a reaction. A soft wind moved over the field and through the trees' rustling leaves. The dish creaked slightly behind him, and a tiny scorpion scuttled over his boot and under a flat rock.

Finally, the sec man relaxed and started to walk again. He had to be far enough away from the mutie that it hadn't heard him. Good. Now all he had to do was walk the three hundred miles back to Shiloh and his problems were over. He had found a working dish! Then it occurred to the man that with the loss of the APC, he might not be welcome in Shiloh anymore. Why not simply leave, head west and become a mercie for some baron.... No, once Sheffield got the Kite under control he would take over the whole continent, and when he found the sole survivor of Alpha team, the punishment he got as a deserter would be a lot worse than merely being eaten alive by any mutie, that was damn sure.

Slinging his rifle, the corporal headed due south. He had a long way to go. Hopefully, Beta team was doing better than his decimated group. They sure as fucking hell couldn't be doing any worse! At least, he was safe. That was something, anyway.

Unexpectedly, a humanoid figure holding a lance rose from the evergreen bushes in front of the startled sec man. Frantically working the bolt of his borrowed AK-47, the corporal swung the blaster around, then paused when he realized that the weapon might not even be loaded. Black dust! He had ammo clips in the pouch at his belt, but those might as well be on the moon for all the good they did here.

Warily, the barb waited for the expected attack, watching for any opening when he could throw the lance and dodge the deathfire of the tube machine. The corporal put on a combat face and waited for the other man to throw, before risking a shot. The bolt had worked, but that might only mean a single live round remaining in the clip. If he missed, it was all over.

Weapons poised and ready, the two opponents stood amid the bushes, each unsure of his next move.

Chapter Thirteen

Much too early, noise came from the mat-trans unit, and the three companions drew their weapons in tense expectation.

"Already?" Jak said, cocking back the hammer on the Colt.

"Something's wrong," Mildred stated, taking a position along the wall near the door. The gren felt heavy in her right hand, the smooth ring of the pin clenched tight in her left.

"Sheffield?" Ryan asked from the doorway across the hall. The man was pale, but his panga was unsheathed and ready. Behind him, J.B. stood with a grim expression, his own knife held in a throwing grip.

Doc braced the LeMat on top of the console, the muzzle pointed straight at the door. "We shall find out soon enough."

As the machinery went still, the companions heard a splash, then nothing else. Going to the door, Doc threw it open and greenish water rushed out over his boots.

"By the Three Kennedys!" he started, then saw his friends laying limply on the floor. "Mildred, hurry!"

Rushing forward, the physician tucked away the gren and knelt in the puddle. Grabbing Dean by the shoulders, she turned him over and pounded the boy on the back. In response, he heaved out a stomach full of thin fluid. Mildred kept hitting his back until some color returned to his face, and he began breathing normally.

"Hot pipe," Dean said, coughing raggedly, then wiping his face with a dripping sleeve. "We...made it...."

Immediately, Mildred went to Krysty and started beating her soundly between the shoulder blades with an open palm. Her damp hair sluggishly flexing, Krysty spewed out the contents of her stomach and shook off the physician, hacking for air.

"What wrong?" Jak asked, helping the boy to stand.

"They're okay," Mildred announced, standing. "Just swallowed some bad water."

The words made Dean go to the corner and retch again, the thought of the rotting corpses filling his mind.

"What is this?" Ryan asked, lifting a canvas bag from the mat-trans chamber. Malodorous greenish water poured from a small rip in the side.

"Grabbed it as we went," the boy said, rubbing his stomach. "Better than nothing."

"Anything useful?" J.B. asked without hope.

Ryan tugged the bag open and inspected the contents. "MRE packs," he said, sounding pleased as he lifted one into view. "Being underwater wouldn't hurt them a bit."

"How many are there?" Mildred asked,

He did a rough count, riffling the packs with a fingertip. "About forty. Enough for another week."

"Must have been field rations for a predark recce squad," J.B. guessed, running a hand over the outside of the bag. Dimly, the faded green letters USMC could be seen on the camou-colored material. "Bad for the Navy boys, good for us."

Lifting a pack, Doc inspected the foil for any holes or corrosion. "Looks perfect, dear boy," he rumbled in delight. "Ah, never before have I so truly yearned for the culinary delights of artificial creamed chip beef on canned toast."

"Pentagon calls it shit on a shingle," Mildred said, smiling.

"Indeed, madam, but they could order out pizza and chicken wings. Ambrosia comes in many flavors these days, some great, some on toast."

Frowning, Jak glanced around, "Hey, where blaster?"

"Dropped it," Dean said, then swallowed to clear his throat. "When we hit the water after the second jump, I lost my grip."

"Second jump?" Ryan said, advancing. "You were only supposed to do one jump."

"Wasn't our choice. Something went wrong with the mat-trans," Krysty answered. "After going to an empty redoubt, we jumped and went to one underwater. We hit the LD button and instead of returning to the empty redoubt came back here. Thank Gaia."

Dean looked at her on the word "empty," but said nothing. It was close enough to the truth.

"Dark night," J.B. stormed, taking off his hat and crumpling it. "We're short enough as it is without losing a blaster!"

"Into the control room," Doc ordered brusquely. "Some hot food will help all of us think more clearly."

Leaving the chamber, the companions were startled

when the door slammed shut behind them and the noise of the mat trans rose and faded away.

"Son of a bitch! You don't think...." J.B. started, when the machinery came alive once more.

As the noise faded away, a furious Ryan opened the chamber door and there was a dripping wet Doc, sitting in an expanding puddle. He was drenched to the skin, and his chest heaved for breath, but the missing Kalashnikov was held loosely in his grip.

Rushing forward, a frowning Mildred slid a shoulder under his arm and helped Doc shuffle from the chamber. "Damn fool stunt," she derided angrily. "Could have chilled yourself doing a double jump that fast!"

"Needed the blaster," he mumbled weakly, struggling to smile. "Besides, I only..." The words faded away as terror clouded his eyes, and Doc flinched as if struck a savage blow. "No! Not into the pit with those animals! I swear I'll kill you, Strasser! Gun you down like Oswald did JFK, like Ruby did Jack... you'll die bloody like the Kennedy brothers..." His strength gone, Doc slumped and could only whisper more wild threats.

"Hush," Mildred whispered, as the man slid into unconsciousness. She knew that name. Ryan had rescued Doc from the evil clutches of Cort Strasser, sec chief to the baron of Mocsin. The madman had been torturing Doc every day for an indeterminate period of time, horrible things that made her feel unclean just to hear, yet Doc had survived through sheer raw determination. He'd stayed alive and mostly sane only by his iron-bound belief that someday he would return to the Vermont of his past, and be reunited with his beloved wife, Emily. Other men would have died or gone completely mad. Doc chose a different route and lived. She admired him a lot more than she had ever told him.

"Tougher than nails," Jak stated, helping to carry the old man into the control room and placing him in a chair. "Who those names he say?"

"Predark barons who got aced," Ryan said gruffly. "Good thing you're out, Doc, or else I'd kick your skinny ass for a triple-stupe move like this."

"He did save the blaster, and it's undamaged," J.B. reported, wiping it dry with a cloth. The Armorer dropped the clip, poured out some water and slapped in a fresh magazine. "This'll work just fine. Mikhail Kalashnikov made a good blaster."

"Better be right," Jak said, taking the longblaster and the spare clip. "Our turn now."

"Keep them warm and get some hot tea down Krysty and Dean," Mildred directed Ryan, taking the other longblaster. "And just let the old coot sleep it off."

"Shot of shine what need," Jak said knowingly. "I find, bring along."

"Blasters first," Ryan said, taking the Colt .45 and gun belt from the teenager.

"Good luck," J.B. added, belting on Doc's huge LeMat.

Nodding, Mildred dropped her med kit beside the door to the mat-trans chamber as Jak walked inside. Following the teenager, she closed the door and soon the complex machines sang their song and faded into silence.

Slow minutes ticked by in endless procession. Always a fast healer, Krysty got to her feet first and fixed some hot coffee for the others. After a few sips,

Dean was feeling better and started to dig into an MRE pack, using the attached plastic spoon to devour an envelope of corned-beef hash. Blasters cocked, Ryan and J.B. waited patiently for the others to return, sipping the strong military brew.

Crossing the control room, Krysty placed a cup of sweet coffee near the sleeping Doc, then turned abruptly, her hair moving in short lashing movements. "Something has happened," she said, walking toward the chamber door. "They're in trouble. I can feel it."

"Malfunk with the machines?" Ryan asked gruffly. He knew Krysty could sometimes sense things unseen, a talent that had saved their lives more than once. But the ability was random, totally unreliable. Just when you needed it most, it went away, which was why Ryan kept his faith in a good blaster. Steel was always reliable.

"Mildred and Jak are fighting," she whispered, reaching for the closed door with fingertips. "Large... no face...they're coming back!"

With those words, the comp monitors scrolled with commands and the hidden machines revved with power.

The AK-47 held level, Ryan walked to the door and froze when he heard the chatter of auto fire. Throwing open the portal, Ryan and J.B. charged in and separated fast, their weapons searching for targets, but they only found Mildred and Jak inside the chamber, smoking Kalashnikovs held in their hands. However, their clothing was torn in places, and Jak was bleeding from a wound in the shoulder. Spent brass was scattered on the floor, and Ryan realized they had to have jumped while firing their weapons.

"What happened?" he demanded, hauling the

woman to her feet. She clung to him for support, panting for breath. "Changing mass in a jump might turn you inside out!"

J.B. knelt and offered the teenager a canteen. "You two know better than to take a risk like that."

"Had to," Jak said between sips, then splashed some on his bloody shoulder. He winced, but didn't cry out.

"They were at the door," Mildred added. "Damn near came through with us!"

Just then, Krysty came in with the med kit, but Dean stayed in the doorway, a gren in each hand.

"What was it, stickies?" Krysty asked, using a knife to cut open Jak's shirt and exposing the shoulder. It was a flesh wound not very deep, just wide and blistered. "That's laser damage."

"Sec droids," Ryan said, recognizing the blister pattern.

Taking a long pull on the canteen, Mildred nodded weakly. "In the armory. Soon as we picked up some ammo boxes they came charging out of the shadows, firing everywhere. Idiot machines destroyed more than we could ever have taken."

"Lucky you weren't chilled," Krysty stated, washing the area and tying on a clean bandage. "Those things are hard to stop."

Ryan merely grunted, remembering when he had been chased across Deathlands by one of the predark mechanical hunters. It was the closest he had ever come to catching the long sleep.

"Stopped them," Jak grunted, gesturing at the mattrans chamber. "Used thermite grens on fuel stores. No redoubt left."

"Thermite!"

Eagerly, J.B. walked over and lifted the lumpy canvas bags to look inside. "Good haul," he said in appreciation. "Additional MRE packs, some med supplies, half a dozen thermite grens, a few AP grens, box of 12-gauge shotgun shells, two Claymores, bottle of whiskey, two flares, full box of 9 mm APC rounds."

Ryan caught the box of ammo as J.B. went into the control room. Taking his S&W shotgun from the corner, the man shoved a 12-gauge shell into the bottom slot and worked the pump to feed in the cartridge. He did this three more times, then filled the empty loops along the shoulder strap. When he was done, J.B. distributed the remaining shells in several pockets.

Ryan was already at the main console, thumbing rounds into the empty clips for the SIG-Sauer. As he filled each, he tucked them into the pouch on his belt, then slapped the last clip into the butt of the handcannon and jacked the slide.

"Better," he said.

"Any blasters?" Dean asked, as the rest of the companions entered the room.

Mildred scowled. "We never got close. Tried to lure the droids away and then double back, but time was too short."

Studying his friends, Ryan made a command decision. "We're calling it a day," he ordered in a nononsense tone. "Let's get some food and sleep. We can start hunting for weapons again in a few hours."

"Dawn soon," Mildred said, glancing at her wrist chron. "Sleep sounds good."

Krysty started for the control room. Doc was still sprawled asleep in the chair, snoring softly. "Thank Gaia we aren't in a rush," the redhead commented, brushing some hair out of his tired face. "If Sheffield and his sec men left this valley, we'd lose our back door."

"Be shit out of luck if that happens," Ryan stated, starting for the hallway. "Come on, let's go eat."

SEARCHLIGHTS CUT through the Tennessee darkness, the bright rods of light sweeping over the Shiloh ville to brightly illuminate each area in an orderly pattern.

Walking patrol along the wide top of the stone block wall, a blue shirt studied the weird landscape surrounding the ville. Not a blade of grass was in sight, nor a tree or even a bush. Just the oddly flowing bed of gray rock. The ground rose and fell in endless irregularities, the acid rain having solidified wind-blown piles of ash into foamy rock harder than limestone. It was as if a gray winter sea had been instantly frozen, catching the waves before they broke upon the shore. He knew it made farming here impossible, and the sec men would have to move to another location, but the thought neither pleased nor annoyed him. It was just another chore to do for Sheffield, easier than some, harder than most. Nothing special.

"Farmers," the guard muttered and lit a cig off a wooden match. Why would anybody bust his ass to plow dirt, when a smart man got anything he wanted by working for a baron? Being a sec man meant all the food he could eat, a soft bed, clean clothes, women for sex whenever he wanted, and with these Ackyfortysevens the blues could chill any invader. Personally, he didn't understand what Sheffield and Collette needed with the dish and Kite. A blaster in the hand was worth more than any predark sat.

Releasing a stream of white smoke, the sec man

continued his patrol along the top of the thick wall. He remembered starting life as a farmer until raiders hit his town. In the midst of the fight, he saw the locals were losing and shifted sides to stay alive. He opened the ville gates and helped hang his own family. It didn't bother him. Civilians, what the hell good were they? All the tasty food came from a can or an envelope. Raw stuff was crunchy and dirty. None of that shit for him.

A movement amid the stony dunes caught the man's attention, and the guard slid the blaster off his shoulder. His thumb slid along the side, making sure the selector was set for full-auto.

He whistled softly, and another soldier stuck out his head from the kiosk at the front gate. The wall guard jerked a thumb toward the outside, then across his throat. Nodding, the private grabbed his blaster off a peg on the wall and advanced carefully to the gate. The steel bars were less than six inches apart and thicker than a soup can. Not even one of the APC wags could ram through the barrier. Damn thing had taken sixty slaves to move into positions, and four died hanging it on the massive hinges. Nobody could attack the ville from that direction. Muties, however, would and could attack from anywhere, usually when you least expected them.

Suddenly, there was a flurry of motion and the blue shirt fired from the hip, the bullets hitting a screamwing that was gliding straight for the gate. The riddled corpse hit the bars and wiggled through before the blue could track his weapon on the animal again. This time the stream of rounds tore it apart, and the screamwing flopped on the green grass inside the ville, keening in pain, its leathery wings beating feebly as its thin lifeblood flowed from the riddled body.

When the thing finally went still, the sec man walked closer and shot it again in the head, then stomped the screamwing under his boot until its body was only a pulpy mass. Little fuckers were hard to chill, and often came back to bite your ass when you were positive they had taken the last train west. Kicking the dead mutie behind the wall, he jabbed it with a sharp stick and tossed its form into an empty fifty-five gallon oil drum half full of similar corpses.

"Welcome to Shiloh," he snorted in wry amusement, then spun with a curse as a loud explosion ripped apart the night.

A fireball was rising skyward by the gap in the wall, the searchlights moving back and forth to focus on the chink in their perimeter. Sirens began to howl as squads of sec men rushed to the area. As they neared, the blues could see that the blast had cleared the hole of barbed wire for yards, the pungi sticks sheared off at ground level.

"Nobody move!" a sergeant ordered loudly, snapping the bolt on a Kalashnikov. "Wait for them!"

The men assumed a firing line just as a dozen humanoid muties shambled through the smoky darkness, the things dripping drool down curved tusks in their eagerness to reach the norms.

"Fire!" the sergeant shouted, cutting loose with a Kalashnikov at the grouped creatures.

The first staggered and tried to dodge behind the predark Army tank that filled the rest of the hole. Then the ground under its claws blossomed into fire as another Claymore detonated, the explosion hurling the limp corpse skyward in many grisly pieces. The concussion slapped the sec man like an invisible fist, the shotgun rounds peppering the tank and stonework. Hoots of agony could be heard in the billowing smoke, and the sec men fired short volleys seeking live targets. More cries of pain announced success, then there was a sudden silence.

"Stupe things are trying the same trick as the last bunch!" the sergeant growled, ramming in a fresh clip. "You, you and you, form a recce squad. Shoot anything that moves!"

Grim-faced, the blue shirts checked their blasters and walked directly into the smoky, bloody, chaos of the gap, the searchlights casting long shadows before them. Soon there came the chatter of blasterfire, but the anguished screams that followed were from norm throats, not the fanged muties. Then dozens of dark shapes appeared from within the gloom and rushed for the astonished blues.

"Breakthrough!" the sergeant shouted at the top of his lungs, hosing the Kalashnikov wildly as the horde of muties swarmed inside Shiloh ville.

"JUST HAD TO GET the stinking slime off me," Krysty said, padding barefoot from the steamy shower. Wrapped in a towel, the beautiful redhead walked across the officers' quarters to the pile of her freshly laundered clothing on a desk.

There was no reply, only a soft snore from Ryan who was sprawled on the bed. A chair had been pulled beside the man, and a cocked blaster rested within easy reach of his outstretched hand.

Patting herself dry, Krysty gazed at Ryan and smiled. He was the only real man she had ever known, and she couldn't imagine life without him. They were more than merely lovers, they were soul mates, two halves forming a greater whole.

Ryan had taken the opportunity to wash his own clothing along with hers and was stretched naked on the bed, his muscular body covered to the waist by the thin blankets. Scars of a dozen types marred his powerful body: the puckered iris of a bullet hole, the zigzag of an arrowhead yanked loose, the smooth slash of a knifeblade and irregular flat areas of white skin, the remnants of fire damage and electrical shock—souvenirs from torture by sec men and barons he later aced.

Although strikingly attractive, Ryan wasn't handsome. But Krysty had seen handsome before, and it usually masked evil underneath the smooth, easy smile. Ryan was a warrior and a survivor, but more importantly, a man who hadn't fallen from the grace of Gaia in the gore and fight for their survival. If possible, Ryan would never kill again, but simply live in peace. It was an impossible dream, but she knew he would never stop searching for some small corner of the world to call home, where edible crops grew in clean soil, and people didn't need to carry blasters every minute of the day and night. Truly an impossible dream, but it was infinitely more than most dared to even hope for.

Dropping the towel, Krysty placed a slim knee on the mattress, and he came awake instantly. There were no jerky movements or gasps of surprise, no outward signs at all that anything had changed. But the woman knew he was fully awake now, had already cataloged they were alone in the officers' barracks, and was listening to her gentle breathing.

"Tired, lover?" she asked, sliding across the bed-sheet.

Turning over, Ryan glanced at the nude redhead sitting on the edge of the military bed. He recognized the expression in her face, and the way her animated hair was moving slowly about her face. She was the most beautiful woman he had ever been with, and the deadliest. Ryan knew that he more than loved the woman. There were no words that could adequately express what he felt for her, and to try would only be an insult. When something like that occurred, both people simply knew it all the way down to their bones. There were no questions, no rules.

As she crawled toward the supine man, her full breasts swinging from the motion, he immediately began to get hard under the blankets.

"Never that tired," he answered, pulling the covers away.

The redhead took his cock in both hands and gently stroked until he was fully erect. Rising on an elbow, Ryan reached out for her, but Krysty pushed him down again.

"Me this time," she said, straddling the man.

He could feel the heat of her pussy as she rubbed it against his shaft, the moisture and curly hair an electric combination. Ryan ran his hands freely over her body as the woman rubbed closer and harder against his shaft until deliciously engulfing it. The hot confines of her tight pussy fueled his desire, then her special muscles contracted in a swirling motion about his cock, lifting and caressing as she moved back and forth, up and down, in a passionate rhythm. Only the sound of their breathing filled the room for several minutes.

Gently, Ryan pulled her close, her full breasts falling warm and heavy across his bare chest. They kissed, tongues intertwining madly, savoring the taste of each other. Her red filaments laced with his black hair as the man and woman shared breath, their hearts wildly pounding. Then Ryan grabbed her around the waist, pinning Krysty in that position as he started pumping hard and fast, using his thighs to drive his cock into her at greater and greater speeds.

"Gaia!" she gasped, biting a lip, galvanized by the overpowering sensations. "Yes, lover! Yes!"

Their bodies gleaming with sweat, Ryan rode the woman from the bottom, maintaining the motions until Krysty trembled all over, her pussy convulsing. He thrust hard one last time, filling her completely, each lost in the sensual world of physical pleasure, and for a few precious moments, there was no world outside of their arms.

Back arched, hair splayed, Krysty waited for the tingling of the orgasm to pass when there was a sound at the door. They both drew blasters and swung the weapons toward the portal, then relaxed when they heard the telltale step-and-click of Doc walking by, using his swordstick.

"Want to go eat now?" Krysty laughed softly, placing the blaster aside and nestling against the big man's chest.

"Later," Ryan answered, rolling over and placing the woman on a clean area of the bedsheets.

Lustfully, Krysty raked his back with her nails, as he spread her smooth legs wide and slide inside the hot satin once more. Their bodies moving together as one, each was lost in his or her own private world of joyful passion and affection beyond the limitations of words.

SEVERAL LARGE-CALIBER machine guns fired nonstop, the burning tracer rounds forming dotted lines through the nighttime sky over Shiloh ville as the rooftop weapons cut down the muties crawling over the stone block wall in every direction.

"They're everywhere!" a blue shirt shouted, running from the front gate. A mob of muties was on the other side of the steel bars, reaching for him with claws and tentacles. It was worse than any nightmare. He fired his blaster at the inhuman creatures, and a few dropped, but others fought to get closer.

A winged mutie landed on top of the wall and was cut down by machine-gun fire, the heavy rounds slamming the body back into the darkness.

Slinking from the gap was a pack of cougars, their fur changing color to match anything they were near. Their fur was cut by the sharp coils of concertina wire, droplets of clear blood oozing from the wounds. Snarling, they converged on a sec man struggling to clear a jam in his blaster. Flesh was bitten off in bloody gobbets, the high-pitched screaming only lasting a few moments as they ate the man alive.

Then the roar of an engine split the night, and a Hummer charged into view, plowing through the cat-like muties, their bodies smashed against the steel fenders with sickening crunches. One survived the attack, and leaped inside to savage the driver. The blue dragged out a handcannon in time blow off its face. Shoving the Hummer into gear, he sped away, leaving the other men behind.

Small-arms fire peppered the darkness, then the

steady chatter of a large-caliber machine gun ripped the attackers to pieces. Dozens of muties died, but the rest spread throughout the base, hooting wildly as they latched upon anybody who got close. Fangs were buried in throats, tongues licking up the hot spurts of blood. The sec man fired from doorways, from between buildings. The dead and the dying were lining the streets, but the muties kept coming, wave after wave, in countless numbers. And as an ammo clip became exhausted, another norm fell screaming to the ground as his flesh was consumed before his heart had time to stop beating.

Inside the armory, sec men fired volleys through slim notches cut in the thick walls. In the shadows of the night, it was difficult to tell their own men from the muties, and often they didn't pause but fired anyway. Sometimes it was a bestial scream, occasionally a human cry of pain.

"Sir, the fuckers are everywhere!" a sec man panted, thumbing fresh rounds into an exhausted clip. He slammed the magazine into his weapon and worked the bolt, chambering a round. Then he started to load a second clip. A case of 7.62 mm ammo was at his boots, and two more full of grens were on the table for easy access. The door was barricaded with the heavy oak throne, and the window shutters closed for the storm were now nailed tight into place.

"Keep shooting," Sheffield snapped, opening a third case of grens. He cast aside the wood slats and ripped off the protective plastic sheeting with bare hands.

"Any flamethrowers?" Collette asked, tossing more wood into the fireplace. The flames licked high up the flue, and something nosily clawed away from the flames.

"No," he spit angrily, stuffing his pockets full. "We used them up in the slave revolt. Silas never had a chance to get any more fuel tanks."

"Shit! Anything in that Quonset hut except these rapidfires and MRE packs? Another APC, or big whatyacallit?"

"M-60? How should I know?" he yelled in reply, going to a gun rack and taking down an AK-47 with an elaborately carved stock. Sheffield inserted a clip and pulled the arming bolt. "I have the inventory sheets, but haven't inspected every fucking box yet!"

Standing, the angry woman stared at the man in disbelief. "Don't the sheets say what there is?"

Unexpectedly, one of the searchlights winked out, and darkness swallowed half the ville.

"Most of it's in military codes, just a bunch of numbers," Baron Sheffield said, going to a chink in the brick wall and chancing a glance outside. Nothing was visible, but tiny flowers of fire winked in the blackness—muzzle-flashes of the wall guards.

"No time for that shit now!" Collette cursed, as a strange dog darted between the buildings. Shoving the stubby barrel of her Ingram subgun out a hole, she sprayed lead at the passing creature. It toppled over, and something rose from its back to scamper away by itself. What the fuck was that?

"Courtyard looks clear!" she said, easing off the trigger.

Cradling the longblaster, Sheffield grunted in reply but didn't relax. Why now? The norms had been here for almost a year building the ville. Why all the trouble now?

"More coming through!" a sec man announced, firing his weapon, short arcs of brass flying into the air to tinkle musically on the cold stone floor. Outside, a flock of screamwings had descended on the bodies of the slain and were loudly feasting.

Switching to single shot, Collette steadily fired the Ingram with lethal accuracy. Each slug took a mutie in the head, skulls exploding, brains splattering outward in a grisly display.

"This has got to be the ash," she said, dropping the clip and ramming in a fresh magazine. "There's no more food around here, but us."

"Fuckers eat each other," a corporal pointed out. "But only after we ace them!"

Outside, the sounds of blasterfire were becoming infrequent, the human screams sounding constantly, as more indescribable things moved past the armory.

Cursing bitterly, Sheffield shoved a Kalashnikov out a hole and sprayed the darkness. Triple-damn Silas and his lust for revenge. "Soon as the scouts report a usable site we're gone!" he stated, spraying a deadly wreath of bullets into the shambling humanoid mockeries. Bodies fell, but a few in the rear struggled to rise once more. He fired again, emptying the clip, and they dropped permanently.

As he reloaded, the man reflected that it almost seemed as if the second group had been using the first to test the defenses. Could that be? No, that was utter crap. He had once heard of a smart mutie that led an army against the norms of some ville, but that was only a campfire story. Something to frighten sluts and babes. Smart muties. Never happen. This was just a bunch of starving animals, nothing more.

"We got to use the Kite!" Collette raged, fumbling

for a fresh clip and finding none. Hastily, she began to load one of the empties on the floor from the pile of loose ammo.

"Can't!" he shot back. "I just tested it a while ago. I'm unable to focus it again for hours!"

"We'll never last that long!" a sec man shouted over the chatter of a Kalashnikov.

"We can inside the blockhouse," Sheffield stated, suddenly sounding calm. "The walls are thicker, the door solid iron."

"Sounds good, my lord," a sergeant replied, but then motioned his head toward the barricaded door. "But how do we get there alive across a hundred yards of open ground?"

The burned bodies of muties who had tried to climb the electric fence that surrounded the armory were a smoking pile on the ground. But there was also a hole in the barrier, and a giant cougar prowled along the brick buildings searching for any opening.

"We cut a deal with the muties," Sheffield said, slinging the longblaster and drawing his handcannon. "Get the kitchen staff."

Collette blanched. "You're going to arm the slaves?"

"Get them!" he roared, spittle flying. "Now!"

A sergeant grabbed a couple of privates and rushed into the back rooms of the armory. Moments later, the blues herded a collection of slaves wearing aprons into the throne room, mostly whitehairs and a few children learning the tricks of cooking for a hundred men at a meal.

"Cripple them," the baron ordered and began to shoot the slaves in the knee.

The men and women fell helpless to the floor, screaming in pain, their legs destroyed forever.

"Muties like their meat alive," he said, dragging the weeping cook to the front door and throwing the bolt. "Okay, let's give them a meal!"

Shoving the wounded outside, the sec men bolted the door closed again. The crying slaves stood in the darkness, looking around in wide-eyed fear. Then the cougar approached and the humans hobbled away in a panic, trampling one another in a frantic bid for life. The giant cat fell on the whitehairs, ripping them apart, blood going everywhere.

While the beast was busy eating, Sheffield led the rush out of the armory, the blues carrying every box of ammo they could. Darting through the hole in the electric fence, the blues shot their way across the compound, using the grens to blow a thunderous path through the carnage until they reached the base of the towering dish.

Sheffield unlocked the door, and the blues piled into the concrete bunker.

"Now what?" a sec man asked.

Heading for a control panel, the baron flipped some switches and grabbed a microphone. "This is Baron Sheffield," he said softly, the words booming outside over the PA system. "Wound the slaves and cut them loose. Let the muties eat them, and get to the blockhouse now! We lock the door in five minutes!"

Soon, squads of blue shirts began to arrive at the blockhouse, hideous screams cutting the night as the crippled slaves were caught by the hungry muties. An old slave wearing a dirty blue shirt tried to sneak inside the bunker, but Collette caught him at the door and stabbed the whitehair in the belly, then kicked him away from the structure. Clutching his wounded stomach, the slave hobbled away into the savage night.

"Time," the baron said, glancing at a wall chron. "Lock it."

The four heavy bolts were thrown and a cross bar dropped into place across the iron door. The noise level from outside lowered immediately. Taking a chair at the control panel, Sheffield sighed in relief, glad that he had decided to reinforce the bunker after the revolt. The man only wished he had done more, maybe lined the outside walls with Claymores, or something, but who could have foreseen a mass attack by starving muties?

"Going to need more slaves after this," a sec man gripped, hugging his longblaster.

"How many made it here?" a sergeant demanded, looking over the assemblage of troops. The bunker was large, but the crowd seemed nowhere near large enough.

"I counted fifty coming in," Collette answered brusquely. "We lost half our guys."

"Better than losing all," a private stated.

"When the muties are finished, they'll try to get inside to us," Sheffield warned. "Try real hard. We just have to hope the door is strong enough to last until the Kite comes back on-line."

"How much longer, sir?" a lieutenant asked, licking dry lips.

Sheffield looked at the wall chron. "Another hour."

Suddenly, something large slammed into the locked

door, rattling the hinges and bolts. Leveling their weapons, the blues retreated from the portal and braced themselves for a pitched battle inside the confines of the bunker.

Chapter Fourteen

A red dawn dispatched the night above North Carolina, and the sec men of Beta team shuffled from the doorway of the overturned dish, yawning and fixing their clothing.

"Now that's why I became a sec man," a private told his comrades as he rubbed his stubbly chin. "Damn near wore myself to a nub."

"All you had in the first place," another chided.

"Fuck you!"

"Not with what you got, stumpy."

"Shut up," Sergeant Campbell ordered, pulling up his suspenders. The night had been long and one of the best in memory. Farmer women lasted a lot longer than slave girls. The man almost felt sorry about capping the bitch he had been riding. She had cried, but they all did that. But this one used his name, and most didn't even know it. That had unnerved him a lot. The sec man didn't like that feeling, so he shot her twice just to make sure.

"Any coffee?" Campbell shouted into the still air, startling a flock of birds covering the corpses of the men.

"Didn't think we'd eat here," a sec man said, wrinkling his nose.

The sergeant was forced to agree. The stink of the rotting bodies was strong. The birds and bugs eating the flesh hadn't helped reduce the reek, only made it stronger.

"Okay, saddle up and let's ride," he commanded, checking the magazine in his blaster.

As the sleepy men stumbled into the rear of the APC, Campbell brushed back his wild crop of hair and walked over to the bearskin on the side of the wag.

"Curing nicely," he said, running a ran over the hide. "I want you men pissing on it more. Going to need a good coat come winter."

A sec man slammed shut the left door as the driver started the big diesels. "What about Collette?"

Campbell climbed inside and took a wall seat. "Screw her. Going to keep it for me. Head north, Sam. And where's the bastard coffee?"

The driver shifted into gear and the LAV-25 rolled out of the hamlet, leaving behind the dead and a rich harvest of spent brass scattered across the bloody ground.

The LAV rolled through the fields and into the woods beyond while a private passed out the MRE packs and another warmed water over a small fire inside a tin bucket, the smoke wafting along the roof and out a series of air vents. Designed for cig smoke, the vents worked just fine for the tiny cookfire.

"How much farther?" Campbell asked.

"Sarge?" the driver asked, confused.

"How much farther to the next dish, asshole?"

Quickly, the driver checked a map taped to the armored wall. "About sixty miles," he answered, working the steering levers. "Say, two hours. With good ground, mebbe less."

"Good. Hey, you! That water hot yet? Then give me a cup."

Breakfast was brief, and Campbell was dry shaving with a Bowie knife when the vehicle passed the ruins of a fishing hamlet beside a raging river of whitewater. The destruction of the flimsy structures was absolute, way beyond anything needed to merely gain entrance. Worse, there were no bodies.

"What could've done that?" a blue asked, working the bolt on his Kalashnikov. "River muties?"

"Don't know. Better bolt the hatch," the sergeant commanded in reply, and unsnapped the flap that covered his handcannon.

Just then something erupted from the river in a geyser of foamy water. Wings flapping, the creature streaked over the smashed kindling and slammed onto the side of the wag. Claws raked the metal, trying to reach the men inside. A black muzzle was shoved to an air vent, and a forked tongue jabbed a good three feet into the wag. The mutie howled in frustration and crawled over the vehicle, searching for a way into the strange egg.

A sec man cut loose with an AK-47 through a blasterport, but the river mutie had already gone under the wag. Suddenly, the belly hatch slammed open and the thing crawled into the transport. A taloned hand slashed at a sec man, who dived out of the way. Another man slammed the stock of his AK-47 into the thing's snarling face, and a third kicked over the tin bucket, fire and boiling water covering the beast.

Keening in pain, the mutie went mad, claws slashing open the seat cushions and a box of ammo, precious rounds rattling across the floor in every direction.

Tripping on the loose ammo, the rest of the sec men scrambled for their blasters, while Campbell knelt and discharged the Colt at point-blank range. The blaster's muzzle-flame extended to touch the beast he was so close. Incredibly, the first round missed, ricocheting off the belly hatch and out of the wag. Riveting its attention his way, the beast reached out and grabbed Campbell by the boot.

"Rad me!" the blue shirt shouted, planting his other boot in the mutie's throat to keep from being dragged any closer, and emptied the blaster at the scaly invader. The .45 slugs blew chunks off the creature's head, and still it tried to haul him out of the wag, the grip on his boot tightening to a painful level.

Dropping the spent clip, Campbell tried to slap in a fresh mag when the APC hit a bump and the clip went flying. The sergeant threw the blaster at the bleeding mutie and drew his Bowie knife. No stinking mutie was getting him alive!

Then a sec man jumped onto the belly hatch, slamming the armored slab onto the beast, knocking it sideways. Partially trapped, it released the sergeant and fought for its own freedom, screaming and thrashing like a demon from hell. Now they could see the gaping, lipless mouth in the palm of each clawed hand.

"Ready, set, go!" a sec man shouted, and pulled the hatch out of the way. In unison, the rest of the blues hosed the beast with their Kalashnikovs, the barrage of 7.62 mm rounds tearing its body apart, black blood spraying onto the walls. Cut to pieces, the mutie screeched and dropped out of sight. Instantly, the wag bumped a few times as the rear wheels crunched over the riddled body, ending the high-pitched yells of pain permanently.

"Bolt that hatch!" Campbell sputtered in rage, retrieving his blaster from the sticky floor. "Bolt every hatch!"

"Freeze," a sec man whispered, and swung his blaster at the sergeant. Before Campbell could react, the man fired a short burst, black blood gushing from the side of his boot.

Weapon in hand, Campbell stopped in the act of squeezing the trigger when he realized he wasn't hurt. Bending, he saw there was some sort of leathery sack attached to the side of his predark Army boot. It was torn apart by the AK-47, but little squiggling things dangled from the base, dripping thick viscous fluid.

"Some sort of egg," he growled, cutting it off with his knife. Then he scraped the residue off the blade with the sole of his boot and ground it flat on the rough metal floor. "Shit-faced little bastard must squirt out eggs when it's about to chill. I heard tell of a mutie down Mex way that did that."

"Cockroaches, too," a sec man added, grabbing a ceiling stanchion against another lurch of the wag. Throughout the whole fight, the driver hadn't stopped or even slowed. Probably just too damn frightened to decide.

Struggling to his feet, Campbell sat down again. "Okay, I want this freaking wag checked from top to bottom! You assholes miss an egg, and we're in deep shit, so don't fuck up!"

Over the next hour, the blues looked hard for any more of the black lumps, checking every nook and crevice inside the wag from under the dashboard to the speakers of the radio, and even inside the barrel of the 25 mm cannon. They found nothing.

"We're clean," a man said with a sigh, slumping into a wall seat. "Black dust, that was a nasty bastard. Sure hope it was a solo. Pack of those could chill an army of blues."

"Shut up," Campbell growled, gingerly massaging his throbbing ankle. It hurt inside, and he was frightened it was more than just a sprain. "And somebody make more coffee!"

WAY OUT OF SIGHT under the wag, attached to the armor flange, safe behind a wheel assembly, was a small leathery lump coated with a mucouslike substance. Speckled with tiny dots of black blood, the sphere pulsated steadily as it absorbed the excess heat radiating from the big diesel engines, growing larger and heavier by the minute.

WALKING HIS tired animal, Baron Henderson slowly proceeded down the predark street through the maze of ruins that surrounded Green Cove ville, the rising sun casting a reddish light over the skyscrapers and office buildings. The man felt as if he were being watched from a hundred different locations, and quite possibly he was, just not necessarily from the outer guards of the ville. Rats scurried underfoot. He had heard of outlanders who preferred to live in the ruins and warned the ville of approaching enemies to get a reward of the supplies when the invaders were chilled. The defensive weapons of Green Cove were as mysterious as they were known to be deadly. Henderson assumed it was merely some sort of poison gas, or snipers with silenced longblasters. But the local sec men would surely have nothing to fear from a lone rider.

The Casanova sec men who had escaped death at Front Royal with the baron had proved less than enthusiastic about his new plan, and so had been set free from his service. The former baron was wearing their blasters and was dressed in their patched clothing, his fine suit of silk thrown into the bushes. Henderson had washed in a creek that morning to cut the smell, since he no longer had access to perfume. His infamous box of jolt and snuff was hidden in the hollow of a tree a few miles farther into the forest. It had been the supreme sacrifice, but revenge was worth any price.

Chewing on a piece of jerky, Henderson walked his stallion down the exact middle of the road, so that nobody could possibly think he was trying to sneak toward the ville. Gaining the trust of Baron Armand DuQuene was of primary importance at this stage of the negotiations. Afterward, things would rapidly change, but that time hadn't yet come. This day, Henderson was all smiles and brotherhood.

The ruins stopped abruptly, and the high walls of the ville rose from the rubble-strewed streets and yards. The debris made it damn near impossible for coldhearts to charge at the ville through all of the wreckage and rubble.

Rusty strips of metal, railroad tracks, led to a large metal-bound door on the north side, and to the south a river flowed through a thick metal grillework. The main gate was fronted by concrete road dividers, again making it tough for enemies to swiftly reach the ville. The door itself was a solid array of barbed arrowheads so tightly packed it was impossible to tell if the material underneath was wood or iron, or whatever.

Composed of bricks and cinder blocks combined in a random pattern, the walls of the ville rose fifteen feet skyward. Armed with shotguns, sec men stood guard behind the top, while wooden towers rose tall within the city, more sec man watching the wall and the ruins beyond with binocs.

Again, Henderson was impressed, although he kept the feelings from his face. This was a fine ville, well designed and built. Tough for any invader to attack. He trembled with anticipation to make it his.

The wall guards were tracking him by now. Henderson stopped well away from the front gate and stepped off his horse, keeping a grip on the reins. To the best of their knowledge, he was just a whitehair solo coming to trade or beg.

"What do you want?" a voice barked from the ground.

Caught by surprise, Henderson now saw there was a tiny man-sized door in the main gates. Standing there was a huge bald sec man dressed in old clothes and sporting a homemade scattergun.

"Morning," he said, smiling as he walked closer. "I am Baron Henderson of Casanova ville and need to speak with Baron DuQuene immediately. Fetch him."

The sec man threw back his head and guffawed. A few more on the walls also laughed, and Henderson had to fight to keep from drawing a blaster and chilling the fools.

"You have a choice, boy!" he boomed, allowing a fraction of his true feelings to show through. "I am either a harmless crazy or Baron Henderson with important news for DuQuene! So choose well, ass! It could mean the total destruction of your fucking rad pit of a ville!''

The hairless guard stopped laughing and cocked back the hammers on his crude blaster. ''Or you're a shammer, trying to trick us,'' he growled, pointing the barrels directly at Henderson. ''Trying to trick us out of food or ammo. Should chill you now.''

''Do it!'' the baron raged, sneering openly at the man. ''You are obviously too stupe to deserve to live! Do it, I command you!''

His face contorted in rage, the guard aimed the blaster and braced himself against the recoil of the colossal homemade.

''Nobody commands anything here but me,'' a new voice said, and the huge gates swung open wide, exposing a second wall of spiked wooden beams. That imposing barrier was raised out of sight to the sound of squeaking pulleys, and Baron Armand DuQuene strode out, flanked by a squad of sec man armed with bolt-action longblasters. Aside from the baron himself, all of the men were shaved bald, making them appear nearly identical. The sec men marched in step around their baron, the blasters gleaming with polish. Henderson admired their precision and couldn't wait until they were his bodyguards.

Baron Armand DuQuene was a huge man, with a dense mane of red hair flowing onto his wide shoulders, a matching mustache and beard covering most of his features. He was dressed as casually as the troops and carried two handcannons, the weapons reversed in their holsters, the butts sticking toward the front. A jagged scar sliced across his face and down his neck, a thin white streak in the redbeard growing over the ancient wound.

"My lord, I—" the gate guard started, but the baron cut him off with a wave.

"How interesting. A baron riding alone, without any sec men," DuQuene said as an opener, hooking a thumb into his gun belt. The man and his guards stayed well within the array of concrete dividers, even though they outmanned and outgunned the lone whitehair. "But I know your face. Your ville is to the east and north of here. Castle Nova, or something like that."

"It was called Casanova," Henderson corrected him, stroking the muzzle of his mount to quiet its nerves. "Not anymore."

"Changed the name, eh?" He shrugged. "It's a baron's choice to call his home anything he likes. What happened to your guards, plague?"

The wall gunners grew tense and worked the bolts on their weapons. The assortment of deadly diseases that had swept the world after skydark were mostly gone these days, but outbreaks of the black cough, or blood fever still occurred. The only cure was to burn everything and run for the horizon. Now the old man noticed that more than a few of the bald men on the wall had lifted into view glass bottles filled with brownish liquid. Rags had been stuffed into the openings. In horror, Henderson realized they were getting ready to firebomb him out of existence.

"I didn't change the name," Henderson explained, controlling his raging temper. "It's gone, the whole bastard ville is gone."

The sec men murmured in surprise but didn't lower the Molotovs or blasters.

"Muties?" DuQuene asked, frowning. It was a natural question. With any major trouble, a person always checked for muties first. The animals were the worst. They sometimes were so bizarre looking a person didn't know what part to shoot at until it was too late. Eagles with tentacles, jellyfish that leaped from trees, and it was getting worse all the time.

"Not muties, or coldhearts, or a wildfire," Henderson stated calmly over his whinnying horse. "It was melted. Melted like candle wax by a sky machine."

"What brand of hot horseshit are you trying to sell?" the red giant scoffed in amusement. "There aren't any more sats. Everybody knows that."

"Then everybody is wrong," Henderson snarled, releasing the stallion and walking dangerously closer. "My ville, and everybody inside it, was reduced to smoke in a matter of seconds by some predark weapon operated by Front Royal!"

More murmurs rose from the crowd of guards, disbelief openly battling with raw fear. Henderson had been counting on this. The common hatred of technology ran deep in people these days. Science had smashed the world, giving them muties, terrible diseases, and a host of other deadly things aside from the acid rain and rads pits. Even simple machines like wags were viewed with suspicion by many folks, and the very word "sat" made even hardened sec men recoil. There was no known defense against an orbiting sat aside from not being there when it cut loose.

Of course, Henderson had no proof it really was a sat that destroyed his ville, but that was the word he had chosen to strike terror in their hearts. And who knew, maybe it was a predark sat. Stranger things had happened.

"You saying Nathan Cawdor can talk to a sat?" DuQuene asked, looking upward. Then he burst into laughter. "I have heard some tall tales before, but this is the best. Cawdor doesn't even have a war wag with armor, but you're telling me that now he got a sat?"

"Yes!"

The baron of Green Cove ville turned away. "Stop wasting my time. Guards, take his goods and whip him into the forest. Goodbye, Henderson."

"And what if I'm right?" the baron hastily asked as the sec men approached.

Halfway through the gate, Baron DuQuene paused to glance over a shoulder. "Never give up, do you?" he snorted.

"And what if I am right?" Henderson repeated, feeling his heart pound inside his chest. "What are you going to do when the top of the ville starts to grow hot, then the walls soften and melt, the molten stone flowing over your screaming people, burning them into blackened bones. What will you do then? Cry? Apologize? You asshole, you don't deserve to be the baron of a latrine!"

The guards growled hatefully and shifted the grips on their blasters, obviously eager to chill the old man.

Baron DuQuene stared hard at the man standing alone but unafraid before the gates of his ville. Henderson was known as a ruthless deviant, a sexual pervert, and worse, a jolt addict, but if his story was true, then the bastard had information vital to the safety of his ville. And what could one lone man do? Slaughter his troops and take over? That was a laugh.

"And you can stop the sat, I suppose?" DuQuene scowled.

"No," Henderson replied honestly, "but we can kill the man who controls it. With him gone, it's useless."

"Cawdor has never bothered me. Why should I take your word?"

"Don't. I could be lying," Henderson said quickly, feeling the fleeting taste of success on each word. He was close now, so very close.

"Send some troops to recce my ville. When they return, then we can talk about how to save your ville. And my price," he added in a flash of brilliance. Nobody gave anything away free. He cursed himself a fool for not thinking of that earlier.

The baron turned and talked with a tall thin sec man. From the man's lack of hair, clothing and stance, Henderson guessed he was the sec chief. The chief wore a wheelgun in a shoulder rig, and some sort of weird blaster strapped to his thigh. The barrel was enormous, twice the size of a shotgun. The stock was new wood, still green in spots, the barrel bound with iron wire as reinforcement. Henderson knew that trick. Heat the iron red hot, then wrap it tight around a weak blaster barrel. When it cooled, it got tight and helped old blasters work for years longer. That weapon had obviously seen long and hard service. Maybe it launched a rocket, or it could be a flare rifle. Henderson once owned a flare pistol. Whatever the thing was, he had no wish to face the business end, and he marked the chief as the first man to die in the revolution.

"As the baron of Green Cove," DuQuene began loudly, "I always have to consider any potential threats to my people. This could merely be a trick to get inside. If it is, you'll hang from a rope with crows pecking out your eyes until we shoot you out of boredom.''

Beaming a smile, Henderson said, "And if what I say is true?"

"We'll discuss your reward later inside," DuQuene growled. "Get his horse, take his blasters and any jolt you find."

"If he resists, chill him," the sec chief said in a raspy voice, as if just risen from a grave.

Henderson allowed himself to be stripped of all weapons, secretly smiling about the bamboo tube of jolt shoved up his ass where few sec men dared to search. He was inside. Now for the second part of his plan.

ORBITING HIGH above Earth, a beautiful black butterfly floated along peacefully in space. The analogy was quite exact, as the inventor of the microwave Kite, Professor Paul Glaser, had collected butterflies as a child and deliberately incorporated the beauty of nature into the orbiting power plant. With a smile, he had always referred to the lovely satellites as Monarchs. But the rest of the predark world soon called the feared machines by the hated designation of Kites.

Miles wide, the graceful wings of the Kite were composed of innumerable tiny glass squares, efficient solar cells that converted the raw solar light falling on them into direct current. The trickle of power flowed into superconductor cables, becoming a stream of electricity that was boosted with a step-up transformer into a raging torrent of power that was converted into safe and harmless microwaves to beam down to Earth.

Originally, the Kite was designed to only emit low-frequency, nonlethal, EM waves that would cascade unnoticed to huge fields of rectennas in the deserts and above the junkyards of North America, the specially treated wire catching and condensing the invisible waves of power, easily convert it into simple electricity to run factories and cities. Once established in its orbit, a Kite would provide limitless, clean power for millions of homes.

Most were destroyed by the hunter/killer sats in the aftermath of skydark. Only a lone Kite remained intact and functioning, floating serenely above the ravaged world.

However, the focus of the microwave beamer had been drastically changed under the austere genius of Silas Jamaisvous, the safeties neutralized, the power grid connected directly to the mighty busbars, and the EM frequency boosted to its highest setting.

Far below the sat, an unseen dish antenna sent coded signals to the machine, and the controls inside the war sat blinked wildly as new commands flooded its master comp. Tiny retro rockets of elemental boron hissed briefly, subtly changing the direction of the silvery cone at the bottom of the Kite. Transformers hummed, its external lights dimmed, and an invisible stiletto of power stabbed through the murky atmosphere, volatizing the heavy layer of polluted clouds until a strange blue could be seen from the Tennessee valley below. Winging through the sky, birds and screamwings burst into flames and plummeted from the deadly air.

Smeared with blood and gore, the feasting muties in the Shiloh ville paused in their gorging to scratch at their skin from the millions of pinpricks stabbing every inch of their bodies. The pain rapidly increased to intolerable levels and the creatures hooted and snarled in agony, blindly clawing at their dead-white eyes. Some tried to run away, others attempted to burrow into the rocky soil, still others sought refuge inside the brick buildings of the two-legs, but nothing helped. Hair burst into flames, skin cracked open, blood flowed from the seared flesh. Dizzy and dying, unable to even comprehend what was destroying them, the insane muties foamed at the mouth and attacked one another, only to weaken and limply topple over, steam hissing from every orifice as their twisted bodies cooked solid.

A clean wind blew over the military ville, and the shrieks of the animals were quickly followed by heavy silence.

MINUTES PASSED into an hour, then two hours before the battered door to the bunker was opened and a sec man held out a hand, testing the air before daring to leave the safety of the armored room.

"All clear," he reported with a sigh.

"Yeah, we know," a sergeant said. "You're still alive."

A scowling Baron Sheffield strode from the bunker, Collette at his side. The base was dotted with chewed corpses, smashed machines, dropped weapons and countless steaming bodies. A few of the muties twitched feebly on the hot ground, their limbs moving as if possessed with a life of their own. The blues started shooting the muties, and Collette shouted for them to cease.

"Get some sledgehammers," she commanded. "No sense wasting ammo on stationary targets."

Shouldering their longblasters, the weary sec men moved in squads to the Quonset hut to get the required tools. At the door, a lieutenant placed his hand on a glowing pad and the door slid aside with the hiss of compressed air.

"Shitfire, we lost every slave with this attack," Sheffield raged, walking among the dead. "You there, Major! I want that fucking gap filled with anything that'll fit! Block that hole or I'll use your corpse! Use a Hummer and get rubble from the quarry to block that hole completely."

The officer saluted and rushed to the task. Overhead the sky was still a clear blue, but a ring of storm clouds was rushing in, the iris of darkness closing above the walled ville. High in the sky, winged creatures were beginning to circle the Shiloh base, many with enormous wingspans and multiple heads. The smell of the spilled blood and cooked meat drew the aerial scavengers like a insects to a searchlight.

"Bastard Kite seems to attract muties," Sheffield grumbled, lighting a cig. "An unforeseen side effect."

"Anything we can do about that, my lord?" a sergeant asked warily.

Collette rested the hot barrel of her blaster against a cheek, savoring the brief sting of pain. "Yeah," she replied. "Stop using it to defend ourselves from simple muties."

"Sec Chief Hogan, have the men prepare to leave the base," Sheffield said abruptly. "It's impossible to stay here anymore."

The use of her last name startled the woman, and it took her a moment to react. "Keep the hammer lifted, Baron," she said soothingly. "We can't leave.

The recce teams haven't found another dish yet. Soon enough we'll leave this rad pit and start taking over the East Coast baronies one by one. And then all of them!"

"Fuck it," the baron puffed, watching the men dispatch the assortment of animals on the ground with grisly thumps. "We have to leave, or the next wave of muties will get us for sure. We can seize some small ville, and stay there until finding another dish. But we leave in the morning. That's an order."

"Sir, the slaves are dead," a lieutenant said hesitantly, "and the men are completely exhausted."

"I don't fucking care!" the baron roared, casting away the cig. "Feed them jolt, use a whip, but we leave tomorrow at dawn!"

The officer saluted. "Yes, my lord."

Sheffield merely grunted in reply, his mind on the closing storm clouds overhead and circling muties above.

IN SPACE, the Kite resumed control over its comps once more and began a diagnostic check. Floating peacefully in orbit, the machine began once more to store the trickle of electricity from its great solar wings in giant accumulators, patiently waiting for its next order.

Chapter Fifteen

"Wait!" Mildred cried, rushing into the control room.

The companions turned as a group, pulling blasters from their clothing and cocking back hammers.

"Something wrong?" Ryan asked bluntly. Squinting, the one-eyed warrior tried to look past the physician to see if she was being chased by anything.

"We...we're out of time," the physician said breathlessly. "I..." She paused to swallow. "I decided to check the outside, using the periscope, just to keep track of how it was going."

"Ash storm still raging, madam?" Doc asked, holstering the LeMat.

Mildred frowned. "God, I wish it was. The valley outside is flat rock. I think there was an acid rain, and it mixed with the ash making a kind of concrete."

"So?" Dean asked, unconcerned.

"Fireblast," Ryan growled, thumbing the safety back on the SIG-Sauer. "Sheffield and his troops will be moving soon. Have to."

"No cover for the ville," Krysty said in understanding. "It's in plain sight now."

"Worse," J.B. stated grimly. "They'll soon be running out of food."

Rubbing a fist into his palm, Ryan nodded. "Silas must have left behind a stockpile of supplies, but even the blues need farmers and hunters for most of their food.''

"Nothing will grow out there," Mildred said. "And there's not a leaf of grass for the local animals to eat."

"Eat each other," Jak said. "Then the blues."

"The more muties attack," Dean said, chewing a lip, "the more they'll be alert and ready for trouble. It's going to make it triple hard for us to nightcreep them now."

"And now we're racing against the clock," Doc rumbled pensively. "Sheffield will know all of this better than us, and could move the computers and his troops to another location any hour of the day or night."

"They move, and we lose our back door into their base!"

"Exactly."

"Shit!"

"So we hit them tonight," Ryan ordered. "Trader always used to say, folks were at their weakest just before a move."

"Sheffield will be low on wall guards because he'll have to send out scouts," Krysty agreed. "And a lot of their ammo will be packed away for the journey where they can't reach it fast."

Glancing at the mat-trans door, Ryan didn't speak for a moment as he mentally reviewed their meager collection of armament.

"Okay, this is the last jump," he stated. "Tonight, we use the tunnel to reach the quarry and hit the blues."

"But not at midnight," Dean piped in. "'Cause

that's when most folks attack. We wait another hour, and then go in. Never do the expected."

"You're learning," his father said with pride.

"We got enough plastique?" Mildred asked pointedly.

"Barely," J.B. replied, resting a hand on the bag of explosives sitting on the control console. "We sure as shit could use another couple of pounds. Every ounce helps at this point."

"Then let's move," Ryan said, and, sliding the Kalashnikov over a shoulder, he walked into the chamber. Once J.B. was seated on the floor, Ryan closed the heavy door and quickly joined his old friend, both patiently waiting for the artificial mists to tear their bodies into subatomic particles and throw them once more into the electronic abyss.

BRAKING THE HUMMER close to the hillock, Collette and a sec man stepped from the wag and quickly drew their weapons.

"Sons of bitches," the private growled hatefully.

"Fire!" the woman barked, and the two cut loose with their rapidfires at the mutie dogs savaging the human corpses on the smooth ground. Startled, the beasts snarled and slavered at the loud noises as they were torn to pieces trying to protect the meat on the ground. The few survivors scampered away over the swells of rock.

Walking closer, the sec men kicked over a tattered body still wearing the rags of a blue shirt. "Rad me, it's Quinn," he cursed. "A cousin of mine from the Shens. Poor bastard."

Collette stared at the face and body of the other corpse. The man was old, with almost no clothing, and shackles still circled his skinny ankles. It was the old slave sent to work the keypad of the door to the redoubt.

"Strange," she said softly, touching the corpse and lifting a broken rib bone into the headlights of the Hummer. "These men weren't aced by the muties. Some sort of blast did this damage."

"An explosion?" The sec man gazed at their Hummer. "Fuel tanks still there, and I don't see any gren holes anywhere. What could have blown up?"

Looking around, Collette soon spied the culprit. Laying in the grass, covered with blood and chewed intestines, was the butt and twisted frame of a predark pistol. Where the metal wasn't burned or shattered, the chrome finish was still mirror shiny.

"I know this weapon," Collette said hesitantly, studying the butt. She spit on the remains of the weapon and wiped the gore on her pants. "Yes, see here. This weird logo on the grip. The blaster is from something called the Anthill. This used to belong to Silas!"

"Dr. Jamaisvous?" the sec man said, scratching his head. "Yeah, I sort of remember him having a shiny blaster on his bed table. After he got chilled, we never found it in his rooms. Figured somebody stole it."

"And why didn't you report a missing wep?" Collette said in a low and dangerous tone.

Nervous under her stern gaze, the blue got formal. "We informed the baron, Sec Chief Hogan. It would be his decision to tell you, or not."

"True enough," she relented, harboring her anger for a more suitable target. Why hadn't Sheffield mentioned it? Was he hiding some plan from her again?

Curiously, the sec man glanced around at the

smooth featureless ground. "No way it could have been in the Hummer," he stated. "Wonder where the whitehair found the blaster?"

Collette snapped her head toward the hill. "Inside the hill," she muttered, feeling a sudden surge of excitement more powerful than any sex. "The slave found the entry code, got inside and found Silas's trick gun."

"What do you mean 'trick'?" the sec man asked, confused.

Ignoring the question, the woman rushed to the black door and ran her hands across its marred expanse, then looked down and found a crumpled mass of paper. Kneeling, she smoothed out the printed sheets. The first eighteen pages had pencil lines drawn through the number-letter combinations. Going on a hunch, she tapped in the first line not crossed out. Nothing happened.

"Smart little fucker," Collette growled in grudging admiration. "The slave found the code and waited for the right time before attacking." Which meant that somewhere within these eighteen pages was the code to enter the predark redoubt. That would give her access to the jump chamber Sheffield had recently told her about, which would be her key away from him and complete freedom. No longer would she have to suck cock to stay alive. She would soon be in charge. If there were any weapon stores inside the redoubt, she could raise an army and take control of the dish from Sheffield. Using the Kite to burn herself more than a ville, or a dozen villes, Collette could become the first emperor of the New America. Everything she ever wanted was waiting behind that black metal door, and the key lay in her hand.

She'd been told that the mat-trans chamber inside the Quonset hut had been sealed in some manner by Silas before he died. Nobody could open the door to the chamber but the old man, and only then after he had placed his face to a hole in the console and let a red light play over his left eye. Sheffield had planned on stealing the eye and sealing it in a jar of alcohol to keep it fresh. But then that bastard Ryan had fried the whitecoat to a crisp and ruined the plan. Now their only hope of gaining access to a mat-trans unit was through the locked door of this redoubt. It was maddening that the blues had a gateway inside their ville, and couldn't use the chamber.

"Big door," the blue shirt commented, ambling. "What is it? Some sort of bomb shelter?"

With a word, Collette worked the bolt on her Inram and turned. Before the sec man could react, she stitched him with a long burst, the copper-jacketed rounds tearing the man apart until he resembled the partially eaten bodies on the cold, smooth ground.

Easing off the trigger, Collette turned to the keypad and began to tap in the first code. She waited, then did the second, then the third. Her anger rose, but she fought it under control. Clearly, this would take some time.

RYAN AND J.B. braced themselves for a surge of weakness, or nausea, but neither occurred.

"'Bout fucking time we had an easy jump," Ryan growled.

"It was a short jump," J.B. said, "which means we're still close to Shiloh."

Reaching out, Ryan touched the wall. "This isn't

armaglass," he stated. "Wonder where the hell we are?"

Looking around, the men noted they were in a small chamber with plastic walls painted a military green to waist height, then a dull navy gray to the ceiling. However, this clearly wasn't a redoubt, but a simple gateway, a mat-trans chamber set outside the subterranean predark fortifications. They had encountered a couple of homemade gateways, which always meant big trouble. Checking their weapons, Ryan and J.B. braced themselves and swung open the door. Both fought back a gasp of surprise.

"Dark night," J.B. whispered, grinning widely. "It's payday."

Ryan wholeheartedly agreed. Stepping out the door, the men could see the gateway was situated inside some sort of huge warehouse, with curved walls and a sharply arched roof, as if a tin can had been cut in two and placed sideways on the ground.

"This is a Quonset hut," Ryan said, studying the distant windows. The glass, or Plexiglas, was frosted white, so there was no way to see outside. The warehouse could be in the middle of a Deathlands desert, underwater, or on the moon. There was no way of telling.

But much more importantly, the entire interior of the structure was jammed to the rafters with military supplies, neat rows of shelving filled with med kits, MRE cartons, satchel charges and endless cardboard boxes of ammo. Huge mounds of crates were stacked along the sloping walls, hundreds of drums of condensed fuel piled conveniently near a small door, and pallets full of tents, bedrolls and huge rolls of concertina wire were everywhere, along with tightly coiled belts of 25 mm shells for APC cannons, .50-caliber bullets for heavy machine guns, long crates full of AK-47 and M-60 blasters and backpacks for carrying LAW rocket launchers. The men had never seen such an incredible collection of weapons like this level since the deadly Alaska redoubt.

"Let's get busy," J.B. said eagerly, shouldering his Uzi and starting down the main aisle.

A forklift was parked in the near distance, obviously used to move the heavier pallets, and it was perfect for their needs. Then a movement at the extreme end of the aisle caught their attention and both men ducked out of sight, but it was too late.

"Hey, who the fuck are you guys?" a distant sec man called out, dropping a clipboard and clawing for the blaster on his hip.

In one smooth motion, Ryan stood, drew the SIG-Sauer and fired. The silenced automatic coughed once, the 9 mm round slamming the sec man backward. He fell sprawling onto an open trunk full of 125 mm AP shells for the main cannon of an Abrams M-1 tank.

"Fireblast, a blue!" Ryan cursed. "This must be the Quonset hut I saw in the middle of their base!"

"Then we better haul ass," J.B. answered, releasing the pistol-grip safety of his Uzi. "The sooner we're gone, the better."

Rushing to a nearby stack, Ryan grabbed a box and used it to prop open the gateway door. Nimbly, J.B. climbed over some coils of electrical cable and into the forklift. The engine started with a purr, and he maneuvered the vehicle to an empty wooden pallet.

"I'll drive, you pile on the goods," he said, trimming the engine and glancing at his wrist chron. "We got seventeen more minutes."

Working fast, the companions started down the main aisle, Ryan slamming entire boxes of Kalashnikovs and ammo boxes onto the pallet. A crate of mixed grens was added, and as they turned a corner, Ryan grabbed a field surgery med kit and a bag of mixed detonators and timing pencils. Next, he added two satchel charges of C-4, then tossed another to J.B., who made the catch and slung it over an arm.

Most of the material had no descriptions or invoice listings as to the contents, but that didn't matter. One of the first things Ryan learned was how to read military code numbers. Often he didn't even have to read the entire sequence before he knew it was something useful, like food or ammo, or predark crap, like paper clips or uniform rank insignia.

"Grab that," J.B. directed, pointing to the left. "And we need that, too!"

Lifting a combo pack of LAW/HALFA rockets, Ryan dropped the missiles and drew his blaster in a smooth, lightning-fast move to fire twice more into the shadows. A sec man fell into the light, with most of his face removed.

"Eight minutes," J.B. reported, grabbing a brand-new can opener off a nearby shelf. There were flashlights on a higher shelf, but they were out of reach without a lot of cumbersome climbing.

"We stay four more," Ryan stated, "then we leave."

"Gotcha."

Pausing at a door, Ryan noted there was a glowing plate set into the wall nearby, exactly like in the more secure rooms of a redoubt. He wasted seconds debating over a quick recce outside, then finally decided against it and moved onward, grabbing a flare gun and box of flares, then a box marked miscellaneous socks. If time had been on their side, the companions would have looted the warehouse down to the floorboards. Silas had to have been compiling these supplies for decades.

"Time," J.B. announced, and wheeled the heavily ladened forklift toward the gateway.

Ryan grabbed small items off the shelves as he approached the gateway, and two men were almost there when the small door at the end of aisle hissed aside and in stormed a squad of blues led by Sheffield.

"God of the atom, it's Ryan!" the baron screamed, pointing with his golden blaster. "Chill them!"

"Ram the door!" Ryan ordered, ducking behind a crate of MRE packs, and cutting loose with the Kalashnikov, sending the blue shirts scurrying for cover. Instantly, he realized he was at a major advantage. The blues only had wall behind them, so Ryan could shoot with totally immunity. But he and J.B. were surrounded by ordnance and fuel. If the blues hit the wrong thing, the entire Quonset hut would vanish in a megaton fireball explosion of cordite and plas.

Comprehending what the big man meant, J.B. floored the accelerator and slammed the forklift directly into the open doorway of the gateway. In wild tumbling chaos, most of the boxes and crates flew off the pallet and into the mat-trans chamber. His chest aching from hitting the steering wheel, J.B. turned in the seat and added the fury of his Uzi submachine gun to the retreat, giving Ryan protective cover as the man darted from box to crate, then behind the forklift and literally dived into the gateway.

Incoming bullets flying all around them, Ryan took over shooting at the blues, emptying the clip in seconds, while J.B. frantically threw supplies into the chamber. Then the friends shifted jobs again, Ryan moving the supplies while J.B. discharged the S&W shotgun. The distance was too great to make the scattergun effective against the blues, but the rain of double-aught steel pellets forced them back into hiding.

Grabbing a sack of grens, Ryan held one out to J.B. so the Armorer could see the safety pin was firmly in place. J.B. nodded, and the two began throwing the deadly bombs wildly into the warehouse.

Shouting warnings, Sheffield and the sec man scrambled to reach the exit. Tossing the half-filled bag into the chamber, Ryan and J.B. each grabbed one more item from the stack of supplies still on the forklift, then slammed shut the door to the gateway.

With pounding hearts, the two men waited for the swirling mists to engulf them, or for the chamber door to swing open again and for them to be brutally cut down by a hail of bullets from the hated blues....

REACHING A RILL in the forest, the LAV-25 of Beta team drove along the woodsy embankment until spying the sprawling ruins of a predark city in the river valley below. To their right was a large flat expanse that sloped inward to a small lake of fused glass.

"Mininuke," Campbell growled, and looked at the dashboard of the APC. Set off prominently by itself was a rad counter, but the red lightbulb wasn't flashing, and no ticks came from the tiny speaker.

"Clean." He sighed.

"If that's working," a private muttered, spooning hash from a MRE envelope.

"Hey!" the gunner called down. "Ville!"

The driver killed the LAV's engines, and the sergeant quickly climbed into the turret with the binocs. This was their last chance at finding a dish. However, a nice ville for Sheffield to move them to would do a lot toward appeasing his anger.

Campbell adjusted the focus until the walls of the ville came in sharp. The ville was situated right in the middle of the ruins, and from that angle the sergeant could see how certain streets had been blocked with rubble, forming a maze around the ville. Unless they knew it was there, coldhearts would simply drive right past the place.

Its walls were the usual mix of whatever was handy, but good and thick, rising twice the height of a man. Inside were rows of houses and huts, all heavily repaired but looking rainproof. Armed sec men walked the walls, with watchtowers set inside the ville to give support fire in case of a successful breech. Damn, this pesthole was well designed. But aside from the defenses, the ville was like any other—civilians walking about talking and doing things, while some wretch hung from a gallow's noose with birds eating his skin. Near a tavern, a couple of bald sec men were having a fistfight in the mud, while an old man across the street was boiling laundry in a bathtub. A crude still was cooking shine over by the barracks, and Campbell guessed the building held a couple of dozen sec men, but that was it. A young busty female butcher was gutting a hog tied upside down to the limb of a tree. Some sluts were hanging their tits out the windows of a gaudy house, trolling for customers. Nice.

The ville looked perfectly normal, except for a fenced enclosure that was filled with rows of long huts whose roofs had been removed and replaced with hundreds of tiny panes of glass. Inside the glass houses were growing plants, a couple of sec men standing guard while workers pulled weeds and tilled the dark soil.

"Fifty, mebbe sixty men," Campbell said to the blues down below. "Got three wags, one up on blocks getting repaired. Sec men got longblasters, but bolt-actions, no rapidfires. Civilians carrying homemades. No slave quarters that I can see."

"Don't like it," the blue shirt muttered. "Too peaceful."

A private blew his nose on his hand and wiped it off on his shirt. "You want us to do a recce? Couple of us could walk to the gate and say we're traders. Give us a handful of ammo and we'll buy some food, lose at dice, talk to the sluts."

"You've done this before," Campbell stated as a fact, narrowing his eyes to mere slits. "Coldheart?"

The man shrugged in a noncommittal manner. "Raided a few villes out west, if that's what you mean. But I work for Sheffield now. As long as he's got blasters and ammo, I stay loyal."

"Which means you keep sucking air," the sergeant retorted hotly. "So watch your mouth about the boss. It's Baron Sheffield, shitface, and don't you forget again."

"Yeah, sure," the private replied calmly. "Anything you say, noble sir."

As smooth and silent as a snake, Campbell lowered the binocs and started to draw his blaster.

"Hey, look over there!" the driver shouted, pointed to the north. "It's a dish!"

Eagerly the men crowded the ob slits, so Campbell stepped outside and walked to the edge of the cliff.

Sure enough, there smack dab on top of one of the crumbling skyscrapers was a nest of dish antennas, each no more than a yard wide.

"I found it, Sarge!" the driver boasted proudly, joining him on the edge of the rill.

Campbell slapped the man on the back side of the head. "You're dumber than a crap sandwich," he snapped. "Those little things are much too small. We need a dish big as the one back home."

"Like that monster over there," a private said, prone in the dirt and looking to the west, cupped hands shading his vision from the sun's glare.

Without much hope, Campbell trained his binocs on the indicated area and saw only jungle, heavy infestations of leafy vines crisscrossing the whitewater river in a dense canopy of greenery. Only the occasional silvery flash indicated water was underneath the covering.

Dropping to the ground, the sergeant could now see under the vines and spotted an intact blockhouse sitting on a small island in the middle of the flowing water. The struts and columns were completely engulfed with leafy vines, past the tops of the trees. Then the dish erupted into view, even larger than the one back in Tennessee.

Holding his breath, Campbell watched as a bird landed on the dish, then launched itself into the sky once more. "Solid as a rock," he announced happily, unconsciously wiggling his boots. "Hot damn, we really found one, boys. And no mistakes this time!"

"That river's going be a bitch to cross," a sec man said. "Probably need to build a bridge to run the power cables and shit."

Standing, Campbell dusted himself off and tucked

away the binocs. "Not our problem. We found the fucker and a rich ville right alongside. Time to go back."

"Sure hope we beat Alpha team," a sec man stated, thinking of the lush reward waiting for them. "Can't wait to start guarding all that pussy!"

"And I hope Brandon got eaten alive," Campbell retorted hotly. "Never did like that butt licker. Sam, how long for us to get back?"

The driver cocked his head in thought. "Be there by dawn tomorrow. If the juice holds, that is. We're pretty low."

"Then strip the wag," Campbell ordered. "Leave everything but one meal of food and half the ammo. We'll make a tent of tree branches to hide the stuff for when we return. That'll cut our weight and give us enough juice to reach Shiloh."

"What are we going to do about Front Royal?" a private asked. "It's only a hundred miles to the north. Damn big, too. Three, mebbe four hundred folks. Plus, sec men."

"Mutie shit," a private replied. "Ain't never been a ville that big in history of the world."

"Baron Sheffield will melt that down to bedrock first thing," the driver stated.

"Not going to do that here, is he?" another sec man asked nervous, glancing at the sky.

Campbell snorted a laugh. "Hell no," the sergeant replied. "Sheffield is going to do a lot worse to Front Royal than just chill them all. A hell of a lot worse."

AS THE TWINKLING LIGHTS inside the swirling mists faded, the door to the chamber was thrown open and the rest of the companions rushed inside.

"You okay?" Krysty asked hurriedly, holstering the Colt.

"No damage," J.B. said, fingering a hole in his shirt where a bullet had come within a hair of blowing off his arm. "Nothing serious, that is."

"Sweet Jesus," Mildred gasped, staring at the piles of supplies and ammunition. "Looks like you hit the jackpot."

"And Sheffield, too," Ryan said. "Doc, don't let that door close! The blues could be right behind us."

Stepping forward quickly, Doc took a stance blocking the jamb with his body. "We are safe now, my dear Ryan. They can not follow you with the door askew," he stated. "And after thirty minutes, Baron Sheffield will not be able to track you at all."

"Hopefully," Krysty stated. "But we'll jam the door open just in case. Silas could operate the mat-trans units in ways we'll never fully comprehend. Sheffield may know some way to extend the thirty-minute window."

Dean hauled a crate of canned goods to the door, and Doc stepped out of the way as the boy chocked the portal open to its absolute widest.

"Sheffield," Jak said thoughtfully. "You go Shiloh?"

Wiping off the sweatband inside his hat, J.B. nodded. "We jumped smack into their warehouse. Stole everything we could before the blues arrived in force."

"Send back satchel charge," the teenager suggested, then he frowned. "Forgot, twenty minutes. Shit."

Ryan understood the complaint. If two groups tried to use a mat-trans chamber at the same moment, there would be a twenty-minute gap between arrivals. That could work in their favor, or against. It was just too big a risk to take at the present.

"Gaia be praised!" Krysty exclaimed, lifting a LAW tube into view. "There's enough MRE packs for a month, a ton of ammo, grens, Claymore mines... Hey, Doc!"

The silver-haired gentlemen turned from inspecting a satchel charge of C-4 plastique. "Yes?" he said politely.

The redhead lifted a cardboard box into view. "Primer caps, black powder, wadding and miniballs. It's for a .45 caliber, though."

"I can easily adapt." Doc smiled, weighting the carton in his hand. "My, my, fifty rounds! It has been quite a while since I last possessed such a plethora of ammunition."

"Here," Mildred said, offering the men a canteen, and they both drank their fill. "And take these. I found some aspirin in the med kit. Haven't seen one of those since the Anthill."

"Thanks," Ryan said, wiping his mouth on a sleeve.

"Here, Millie," J.B. said. Digging into a pocket, he unearthed a small cardboard box and passed it over. "For you."

The physician took the box and slid it open. It was full of .38 solid steel Maxim Express rounds. Immediately, she began loading her empty ZKR target pistol. J.B. had gone out of his way to get those for her. In her skilled hands, that slim blaster was more deadly than a barrage of predark rockets. What he could do with explosives, Mildred did with her handgun.

"Let's haul the supplies out of here," Ryan stated,

lifting a crate of grens to his chest and stepping around the military jumble covering the floor. "We have a lot to do before we hit the blues tonight."

"We going to recce first?" Dean asked, hauling a pack of six LAW rocket launchers to his back.

"Nightcreep," Jak stated, sliding a knife from its sheath and testing the edge of a thumb.

"Mass slaughter," J.B. corrected him, carrying a box of Claymore mines into the control room. "Now here's the plan...."

Chapter Sixteen

The predark office building rose five full stories above Green Cove ville in Virginia. It had been much taller originally, until the shock wave of a nuke blast that annihilated a coastal Navy base sheered it off clean at the fifth floor. However, the nameless structure was still the highest building in the ville, proudly dominating the crumbling ruins outside and the dense forest beyond.

Sec men stood guard on top of the structure, smoking cigs and walking patrol around the towering building. From that vantage point, they could see everything in the ville, down the river to The White Ear of God, and over the high rill to the grasslands of the south. There had been reports of outlanders sneaking through the bush toward the ville, but no sign of invaders had been found by a recce team. However, Baron DuQuene had still ordered an increase in the patrols and even a roof watch. It seemed pointless to the troopers, but a lot better than walking the wall, or standing guard in the dungeon where the prisoners wailed and begged to be killed instead of being slowly tortured for their petty crimes.

The lower levels of the building housed the workshops of the ville, looms to make clothing from dog hair, a potter's kiln and wood shop to make spoons, combs and other useful items. The first floor was the barracks of the sec men, and the top floor the private rooms of the baron and his family. The windows were boarded shut with thick planks, inside and outside. There was no way for a mercie to sneak in for a night-creep without using the stairs and going past a score of armed guards. So far, three assassins had tried, and each failed miserably.

In the middle of the baron's floor was a spacious ballroom decorated with velvet wallpaper and large mirrors, which made the room seem even bigger than it truly was. Clusters of alcohol lanterns hung from the ceiling above a huge circular banquet table that filled most of the ballroom, yet the center of the round table was wide open, leaving enough space for a dozen people to dance without bumping the wood and rattling dishes.

Drinking and talking, the baron and senior sec men of Green Cove ville were discussing battle plans while lunch was being served by a bevy of young, half-naked, serving girls, their budding breasts scarred from splattering grease. As the servants brought heaping platters to the table, the two barons would fondle each in turn and discuss her merits with cruel exactness. Trying not to cry from the pain of the pinches, the girls would smile in return and thank the men for the compliments.

Standing in the corner where he could keep a watch on everything was the sec chief, Seaton Crane. The bony man was sitting in an armless chair, with his back to the stone wall, an oversized blaster resting in his lap. Henderson knew that with a word from the baron, he would be shot dead on the spot. Oddly, the danger excited him and found little urge to sneak a dose of the jolt hidden up his ass. Maybe this was what he had been needing all those decades, a sense of danger to keep up his interest. How amusing that would be to discover at this stage of life.

The two barons were seated near each other for the sake of conversation, DuQuene with armed guards standing behind his chair and seated on either side. Henderson had the same, but his entourage seemed oddly uninterested in the meal and merely watched the visitor very closely. Henderson accepted the scrutiny as a logical precaution. In similar circumstances, he would have placed the visitor in chains. Their mistake.

Henderson felt uncomfortable in his freshly washed clothes, his hair still damp and soapy from a hot bath. But this wasn't his ville yet, and he needed to get on the good side of the local baron as quickly as possible. People put such stock into bathing. It was ridiculous. Animals didn't bath, why should humans?

The food was barely adequate by his standards, but there was plenty and it was decently hot. There was the expected communal bowl of stew, a mainstay in any ville, and the meat tasted more like squirrel than rat or dog. That was a pleasant change. However, there were also several heaping platters of fried fish, with the heads still attached, some local crap about it improving the flavor. It was repugnant. They washed, but ate fish heads. Where was the logic in that?

Loaves of fresh acorn bread lay on wooden boards to keep the heat, along with small dishes of honey, but no butter. Henderson knew the ville had goats. Why weren't the servants milking the animals? Didn't they know how? It was pathetic. These people desperately needed him to take over. The only thing he liked about the banquet hall was the three skulls on the table for decorations. Those would stay.

Scattered about the circle of wood were small bowls of salt, but none of pepper. Pity. Uncaring of the layer of hot grease, the sec men used bare hands to take servings of fried corn-mush cakes. Henderson took a small one and fed it to one of the many dogs laying under the table, probably for just such a reason. The single bright note was a heaping bowl full of stewed dandelion leaves. Merely being polite, he tried a leaf and was stunned to discover the weeds were delicious. There was water and green beer to drink, barely fermented and tasting strongly of wheat. Didn't these idiots know how to plant rye? Probably not.

"Is the food to your liking, Baron?" a sec man asked with his mouth full, a partially chewed fish head peeking out from between his lips.

Henderson finished chewing some fried mush before answering. It was as tough as fried shoe, and almost as tasty, but he smiled and speared another piece with his fork, transferring it to his plate for dissection before the long and arduous process of consumption. They could patch holes in the roof with these things. Simply horrid.

"Best I've ever had," he said with a smile. "Pity there are no onions. Always loved the things."

"Onions?" DuQuene asked, as if never hearing the word before. "That's servant food. Onions and fish guts."

The sec men laughed at the witticism and pounded the table to encourage their baron for another.

Henderson damned them all for idiots. Trying not to scowl, the whitehair baron pushed away his plate and took a sip from his mug. "Oh no, my dear friend, food fit for a baron! Dice the onions, dip them in beer, roll them in breadcrumbs and fry them in fat. Utterly delicious and very healthy. Good for the blood.''

"Yes, well, we'll have to try that sometime," DuQuene said in a manner indicating that Deathlands would become a lush green jungle before that happened.

Suddenly there was a commotion in the hallway leading to the banquet hall, and the sec men stationed along the walls drew weapons and filled the doorway with their bodies. There were some shouted words, and the guards quickly parted to admit a panting sec man covered with road dust and a strong reek of horse.

"My lord! I have just returned from Casanova," he exploded in a single breath. "And the story the old pervert tells is true!"

Henderson narrowed his eyes at the words, but said nothing. There would be plenty of time for retribution later, but the scout just went to the top of his shit list.

"His ville was melted?" DuQuene demanded, arching an eyebrow.

The man nodded excitedly. "Yes, my lord. The area is flat stone with bits of huts and bones sticking out, and still warm to the touch! It's true!"

The sec men muttered among themselves at the pronouncement, and most drained their mugs, eyes full of worried thoughts. Seaton made no reaction to the dire news, the sec chief as calm and cool as a winter corpse.

"So it's real," Baron DuQuene muttered, putting aside his knife and fork.

"Of course," Henderson replied softly.

"Wine!" DuQuene said, snapping his fingers. "We

need a toast for our valued guest and adviser in the coming war on Front Royal.''

The young girls scurried aside as an adult woman hurried into the dining hall with a silver tray bearing goblets and dark bottles. Inspecting the wine as it was placed on the table, Henderson saw in dismay that the cork wasn't flared and knew this was no predark vintage, just some damn local brew. Gods of the atom help him survive another meal with these barbs. Raw pig with cannies couldn't be worse then this horrid slop.

''Splendid idea,'' Henderson beamed in a calculated fashion. ''My pleasure.''

The servant opened each bottle and filled the crystal goblets, painstakingly careful not to spill a single drop.

''To the death of Nathan Cawdor!'' a sec man exclaimed, raising his goblet and sloshing some wine on the table.

Henderson smiled and reached for his own glass when there was a shattering crash at the window. Everybody turned and saw a screamwing partially impaled on the wooden splinters of a plank, halfway into the room. The leathery mutie shrieked and struggled, tiny rivulets of blood trickling down to the floor.

''Fucking hell!'' Seaton cursed, and, holstering his large blaster, drew a wheelgun and fired. The slug plowed through the winged animal, blowing its head out its ass. The wings fluttered wildly for a moment, then the mutilated body plummeted out of sight into the ville below.

''Damn things are always attacking the windows,'' Baron DuQuene said, holstering his own blaster and sitting again. ''We have no idea why.''

"Cracks," Henderson explained.

"What was that?" the baron snapped, glowering at the man.

"Cracks, openings between the wood planks," the whitehair explained slowly. "The light from the lanterns must sparkle off the glass, making the muties think it's water underneath."

"And we're the fish? How very amusing," the baron stated.

Only to you, half-brain, Henderson shot back mentally. Lifting his glass, the old baron then paused in the realization that his attention had been off the goblet during the whole screamwing incident. Could it have all been a trick?

Glancing casually over the sparkling rim of his drink, Henderson saw DuQuene sniffing hesitantly at his own goblet.

"We have a small problem here," the baron said. "I, ah, think the wine has turned bad. Fresh wine, woman!"

"At once, my lord," the servant replied and raced from the room.

"No need for that," Henderson said, drawing the bowl of fruit closer. He poured the apples and pears onto the floor, the fruit rolling about randomly. Then he poured his drink into the bowl and pushed it toward the other baron. DuQuene did the same, then lifted the bowl and poured half of the combined wine back into his goblet. Henderson finished the process and they clinked glasses.

"To victory!" DuQuene said without rancor, taking a drink.

"Death to our enemies," Henderson replied with a

smile, releasing his grip on the .44 derringer hidden in his jacket.

A SOFT WIND BLEW over Shiloh ville, as Sheffield stood outside the Quonset hut and watched through the open doorway at the team of sec men smashing the delicate gateway with sledgehammers. As men carried the pieces outside, a sergeant cut each into even smaller segments with an acetylene cutting torch. Privates would load wheelbarrows with the debris and cart the material across the compound, through the southern gate, then dump the trash over the cliff into the abandoned stone quarry.

Sheffield still couldn't believe that Ryan and one of his sec men still lived and raided the warehouse right in the middle of his ville. In broad daylight! With Silas dead, this was all of the predark supplies Sheffield would ever have. Luckily, Ryan wasn't as smart as Sheffield had been led to believe and had thrown grens without priming them first. Triple-stupe. And Ryan was supposed to be the son of a baron. Ha! Son of slack-jawed mutie was more like it.

Cheering sounded from the distance, and Sheffield whirled with a hand on his blaster just in time to see a battered LAV-25 roll through the front gate and into the Shiloh base. The vehicle parked near the blockhouse, and the baron started to walk that way. Four of its eight tires were missing, the body armor was scorched, the Plexiglas cracked, but a smiling sergeant stood in the open turret of the wag, waving at the other blues and beaming as if he had just invented fucking.

The war wag pulled to a halt directly before the

baron, and the sergeant ducked inside the turret to climb out the back along with a handful of men.

"Well?" Sheffield demanded impatiently. They were smiling and happy, but that could mean anything. "Did you find a dish? Answer me!"

"It was a bitch of a trip, sir," Campbell said, giving a salute. "You wouldn't believe what we—"

"Well!" Sheffield roared.

Campbell's smile faded and he saluted again, with a bit more of a snap. "Sir! Success, my lord!" the sergeant shouted. "We found a dish. Complete and intact. Right near a juicy ville just waiting to be taken."

"Piece of cake, sir," a private added with a grin.

Sheffield crossed his arms. "You've been gone too long for it to be in Georgia, or Carolina. Was it Front Royal?"

"Green Cove ville, sir. In Virginia, near the river and the rill."

"Better," the baron said, a wan smile playing across his tired face. He had been looking forward to melting Front Royal down around the ears of Nathan Cawdor. If he couldn't chill Ryan, then his nephew would have to pay for the man's crimes. Blood for blood—that was the first rule of Deathlands. Never forgive and never forget.

"You did well, men," Sheffield said loudly. "Go wash and get some hot food. You'll be the point men for our convoy on the return trip out there tomorrow morning."

His feelings of elation fading, Campbell blinked at the news. "That soon, my lord?"

Sheffield turned away to look over the assemblage of sec men. "Even sooner would be better," he said bluntly, then found the man he wanted. "You there, Lieutenant Harris!"

Busy congratulating the Beta team blues, the sec man stopped shaking their hands and hurried to the baron. "Yes, my lord?" he asked, saluting and clicking his boot heels.

"How are the preparations for our departure?"

"We can leave anytime, sir."

"Excellent. Any word from Collette yet?"

The officer hesitated, then plowed on. "I sent a recce team to check, what with her and Dickson being gone for so long." He swallowed. "They found only bones, dead muties and burned wreckage. Wild dogs got them."

"Four bodies, two hummers?" the baron pressed, a sudden feeling of dread welling from within.

"Impossible to say, my lord. The mutants had been feasting, and the wreckage of the explosion was thrown all over the area. The ammo must have cooked off from the fire."

"Mebbe," Sheffield muttered. Unless the slave had found the entry code and that bitch Collette was now inside the redoubt. It was a chance he had been forced to take, and it might have bitten him in the ass. Shitfire! He never should have trusted the traitorous bitch.

"Get a squad to the boilers and start stoking the fire," the baron decided aloud. "I want maximum steam as soon as possible. Hopefully before nightfall."

"Yes, my lord!"

"And triple the wall guards," Sheffield added almost as an afterthought. "Just in case."

"More muties?" the sec man asked, worried.

"If we're lucky," Sheffield growled, heading for the control room in the blockhouse at the base of the dish.

THEIR MEAL OVER, the baron of Green Cove ville and his men had adjourned to the war room to plot the attack on Front Royal. Racks of longblasters lined three of the walls, along with spears, swords, longbows and quivers of arrows, while hand-drawn maps of the area adorned the fourth wall. The baron and his troops studied the plastic sheet carefully. Meanwhile, Baron Henderson was sketching on a tabletop with a piece of charcoal.

"The drawbridge is here, not there, as your maps say," he stated, drawing neat square figures on the smooth wood. "There is a hill back here perfect for launching an attack, but it's a trap. They have some sort of secret chamber in the trees, possibly a tunnel, and can release those monster dogs at will."

"How do you know all this?" DuQuene demanded gruffly, pinning some predark medals to his shirt. One of the many treasures found in the ruins where his grandfather had built the ville was a military supply store. All of the ammo and blasters were gone, but many other useful items remained: uniforms, medals, lots of swords and countless books on warfare. DuQuene had never learned to read, but he wore the medals and they made him feel brave and confident, as he had earned the right to wear the decorations through simple birth. Aside from the fancy ribbons and medals, the baron was wearing a helmet from some predark war. Made of heavy steel, it was round with a very wide brim and a chin strap to keep it in place. DuQuene had many others helmets from different wars. Some were more lightweight, others formfitting and sleek, but this antique was made of heavy steel with several deep dents, showing it was protection against large-caliber rounds. The sec men got the fancy helmets for battle, but the steel was reserved solely for the use of the baron.

"I know," Henderson replied coldly, "because Cawdor obliterated my troops with those blasted dogs."

"So we need a strategy to remove them first off," a sec man said.

"You have the answer right here," Henderson replied gesturing at the assortment of weapons. "Pike to hold the dogs off while archers feather them with poisoned arrows. Once the dogs are gone, the battle will be easy."

"Perhaps," DuQuene demurred, hands clasped behind his back. "But their front gate is formidable. It would take a lot of explosives to blow through, and why wouldn't they use their sky machine on invaders outside the walls?"

Putting the charcoal aside, Henderson knew he had no answer to that simple question and so lied outrageously. "It's too close," he said smoothly. "They try and melt us, they'd only destroy themselves."

"And you know this for a fact?" the baron asked, not looking in his direction.

Baron Henderson grinned anyway. "Of course."

"Good." DuQuene turned. "Because you will be leading my troops into battle."

"That wasn't part of our deal," Henderson snapped.

"It is now," Seaton replied, eyeing him with disdain.

Suddenly, a sec man burst into the room and drew

his blaster. The sec men closed around the baron, but the newcomer had his weapon pointed at Henderson.

"What is the meaning of this outrage!" he sputtered, sticking a hand into his pants and grabbing the squat derringer.

"Well?" DuQuene demanded.

"Report, trooper," Seaton added, a hand on his own weapon.

"Bind that son of a bitch!" the sec man ordered, cocking back the hammer of his handcannon. "He's a fucking liar, my lord! I just rode back from Front Royal and found them hard at work repairing damage from an attack. I bought some of the civilians drinks in a bar and got the whole story. There was a revolt. Some man named Overton pretended he was the bastard son of a Cawdor and tried to take over."

"If he was strong enough to do so, good," DuQuene stated. "Only the strong should rule."

While the sec men murmured approval at the statement, Henderson edged a little closer to a gun rack. His derringer would buy him a few seconds, but after that, he was in for a fight. The whitehair had no intention of getting captured alive and letting DuQuene do what he had done so often to his own prisoners. The very thought made him feel ill, and Henderson fought back a wave of nausea. Some of the sec men noticed his movement and moved to intercept him. Henderson changed his course, a new plan already forming in his mind.

"He had lots of blasters and a war wag in perfect condition, but Ryan Cawdor stopped the man. They have no intention of attacking anybody. They're building their walls and planting crops."

"Not what you do when planning an invasion,"

Seaton stated, drawing his oversized weapon and pointing the business end at Henderson. Everybody behind the old baron moved away quickly.

Going backward to the wall as if terrified, Henderson quickly drew his tiny derringer. The sec men laughed at the miniature blaster, until the old baron thrust it against an alcohol lantern and fired. The glass reservoir shattered, spraying burning fluid over a gun rack and the stack of ammo boxes underneath.

The sec man yelled as they scrambled for cover. Seaton kicked over the map table for protection, and DuQuene pulled a guard in front of him as a shield while Henderson dived for the open doorway and sprinted down a hallway just as the first of the bullets began to ignite from the spreading flames. In seconds the war room was under a barrage of ricochets, the flames spreading across the carpeting toward the kegs of black powder....

EVENING WAS starting to darken the sky over Green Cove ville, and the sec men on top of the baron's building grew tense as they heard the sounds of distant blasterfire. Only the noise was muffled, and they weren't sure from what direction it was coming. All looked quiet in the streets below. Just then, the guards felt a warm wind wash over them and noticed a sudden increase in the waning daylight.

"What the fuck is that?" a sec man asked, looking straight upward. There was no lightning in the sky, no sounds of thunder. But as he watched, the red and orange clouds began to thin and within moments a clear blue sky was visible.

"Nuke me," a corporal whispered in astonishment,

rubbing at his itchy cheek. "Never seen nothing like that before!"

"A clear blue sky," another agreed, twitching at the gnats biting his skin. "Got to be a good sign."

"You think?"

"What else could it be?"

"Mebbe so," the first man muttered, idly scratching at his exposed forearms, then doing so with more force. What was going on? He felt as if ants were crawling over his body, but nothing was visible on his skin. Maybe he caught something from those travelers he raped last week. Damn farmers, weren't even good for a decent hump.

Then the guards jumped as something moist smacked onto the roof nearby. Working the bolt on his longblaster, the corporal walked over and was stunned to see a dead eagle sprawled on the concrete, wisps of steam hissing from within its curved beak.

Starting to twitch badly, the puzzled sec man stared at the other guards and saw their eyes turn solid white a split second before his own vision went completely black.

Wild panic seized the men, and they dropped their blasters to rub their eyes in the desperate hope something was merely covering their faces and blocking the light. But nothing was there, and they began to twitch from the painful tingling now covering their entire bodies. Abandoning his friends, one sec man darted for the stairs and ran straight off the edge of the roof, wailing all the way down to the street where he landed across the top of an artesian well, the brutal impact shattering his spine and shoving pieces of bone through his chest. Blind and paralyzed, the sec man couldn't even scream anymore as he felt his lifeblood flowing along his limbs and into the water below.

Crawling along the roof, the other sec men made it to the stairs and soon were tumbling down the steps in their haste to escape. As they reached the fourth floor, the sounds of blasterfire became noticeably louder. They stumbled along a hallway, shouting for help until the corporal accidentally bumped into an alcohol lantern, spilling the fuel all over himself and bursting into flames. The burning man screamed in agony and madly dashed around, igniting wallpaper and tapestries until finally collapsing to the carpet, the predark shag whoofing into flames as if it had been designed for such a purpose. Backing away from the growing conflagration, the third sec man found himself trapped in a corner with nowhere to run. Clawing the wall to try to find a door or a window, the trooper felt his clothes catch fire and grew strangely peaceful as he drew his handcannon and shoved it inside his mouth to blow out his brains rather than burn to death. But the bullet only grazed his skull, removing an ear and a lot of flesh. Badly wounded and unable to make a sound, the sec man was horribly alive as the flames claimed a new victim.

Somewhere in the ville, the alarm bell began to ring, as thatched roofs on the servants huts started to smolder and smoke. In the streets, horses screamed and ran blindly through crowds, knocking over the twitching civilians before dashing out their own lives against a stone wall. More birds fell from the terrible blue sky as the people began to understand they were blind and insanely screamed for help.

TAKING THE STAIRS two at a time, Henderson reached the next floor of the building and hid in a closet to drop his pants and extract the bamboo tube of jolt from its hiding place. Taking a deep sniff up each nostril, the man instantly felt years younger, stronger, smarter, his heart pounding with renewed strength inside his old chest. As he buckled his belt, he could hear the constant explosion of live rounds from upstairs, and an alarm bell was ringing. He wondered how anybody could have learned of his escape so quickly.

Going down the hallway and through the kitchen, he passed the cringing servants and reached the banquet hall, heading straight for the damaged window. It was his only chance of escape. The first floor of the building was the barracks for the sec men. He'd never get out that way. Grabbing a chair, the whitehair battered at the weakened planks until they came free and fell to the floor.

"Hey!" a female voice said, shuffling forward with a strange expression on her face.

Ruthlessly, Henderson fired point-blank, the .44 round opening up the belly of the serving girl like a bag of rope. Returning to his work, the old baron tore fingernails as he struggled to remove the last of the planks and kick his way through the glass. More planks covered the window from the outside, but those were easy to remove, and soon Henderson was able to climb onto the ledge. He was bleeding from both hands, but the river was almost directly below. As he tested the wind and tried to gauge the distance, the old baron felt itchy all over, the tingling sensation oddly pleasant mixed with the effects of the jolt, and then he went stone blind.

Startled, he slipped off the ledge and fell, going into

a dive as he tried to angle for the river. Baron John Henderson slammed headfirst onto the cracked pavement of Green Cove ville, missing the rushing waters of the cool river by less than a yard. Death was instantaneous. He was one of the lucky ones.

WITH ALL OF HIS MIGHT, Seaton threw the spear across the fiery war room and hit the last keg of black powder, cracking it apart a split second before the raging fire got through the wood. Instantly, the black powder flared brighter than the sun, producing volumes of acrid smoke, but the deadly explosion was avoided.

"Follow me!" DuQuene shouted, heading for the doorway and holding the map table as a shield. With slugs slapping into the tabletop, the baron backed out of the war room, herding the rest of the sec men to safety.

Reaching the next room, Seaton slammed the dividing door shut and threw the bolt, sealing the fire on the other side. The sec men sighed in relief, then started to rub vigorously at their faces.

"I want Henderson found and skinned alive!" Baron DuQuene railed furiously, casting the table aside. "I'm going to make him watch as I eat his balls for breakfast! We'll get wild muties to fuck him after we stitch his mouth shut!"

He waited for the expected response, but the others were too busy scratching themselves. Suddenly crying out, the men began to tear at their faces, weeping and waving their hands as if the very air were attacking them. They started to bump into one another and to twitch uncontrollably, shouting obscenities and clawing bloody gouges in their skin.

Rubbing at his slightly itchy forearms, DuQuene

could only stare in bafflement at the convulsing people. His men was acting as if they had gone blind!
Watching in horrid fascination, the baron slowly came
to comprehend that the analogy was correct. They
were blind, but how? Something in the smoke? Had
Henderson poisoned the food? If so, then why wasn't
he affected?

This was when DuQuene noticed the antique steel
army helmet on his head was becoming uncomfort-
ably hot. He started to remove it before realizing the
metal had to be somehow protecting him from whatever was happening. There were more helmets in the
war room, but the flames were licking at the ceiling,
bullets discharging constantly. Return was impossible.

Accepting that, DuQuene picked up the battered table and plowed a path through the screaming people
to reach the door to the stairs, only to find a snarling
Seaton clawing at the locked door, trying to dig his
way through. Without a qualm, the baron shot the man
and left him dying on the floor to be trampled by the
others while he slipped through and locked the door
behind him. There was no sense allowing the others
to get in the way of his escape. Blind, they were dead
already as far as he was concerned.

Heading quickly down the stairs, DuQuene heard
the alarm bell ringing over the blasterfire from above.
What the hell was going on in his ville? Was this
some sort of an attack? Maybe Nathan Cawdor heard
of his intent to attack Front Royal and was melting
Green Cove first. Damn the man! Not even an offer
to surrender first! The man would pay for that with
his life.

On the ground floor, he found only chaos in the
barracks, the sec men stabbing and shooting one an-

other for no sane reason. It was literally a blind panic. Faintly from the dungeon below, DuQuene could hear the prisoners begging for help and he dismissed them all without a thought. If he couldn't help his sec men, why should he care about thieves and murderers?

The smell of his singeing hair was beginning to choke the man, the antique army helmet becoming almost too hot to touch. But DuQuene accepted the pain and watched the armed mob chilling one another as the men fought to escape through wide open doorways. Covered in blood, one man simply clawed at his faced until the flesh was in tatters, endlessly yelling that this was all a dream and couldn't be happening. DuQuene leveled his blaster at the beleaguered soul, then decided it was stupe to waste a round on a walking corpse.

The baron itched horribly on his arms and legs, but through sheer force of will kept his hands from tearing at the flesh. This wasn't what Henderson had described. The stone walls were cool to the touch, and there was a smell of smoke, but not fire in the air. Front Royal was doing something new. However, if this was a sky attack, then he better get as far away from the open air as possible.

For a split second, he debated trying for the river, then changed his mind and headed for the stairs that led to the dungeon. Deep underground he should be safe from the sky machine. And when the attack stopped, he would take all of the supplies he could pack into a wag and leave the rest of his people to await the arrival of the enemy troops. The survivors would probably be taken into chains as slaves. But not him. That wasn't how Armand DuQuene would exit the world.

Reaching the basement of the predark building, DuQuene felt the terrible itching noticeably lessen and sighed with relief. Then he heard the telltale click-clack of cell doors opening and saw the ragged prisoners walking out of their cells, carrying the blasters and keys of the prison guards.

Snarling, DuQuene swung his blaster around and fired, chilling half a dozen before the rest swarmed over him, yanking away the blaster and knocking off the steel helmet. DuQuene braced himself for the onslaught of blindness and was shocked when it didn't occur. The walls had to be too thick down here. He was protected from the ravages of the sky machine, but then he realized it also meant that the prisoners were unaffected. They could see! The men and women he had been brutally torturing for months, years, were loose and armed, and could see!

His pitiful wails for mercy were swamped by the gleeful howls of the starving prisoners as they savagely ripped away his clothing and began to tear the hated baron apart with their bare hands. DuQuene's ghastly screams of agony rose in pitch as the starving men and women began to gorge themselves on raggedy gobbets of his tender flesh.

Chapter Seventeen

In the bottom level of the redoubt, the companions checked their equipment one last time.

"Ready?" Ryan asked, shifting the weight of the heavy pack on his back. The fluted plastic tubes of a couple of LAW rocket launchers jutted from the pack, along with a single HAFLA. The attack was going to be a nightcreep, a silent penetration, but in case of trouble, Ryan wanted some big ordnance to help blast their way to freedom. As the Trader always said, a man could never have too many friends, or too much explosives.

"Ready as we're going to be," J.B. replied. He felt more like himself again with the S&W shotgun and an AK-47 strapped across his back, the Uzi hung at his right side and a bulging bag of explosives serving as a counterbalance on the left side of his body.

In preparation for the assault, the companions had enjoyed a good meal and gotten a few hours of sleep during the day. Fed and rested, every companion carried a Kalashnikov, a bulging ammo pouch either on their belt or slung over a shoulder. Jak also toted the remaining crossbow with an arrow notched under the string and two more taped to the either side of the stock for fast loading. These were the last three of the homemade arrows, and only two had steel arrowheads. But the weapon was silent, and in the teenager's deft hands would chill from a very great distance.

Only Dean wasn't burdened with plas charges. He had hauled down a chair from one of the offices upstairs and was piling boxes and bags in front of it to make a crude barricade.

Rotating the cylinder of his LeMat to visually inspect the charged chambers, Doc set the selector pin and slid the mammoth handcannon into its holster. "You know," Doc said from out of the blue, "sometimes I am sorry about throwing my hat into the Hudson River. A hat makes a man feel more protected, fully clothed."

"It was a damn silly thing," Mildred chided playfully, stuffing more rags into a duffel bag sitting on the floor. "Made you look a little like Lincoln."

"A wise and great man."

"Who got shot in the back of the head."

"Bad luck," Jak added.

"Man makes his own luck," Dean stated, sounding exactly like his father.

Ryan nodded. Amazing good luck hadn't gotten him the 7.62 mm rounds now loaded into his Steyr SSG-70. He had searched for sniper rifles among the weaponry in the Quonset hut, and near a Barrett 1-A had found a case of Steyr longblasters and boxes of ammo, along with the rotary mag they used. Nothing lucky about it, just hard work and brains, that's all. Silas was mad, but not a fool, and he had stocked only the best weapons in the armory of his Shiloh base.

Mildred was struggling to balance her load of ammo pouches, plas charges and the med kit. Incredibly, it was from a time after she went into cryo-sleep and had some items she couldn't identify. That made it worth more than anything imaginable. What fantastic breakthroughs had been accomplished just before skydark while she slumbered in her frozen coffin?

"Hey, what was that?" Krysty asked, snicking off the safety of the longblaster with a sweep of her thumb. She started toward the stairs in a crouch and paused at the bottom step.

The rest of the companions braced for an attack, and the redhead tensely waited, her hair motionless about her lovely face as the woman strained to catch the sound again. Minutes passed, and she slowly, reluctantly, relaxed.

"Must have been some of the automatic machinery," Krysty said hesitantly, then glanced at the silent water pump across the room. The base did a lot of repairs all by itself, monitoring water pressure, and the elevator ran up and down every few days to keep the cables greased. Was that what she had heard?

"What did you think it was?" Doc asked, tightly gripping the AK-47. The scholar was well versed in the operation of automatic weapons, even though he much preferred the solid reliability of a revolver. Blasters like his LeMat and Jak's Colt Python .357 Magnum didn't even have a jam factor. They couldn't jam, unlike a rapidfire. A person could load a revolver, stick it somewhere and pull it out ten years later to shoot. Good as gold, they were. With an automatic, a person was forced to unload the clip and ease off bolts constantly. Damn things required more maintenance than a Thoroughbred colt. But in the forthcoming donnybrook, Doc knew this was the tool needed to assure success. So be it, the LeMat was ready to go if the Kalashnikov failed.

Krysty started to speak just as the water pump for the fusion reactor began to thump softly. "Just the pump," she replied with a sigh, her hair moving in gentle waves. "Guess I'm a little on edge. Too much coffee at breakfast."

"You sure?" Ryan demanded, glancing up the stairs. Nothing was in sight, and no noise could be heard over the steadily working pump.

She smiled. "Yeah, I'm sure. Come on, let's get going. We have a long walk to reach the quarry."

Lighting their torches, the companions opened the door and were startled to see a couple of runts curled into fetal positions on the rocky ground, snoring soundly. As the fluorescent light washed over the muties, they awoke with a start and backed away, bowing and scraping to the tall norms.

"Machine god!" one cried out fearfully. "We waited!"

Ryan glowered down at the diminutive being. "As I ordered," he said. "Has all been done that I asked?"

"Yes, god!" the other said, holding a three-fingered hand before its pale face to block out the bright illumination of the redoubt. "We obey all!"

"Show me," Ryan commanded, and strode down the tunnel, making the runts race to keep abreast of the big man.

Once more, Dean stayed behind and watched the adults proceed deeper into the underground. Somebody had to make sure the entrance to the redoubt was still available when they returned. The heavy door didn't even have a handle or lock on the outside. If it closed, the companions would have been forced to go outside and cross open country to enter the redoubt through the front door.

Settling in his chair, Dean rested the Kalashnikov in his lap. Taking out his pocketknife, he started to cut slices off a brick of military cheese from a MRE pack and prepared for a long wait. Then something bounced down the stairs, clanging and banging on every step and issuing volumes of gray smoke.

The boy gasped at the sight of the military gas gren, then realized his mistake, but it was too late. Trying to force limp fingers to trigger the longblaster, he slumped over and lay unnaturally still within the billowing gray cloud.

ONE LEVEL ABOVE, Collette smiled in satisfaction at the sound of the body hitting the floor. Sliding combat boots back on her bare feet, the woman drew a knife, impatiently waiting for the life-support system of the redoubt to clear the air and allow her to finally reach the staggering pile of weapons and supplies so tantalizingly close below.

REACHING THE END of the tunnel, the companions and their mutie guides went down the incline to find even more runts waiting for them with offerings of mushrooms, smoked rats and baskets of fluffy moss.

"Gifts!" the chief announced, gesturing at the baskets. "Much food!"

Ryan looked over the assortment and pointed the Kalashnikov at the attending runts. They went deathly still, until he laid the longblaster on a shoulder. "I am pleased," he announced, "but we don't need more food yet. You may keep and eat."

"Hail the machine god," a female warrior whispered in shock, then she shouted it to the cavern roof. "Hail the machine gods!"

The runts cheered wildly at the magnificent gift, only a few of their numbers glowering in open hostility at the norms. But those muties also stayed well away from muzzles of the deadly blasters.

"Now take us to where your old god died," Ryan commanded loudly, his words echoing among the stalagmite forest. "And I want fifty of your strongest workers to follow. We have much to do."

"Will this bring more food?" the chief asked hopefully.

"Better," he replied.

On cue, J.B. tossed a cloth bundle at the feet of the little mutie. It came apart as it hit the ground, spilling out dozens of knives. The runts stared at the steel weapons and reached for them, then looked at Ryan for permission. The Deathlands warrior nodded, and the chief lifted a blade, marveling at its shine, then testing the edge of a palm. A line of blood welled from his skin and flowed along his hairless arm.

"Magic knives!" the chief shouted, brandishing the Bowie knife, and the runts chorused the words over and over in a wild frenzy.

"It shall be done as you command, god," the leader of the runts breathed, hugging the knife and bowing deeply, his twin tufts of hair brushing the pile of weapons.

The companions waited while the chief distributed the knives to the female warrior and a select few of the males. Then, choosing his work force, the proud runt lead the norms from the cavern into a warren of caves. Zigzagging through a maze of cracks and hewn tunnels, the runts led the companions back to the crashed wag. Once there, Ryan had the muties start a relay line, hauling the smaller of the rocks from the pile until the tiny pinprick of light from the outside world was enlarged to a medium-sized hole. Satisfied, Ryan dismissed the runts, sending them back to their ville. The chief was the last to go, dragging his feet and stalling, obviously hoping to be allowed to stay. But when Ryan began to frown, the chief took flight and disappeared into the subterranean darkness.

"Twilight," Jak said, studying the purplish illumination outside. "Got to wait some."

"Mebbe an hour or so till night," Ryan said, checking his wrist chron. "Time to get ready."

Dropping their packs, the companions gratefully stretched their muscles, working out some kinks. Meanwhile, Krysty opened her duffel bag and started passing out the long strips of blue cloth.

"I never asked where you got it," J.B. said, tying a length around his head pirate fashion.

"Officers' quarters," she answered, removing the chron from her wrist and attaching it farther up her arm safely under a sleeve. "Lots of Navy and Air Force uniforms still hanging in the closet. Army camou is the best, but this blue is dark enough."

Opening the door to the wag, Ryan went behind the seats and got a tire iron, then proceeded to remove the lug nuts off both front tires. Rocks under the wag prevented it from lowering to the ground, and the man had no trouble removing the castle nuts on the axle and sliding off the main bearing assembly.

"Use it sparingly," he said, proffering the handful of grease to the others. "This is all we have."

Krysty dabbed in a finger and smeared the cold grease over her cheek, leaving a wide black streak. J.B. followed her example.

"Me next," Jak said, tying back his long snowy hair. "Need rag for this."

Krysty passed the teenager a cloth for his hair.

"I do believe that I shall need similar protection myself, madam," Doc rumbled, brushing a hand over his waves of silvery hair. "This will reflect light like a mirror."

"Hey, boots," Jak said to Krysty, pointing downward.

The redhead looked and cursed. The silver embroidered falcons on her blue cowboy boots would stand out in the darkness like a neon banner. Ripping another uniform to strips, she bound her footwear until the silver was properly masked.

"Bombs prepped?" Ryan asked, smearing grease over his face. Strips of cloth were already wrapped around the barrels of their weapons to prevent any reflection. He had passed by dozens of Parkerized automatics in the Quonset hut, and those were perfect for this kind of attack. But the metal also corroded easily, and so he hadn't taken any. That had been a mistake on his part. Hopefully not a deadly one.

The Armorer patted the heavy bag at his side. "Don't know how many boilers the ville's power plant has," J.B. said, "so I used all of the plas from the Claymore and spare grens to make six bombs. When these go off, the boiler will erupt, taking out most of the ville, and the rest will be washed with steam. Not many folks are going to be alive after that."

"One should go on the main support column of the dish," Ryan stated, greasing up his neck, then the back of his hands. "Buckle that and gravity will finish the job."

"And then we go in and remove any survivors?" Doc asked, tucking another blue cloth into his shirt to hang down like a bib and cover the white linen frills.

"Got it covered," J.B. said, lifting a squat package. "This one goes on the outside of the Quonset hut, just to the left of the door. It should blow a hole through the corrugated wall and ignite the pile of fuel barrels on the inside. That'll start a chain reaction among the stores of ammo, finishing the job the boilers begin. Actually, this charge will ignite first so nobody can try and escape through the gateway."

"If they haven't already."

"Yeah, true enough."

"No danger of that," Krysty said, stretching her arm out the hole in the rock pile. She crawled partially out of the opening, then came back with an expression of success. In her hands was what appeared to be a retinal scanner. "Looks like they took that gateway apart."

"To stop us from trying to gain entry again," Ryan said. "Only do that if they were never coming back here again."

"Mebbe be gone already," J.B. observed.

Just then a rain of rubbish crashed into the quarry, starting a small landslide of ruined technology.

"Still here," Jak said grimly, tying a strip of cloth around the six-inch shiny steel barrel of his .357 Colt Python.

While the others finished their preparations, Mildred placed the med kit inside the crushed wag. She hated to leave it behind, but it was much too heavy for her to carry along with the assorted weapons and explosives. Besides, the companions would be coming back this way. Nice to know it was here to patch any

wounds in case they caught some lead blowing the
ville to hell.

"Any chance the blast will cause a cave-in down
here?" she asked suddenly.

"No way," Ryan stated, adjusting his bandoleer of
loaded rotary clips for the Steyr. "The ceiling is supported by the same metal as the nukeproof door of
the redoubts, same stuff that forms the outside armor
of the redoubts themselves. These tunnels will hold."

"Cavern?" Jak asked, looking down the long dark
tunnel.

"That could be trouble," J.B. admitted. "But we'll
have plenty of time to get past the cavern before the
charges blow. I set them for thirty minutes."

"More than enough," Ryan said, going to the hole
and glancing outside. The shadows from the high
walls of the quarry made it difficult to determine if
true night had fallen yet. Drawing the SIG-Sauer, the
one-eyed man settled down on a rock and patiently
waited until the darkness was near absolute, softened
only by the cold moonlight.

"Good enough. Let's go," he said, and started to
climb into the ragged hole.

Crawling over the smashed rocks, the companions
exited the tunnel and moved silently through the jum-
bled remains of the quarry. Bits and pieces of crumpled machinery jutted from the piles of stones, along
with an occasional human arm or leg, most of them
still wearing the chains of their servitude.

Watching the cliffs above for any sign of movement, the companions proceeded a few yards and
paused, repeating the process until reaching a sloped
road. They followed it to the top of the quarry and
saw the wall of the ville rising before them. There

didn't seem to be any sec man walking patrol along the top of the wall, and only a single searchlight swept over the ville. Then the revolving beam washed briefly across the dish, rising majestically into the sky. At that close range, the predark antenna looked impossibly huge. Directly ahead of them was a gate set in the limestone wall, banded metal of some kind with hidden hinges, with no lock or handle. They instinctively knew it would take explosives to get through that portal. Thankfully, they had another way inside the Shiloh base. That was, if Ryan and J.B. remembered the layout of the ville correctly. If not, the mission was a bust from the start. The backup plan was to simply shoot the dish with the LAW rockets from outside the wall, then run for cover and hopefully get back inside the underground tunnels before sec men arrived in an APC and shot them to pieces. The plan bordered on suicide, and they all knew it, but the destruction would stop the blues. At least, for a little while.

Raising a hand to signal for a pause, Ryan pulled the lone HAFLA rocket launcher from his backpack and placed it on the ground next to a whipping post for slaves. He laid a strip of dark cloth on top, then sprinkled some dirt over both. In the darkness, the lump was nearly invisible from only a yard away.

Ryan gestured at the hidden weapon with a stiff finger, then slashed a hand sideways across his throat. The masked companions nodded in understanding. The launcher was for life-and-death emergencies only. Ryan gave a thumbs-up and gestured to the western side of the quarry, slightly away from the imposing wall.

Following the edge of the cliff, the companions

spotted dark shapes in the wan moonlight and found a line of broken wags. Sheffield and his people were still here. Jak and Ryan stood guard with their silenced weapons, while J.B. found a vehicle in decent shape and put it into neutral. He steered while the rest pushed the wag toward the wall, its flat tires crunching over the loose gravel. Coming abreast to the wall, J.B. parked the wag and set the brake. Weapons at the ready, the companions walked for a minute, listening for any reactions or alarms, but all was still.

Going to the rear of the wag, Krysty tied a rope to the main axle, loosely coiling the rest of the length over a shoulder. The strong cotton rope had been machine washed in hot water with dark clothing of different colors found in the redoubt and came out a murky camou pattern that was barely visible.

One by one, they climbed up the wag and onto the top of the wide stone blocks. Krysty was the last, trailing the rope behind her as she joined the others, and they stood gazing upon the ville of the blues. There seemed to be some damage to a few of the buildings, and each attributed it to possible mutie attacks. The rad-blasted animals of Tennessee were the wild-card factor in the whole operation. If there was an attack by screamwings or stickies while the companions were planting the charges, the chances of their getting out were slimmer than a baron keeping a solemn promise.

Crouching, the companions waited on the wall while Ryan headed to the left, Jak to the right. The masked teenager traveled only a hundred yards before a figure appeared on the wall before him. Without pause, Jak fired the crossbow, the bolt taking the man in the throat. Dropping his blaster, the sec man staggered and almost fell inside the ville, but the albino teenager rushed forward, grabbed the man by the shirt and shoved him over the wall. He toppled over the edge and inside the ville, but Ryan fired a fast four times, the silenced slugs slapping the man backward until he fell outside the wall. The body landed with a crunch, and Jak moved on. Reaching the gap in the wall, the teenager headed back along the top until rejoining the others. A few seconds later, Ryan returned, sliding a fresh clip into his empty SIG-Sauer.

Suddenly, the searchlight was coming their way. The companions hurried to exterior edge of the blocks and lowered themselves over the side, holding on by their hands. The brilliant beam swept over that section of the wall and moved onward without even pausing.

The companions pulled themselves up and moved to the inside edge. Krysty now uncoiled the colored rope and lowered the knotted length to the ground below. Ryan went first to anchor the rope with his weight, and the rest followed. They reached the scorched earth and spread out so as not to offer a group target to any unseen enemy. Overton had been a sharp military commander, but they didn't know if Sheffield was any good. Underestimating an opponent was a fast way to taking the forever sleep. Fools thought they were invincible and died, a true warrior feared death and so lived to fight another day.

Stabbing a wooden stake into the ground, Ryan tied off the rope to keep it still, then took a handful of dirt and rubbed some of it between his fingers. The soil was badly burned. Even the roots of the grass were charred dead. Sheffield had to have used the Kite on his own base. If he could do that... For a moment Ryan weighed calling off the assault, then decided they would never have another chance to finish the job. In every fight, every battle, an opportunity would come for a telling strike that would end the matter. If the chance was missed, the odds might turn against you. Ryan touched the long scar on his face and frowned, then raised an open hand, closing it into a fist to summon the others.

Passing out the plas charges, J.B. whispered brief instructions on how to set the timing pencils embedded into the huge wads of sticky C-4. Accepting the charge, Jak gave Mildred the crossbow and drew one of his many knives, the steel blade blackened with soot from a candle flame. Then Jak moved off into the darkness and was gone from sight. The young hunter worked best alone on a nightcreep and they all knew it.

Krysty and Doc were assigned the dish. She took the charge, and they headed around the silent slave quarters to swing behind the blockhouse underneath the antenna. Holding the crossbow and a Kalashnikov, Mildred stayed with the rope to act as anchor for the group, while J.B. and Ryan moved stealthily through the night towards the noisy power plant full of sec men.

Chapter Eighteen

In the cool quiet of his private bedroom, Baron Sheffield sat in a comfortable chair and sipped a glass of whiskey. The amber-colored liquid swirled over the miracle of ice cubes from his small electric fridge in the corner. It had been a long day, and the next one would be even longer, but success was spread before them like a path through the woods. Where Silas had so sadly failed, there was no way Sheffield could do anything but succeed.

The table before him was stacked with maps of Virginia, both predark and modern. The civilians and sec men of Green Cove ville were probably still chilling one another, finding an easy release from their blindness. Melt a ville, what crap! Where was the profit in that? Corpses made poor slaves. But blind men could still be chained to a plow, or a waterwheel.

Sheffield took another sip of the whiskey, marveling over its smoothness and savoring the rich flavor on his tongue. The ancient stuff tasted nothing like homemade shine.

The next day, his small army of blue shirts would leave this rad-blasted hellhole and seize their new home at Green Cove. He would immediately send out a scout to talk peace with Nathan Cawdor of Front Royal to buy them the week necessary to get the new dish functioning properly. Then he would blind Front

Royal, chill Cawdor, take his bitch as his personal
slut, loot everything there was, especially any puppies
of those mutant dogs so he could raise them as his
own guards, and then melt the place to the ground. It
made no sense to leave a stronghold like that so close
to his new ville where enemies could hide and prepare
to launch an attack. The world was full of fools, but
the thinking man ruled them all.

Setting down the glass, Sheffield rose from his
chair and began to strip for sleep. With the destruction
of the gateway, Ryan had been neutralized, Silas was
dead and he had a new ville and dish. A new era
would soon begin in Deathlands, making the current
days of bloody chaos seem like a pleasant afternoon.
The whole world was in the palm of his hand, and
soon he would start to squeeze.

KALASHNIKOV IN A STEADY grip, a sec man walked
among the brick buildings of the Shiloh base, listening
for any suspicious noises. The muties hadn't attacked
for a while, and he was part of the new increased
patrol to make sure the creatures didn't get inside the
base again. And flying over the wall was just about
the only way they could get inside. The hole was jam
packed with barbed wire and miscellaneous junk. Nobody and nothing was getting through that crap pile
of explosives and glass.

Watching the searchlight swing by overhead, the
man glanced around and stepped into the shadows behind the Quonset hut. He lit a cig and drew in a lung-
ful of smoke with a satisfied sigh. Then he went motionless.

Someone stepped in and gently lowered the corpse

to the ground, removed the cig and crushed it under a boot.

In a faint sucking noise, Jak removed the knife from the sec man's neck where he had expertly inserted it into the man's brain. The blade was shiny clean now, so the teenager rubbed some dirt on the bloody blade to keep down the sheen, then moved on to the Quonset hut.

A light was on above the only door, and two sec men stood guard. But that wasn't his goal. Spotting some crates and barrels that generated a tiny pool of darkness near the back of the hut, Jak crawled along the ground until he was safely within the shadowed area. Sliding the charge off his back, he placed it against the cool corrugated metal of the hut, the plas molding itself to the irregular surface and firmly adhering. Inserting a timing pencil into the bottom of the wad where it couldn't be seen, he snapped it off at the correct length starting the silent chem fuse. Then he stabbed another timing pencil into the top of the wad where it couldn't help but be seen, and set the timing pencil for two hours. If a sec man found the charge, he would remove the wrong pencil trying to defuse the bomb and think he was safe.

One of the guards coughed and the other softly made a rude comment of some kind that started both men laughing. Jak crawled backward from the ticking bomb, and the night swallowed him whole.

LUNGING INTO THE POOL of light, Doc skewered the sec man through the throat, removing any possibility of a cry of alarm. Startled, the dying man dropped his longblaster, and Krysty caught the weapon before it clattered onto the hard ground. Then she grabbed his booted feet while Doc got the shoulders, and they hauled the man where nobody could see and neatly finished the job.

Returning, Doc rubbed out the spilled blood with his boots, while Krysty studied the surrounding buildings to see if anybody noticed the absence of the guard. No one had.

Deciding the area was clear for the moment, they dropped to the ground and crawled across the few yards of open land to reach the closest support column. Safe in its web of shadows, they closely inspected the thick girder. The imposing array of riveted steel was strong enough to not only support the dish, but to also completely resist the push of any wind against the titanic mass.

Finding a junction, Krysty cupped her hands and boosted Doc up into the maze of metal. Using fingertip pressure, he molded the wad of plas into a long strip. Its job wasn't to blow a hole in the support column, but to weaken the strut sufficiently so that gravity would pull down the dish and complete the destruction.

Hearing the sound of bootsteps coming their way, Krysty tapped Doc's shin, urging him to hide. Releasing the plas, the old man chinned himself into the struts while Krysty curled into a ball on the ground, making herself as small as possible.

Smoking cigs, four sec men walked by the companions less than a yard away. Unseen blasters tracked the blues from the shadows until they crossed the street and went inside the barracks. Her hair writhing under the confining bandanna, Krysty hissed at Doc, and he redoubled his speed. He pressed the plas into place, stabbed in the two timing pencils, setting the alternate times, and gracefully jumped to the ground.

Glancing upward, Krysty could see nothing amiss in the struts overhead and nodded in satisfaction as they stealthily moved into the night once more, just as the searchlight swept over the blockhouse and support columns with its brilliant white light.

CROUCHED OUTSIDE the power plant, Ryan and J.B. could hear the steam boilers hissing loudly and the massive pumps pounding as they turned banks of generators to make the electricity to power the comps and the motors that operated the dish. This was the hard job. The others could plant their charges on the outside of the buildings, but that wouldn't work here. These explosives needed to be planted directly on the boilers.

The taste of coal was thick in their mouths, as the two men peered through a grimy window. Inside was a group of blues in T-shirts playing cards and drinking cold beer taken from a small fridge, their shirts hung over the backs of their chairs, Kalashnikovs standing along the wall in a tidy row for fast access. Retreating from the window, Ryan tugged J.B. on the cuff and made a knocking motion. The Armorer nodded.

J.B. knocked softly. A grumbling voice demanded to know what the fuck was wrong now and shoved the door aside. Ryan fired the SIG-Sauer twice in soft chugs, blood exploding from the sec man's throat and left eye.

The man staggered backward, and the masked companions rushed inside the office, using the body as a shield. The blues stood up, shouting in surprise, only one of them going for a blaster. Ryan kneecapped the man, and he hit the floor inches short of the deadly rapidfires. They pushed the corpse into the others and pulled their knives, slashing throats and stabbing into armpits with deadly results. In under a minute the floor of the office was awash with blood.

The heat from the boilers was stifling. Reluctantly, Ryan and J.B. removed their bandannas and loosened their shirts, sweat already trickling the axle grease from their faces.

A wall of glass windows fronted the office, but the glass was yellowed from the soot and condensed creosote, almost too dingy to see through. Ryan took a bloody shirt and rubbed a spot clean to peek inside the power plant. Apparently, they had chosen the right spot to strike. Beyond the office was the main floor of the boiler assembly. The chimneys were brick, but the boilers were seamless vats containing countless tons of pressure. Steam hissed from a hundred joints in the feeder pipes and from the ever cycling pistons. Ryan couldn't imagine how Silas got it here through the little gateway. It had to have already been here, something from predark days that Silas repaired into a functioning power plant. What other explanation could there be?

Testing a bottle, J.B. found the beer on the card table was still cold, and each man took a refreshing swig. Then, stepping out of the office, they began a security sweep of the place. J.B. and Ryan encountered five more sec men who quickly surrendered to their ready blasters, and died anyway. The companions moved on with ugly expressions. Chilling somebody who had given up was a hard task, but there could be no prisoners or quarter given on this night. Their job was extermination; nothing less would do.

But each man looked a little older as he finished the security sweep, and neither spoke, their minds focused on the completion of the job at hand and nothing more.

Going around the blazing furnaces, the companions found a group of people shoveling chunks of coal from huge bins and tossing them directly into the open hearth of the furnaces. They were bare-chested and covered with soot and sweat. Ryan almost lowered his blaster to set them free when he noticed how well fed they were, and with no whip marks on their muscular shoulders.

"Blues!" J.B. cursed and cut loose with the Uzi submachine gun, sending a wreath of 9 mm lead into the workers. The chattering of his blaster was barely discernible over the noise of the boilers and the pistons.

Half the sec men died on the spot, while the rest dived for their weapons as Ryan emptied the Kalashnikov at them. Most dropped, but a 7.62 mm round zinged off a thick shovel blade, and the snarling trooper managed to reach onto a shelf and grab a handcannon. Ryan aimed high, while J.B. swept the sec man's legs with the Uzi, the mixed assault peppering the man and tearing him apart.

Freed from the necessity of silence, the companions strode through the building shooting freely, chilling everybody they saw until the power plant was a morgue full of the dead and the dying.

Returning to the first boiler, Ryan stood guard while J.B. extracted a huge plas charge and placed it directly under a main steam pipe and set the double pencils. He couldn't place the plas directly on the pipe or the mounting heat would soften the stuff until it liquefied and dribbled off. But with this much explosives, a few feet of distance wouldn't make any real difference. When it ignited, the whole building would be blown sky-high, hopefully taking the rest of the ville along for the ride.

He did the same with the other four boilers, and spent a precious few minutes barricading the doors to the power plant with heavy drums and placing a live Claymore mine attached to a trip wire. Exiting through the back door, J.B. rigged grens on both sides of the threshold. The two men tied the dark blue bandannas on their heads once again, then smeared fresh grease over their faces and melted into the night. The trap was set, the mission complete. All the companions had to do was to leave and the rest would take care of itself. Baron Sheffield and his triple-cursed sky machine were already dead and buried. They just didn't know it yet.

FOLLOWING THE WALL, Jak moved from shadow to shadow, heading back for Mildred, when a door unexpectedly swung open in the slave quarters, catching him in a bright light. Instantly, he raced around a corner of the brick building, then paused and drew a knife. Maybe they hadn't seen him. It could be only a single overseer checking the slaves. Then Jak heard the sounds of boots on gravel coming from both directions and knew he was caught. Sheathing the blade, he softly worked the bolt on the Kalashnikov, a spare clip already in his hand. Anything less than twenty and he could chill them all.

"I got him!" a sec man cried from above.

Lightning fast, Jak realized the danger and tried to

dodge, but somebody fell on him from the roof and the Kalashnikov went flying.

Head butting his assailant, Jak drew a knife and slit the man's throat from ear to ear. A hand grabbed him by the hair, but only got a fistful of blue cloth. Rolling free of the corpse, Jak stood and fired the Colt Python, the booming .357-Magnum round illuminating the alleyway between the two buildings. The heavy slug drove a blue shirt backward, with most of his face gone. Then another assailant tackled Jak around the ankles, and he hit the wall, losing the handcannon. A third sec man kicked the blaster away as a dozen more raced into the narrow passageway. The albino teenager was knocked to the ground and the blues piled on, driving the air from the teenager's lungs.

Partially pinned, Jak clawed desperately in the grass for his blaster, but it was nowhere to be found. Cursing vehemently, he pulled out a pair of knives and wildly stabbed anything nearby, arms, legs, butts and ribs. Men cursed and started pounding him with fists. They wanted him alive! Somebody stomped on his wrist, pinning his left hand, Jak sliced with the right, opening the belly of a snarling sec man, warm blood and entrails pouring out from the ghastly wound.

That bought him some space and Jak pulled out another blade, doing his worst. Screaming in pain, the blues scrambled to get away and he was free. Rising to his knees, Jak stabbed a man in the groin. The blade opened a vital artery, and the man paled instantly from blood loss. The neutered sec man writhed in agony, clutching the blade that had removed his manhood. Jak tried to yank the knife free, but the man's death grip was too strong. Releasing the trapped knife, Jak drew another leaf-shaped blade when somebody grabbed him from behind. The attacker released the teenager instantly as his fingers fell to the ground, the razor blades sown into Jak's collar neatly severing them.

Spinning, Jak threw the knives. A blade caught a short sec man in the chest, and he fell. But the other trooper took the knife in an arm and turned sideways to kick Jak in the face.

Blood filled his mouth, and Jak spit it into his adversary's face, drawing his last blade while digging for a gren in his pocket. The bombs were ticking; he had to leave before this whole complex went skyhigh.

Then something slammed into him from behind and the world started to spin out of the control. A blaster fired, and he felt white-hot pain in his leg. Dropping the knife, he clutched the wound and tried to shout a warning to the companions, but blood was pouring down his throat from his broken nose and all he could produce was a horrid gurgling.

As he got the gren loose, another sec man rose before him and shoved a rifle butt toward him. Jak tried to duck out of the way and caught the blow on his wounded shoulder. Pain erupted and his arm went limp, dangling loosely. Then the unprimed gren fell to the ground from his numb fingers, useless and inert.

Jak tried to run again, but the blues swarmed over the teenager, pounding him with rifle butts and fists until there was only the sound of meaty thumps in the Tennessee night.

WHEN RYAN AND J.B. returned to Mildred and the rope, the men found the other companions waiting for them nervously.

"Trouble?" Ryan asked, looking out into the ville. All was quiet with no outward sign of undue activity from the blues.

"Where's Jak?" J.B. asked.

"I think the blues got him," Mildred answered with a hard edge to her voice. "Saw some muzzle-flashes in the western section of the ville, and then heard Jak cry out."

"Can't be dead," Krysty said, looking at the dark buildings, a hand partially raised as if feeling the air.

"Anything, madam?" Doc asked hopefully.

"Nothing."

Biting back a curse, Ryan glanced at his wrist chron. Twenty minutes remained until the whole valley was one huge fireball of steam and shrapnel. Clearly, the others wanted to go after the teenager, but they always followed his lead. Every cell in his brain told Ryan to leave the teenager as a causality of war. Friends died, that was a fact of life. Finnigan was gone, old Pete, Hunaker, maybe even the Trader himself. Everybody died eventually.

Soft thunder rumbled overhead, the clouds sealing off the moon and extinguishing its silvery light.

In spite of logic and reason, Ryan already knew the answer. Maybe Sheffield and the blues could leave a friend alive in the hands of the enemy, but not him. This wasn't a question of tactics, it was a matter of honor.

"Well, what the hell are you waiting for?" Ryan whispered, working the bolt on his Steyr SSG-70. "Let's go get him back."

Chapter Nineteen

"Twenty minutes until the first charge goes off," J.B. said bluntly, checking his wrist chron. "That's mighty tight."

"Buy us another ten," Ryan ordered gruffly. "Then get out. We'll meet you at redoubt."

"Do my best," the Armorer said offering his hand.

Ryan took it and the men shook, saying goodbye in the only way they could. Neither expected to see the other alive again.

"Want some company, John?" Mildred offered, stepping closer.

Smiling, J.B. touched her cheek. "Only slow me down, Millie. Cover your ass, and I'll concentrate on mine."

She nodded, and he took off into the night.

"Gaia be with you," Krysty muttered in prayer.

"Come on," Ryan stated, heading toward the Quonset hut. "Let's see what we can find."

Staying low to the ground, Ryan followed the tracks the teenager had made in the hard ground. The light was poor, but he had been carrying a lot of explosives and that made the difference. They were halfway to the hut, near the slave quarters, when Ryan stopped cold and knelt on the soil.

"Three men, no, four killed," he said, studying the

tracks. "Mebbe ten more. Jak lost his blaster, was wounded, tried to run and they got him from behind."

"Still alive, then?" Krysty asked.

Ryan stood. "He's alive. They dragged him away, limping, then lifted him off the ground."

"Probably fainted. How the hell did they beat Jak in a knife fight?"

"Mebbe they hit his bad shoulder," Mildred suggested, the crossbow steady in her grip as she watched the shadows for any suspicious movements. "It was hurting more than he would admit."

"Time," Doc demanded, Kalashnikov at quarter-arms, his swordstick stuck through his belt in lieu of a scabbard.

"Fifteen minutes," Mildred replied.

"Where now?" Krysty asked. "The tracks go in a dozen directions from here. Which one has Jak?"

Ryan couldn't tell and chose one at random. The boots were in the best condition, so those were most likely the officers who would be interrogating the youth.

"This way," he said and took off at an easy lope. Time was against them now, and every second counted.

WHEN J.B. ARRIVED at the power plant, the noise of the pistons inside was steadily growing in volume. Worried, he glanced through the filthy windows and saw that several of the safeties had blown and steam was filling the building from floor to rafters. The grime on the office windows washed away under the boiling assault. The temperature inside was lethal. Without anybody at the controls, the boilers were running away, building to an explosion of their own, even without his charges.

As he watched, another valve burst, shooting through the steam on a white jet and smashing through the office window.

Backing away, the Armorer paused and started to go for the trip wire of the gren at the back door, then stayed his hand, turned and walked away. Even if he could cut the booby traps fast enough, there was no way through that cloud of steam. It would ace him in under a heartbeat. The plas would be okay. The charges were out of the way of the direct venting, but the only doors were smack in the path. The plant had to have been designed that way so that the doors could be blown from the exterior and the power plant would cool down naturally without any loss of life. Now it only meant the place was death for anybody trying to sneak inside.

The bombs would explode in twelve more minutes, and there was nothing anybody could do about it.

JAK LAY LIMPLY on the rough-hewn wooden boards, one eye swollen shut, but his teeth were still in place. That had seemed to enrage the blues, and they converged again to concentrate a lot of their kicks on his mouth.

''That's enough,'' a sergeant ordered, and the gang of men stepped away from the bloody form on the floor. ''You going to talk now, mutie?''

Although both lips were swollen and cut, Jak managed a smile, the taste of blood filling his mouth. One blue snarled and stabbed Jak in the thigh with a fork from the dining table. The teenager shuddered, but didn't speak.

"Strip him, then chain him to the wall," the sergeant ordered brusquely.

Jak was stripped, then hauled across the room and chained spread-eagled to the brick wall. Cold suddenly washed over the teenager, and he found himself rudely awake, his dripping hair blocking most of his vision.

"Again," the sergeant said, and another bucket of icy water was thrown over the prisoner. Most of the blood was sluiced off his lean body.

"Now me," a sec man growled, and a whip cracked.

Jak flinched as a white-hot pain hit his wounded shoulder, the flesh swelling red immediately.

"Gonna take his eyes," a sec man growled. "He cut off Digger's balls with that fucking knife. I want his eyes!"

"Digger still alive?"

"Christ, no. I blew his brains out. Had to, he was my bud."

"Fucking mutie," a corporal snarled, slamming a knee between Jak's legs.

Pain filled his world until the teenager couldn't hear or see anything. Swirling clouds of red cloaked his vision. Slowly, the mists faded and Jak vomited on the floor, heaving and retching.

"Make you eat that later," the sergeant growled. "Better yet, make the freak eat some glass and watch him die from the inside."

"Just set him on fire!" another man snarled.

"Talk, mutie!" a sec man demanded. "What are you doing here? Stealing food? Trying to free the slaves? Ace the baron?"

"Are there any more of you?"

Summoning strength from somewhere, Jak pursed his bleeding lips and started to whistle a happy tune.

Infuriated, a corporal slapped him in the face.

"Call your sister," Jak mumbled around the puffy lips. "Or small child. Either hit harder."

Grabbing a chair, the sec man charged forward, but the sergeant shoved him aside. The furniture smashed on the brick wall beside the teenager, splinters spraying from the crash.

"You fool! How are we going to ask a corpse anything?" the sergeant bellowed. "Get out of here and get a kid."

Smiling at the suggestion, the blue hurried from the room, glaring at the prisoner as the door slowly closed.

"As for you," the sergeant said, grabbing an ear and hauling Jak around, "you're going to tell us what's going on, or we'll have to get nasty."

Jak said nothing until the sec man returned with a small kid in tow.

"We lost most of the slaves to a mutie attack," the sergeant said, stroking the trembling child. "But not all. We found her hiding under a pile of rags. Too small for cooking or sex. What are we going to do with a little kid? Got no use for her."

The little girl looked at Jak with eyes of terror as the sergeant leveled a blaster to the child's head and clicked back the hammer. "Talk," he said.

Jak slumped in the chains. He had been tortured many times before, but this was a new tactic and one he had no defense against. He couldn't talk. It would mean the deaths of his friends. The child was a stranger, and his first allegiance would always be to his friends.

"Talk!" the sergeant roared in unbridled fury.

Jak looked him straight in the eye. "No," he said with as much conviction was he could muster. Maybe, if they thought it was hopeless, they'd wouldn't chill the child. It wouldn't serve any purpose then.

The blaster roared, and something wet slapped the wall.

"What a mess," a sec man roared. "Blame yourself, Whitey. We didn't have to chill her. You made us."

Staring at the monsters, Jak put every ounce of strength he possessed into a long string of gutter curses, damning them in every way he knew, his ruby eyes staring at the men and radiating a savage intensity that almost broke their nerve.

The sergeant pulled out a knife with a serrated edge, turning it so that the jagged steel caught the lantern light and threw a rainbow of colors across the tiny room. "I'll make him sing."

REACHING THE LARGEST brick building in the compound, the companions watched a tall man in a blue shirt leave the building through an electric fence and head into the darkness with a gangly stride.

Ryan pointed the SIG-Sauer at the insulated wires touching the fence and fired twice. The coughs were lost in the gentle mountain wind, but a pair of wires fell from the sky, sparking briefly at the contact, then stopped.

A guard stepped from the shadows, zipping up his pants at the noise and walked closer. Mildred fired from the ground, and the man staggered backward with the feather end of an arrow jutting from his jaw, the rest of the shaft going through his mouth and pinning it closed. Ryan fired again, and the corpse sat on the ground and stayed there, as if he were merely tired and taking a rest.

Sliding through the fence, the companions reached the front door and Krysty listened carefully. She held up an open hand with splayed fingers, then closed it into a fist, next raising one, two, three fingers. Ryan gestured back and forth, and she replied by pointing two fingers to the left, one to the right.

Nodding in understanding, Ryan stepped closer to the door and eased out the half-clip in the SIG-Sauer, gently sliding in a fully loaded magazine.

DROPPING HIS SPOON into the bowl of stew, a blue shirt grabbed his blaster and snapped the bolt.

"What's wrong?" asked his comrade, taking the corncob pipe from his mouth and exhaling a long stream of smoke at the ceiling.

"Heard a noise," the corporal replied, rising from the table and heading for the door.

Sitting on a low stool, a private glanced up from stropping a knife. "Wasn't me," he said. "Mebbe it's Collette finally coming back."

"Bad for her if it is," the sergeant puffed, crossing his arms. "Baron wants her dead now. Guess her special pussy ain't so special as we heard, boys."

"Fist, mouth, cunt, ass, it's all the same to me," the corporal snorted, then paused near the door, his hand almost touching the handle.

There was an odd smell in the air, and he sniffed. Grease. Smelled like axle grease from the wheelbearings of a wag. The private was spitting on the whetstone sharpening his new knife again. The sergeant smoked his pipe contentedly in the corner. Nobody here had been working on a wag today, so where was the smell coming from? Then he vaguely recalled Collette saying how axle grease made for a good stain if you were doing a nightcreep.

"Oh fuck!" he cried, and dived for the locking bolt. The door burst open, driving him backward. A big man stepped into the room, a sleek blaster at his side blowing silent flame.

The private grew a third black eye in his forehead and tumbled off the stool, the knife and whetstone flying into the air. The sergeant cursed and stood, trying to draw his own handcannon, when his nose disappeared and an arrow thumped into his chest. The grizzled veteran slammed against the wall, and still managed to draw his weapon when the big man fired his fancy blaster three more times, the impacts slapping the sergeant around and around until he collapsed in the corner on top of a bloodstained chair covered with chains.

Scrambling under the table for his blaster, the corporal grabbed the weapon and rolled, attempting to fire from a prone position. The longblaster spoke once, the slug ricocheting off the wall near a stocky woman who was entering the armory holding a crossbow. Shitfire, his weapon was still set on single fire! Desperately, he thumbed the selector to full-auto and he saw the woman cast the crossbow aside and draw a revolver with amazing speed. He swung the longblaster toward her as she did the same. He saw her weapon spit fire first, then everything went black.

Suddenly, the interior door slammed open, and Ryan stitched the sec man standing there with a Kalashnikov. The body flew back into the room, and the companions followed.

Sheffield was at a gun rack with six other sec men, hastily loading blasters. Ryan and Krysty hosed the group with streams of bullets, bodies falling in every direction.

Only Sheffield still moved on the floor, clawing for the blaster at his hip. Ryan fired again, the floorboards splintering between his hand and the revolver.

"Thought you'd be wearing a bulletproof vest," Ryan said, hauling the man up by his shirt.

"Where's the whitehair?" Krysty demanded, nudging the baron with her longblaster.

"Silas is dead," Sheffield spit, twisting to get away. "One-eye here chilled him days ago."

Ryan slapped the man across the face with his pistol, and teeth landed on the floor. "We got no time for horseshit," he snapped, breathing into the baron's face. "So speak fast or die. Where's the albino being held captive? Long hair, lots of knives."

"If you don't know," J.B. stated, walking into the room, cradling his S&W shotgun, "then you aren't any good to us."

Glancing toward the power plant, Ryan asked the Armorer a silent question and J.B. shook his head. Fireblast! Ten minutes before all hell broke loose.

"Fuck you," Sheffield snarled. They seemed rushed, nervous. Maybe his troopers were on the way. He decided to play for more time.

"Where is he?" Ryan demanded, firing the blaster and scoring a bloody graze along the man's head, then pressing the hot barrel against the baron's cheek. The flesh sizzled from the contact.

"All right!" Sheffield shouted, recoiling, almost tearing from the awful pain. "He's in the small room at the far end of the slaves quarters."

"Is that your prison?" Krysty asked, filling her pockets with loaded clips from the gun rack.

"Interrogation room," Sheffield muttered, drooling blood from the side of his mouth.

Ryan hauled the man upright and threw him toward the doorway. "Show me," he commanded, jabbing the man along with the fluted muzzle of the Kalashnikov.

ANNOYED, THE SEC MEN stepped away from their prisoner, their knives dripping blood.

A hundred shallow cuts crisscrossed his chest, warm blood running down his stomach and thighs, but Jak still refused to speak. Once you started, it was impossible to stop. He had been tortured enough before to know that for a fact. And he only had to stay alive for another ten minutes or so. Just long enough to see their faces when the boilers blew and the base was obliterated.

Unfortunately, something had to have shown on the teenager's face as the sergeant frowned.

"This ain't balls," the sec man said in a worried tone. "The freak knows something."

"Crap, mebbe there are more of them!"

"Got a rescue planned, or something."

"Sound the alarm," the sergeant decided abruptly. "Rally the troops. Let them come. We'll blow the coldhearts to hell and back."

"Yes, sir!" a private said and threw open the door to shout when a thundering gunshot shook the room and the sec man slammed into the far wall, minus a head.

With a supreme effort of will, Jak forced his vision to focus and saw his friends enter the room with every weapon firing. Caught by surprise, the sec men where slaughtered where they stood.

"Jak, my boy, are you still alive?" Doc asked, working on a chain.

As the wrist came free, the teenager start to slump, and the old man caught him before Jak hit the floor.

"Hey…" the teenager whispered softly.

The clothes of the dead men were too bloody to use, but Krysty spotted a bearskin attached to wall. Ripping it down, she draped it over the naked youth and lifted him into her strong arms.

"Leave me," Jak wheezed, trembling. "No time. Bombs soon."

"Think we're going to die just to save you?" Ryan asked. "We have a ticket out of here. Say hello to Baron Sheffield."

Jak looked up, then fainted dead away.

Mildred checked for a pulse. "He's okay."

Ryan glanced at his watch. Seven minutes. No time to reach the slave gate and climb over. They were on the other side of the ville.

"Head for the garage," Ryan commanded, going for the doorway with Sheffield in tow. "We need speed, and that's our best bet. Krysty, grab Jak's clothes there."

"Why not use the hole in the wall?" Krysty asked, jostling Jak's limp body as she stooped to carefully grab what she could.

"Too good a spot for snipers to pin us down on foot," Ryan countered. "We're driving out."

"The garage is right near the Quonset hut!" J.B. admonished. "When that baby goes—"

"There will be no more sec men to chase after us," Mildred observed. "Hurry! Seven minutes to go!"

Sheffield had no idea what was going to happen in seven minutes, but he already knew he wanted no part of it.

As the companions raced across the ville, a whistling sec man ambled out of the night contentedly munching an apple, an AK-47 slung over his shoulder muzzle downward. Without pausing, Ryan shot the man from behind and kept running. "Move faster, fatso!" he ordered the baron.

Pretending to be more frightened than he was, Sheffield did as requested, a plan for revenge already forming in his mind.

Reaching the garage, the companions raced directly through the open doorway. A couple of mechanics were tinkering with a wag and turned with their blasters leveled at the invasion, but then paused at the sight of Sheffield. The companions didn't hesitate and the men died on the spot.

Surveying the place, Ryan saw a dozen U.S. Army 4x4 trucks, five Hummers and one APC, all loaded with supplies. The war wag looked in good shape even it did have only seven tires. The installation of the eighth had been interrupted by death.

"One of these trucks will hold all of us," Doc stated, grabbing a roll of duct tape off a workbench.

"Take too long to unload," J.B. said.

"And too slow." Ryan frowned. "We're taking the LAV. Right out the front gate."

As Doc started to wrap the baron's arms to his sides with the tape, Sheffield stared at Ryan as if he were insane. The front gate was the strongest point of the whole ville. How could they exit there?

Krysty tried the rear door. "Locked!"

Without comment, J.B. doffed his fedora and dived

underneath the wag. As his legs wiggled out of view, he cried out and started to fire the Uzi on full-auto, the muzzle-flashes strobing from beneath the LAV-25.

Ryan hit the concrete floor, his Kalashnikov searching for targets, but only spent brass and J.B. were in sight. Plus, a lumpy pile of bleeding leather.

"Some sort of egg sack under the wag," the Armorer said breathlessly, working on the belly hatch. "Damn thing started to hatch when I arrived." The small door yielded to his touch and the man wiggled inside the APC.

Seconds later the rear doors swung open wide, and the companions piled inside. J.B. took the driver's seat and started the engines. Ryan slammed the baron into a wall seat and buckled him in painfully tight. The man glared but said nothing. Going to the turret, Ryan checked the cannon on top of the wag. It seemed to be in perfect condition, but it was unloaded.

"Ammo!" he called down as the wag rolled out of the garage.

Using both hands, Krysty passed up a weighty roll of 25 mm shells for the electric-driven Gatling. Mildred got busy strapping Jak across several wall seats, then started to wash his wounds with the water from her canteen. Once she got her med kit back, the boy would be fine. Other than the broken nose, none of the wounds were serious, or the cuts very deep. The blues had been going purely for pain, nothing more.

As J.B. headed straight for the front gate, lights were flickering on all over the base, brightly illuminating the buildings and streets. Doors were flung open by unshaven men with blasters, rubbing sleepy faces. Some started running around madly, shouting orders and questions. The companions opened fire with their AK-47s through the blasterports of the APC, cutting down the men mercilessly.

"Two minutes!" Doc warned, slapping a fresh clip into the Kalashnikov.

In a crash of splintering wood, the LAV plowed through the kiosk, men inside yelling for only an instant. Then the gate loomed before them. Ryan concentrated the roaring 25 mm cannon on the hinges, the HE shells chewing a path of destruction along both sets. Shards of metal flew in all directions under the furious bombardment. Ryan never stopped shooting until the gate was too close, then he was forced to drop inside or risk being sheered in two.

"Hold on!" J.B. shouted, shoving the gas pedal to the floor.

The wag seemed to exploded as it struck the steel bars, the passengers thrown forward as every loose item went flying. The front of the armored wag lifted into the air as the sound of screeching metal assaulted their ears. Then there was a tremendous crash and metallic ringing as the LAV straightened its keel and rolled over the fallen barrier. The engines sputtered, and J.B. fought to keep them alive as the wag raced over the hardened landscape, putting as much distance as possible between it and the doomed ville.

"Angle away from the gate!" Ryan ordered, grabbing another belt of ammo from the locker and struggling up into the turret. "Then stop!"

"Stop?"

"Do it!"

Sec men were appearing at the ruined gates, the muzzle-flashes of automatic blasters making bright flowers in the night. One big man seemed to be struggling to operate a LAW rocket launcher, which was exactly what Ryan had been worried about. In the background, a Hummer darted from the garage and headed for the new hole in the limestone wall, a .30-caliber machine gun spitting fire.

"We got to keep them inside those walls!" Ryan shouted and cut loose with the cannon. The shells tore the sec men apart, and the Hummer veered out of sight.

"Are we far enough away to survive the blast?" Mildred asked, peeking out a rear blasterport while bolting the rear doors tight.

"How should I know?" J.B. shot back irritably. "I tried to make as big a bang as possible. Didn't calculate the kill zone."

Sheffield stared above his gray tape bindings, no longer struggling to get loose. Were they talking about a bomb?

"How much longer?" Krysty shouted, firing her AK-47 out a blasterport.

Reaching into a pocket, Doc glanced at his antique pocket chron and rumbled, "Any second now, madam."

Chapter Twenty

Buttoning his shirt closed, Sergeant Campbell stared at the outlanders herding the baron into the garage, watching as they drove away in the APC firing weapons in every direction.

"Son of a bitch, they got Sheffield," he muttered, grabbing a blaster from the wall and running to the garage.

A group of officers and troopers were already there, throwing the cargo out of a Hummer and piling inside the wag.

"Hop in!" a lieutenant ordered, starting the engine. "We're going to catch them at the gate!"

Along with the others, Campbell's men started forward eagerly, but he held up a restraining hand. "We'll be right behind you, sir!" the sergeant told the officer, saluting.

"Good man!" the lieutenant shouted, and threw the Hummer into gear. Revving the engine, the sec men charged toward the gate, steadily firing their blasters.

"Idiots," Campbell said aloud once the man was gone. "The fucking 25 mm on that LAV will chew a Hummer to pieces."

"So what are we going to do, Sarge?" a private asked, a longblaster balanced in his hands.

"Head for the slave gate," Campbell ordered.

"We'll circle around the whole damn ville and catch them from behind and rescue Sheffield."

"Grab some heavy weapons," Campbell directed. "Take that one there, and the LAW, too."

With the searchlights sweeping the sky overhead, Beta team got busy clearing a Hummer of excess cargo, piled in and took off racing across the ville. Stopping at the slave gate, a sec man hopped out, threw the heavy bolts and climbed back into the vehicle. Campbell nosed the door out of the way with the armored grille of the wag, then hit the gas and powered along the cliff of the quarry, steadily angling westward around the high wall.

"They'll never see us coming," Campbell growled, driving with one hand as he awkwardly shoved a 40 mm round into the breech of the M-79 gren launcher held tight between his knees.

As RYAN WORKED the bolt on the Gatling to clear a jammed round, there was a sharp explosion somewhere within the ville. In slow majesty, the dish started to tilt, then lean and finally to fall toward the ground, building speed. It dropped behind the wall, then broken bits sprayed into the sky.

"That's the diversion," Ryan said, dropping inside the wag and bolting the top hatch shut. "Get ready for the big one!"

Suddenly, a blinding light flash filled the entire valley, and boiling flame extended over the wall and stretched out through the ruined gate. The companions opened their mouths and covered their ears just as the concussion of the detonating Quonset hut washed over them like a tidal wave, shaking the world and drowning them in its power. The LAV was slammed side-

ways for yards by the force of the blast, ripping open
the top hatch, as a hot wind tore through the vent and
ports, stealing the words from their mouths. Minutes
passed in strident fury, but slowly the reverberations
of the explosion faded and sound returned with a ven-
geance as a rumbling mushroom cloud formed over
the annihilated ville.

"Mother of God," Mildred whispered. Then she
relaxed, remembering that any hot ground explosion
of sufficient size would form a mushroom cloud. It
wasn't a proprietary symbol of only a nuclear blast.

The winds continued to buffet them for several
more minutes, smaller detonations barely discernible
within the roiling hell of the fiery ville. Daring to open
the rear doors, the companions stepped out of the APC
and looked upon the destruction. The men and wags
at the gate were gone without a trace, vaporized by
the blast. Pieces of the stone blocks were missing, and
gaping cracks ran along the expanse of the limestone
wall, the mushroom cloud hellishly illuminated from
below by countless small fires. It was unlike anything
they had ever seen. Only Mildred shivered, recalling
the old vid of the nuke blasts at White Sands and
Hiroshima.

Then something bounced off the top of the wag
with a ringing clang.

"Fallout!" J.B. cried, and started racing for the
LAV. "Back inside the wag!"

The companions followed the man and piled into
the vehicle, slamming shut the doors, just as the first
of the debris began to plummet from the tortured sky.
Bits of wood, pieces of brick, body parts, chunks of
the dish and assorted junk rained across the landscape,
making the LAV sound as if it were caught in a never-

ending shotgun blast. A cooking pot slammed into the wag through the missing turret hatch, followed by a smoking toilet seat and a brick that shattered into reddish dust on the dented floor. In desperation, Mildred covered Jak with her body and cried out as the particles hit her back.

"Move this thing!" Ryan commanded, holding on to a ceiling stanchion.

Already in the driver's seat, J.B. fought to start the engines, but the diesels were uncooperative. "Come on, you piece of shit," he cursed, adjusting the controls, as a chunk of burst steam boiler melted doors and gigantic pieces of foundation slammed around the wag with meteoric force, shattering the landscape for hundreds of yards.

With a roar, the diesels finally caught. J.B. slammed the ten-ton wag into gear and stomped on the gas. The LAV rolled straight for the smaller debris, rolling over the pieces, zigzagging its way across the broken landscape.

"John Barrymore, what are you doing?" Doc shouted from the rear.

"I'm dodging the falling debris!" J.B. replied, tugging and shoving the steering levers frantically. "It rarely lands on the same spot twice. By going from wreckage to wreckage, we probably wouldn't get flattened."

"Probably?"

"Best I got!"

"Then haste thy chariot, Hermes!"

Soon they reached the rim of the debris, and the APC charged on a straight line for the redoubt.

"Goodbye Shiloh," Ryan growled, removing his bandanna and using it to wipe his face clean. Tossing away the rag, the Deathlands warrior turned to look at Sheffield.

"Which only leaves you," he said, drawing the SIG-Sauer.

"Chill him later!" Krysty cursed, watching out the rear ob slit. "We got company."

The starboard ob slit had been hammered shut by concussion, so Ryan went into the turret to look behind. Sure enough, there were bobbing headlights. A vehicle of some kind was in pursuit. In the background, the flames of the burning ville seemed to reach the clouds, the black smoke rising to the distant stars.

"That's a Hummer," Ryan shouted to the others. "No prob. I'll chill it with the —" The man stopped talking as he saw what remained of the electric 25 mm Gatling cannon. The rapidfire was bowed in the middle, almost bent in two.

Just then there was a flash from the Hummer and something exploded on the rear doors, making them rattle and loosening several of the hinge bolts.

Sheffield beamed in delight behind his gag, and continued working on getting the rope around his wrists loose. There was a jagged piece of metal that had penetrated the seat cushion beside him, and he had managed to steal the sliver before the others noticed. He had already cut halfway through the safety harness holding him in the seat and was steadily working on the sticky layers of duct tape. His fingers were slippery with his own blood from using the razor-sharp sliver, but wounds would heal. A bullet in the brain was forever. He had to get loose quickly, before Ryan turned his attention on the baron for one last time.

Shoving a Kalashnikov out a rear blasterport, Doc cut loose, spraying rounds wildly all over the place. He knew there wasn't a chance in hell of hitting the other wag, but it would certainly slow them. Krysty tried the same with her blasterport, but found it blocked with slivers of metal, more flying debris from the devastated base.

Slamming a fresh clip into his exhausted blaster, Ryan glowered at the swerving vehicle chasing them. He knew what somebody was doing below and heartily approved. Unfortunately, the driver of the Hummer was already anticipating retaliation by swerving back and forth, making the wag damn hard to hit. Holstering the piece, Ryan called down, "Pass me a LAW!"

There was some rummaging about by the companions, then a sealed plastic tube was handed up to him. Yanking out the safety pin made the sights pop up automatically. Zeroing the aft port, Ryan checked to make sure it was clear behind him, then placed the crosshairs of the scope on the veering wag, resting his finger on the firing button placed on the top of the launcher tube.

Counting under his breath, Ryan tried to find a pattern to the driving, and had to accept it was purely random. Whoever was behind the wheel was smart. But not smart enough.

The LAV was struck again by a powerful explosion, and he could see the reflected light of the blast underneath him. There was no contrail of flame, so it wasn't a LAW, and not powerful enough for an Armbrust or HALFA. Someone was firing a gren launcher. The Bradley was a light armored vehicle, but it could easily take a hundred 40 mm grens without damage.

The black night sped by without details to the landscape, while Ryan tried to catch the Hummer again in his crosshairs, but between the LAV rolling over the irregular ground, and their pursuers nimbly dodging, there was no way he could track the target.

"Find some flat ground!" he shouted into the wag. "Give me ten secs of straight driving!"

"They'll get our range!" J.B. shouted back in warning.

"Already got it," Krysty retorted angrily, as another gren brutally slammed the LAV.

Squinting through the cracked Plexiglas of the ob slit, J.B. drew his blaster and blew it away, clearing his vision immensely. A cold wind streamed into the wag, but his glasses protected his eyes, preventing J.B. from blinking blindly. There seemed to be more rolling hills to the south, but the land to the north appeared to be more level. Taking a chance, the Armorer headed that way and the LAV picked up speed as the ground leveled to a smooth plain.

Caught unawares, the Hummer stayed still for a split second. Ryan laid the crosshairs on the wag and pressed the launch button. A dart of fire flashed from the front of the tube, streaking toward the Hummer. Just then something detonated under the LAV, making it lurched violently to the right and start to tip over.

Already on its way, the armor-piercing missile streaked past the Hummer and struck the ground, harmlessly blowing chunks of the hard soil skyward. Tossing away the spent LAW, Ryan bruised his shoulder and jaw as he dropped back inside the armored wag just as it slammed into the ground, skidding out of control. Boxes were bouncing about inside the vehicle. Mildred was sprawled fully over Jak, and Sheffield was dangling from a broken safety harness, almost free. Snarling, Ryan grabbed for his blaster only to find it gone.

"Fireblast!" he roared in frustration.

With a triumphant cry, Sheffield snapped the ropes binding his wrist and dropped to the opposite wall. On his knees, Doc turned as the baron slammed him against the rear doors. Doc was astonished by the man's strength and realized the baron wasn't a norm, but a mutie with superior strength. Gasping from the blow, the old man rapped the stock of the AK-47 into the baron's face.

Sheffield merely grunted from the strike and pulled the huge LeMat pistol from its holster. Shoving the weapon into the whitehair's face, he pulled the trigger. Nothing happened. The baron couldn't believe it. A sec man in battle with a dead blaster? What sense was that? He fumbled to find a safety as Doc smashed the stock of the Kalashnikov on the baron's head, making him drop the Civil War blaster.

Sheffield slapped Doc aside and clawed at the bolts, managing to open the door. It slapped onto the ground, throwing off a spray of sparks. Without a pause, Sheffield dived from the wag and hit the ground hard, rolling end over end, hitting his head a dozen times before coming to a stop. Dizzy, the man forced himself to stand and lurch away. Blood trickled down his face, and the whole left side of his jaw was numb. He probably broke the bone, but he was free!

Somewhere in the background, blasters were firing, autos chattering as handcannons boomed in reply. A man screamed in pain, followed by the dull thud of a gren. The fight was going full force. If his side won, he would be safe. But if they lost, this would be his only chance at escape.

Then Sheffield tripped over something, and, fumbling in the dark, was astonished to discover it was the dropped LAW. Baring his teeth in a savage grin, he checked the rocket launcher, trying to find the controls and make damn sure it was in workable condition. He was armed now, and the tables had just turned on Ryan and his pack of coldhearts.

FINALLY GRINDING to a halt, the companions climbed out of the LAV-25, steadily firing their blasters at the oncoming Hummer. The wag bounded over the rough terrain, blasters firing from both sides and over the windshield. Crouching in the open rear door, J.B. cut loose with the Uzi, spraying the enemy vehicle. The windshield shattered and a headlight winked out. But the return fire continued unabated as the Hummer started to circle the crippled LAV, peppering it with bullets from every direction.

Dragging a bag of grens free, Krysty started to pull pins and lob the spheres at the attacking wag. She understood they were hesitating about a hard kill because they thought Sheffield was still on board. However, if they found out he wasn't anymore, the fight would take a sharp turn against them, and it was a disaster already.

The grens bounced through the darkness, exploding into fireballs always just behind the racing Hummer. A man cried out and fell off the wag, but it was only one out of many.

Tossing everyone a longblaster, Ryan formed the companions into a tight group and they tagged the wag with concentrated fire, until the driver turned off the lights and engine. In near silence, they could barely hear the armored wag coast along through the night and disappear.

Ryan grabbed Krysty and jerked a thumb. She touched her ears and nodded, pointing in a specific direction. Moving fast, the companions grabbed their backpacks and got Jak loose, then slipped quietly out the belly hatch of the sideways LAV, putting it between them and the Hummer. Trying to buy his friends some yardage, Doc stayed behind, firing two Kalashnikovs in an alternate pattern to make it sound like several people were shooting back.

Reaching a safe distance, they waited on a rill for Doc to tie off the trigger of a fully loaded AK-47 as a diversion, then exit the belly hatch to join them.

"Now we'll see how smart the blues are," J.B. commented, tilting back his fedora with the barrel of the Uzi.

"Only have to be curious," Ryan said. "We'll do the rest."

A hundred yards away, the rigged Kalashnikov finally died and silence ruled the starless night. On the horizon, even the terrible flames of burning ville began to slowly diminish.

"THINK THEY'RE ACED?" a sec man asked, pausing on the ground.

A blaster in each hand, Campbell rested his chin on a forearm and chewed over the possibility. "Mebbe," he replied hesitantly. "Or they could be trying to lure us in closer for an ambush."

"Keep going?" a sec man whispered.

The hairs on his nape were going stiff. Campbell sensed a trap and crawled away from the toppled

APC. "Back to the Hummer," he commanded softly. "We got some willy peter grens in the locker. We're going to lay down a ring of flames that'll light the night. Then we can pick them off, one at a time, and save the baron. They'll try to cut a deal at the end. We'll agree and shoot them in the back."

"About fucking time," another man growled in agreement.

As the handful of sec men crawled toward their wag, the single headlight switched on, bathing them in brilliant illumination. Dimly, Campbell could see the one-eyed man behind the wheel, holding his M-79 gren launcher. How had they found the wag in the pitch dark? It was impossible!

Somebody worked a bolt chambering around, and both sides started firing simultaneously. However, the companions were shrouded in blackness, protected by the armored body of the Hummer. The blues were in the open on flat ground. The exchange was brief and permanent.

Mildred checked to make sure Jak was okay in the rear of the wag. Some of his minor wounds had opened again, but the blood loss was minimal.

"How are you feeling?" she asked, wiping his brow.

"Blues dead?" he wheezed.

"Yes, they are."

The teenager gave a wan smile. "Then fine."

"J.B., cover me," Ryan said, walking toward the bodies. He found two still breathing and finished them off with head shots.

"By the Three Kennedys," Doc rumbled in annoyance, moving to the other side of the Hummer for protection.

Standing on a low rising hill was a dim figure faintly silhouetted by the dying fires of the Shiloh ville. The person was carrying a longblaster of some kind.

"Now you fuckers are mine!" Sheffield shouted, and pressed the launch button on top of the LAW. The device gave a resounding click, but nothing more. Empty. It was empty? When had Ryan fired off the rocket?

Frantically tossing away the tube, Sheffield sprinted for a nearby rill, planning to throw himself over the edge no matter what was on the other side.

Holding the SIG-Sauer in a steady two-handed grip, Ryan fired a full clip after the racing baron. This wasn't the time for halfway measures. When Sheffield died, the danger of the Kite was gone forever.

The baron stumbled over the uneven ground when a white-hot pain punched into his side. He fell to his knees, then rose again and continued for the rill. He had to quickly get out of the range of their blasters. But his blood was everywhere, and the man felt terribly cold.

Cutting loose with Uzi, J.B. angled high, trying for the running man. Krysty fired at him with the AK-47, and Mildred did the same, but he was out of range for the blasters. Ryan unlimbered the Steyr and chambered a round, when the night split apart with a thunderous discharge, a foot-long lance of flame reaching out from the pitted maw of the Colt Python held in the bloody hands of a grim-faced Jak Lauren.

With a gaping hole in his shoulder, Baron Sheffield flew forward with his arms outstretched and hit the top of the rill. On the other side was a babbling river, water to hide in and wash his wounds. Escape was only feet away.

Exhausted from the effort, Jak collapsed once more, as the indomitable baron rose again, clutching his stomach and shuffling for the crest of the rill. He was going to make it, going to live!

His long frock coat billowing in the breeze, Doc cocked the hammer on his LeMat, which advanced the trigger a full half inch, then fired. Throwing flame and smoke, the handcannon blasted a .44 miniball straight into the baron just as he reached the rill, blowing away most of his neck. The Steyr spoke twice, finishing the job, and Sheffield hit the ground hard, his head freely rolling away to splash into the dark waters.

"It's finished," Ryan said, resting the stock of his longblaster on a hip. "Come on, let's see what's salvageable in the LAV."

As the companions headed for the APC, Krysty nudged Doc. "Good thing your blaster did a malfunk before," she said, slinging the AK-47 over a shoulder. "Sheffield would have chilled you for sure."

"The LeMat is operating perfectly, my dear Krysty," Doc retorted, waving away the volumes of smoke pouring from the muzzle of his black-powder weapon. "This is a single-action pistol. You must cock the hammer first or it will not shoot, unlike your double-action revolver."

"Sort of a double safety?"

"Exactly."

"I didn't know that," Krysty said, mentally filing the information away.

Doc smiled, displaying his oddly perfect teeth. "And most assuredly, neither did the good baron."

Taking what they could from the battered APC, the companions filled the Hummer with ammo, MRE packs and assorted supplies, then started the long drive back to the redoubt. There was a lot to tell Dean once they got back.

EPILOGUE

As the door to the redoubt slid open, J.B. drove the Hummer along the antirad zigzagging tunnel and into the garage. Immediately, the companions piled out of the wag and charged across the floor. A dead woman lay near the stairwell door, surrounded by a pool of blood. Sprawled on top of her was Dean, his fist still clench around his pocketknife, which was buried to the hilt in her left ear.

"Son, what happened?" Ryan demanded, going to his side.

Weakly, Dean looked upward, his eyes a blazing red in color. The irritation had to have been severely painful. "Stu—" He swallowed and tried again in a whisper. "Stupe bitch didn't know the difference... between a tear-gas gren and a poison-gas gren."

"Couldn't read the color codes, eh?" Ryan mused, helping the boy to his feet.

"Guess not," Dean wheezed. "I waited for her to come get me...and jumped her."

"On the bottom level," J.B. asked for clarification.

"Yeah."

"And it ended all the way up here?"

The boy nodded.

"Hell of a fight," Krysty observed.

Ryan gave a rare smile. "Expect no less of a Cawdor."

Smiling in appreciation, Dean then got a serious expression and walked over to Mildred. "Sorry," he apologized. "But she shot up your fancy med kit. It's all busted to pieces. Along with a lot of our other stuff."

Mildred tightened her lips to a thin line and closed her eyes for a minute. Then the physician opened them and sighed. "Better to lose the med kit than you. And some of the equipment should still be usable. I'll go check."

"Coming with you," J.B. said, and the two went down the stairs, the door swinging closed behind them.

"Wonder how she got inside?" Ryan muttered, then spied a piece of paper covered with numbers sticking out of her pants pocket. Retrieving the sheet, he found it was filled with alphanumeric codes, most of them crossed out. At the top of the page was a heading: From the desk of Silas Jamaisvous.

"Should have chilled you twice, you old bastard," Ryan stated grimly, pulling out a butane lighter to set the papers on fire. Then he crushed the ash under his boot.

Rummaging through the pockets of the dead woman's clothes for any further documentation, Doc got an idea and started to check the labels instead. "Let us take her clothes," he suggested. "We could only salvage Jak's camouflage jacket and vest. The boots and pants should be about the right size for him."

"Save the bearskin for me afterward," Krysty directed. "I need a new coat, and that hide will do nicely once I cut and sew it some."

J.B. and Mildred returned just then with their arms full of supplies, and the companions got busy relaying the goods to the mat-trans chamber. The consensus was that they wanted out of this particular redoubt as soon as possible. Hopefully, the next would be completely deserted and they could spend a few days resting and letting Jak heal.

Within the hour, they were ready to go. The friends climbed into the chamber, and Ryan closed the door. He sat quickly and impatiently waited for the electronic mists to take them someplace, any place, far far away from war-torn Tennessee.

DAWN WAS BEGINNING to break on the Pennsylvania mountains, when the exhausted barb decided to break his stance. Lowering his lance, the naked outlander waited for the reaction of the strange male in the blue shirt. For two days they had faced each other poised to chill, but neither struck first. After so long a period, the barb could only grant a warrior's boon to the blue shirt. He offered peace. Hopefully, it would be accepted.

Utterly astonished, the corporal could barely believe what he was seeing. The damn fool was giving up! As the sec man watched, the barb turned and started to walk away. Two days of standing motionless in a Deathlands standoff, and he was done. The barb was just a yellow-belly coward and he deserved to die.

Curling his lips in a disdainful grin, the sec man leveled the blaster and pulled the trigger. The Kalashnikov fired once, winging the barb in the shoulder.

Frantic, the blueshirt hit the ejector switch to drop the dead clip, then fumbled for the bulging ammo pouch at his side. But the barb had already spun at the traitorous action and thrown. Straight and true, the lance pounded through the sec man's chest, busting bones and exploding out of his back, carrying pieces of internal organs along with it into the ground.

Impaled motionless, the sec man exhaled and dropped the AK-47, hot blood pumping along the shaft of the weapon. Watching the hairy stranger quickly die, the barb reclaimed his lance, then took the longblaster as a trophy. Time was short. Already the grass was starting to ripple this way.

Jumping from rock to rock, the warrior raced for the safety of the tall trees. With a bound, he launched himself into the air and caught a low hanging limb, hastily climbing into the upper branches just as ropy tentacles snaked from the soil and dragged the gory corpse away to the mutie's hidden den.

The barb waited awhile to make sure the ground was clear before continuing his interrupted journey. The machine was a great totem, a mighty trophy, yet the warrior was a bit sad. He had come to respect the hairy stranger as a fellow warrior, and assumed he had done the same. Was the mistake his, or some flaw in the dead man? It didn't matter really. Only a fool forgave a betrayal, and death was the only coin of the realm used for paying debts of honor in Deathlands.

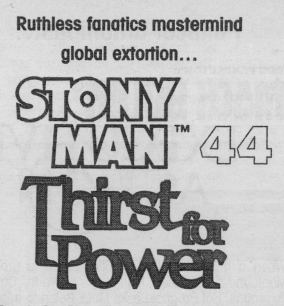

James Axler

OUTLANDERS™
WREATH OF FIRE

Ambika, an amazon female, has been gathering groups of Outlanders in the Western Isles in an attempt to overthrow the Barons. But are her motives just a ploy to satisfy her own ambition?

Journey back to the future
with these classic

DEATH LANDS®

titles!

#62535	BITTER FRUIT	$5.50 U.S.	☐
		$6.50 CAN.	☐
#62536	SKYDARK	$5.50 U.S.	☐
		$6.50 CAN.	☐
#62537	DEMONS OF EDEN	$5.50 U.S.	☐
		$6.50 CAN.	☐
#62538	THE MARS ARENA	$5.50 U.S.	☐
		$6.50 CAN.	☐
#62539	WATERSLEEP	$5.50 U.S.	☐
		$6.50 CAN.	☐

(limited quantities available on certain titles)

TOTAL AMOUNT	$
POSTAGE & HANDLING	$
($1.00 for one book, 50¢ for each additional)	
APPLICABLE TAXES*	$ _____
TOTAL PAYABLE	$ _____
(check or money order—please do not send cash)	

To order, complete this form and send it, along with a check or money order for the total above, payable to Gold Eagle Books, to: **In the U.S.:** 3010 Walden Avenue, P.O. Box 9077, Buffalo, NY 14269-9077; **In Canada:** P.O. Box 636, Fort Erie, Ontario, L2A 5X3.

Name: _____

Address: _____ City: _____

State/Prov.: _____ Zip/Postal Code: _____

*New York residents remit applicable sales taxes.
 Canadian residents remit applicable GST and provincial taxes.

GDLBACK1

GOLD EAGLE®